DEMONSTORM

BOOK TWO 🕊 DEMONSTORM

LUKE CHMILENKO &
HARMON COOPER

All rights reserved. No part of this publication may be reproduced, stored in a retrieval system, or transmitted in any form or by any means electronic, mechanical, photocopying, recording, or otherwise without prior written permission from Podium Publishing.

This is a work of fiction. Names, characters, places, and incidents are either products of the author's imagination or used fictitiously. Any resemblance to actual events, locales, or persons, living, dead, or undead, is entirely coincidental.

Copyright © 2026 by Luke Chmilenko and Harmon Cooper

Cover design by Mario Teodosio

ISBN: 978-1-0394-6622-7

Published in 2026 by Podium Publishing
www.podiumentertainment.com

DEMONSTORM

CHAPTER 1

All stabilizing wards remain within acceptable deviation parameters. Core absorption capacity is estimated at 93 percent, assuming optimal leyline flow. While the Heart of Creation was never specifically designed to withstand a full-scale Beast Tide, we are confident in its ability to endure significant aetheric pressure. Extremely confident.

—Memo from the New Albion Crafters Union to the High Council and Master Weaver Patrjohn Granadam, Magistor of Gilded Radiance and current Dean of the Great College

Lightning cracked open the sky above New Albion, the city lurching awake to a shrieking wind. A low boom followed, rolling forward like the start of an avalanche.

"Wh-what?" Callum Stross shot upright in bed, heart pounding, the afterimage of violet lightning searing his vision and leaving bright sparks across the room as he came out of a deep sleep aided by his Empowerment of Rejuvenation core.

"I'm on it!" Fen appeared beside him in a flash of brilliant magic, the Radiant Fox leaping onto the desk near his rattling window frame to get a better view of the Great College. Another bolt lit up the room, followed by thunder that pounded through the stone and the sound of lashing rain. "It can't be . . ." Fen said, his tail stiffening as he turned back to Callum.

"Coming!" Callum threw off the blanket and swung his feet onto the cold stone floor.

A shiver ran through him as he joined Fen at the window, the storm overhead far too familiar, too much like the aetherstorm that had struck his family's farm and driven him into the ruins of the East Manor, straight into Fen's path.

The next bang wasn't thunder. It was a fist on the door.

Callum turned just in time to hear Marcella yelling over the storm. "Wake up, Callum! Can you hear me?" She banged again. "Something's happening!"

He rushed to the door and yanked it open. "I'm up. You . . ." His words faltered at the sight of the tall woman from Aveiro—long skirt, armor from the waist up, sleek and reinforced, strikingly similar to the style Princess Selene favored. "Where did you get that?"

"My skirt? Does that matter right now?" She nearly shoved him. "What are you waiting for? Put something on! We need to get out there."

"I don't want to say it," he told her, running a hand through his hair, "but this looks like an Aetherstorm."

"In that case, you said it, not me." She shot him a teasing grin that turned serious when more lightning struck, thunder slamming through the room in a single, heavy pulse.

Fen hopped over to them, voice tight. "Where there's an Aetherstorm, there are aetherbeasts. We need to go!"

"The Heart of Creation should be able to handle it," Marcella said.

"It should," Fen told her, "but the storm is massive."

"Still." Her eyes darted from Callum to the fox. "Let's just get outside. That's where everyone's going. I'll meet you out front—"

"Wait!" Callum told her before she could leave. "This will only take a second." He grabbed a tunic and pulled it over his head. "Ready!"

Marcella glanced down at his bare feet. "You're joking."

Callum looked down. "Right. Um, I'll put on shoes."

"And pants?"

"You said to hurry. On the farm, if something needs doing, there isn't much time to think about fashion."

She laughed until another crack of lightning cut her short. "Well, that ruined that moment. Pants and shoes, Callum, overcoat too. You're representing the Great College now, not just stomping around Weatherby."

"Fine. Just give me a second."

"See you down there!" She vanished down the corridor.

Callum moved fast, yanking on a pair of pants, lacing his boots with stiff fingers, and giving his room one last glance before turning toward the stormlit hall.

"Ready," he told Fen, who dissolved into him in a streak of light. Warmth flooded his limbs, their heartbeats synchronizing. A familiar power settled into his frame, alive and just shy of wild now that Fen was with him.

<*Whatever is happening out there is going to be trouble,*> Fen told him. <*I can sense it. We need to move!*>

<*That's the plan.*> Callum threw on his overcoat and bolted out of his room. A few students from his cohort rushed toward the stairwell, some shouting, others still trying to figure out why everyone was evacuating the dormitory.

The wind screamed even louder now, not through cracks or gaps, but from inside the building itself. Raw mana seemed to leak through unseen fractures in the world, turning the air strange and sharp as Callum reached the front entrance and shoved the door open.

"This is bad," he said as he looked up to the sky, which was a twisting mass of clouds and color, lightning arcing through it in spirals of purple and black. In the distance, the Heart of Creation pulsed in the center of Valestra's capital city, pulling the storm inward—but not fast enough.

Callum spotted Marcella near the outer steps, just ahead of Quinn, who shoved a silk sleep mask into his overcoat pocket with a sheepish look on his face. Tuck, Quinn's pacted Darkmoor Cat, was perched on his shoulder, fur bristling, the aethercat's ears flat against his skull.

"Callum!" Quinn called.

"I'm here!"

Marcella turned to speak but stopped as a figure cut through the storm's haze. Master Cruedark stood firm and unyielding against rain that slashed sideways, battering him like a barrage of needles.

The broad-shouldered combat master wore a grim expression as he looked the students over. "I've never seen a storm this bad over the city," he began, his voice cutting through the wind and thunder as if it was magically amplified. "Fan out, all of you. Be ready to protect New Albion with everything you have. This is going to be a fight."

"The Heart of Creation won't stop it?" Marcella asked, barely able to contain her shock.

"Eventually," he said, scanning the horizon. The wind howled behind him as the storm tore through the campus grounds, flinging banners from their posts and hurling debris across the stone paths. "But not before things get through. And if it fails—"

The ground shook as a bolt of lightning struck just ahead, which cut into the ground near one of the gateways to an abandoned campus. They all turned as a monstrous aetherbeast solidified, the creature an amalgam of a broad-backed ungulate and something cruelly feline, its body formed of seething, corrupted mana.

Plates of mana jutted through taut flesh along its spine. Its elongated limbs moved with a terrible, unnatural grace as tendrils unfurled from its shoulders, barbed like whips. Three tails coiled behind the aetherbeast, each ending in a vertical maw that opened in a wet, silent shriek.

"This one is mine," Master Cruedark said, his tone flat, dangerous. Light surged down his arms and a pair of blistering horns erupted from his forehead—jagged, black-edged, steaming in the stormlight.

Several students gasped. None of them had seen him like this. Not truly.

Master Cruedark stepped forward, gaze locked on the beast. "Go. Into the city," he said to the students, horns flaring with power. "Protect the people, and make damn sure New Albion still stands by dawn."

Then he charged, and the terrifying aetherbeast bowed to meet him.

CHAPTER 2

The mana shard recognizes decisive force. It binds to the one who delivered the final blow, regardless of intention or teamwork.

—A quote from *Mana Basics: A Guide to Mastery, 3rd Edition* by Jez Sageglow, Master Weaver, Core Lector

Callum caught a glimpse of the Heart of Creation as he sprinted through the wet streets of New Albion, Marcella and Quinn close behind him and Fen running at his side. The famous structure rose from the city's center like the spine of their kingdom, gleaming with a serene inner light. Waves of magic rippled down its mirrored surface, mana swirling around its spire in looping patterns of purple lightning, striking and dispersing across its surface, held at bay by ancient wards.

"I've never seen it so active," Quinn said as he caught up to Callum.

"Same."

"It's crazy," Marcella said, eyes wide as she took in the Heart.

They didn't have long to look.

A blazing arc of light scythed across the sky and smashed into the street just outside the north gate of the College. It flattened a bookstore in a burst of violet fire and shattered stone, the blast sending a wave of heat across the square, followed by a low hum that vibrated in Callum's chest.

Another aetherbeast, Callum thought as Lynnafer Sunsouth and Godric Rush rounded the corner from the opposite side, their Armorcores gleaming. Godric skidded to a halt and locked eyes with Callum.

"We've got this one!" he called to Godric.

"Right," Lynnafer said, adjusting her goose-headed Weaponcore. "Come on! We'll check the south curve toward the Belldrum District," she said after a quick exchange with Godric.

The two took off just as Marcella shifted into her meldform. "Thanks, Harold!" she called as shimmering heron wings unfurled down her back, each feather edged with glimmering mana. Light spilled from her shoulders as her feet lifted from the ground. A translucent, beak-like protrusion of glowing energy formed over her face, her silhouette blurring at the edges.

<Something is coming!> Fen said as the smoke from the impact site ahead began to lift.

He melded with Callum in a flash of white-gold light, his aura flaring outward as Callum conjured his Armorcore. Shards of radiant plating formed across his limbs and chest, locking into place with a hiss of heat, the weight of it settling in an instant. Familiar now. Natural.

The Weaponcore of the Sunsteel Ram flared to life in Callum's palms as a blade shaped like a ram's horn. He split it in two, as Master Cruedark had shown him, causing a golden pulse of mana to run along the edges of the two ribbed blades.

<Ready to see what these things can do?> Callum asked, looking down at his newest weapon, which he had picked up in the ruins beneath an abandoned campus, thus knocking another unique item off the Great College's hidden Powercore list.

<Always!> Fen said as the smoke parted ahead.

Floating above the shattered remains of the bookstore was a creature that barely conformed to the laws of form, its massive body translucent and amorphous, vaguely shaped like a whale suspended midair. Its underside sagged with squid-like tendrils that trailed beneath it, their slow, drifting motions dragging the creature downward with a kind of lazy menace.

Three yellow eyes opened midair, too slowly, too wide, their glow rippling like oil across water.

"This thing's big!" Marcella said, her wings fanned wide as the rain pouring from the aetherstorm intensified.

"And ugly," Quinn added. His cat claws formed, sleek, blackened talons extending from reinforced armguards.

The aetherwhale let out a low, reverberating groan that echoed off the nearby buildings and made Callum's armor vibrate in protest. It glided forward, reaching down in slow, looping arcs like a spider dipping toward prey.

Callum dashed in first, closing the distance in a fury of motion. The monster snapped toward him; he parried, sparks flying from the impact, and slipped beneath it, where he was able to carve a deep gouge along the beast's semisolid flank.

The aetherbeast shrieked, high and distorted, as Marcella darted past it and loosed a flurry of strikes from her wings. Each bolt slammed into the creature's back and forced it to twist toward the ground.

Dropping to all fours, Quinn charged through the gap, fast and low. He vaulted by the beast just as it smashed into what was left of the west wing of the bookstore, his watery Armorcore actually making a splash as he leaped through a flurry of flying books and straight toward the aetherwhale.

"Quinn, what are you—!" Callum started, but it was too late.

Quinn latched on, claws biting into the creature's flesh. The monster reacted violently, thrashing and slamming him toward the ground. Quinn held fast, dragging it lower with him, using the momentum to force the thing off-balance.

"There's a method to my madness!" Quinn finally shouted to Callum, his voice strained as he pulled the aetherwhale closer toward the ground.

"Sure doesn't look like it from up here!" Marcella called, circling wide for another angle.

The creature bucked, struggling to keep altitude. It slapped against the ground and barreled to the right as it tried to whip Quinn off.

<*Is he really that heavy?*> Callum thought to Fen as he took a step back, looking for his next opening. It became clear that whatever Quinn was doing, it was Powercore related.

<*Some sort of deadweight ability,*> Fen surmised. <*Has to be.*>

"Go, go, go!" Quinn yelled to Callum, who pushed forward again, Ram swords blistering with power.

Callum drew both blades back and pushed them forward, flashing in a crisscross arc as he carved deep into the beast's exposed core. The monster reeled to the right, its entire body convulsing as light bled from the twin gashes across its chest.

With a violent shudder, it made a second attempt to free itself by whipping to the other side, its massive fin catching Quinn and lifting him briefly off the ground. The beast's tendrils flailed and limbs spasmed as it reared back.

A pulse of light surged up the creature's spine, gathering at the blowhole atop its back. In the next instant, mana erupted skyward with a deafening crack, splitting the air like a thunderclap. The focused beam of searing energy lanced straight toward Marcella, who barely had time to register the attack, let alone move.

The shockwave struck her mid-flight, slamming her into a crumbled stone archway of the ruined bookstore. She vanished in a flash of feathers and dust.

"Marcella!" Callum shouted, staggering. He pivoted toward the wreckage, eyes wide—

<No!> Fen snapped. <We have to focus. Harold will protect her—finish this!>

Callum gritted his teeth, forced down the panic, and turned back to the aetherwhale just as it flopped toward him.

The whale's fin struck him, the force sending Callum flying through a broken fence and into the remains of a flower cart, where he cracked his side against a toppled barrel. Wood splintered and pain bloomed down his ribs but his Armorcore took the worst of it.

"Damn it," he gasped, rolling back to his feet.

Before the beast could rise higher, Quinn was already moving, locked in with purpose. He drew a short dagger from his belt, its hilt flickering with sigils—another Weaponcore, compact and volatile.

Quinn drove it into the base of the aetherwhale's side with a shout.

The moment the blade pierced, a burst of mana erupted from within the creature, arcing outward like a contained explosion. Its body lit up from the inside, veins of corrupted energy flashing, cracking, and then collapsing in on themselves.

The aetherwhale let out a final, fractured cry as its body lost shape almost instantly. It dissolved into collapsing strands of magic that hissed against the ground like steam. One by one, the tendrils fell, the air trembling with the release of shards, which poured into Quinn, followed by silence.

Callum pressed forward, the light of his blades slowly fading.

"You good?" he asked, reaching Quinn as the other man stumbled back, eyes wild.

"Been better," Quinn said, sucking in a breath. "Good haul, though. Two Water Affinity Shards, one Empowerment of Might Shard. Nothing whale-related, sadly."

"Marcella?"

As if on cue, a cough came from the rubble. Marcella emerged a few seconds later, covered in dust and wiping her hands on her skirt as she swore under her breath. Harold glided above her head, the heron moving in a protective arc.

"You're lucky Harold caught most of that," she told Quinn. "Or I'd be dragging that whale corpse over your grave."

"You're blaming its blowhole attack on me? Seriously?"

"Who else was latched onto the thing, throwing it off course and directly into my line of flight?"

"Less arguing," Callum said, squinting toward the next street. "There's going to be more."

All three turned as a fresh shockwave rippled through the air. The Heart of Creation was still holding, but the storm wasn't done yet.

More comet-like flashes landed ahead, signaling a new wave of aetherbeasts.

"Let's keep going," Marcella said with a quick breath out. "And . . ."

"Yes?" Quinn asked as she turned to him.

"Just out of curiosity, what did you do back there anyway?"

"What do you mean?"

"That aetherwhale was massive. How did you pull it to the ground?"

"Oh, *that*. It's a power that Tuck has," Quinn told her.

<*I knew it!*> Fen said privately to Callum, as Quinn continued:

"It's called Gravitail and it amplifies my weight. Think of it as Tuck lending me some of his stubbornness—" It was clear that his pacted aetherbeast said something in Quinn's head as a smirk traced across his face. "Anyway, I never thought it would be useful but, apparently, it helped."

"Keep telling yourself that," Marcella said as she glanced around. "Where to now? There is so much going on that it's hard to pick any one path."

Callum stepped up. "Everyone will likely be in the districts closer to the Great College. Perhaps . . . Stadacona? That would be closer to the storm's edge." He glanced skyward, watching as rain lashed down in unrelenting sheets. "I think we might get lucky out there."

"If by lucky, you mean get a bunch of shards and maybe a few Power-cores, I'm game," Marcella said, her wings appearing as Harold melded with her. "Lead the way, or maybe I will this time."

CHAPTER 3

Even in shadow, the spires do not fall. The College endures, and the Heart beats strong. New Albion—city of ages. The Valestra Kingdom—most noble of them all. Built by the strength of legend and archmages.

—Kay Fife, poet

The three students reached the edge of Stadacona just as the wind settled into a heavy, unbroken drizzle. The storm had already carved its signature into the city—walls scorched by lightning, stones cracked from fallen debris, and craters marking the places where aetherbeasts had struck.

For the past hour, they had pushed through the nearly flooded streets of New Albion, slaying corrupted beasts and hauling in shards. Battles flared and faded in every district, and shards flew like sparks, scattered and claimed by whoever landed the final blow. Callum now carried three Air Affinity Shards, two Fire Affinity Shards, and two Attribute Shards, a Vigor and a Might. He had yet to distribute the shards he had claimed in his excursion with Princess Selene, considering he had only returned two nights ago, and his pouch was starting to get heavy.

Quinn hopped down from a collapsed cart just as his feline meldform disappeared in a sizzle of magic. "We've done pretty well for a rescue crew, and we haven't had to deal with many people. Not bad! Tuck says it's not bad."

"Which probably means the people cleared out *before* the monsters showed up," Marcella told him. "That's the first lucky thing that's happened all night. Tell Tuck that."

Rather than listen to the two playfully bicker, Callum scanned the open plaza ahead, where rain traveled in narrow channels through the cobblestone at their feet, thick with ash and splinters.

<We might be in the clear when it comes to civilians,> Fen said, *<but the storm hasn't cleared up yet.>*

<No, it hasn't.> Callum glanced back toward the Heart of Creation, now a distant shape in the skyline—still towering, still pulsing, but softened by the thick rain between them.

The air around it shimmered with residual power, a magical mist drifting around it in a spiraling pattern. Bolts of mana still arced toward its mirrored surface, each one absorbed in silence, feeding the tower's slow, relentless pull. The worst of the storm might have passed, but the power it left behind still circled the Heart, refusing to scatter.

Callum turned back to the Stadacona market, where the air still carried the sharp scent of rain and lightning-scorched stone.

<You sense it too?> Fen asked.

<I do.>

The district's main square had been reduced to partial ruin. What remained were ripped canopies and broken frames, stalls torn to shreds, and crates overturned and emptied by wind. Here and there, stubborn lanterns still burned from iron hooks, casting golden puddles of light into the gloom, as if refusing to give in.

Something crashed through a row of spice barrels near the fountain.

"Heads up!" Marcella said as a corrupted aetherbeast tore out of the center of the square in a snarl of splintered wood and warped mana.

It was shaped like an elk, massive and powerful, but its antlers were jagged, sharp, and branched far too wide. Instead of hooves, the monster had wide, curved claws that gouged the stones with every step. Beneath its skin, faint lines of glowing silver-white light pulsed rhythmically, magic stitched into muscle. The aetherbeast turned toward them and charged, shattering the remains of a fruit stall in its wake.

Callum didn't wait.

He summoned his claws in a burst of wind and dove to the side, using Zephyr Strike angled toward its flank. Callum raked his Radiant Claws across its hide; the beast twisted mid-step and retaliated with a side kick that sent Callum tumbling, his Armorcore flaring with light as it strained under the impact.

<Let's pin it!> Fen told him.

Callum called on his Roots of the Willow Aethertree Powercore, which summoned mana-laced vines from the cobblestones beneath the aetherbeast's feet. They coiled upward with preternatural speed, wrapped the monster's legs, and yanked them downward, just enough to break the aetherbeast's momentum.

"I'm going in!" Quinn lunged, claws flashing.

He landed on the beast's back—but only for a moment.

The creature bucked hard, launching him into the air like a loose sack of grain. Quinn flew backward, narrowly missing Marcella as she soared overhead. She dipped to avoid him, wings faltering slightly before she regained her balance.

"I'm fine!" Quinn yelled from the mud, flat on his back.

Callum's Ram swords appeared mid-step, seething with brilliance. He leaped forward, blades raised, ready to drive them into the creature's exposed shoulder.

A scream split the air above him.

Callum jerked his head up as a new shape tore through the rainclouds.

The approaching aetherbeast stretched unnaturally thin, its wings made of sheer aetherlight, taut and alive with flickering power. Each beat sent arcs of energy rippling through the storm. Its long, sinuous body twisted through the air, trailing tendrils that lashed behind it like whips of lightning, carving streaks of brilliance across the darkened sky.

Callum had to abort mid-strike, twisting away just as the monster passed overhead in a shriek of wind and venom.

"Above you!" Marcella shouted as he landed.

With Fen's help, Callum jumped again to dodge the aetherbeast. He came back up with his Piercing Air Spear, which flared to life in his grip as the beast wheeled midair, rising sharply to arc back toward him.

Callum didn't give it the chance. His spear tore through the air, straight through the creature's open chest. The beast convulsed once mid-flight, its wings folding inward, then crashed into the side of a nearby tower in a shower of sparks and dissipating mana.

A Powercore flew into Callum's hand and he briefly checked the details before sending it to his Soul Heart.

Gale Pulse of the Skyrend Screech
Type: *Ability*
Grade: *Uncommon*
Infusion Requirements for Grade Increase:
0/20 Air Affinity Shards
0/10 Might Shards
0/5 Resilience Shards
Affinity Requirements: *Air*
Effect: *Unleashes a concussive burst of wind in all directions, knocking enemies back and interrupting spellcasting or movement.*

Callum looked back at the other aetherbeast to find Marcella hovering in the air above it, wings extended but still, motionless.

<*What's she doing?*> he asked Fen.

<*Wait—!*>

Callum stepped back as Marcella's aura condensed into a silhouette of glimmering magic. The plaza went quiet around her, the rain itself seeming to pause for half a breath.

She flickered forward in a blur, her form vanishing, then reappearing behind the aetherbeast, one hand extended as if she'd thrown something invisible.

The beast staggered.

A ripple of force cracked through its body, and its antlers shattered, the monster collapsing forward in a heap, unmoving.

Marcella touched down lightly on the wet stones as several Attribute Shards rushed toward her. She turned to Quinn and offered him a hand. "You alright?"

"Define 'alright,'" he groaned, taking it.

A flash of concern painted across her face. "Do you need a Regeneration Shard?" Marcella went for her shard pouch.

"No, no, I'll survive." Quinn smiled at her. "Thanks, though. Tuck says thanks as well."

"What was that attack you did?" Callum asked Marcella as he joined the two of them.

"I've been meaning to try it," she said. "It's called Pierce of the Still Beak. It's a Powercore I picked up at the Emporium when we got back from our trip. Good, right?"

"Amazing," Callum said. "I don't even know how to describe what you just did."

She winked. "Watch and learn." Marcella stepped away, only to stop and turn back to the two of them. "I guess that would have been more dramatic if I had somewhere to go."

"Campus?" Quinn asked.

Callum glanced around at the quiet that had finally settled over the square. The storm was breaking apart overhead, its heavy black clouds retreating in pieces. Blue light stretched across the buildings, soft and pale, the first breath of morning.

He exhaled once. "Yeah, let's get back to campus."

As Callum walked back to the Great College, and as Marcella and Quinn spoke about all that had just happened, he used Soul Sense and quickly scanned the information:

Soul Sense:
Status:
Health: *Uninjured*
Mana Reserves: *Steady*
Soul Heart Rank: *Wielder*
Soulbonding Capacity: *15 Powercores, 2 Aethercore*
Attributes:
Might: 5
Deftness: 4
Vigor: 4
Resilience: 4
Regeneration: 4
Mind: 4
Soulbound Cores:
Ability: *Empowerment of Zephyr Strike*
Ability: *Gift of the Luminous Lance*
Ability: *Inner Light*
Ability: *Roots of the Willow Aethertree*
Ability: *Onslaught of the Thunderhoof Shadowbull*
Ability: *Gale Pulse of the of the Skyrend Screech*
Accessory: *Weaponcore of the Tempest Fang*
Accessory: *Piercing Air Spear*
Accessory: *Weaponcore of the Sunsteel Ram*
Support: *Empowerment of Sustenance*
Support: *Armorcore of the Brightflame Falcon*
Support: *Empowerment of Sustenance*
Pact: *Pact of the Radiant Fox*

Now that I've reached the Wielder Stage, I can pact with another aetherbeast, Callum thought. *But with the tournament coming up, and classes, I don't even know where to begin looking for a new Aethercore.*

As they climbed a flight of steps, his thoughts drifted to the statue of his forefather at the Great College. Five pacted aetherbeasts: a fox, a gryphon, a wolf, a phoenix, and a dragon.

Obviously the gryphon made the most sense, but where would he even start looking? He let out a quiet breath and glanced over as Quinn knelt beside a man slumped against a barrel.

"I'll be fine, sonny," the man said, waving him on.

"Are you sure—?"

The man wiped water from his brow and flicked it onto the ground. "This isn't my first aetherstorm. Why do you think I moved here from Weatherby."

Callum stopped. "Did you say you were from Weatherby?"

"I did," the man said, offering up a toothless grin, "But I haven't been back in years."

"That's where I'm from."

The man gave Callum a once-over, eyebrows knitting together. "Weatherby? The only nobles from that patch of nowhere are the Strosses."

"That's me!" Callum quickly tempered his enthusiasm. "I'm a Stross. Callum Stross—"

"Little Cal?" The man's eyes bulged slightly. "The last time I saw you, you were six, maybe seven years old." He grinned. "Small world, I guess." Something shifted in his posture. "I know your pappy had it hard back there on accounts of what happened with your mother, but I'm glad to see you making something of yourself, and I'm glad to see that the city still stands." He waved them on. "Now back to the college, heh, and don't worry about Ol' Lyrian here. I'm sure you all have some regrouping to do."

Marcella shouldered up next to Callum after they passed. "Little Cal, huh?"

"Please don't . . ." he started to say.

"Your secret is safe with me." She pretended to lock her lips and throw away the key.

They came to the gates of the Great College, passing upperclassmen assigned to deal with the storm's aftermath. A water-aspected aetherbeast snaked through the scorched courtyard, its fluid form weaving between stones as it doused smoldering patches with controlled jets. Nearby, a student guided a windbound hawk, its wings flicking out sharp gusts that swept ash and broken tiles into neat piles. Others moved between cracked stones and shattered arches, conjuring light to inspect deep fractures or calling on earth-aspected cores to brace weakened walls.

A few students sat on overturned benches, mana reserves clearly spent, hands trembling as they passed canteens or slumped forward to rest. Someone had chalked inspection marks along the base of a collapsed tower, and off to the side, a fire-aspected salamander hissed quietly while a student used the light from its forked tongue to peer into the hollow beneath the rubble, where smoke still curled.

As they pressed through the gates, the three saw the students from their cohort gathered around Master Cruedark. Callum scanned the group, catching some of Draven's friends, none of whom made eye contact with him. He hoped to see the princess, but he knew that she had stayed behind after their last excursion at the request of Sir Trindade, who wanted them to brief the High Council, which was currently holding court in Ontaria.

Lynnafer and Godric waved to them, Godric the first to speak. "Did you all hear what happened to Victrin?" He went ahead and told them before they could respond. "He was launched into the air and hit his head on the lip of a well and somehow, I sort of wish I had seen it—he's fine—flipped into the well and had to be fished out by Demandra, *literally*."

Callum looked over to the blonde-haired woman, whom he once bested in a sparring match. She hadn't spoken to him since he'd taken out her pacted koi fish.

Before Godric could say anything else, Master Cruedark clapped his hands together once.

"Listen up, everyone," the big man said in his booming voice. "I know that this storm pushed many of you further than anything you've faced before. But what you did—stepping into chaos, facing the unknown, protecting this city—is exactly what we expect from the next generation of Great College archmages."

Master Cruedark beamed a smile at all of them.

"Now, it's practically morning, so get yourself some sleep. Classes are canceled today. I suggest tallying up your shards and visiting the Emporium, which was thankfully spared. Sundering, fusing, training, resting, writing a letter to your mum—whatever it is you need to do to prepare for the upcoming tournament against the Geshwine Empire. Details to follow. And do not worry about New Albion. She will survive. The Heart of Creation stands. And luckily, so do we."

CHAPTER 4

Every archmage remembers the first Powercore they received in the field. Few keep it. The ones who rise? They learn to love the upgrade more than the memory.

—A quote from guest lecture at the Great College, Year 517, by Jez Sageglow, Master Weaver, Core Lector

Callum lay on his back in the dormitory's upper loft, eyes open, pillow pressed uselessly against his face. Sleep wasn't happening. Not after everything—the shock, the fights, his nerves still buzzing like the aetherstorm had left something burning inside him.

Morning light spilled through the high windows, casting a soft wash of blue across the ceiling. With a groan, Callum rolled over and sat up.

<*Someone can't sleep,*> Fen said, not even bothering to sound surprised. He appeared in a dazzling flash of mana and stretched.

<*Nope.*>

<*You need the rest.*>

<*Maybe this will help.*> Callum pulled on the cloak his father had made him buy and dropped into the meditation position on the floor. As he closed his eyes, Mastress Lucerne's words came to him: *Quiet the body. Quiet the mind. Calm the breath. Calm the thoughts.*

The Great College's Soul Pythia had drilled the fundamentals of cycling into them during Soul Heart cultivation: breathe, find stillness, release the hands, ignore the impulses, and unclench the jaw. Proper cycling, she had explained, wasn't just about survival—it was dialogue. A conversation between power and self.

Let the breath guide the mind. Open the channels.

He focused inward, past the surface of any strain he still felt from the previous night. Callum imagined his Soul Heart kindling to life, mana streaming from it in smooth, unbroken lines.

Draw in ambient mana . . .

The dorm room wasn't rich with leylines, but after last night, the air still carried a trace of power, a storm-churned energy that he could feel. Callum pulled it in gently, not too fast. His professor had warned them that cycling wasn't about devouring. It was about rhythm. Balance. Respect.

And she's the Soul Pythia; she knows what she's talking about, he thought as his mind jumped to the trials he had faced when joining the Great College, how they had all taken place in his head.

He fidgeted until Fen noticed.

<*Focus.*>

"Sorry," he whispered, once again returning to his breath.

He soon found himself in a strange state, somewhere between awake and a deep reverie. The state came coupled with passing images, from his farm back in Weatherby to his recent journey with Princess Selene, when they had passed through a portal hidden in a portrait into what felt like an entirely new world.

He pushed the memories aside as energy flowed into his Soul Heart and out again, looping back through his system in practiced spirals.

It was working. The slight ache in his limbs eased. His thoughts settled even further.

Circulate mana through the Soul Heart and back out. Let the cracks smooth. Let the flow move through you . . .

The spiral continued for several more breaths, steady and—

Then the thought struck. *I was in Stadacona and I didn't even check on the barn!*

Callum's eyes snapped open. <*Telluride. I need to check on him!*>

<*Oof, probably a smart idea. Now?*>

Rather than answer, Callum stood, already moving as he slipped on the cloak, into his boots, and back into the Great College overcoat that all the students wore. The mana still cycling through his core gave him a strange clarity as he left his dorm, a surge of focus he hadn't felt before. Each step felt light, balanced.

Callum sprinted through the Great College's outer gates and down the winding path into the wider city, not bothering to stop to look at any of the smoldering buildings, New Albion passing in streaks.

He took the quickest route toward the outskirts, weaving through the battered edge of the Belldrum District. The storm had hit hard here. Entire ceramic furnaces lay in ruins, their brick shells collapsed inward, scorched and rain-soaked. Shattered pottery was strewn in heaps along the road, bright fragments of glaze catching the morning light. Amid the wreckage, men and women in leather aprons had already begun the slow work of cleaning up, moving with the quiet determination of those too exhausted to despair.

He barely slowed.

Within minutes, Callum reached the red barn Telluride called home, where he found the door already open, warm light flickering from inside. He stepped inside to the sound of gentle whistling and the unmistakable scent of frying butter and eggs.

Telluride stood near the hearth, sleeves rolled, a pan in hand, his pipe near the cutting board. His eyes shot over to Callum. "Ah, I was wondering how you fared," he said, grinning.

"I came to check on you. I'm sorry, I should have—"

"Sorry for what?" Telluride interrupted. "Aetherstorms are terrible things, and I'm sure the Great College kept you busy."

"It did."

"The damage is mostly over. There will be the usual issues that follow a storm like that—"

"Once in a lifetime, right?"

Telluride pursed his lips as he considered this. "Maybe not. There was one that was rumored to have been stronger back when I was a student at the Great College. They have instruments to measure them you know. But in the end, we survived." He breathed in deeply, gesturing at the gentle shimmer of mana still clinging to the wooden rafters. "And the magic they leave in the air, heh, you can *taste* it."

Only then did Callum realize something felt off. His energy levels were unusually high. He had crossed the city with barely any strain, almost like the mana in the air had carried him, his steps lighter than they should have been.

He turned toward the older man, blinking. "How come I didn't feel that after the aetherstorm in Weatherby?"

"Well, for one, you were pretty new to this at the time, if I'm not mistaken."

Fen appeared beside Callum, his mana form flickering into view with a soft pulse of light, shaped like a fox made of essence and flame. "We both were. Well, sort of."

"And good morning to you too, Fen!"

"Morning," the fox said.

"As for the power you feel, you're much closer to the Heart of Creation than you were when you were in Weatherby. It has a way of absorbing and radiating mana outward." Telluride returned to the eggs he was cooking. He flattened them into a pancake and painstakingly flipped them. "Take a seat, I'll make you one as well."

"I just came to check on you."

"Nonsense," Telluride said. "We'll eat first. Then we begin."

"Begin?"

"If your experience was anything like mine, your teachers gave you the day off and told you to deal with your shards and Powercores, right?"

"How did you know?"

Telluride gave him a knowing look.

"Right, you were a student too. Actually, maybe it's good I stick around for a moment. I have something to catch you up on," Callum said, "A lot, actually."

"Good. Breakfast and a chat first, then we fuse and sunder. Better here than the Emporium. Every student's going to be there, and the shard dealers know it." He pinched his fingers and flicked them upward, the signal for gouging prices. "Shardcrafters always profit after a storm."

After breakfast, and after stepping outside to smoke his pipe for a few minutes, Telluride ushered Callum into the cramped workspace where he did his shardcrafting. He settled onto his usual cushion behind his grooved table. Callum joined him and unclipped his shard pouch, the contents jingling softly as he set it down on the etched surface between them.

"That is quite the haul," Telluride said as he started going through the shards. "You have three Air Affinity, two Fire Affinity, three Shadow Affinity, three Death Affinity—which I will destroy—and two Earth Affinity, not to mention . . ." he shifted through Callum's Attribute Shards. "Three Mind, one Deftness, one Resilience, one Vigor, two Regeneration, and two Might shards. Why didn't you use any of these last night?"

"I didn't feel the need to. The aetherbeasts we faced were intense, but . . ." Callum relaxed a little more. "It still feels strange to simply use an Attribute Shard, if we're being honest. I always think back to my time on the farm, when we used them like once a year."

"And then you go on an excursion with Princess Selene and your friends, and everyone is using them, right?"

"True," Callum said, recalling he had taken a cocktail of shards back at the abandoned campus. "I barely used my meldform abilities last night, like Radiant Inferno."

"They weren't needed," Fen assured Telluride. "Or, better and not to sound cocky, they may have been had it been just the two of us facing off against the aetherbeasts. But Marcella and Quinn were there."

"Yes, strength in numbers, generally an advantage." He stroked his patchy beard stubble. "Well, if you ask me, and you sort of are, I would tell you to preserve them when you can, but don't be afraid to use them. You're at the Wielder Stage now, yes?" he asked Callum.

"That's right."

"Which means you can have how many cores?"

"Fifteen."

"And the cores you do have will be more powerful if you upgrade them. You know the breakdown?"

"Kind of," Callum said. "I know that the rarer ones get stronger depending on my Stage."

"Correct. At the Wielder stage, a Common Powercore operates at the 120 percent level; an Uncommon core operates at the 110 percent level; a Rare core operates at the 100 percent level; Exalted at 85 percent; Sublime at 65 percent; Legendary at 45 percent; and finally, Mythical at 45 percent. Let's try it another way: what's the most powerful core you have based on its grade?"

"Empowerment of Rejuvenation," Callum said.

"Which you got by . . ." Telluride squinted at him. "No, don't tell me. The Archive of Destiny, that's what you said before, right? You went there and it led you to a core given to you directly by your forefather. Lucky, you are! And lucky I am for having a good memory!" He sighed. "Alas, if only my forefathers had been so prescient to leave me a divine inheritance. Anyway, I digress because I can, Empowerment of Rejuvenation is now operating at 45 percent of its max power, which oftentimes, is stronger than a Common core operating at 120 percent of its max power."

"Yes, Mastress Lucerne mentioned that. If you strictly look at the numbers, upgrading a Core seems to downgrade it based on whatever Stage you are at, but this isn't the case."

"No, it is not. So don't let these percentages fool you. And don't be afraid to sunder a few cores to reap their powers." Telluride motioned to the Affinity Shards. "You shouldn't be carrying this many around. The Attribute Shards? Sure, carry some if you plan to use them, but you should be fusing as quickly as you can. It's a better way to store them."

"I know, I know, it's been a wild couple of days."

"Understandable, and now that you're at the Wielder Stage, your main goal should be bringing Fen's Aethercore up with you. So let's focus on that first. Let's see what you need to upgrade it, and then we can look through your cores to see what I could potentially sunder."

Callum accessed that information:

Pact of the Radiant Fox
Type: *Pacted*
Grade: *Uncommon*
Infusion Requirements for Grade Increase:
4/10 Air Affinity Shards
0/10 Light Affinity Shards
1/10 Deftness Shards
7/10 Might Shards
5/5 Resilience Shards
Mana Affinity Granted: *Air, Fire, Light*
Meldform Benefits:
Attributes:
+3 Might
+4 Deftness
+3 Vigor
+3 Resilience
+3 Regeneration
+1 Mind
Radiant Claws: *When melded with the Radiant Fox, the wielder gains powerful claws made of burning light, which can not only be used to attack its enemies, but also empower further, unleashing blazing slashes of fire and light a short distance before them.*
Radiant Inferno: *When melded with the Radiant Fox, channel pure radiant energy into flames that create a white-hot fire capable of melting through armor and dispelling darkness. The flames burn brighter than natural fire, blinding enemies with their intensity.*

"Good, good," Telluride said. "Let's now focus on what you already have first. You had three Air Affinity Shards, so fuse those, the Empowerment of Deftness and the two Might Shards."

"Will do," Callum said as he brought out Fen's Aethercore. The surface of the palm-sized orb of prismatic light flickered with a foxlike motion, as if a radiant tail swirled just beneath the surface. He fused the shards, then pressed the core back into his chest.

"Always check," Telluride reminded him.

Callum used Soul Sense again and saw that the shards were now fused.

Pact of the Radiant Fox
Type: *Pacted*
Grade: *Uncommon*

Infusion Requirements for Grade Increase:
7/10 Air Affinity Shards
0/10 Light Affinity Shards
2/10 Deftness Shards
9/10 Might Shards
5/5 Resilience Shards

"Everything in order?"

"It is," Callum toll Telluride.

"Now, let's look at all your Powercores and see which ones we can get rid of." Something flashed across the older man's eyes. "Well, that's an easy one. You have Gift of the Luminous Lance, which is a Powercore, and Piercing Air Spear, a Weaponcore. These have a similar function. You need Light Affinity for Fen's Aethercore and Might. If we sunder Luminous Lance, that should get you part of the way there."

"That was the first Powercore I got on my own," Callum said.

"Treat Powercores as tools, not treasures. It's the parts inside that usually matter most."

"The thing is, that core specifically came from a man named Brock who died defending the caravan that brought me to New Albion." Callum shook his head as he remembered the fight against the bandits, the first time he had killed someone.

Though Fen sat next to him, his voice spoke straight into Callum's thoughts, clear and steady. <*He's right, we can't get attached to these things. Brock would want you to do what's best.*>

<*I know, I know. I didn't expect to feel sentimental about a power.*>

<*It happens. You've been through a lot since my rebirth.*>

"Let's do it," Callum told Telluride as he looked back up at the shardcrafter.

"You sure? You seem to be debating it."

"I can't get attached to these things. Fen's Aethercore is more important."

"Correct. It will augment your overall power, and Piercing Air Spear will take something out just as easily." He bit his lip. "Well, in theory. Aetherbeasts do have weaknesses to certain powers, but this isn't something that has been fully documented when it comes to the corrupted ones."

"Many of the corrupted ones seem to be amalgamations," Callum said as he summoned his Luminous Lance core. The glowing orb floated over to Telluride, who examined it for a moment.

The shardcrafter grew serious.

Callum couldn't see it clearly, but he noticed something anchoring the core to the worktable. Telluride's unkempt eyebrows drew tight as he studied the orb. He lifted a finger and it shattered, the fragments falling neatly into a carved recess in the wood.

"Ah, good, five Light Affinity Shards, and two Might Shards," he said. "You only needed one Might Shard, so you can pocket the extra one for now. The rest?"

". . . should be fused." Callum once again brought Fen's Aethercore out and fused the shards into it. He checked to find they were all in place.

"Correct. You still need Deftness, but it's a start," Telluride said. "Now your Weaponcores. You have a wind sword, a ram sword—"

"You should see that one in action," Callum said, lighting up a bit. "It's amazing. The weapon splits into two."

"Two swords?"

Callum nodded.

"Well, I can imagine that would be quite helpful, wielding two weapons. Never tried it myself. Was bad enough with just the one!"

"Master Cruedark gave me a few pointers on wielding two weapons. I used it last night."

"And can the sword operate as a single blade?"

"It can. We tested it," Callum said. "It has more finesse as a single weapon, but it seems deadlier as two."

"I bet it looks that way as well. Huh. What about your wind sword, Weaponcore of the Tempest Fang, it has synergy with Zephyr Strike, does it not?"

"It does," Callum said. "I can conjure the power through it."

"Which can amplify the effect. Worth keeping for now, although you'll need Air Affinity, Vigor, and Might shards if you want to bring the sword up from Uncommon to Rare." He glanced over at the spare shards Callum had. "Yes, definitely worth it for the synergy alone."

"I can put the Vigor and Might there now."

"Smart move." Telluride waited for Callum to fuse the two shards. "A little housekeeping never hurt anyone." He glanced around the shabby room and laughed. "I really need to take my own advice; that or get the hell out of this shardforsaken barn."

CHAPTER 5

The modern Core Emporium was rebuilt following the Shatterwake of Year 427, which triggered a cascading mudslide that buried much of the original Emporium's foundation. Rather than demolish what remained, the Crown sanctioned an elevated reconstruction, resulting in its current multitiered design. The lower levels—now often the booths of unlicensed shardmongers and enterprising renegades—are remnants of the original arcane market, still etched with trader-marks and old warding glyphs.

—A quote from *Brick to Breath: A History of New Albion's Living Architecture* by Sir Eligus Ruthsep, Duke of Livingston, High Council historian

Callum stopped in front of the Emporium, its arched doors flung wide to the morning bustle. The building looked much the same as always, an enormous structure built from wood and stone, anchored into the hillside just off the eastern campus path.

The storm had left its mark. Twigs and broken branches still clung stubbornly to the roof's edge. Orange autumn leaves plastered the stone walls and fluttered from torn campus banners. A cracked upper window had been hastily covered with a swath of leather, and near the front steps, faint gouges in the stone and a smear of blackened residue marked where something had fought the night before.

<Lively,> Fen commented as Callum stepped forward, and let the buzz of student voices wash over him.

The Emporium's upper floor was in full swing. Students in overcoats leaned across countertops discussing shard values and Powercore properties. Sparks leaped from sundering tables, and the mingled scents of parchment, fresh ink, and spent mana hung heavy in the air. Farther back, a pair of upperclassmen debated animatedly while holding a flickering Memorycore between them.

Callum's eyes swept across the vaulted interior as light spilled through stained-glass panels overhead, casting bands of amber and teal across the floors.

<*I don't think we've ever seen it this busy,*> Fen said from within.

<*Telluride was right about that,*> Callum told the Radiant Fox as he moved toward the back. His feet knew the way, boots clicking down polished wooden stairs as the light dimmed and the gleam of the main floor gave way to worn boards below.

Only hushed conversations filled the basement. This was where the real deals were made, tucked behind curtains, at private counters, and in rooms with cushioned seats that likely weren't listed on any official map.

Where could she be? Callum thought as he scanned the basement for the shardcrafter Quinn had introduced him to.

He pushed through a beaded curtain and turned left, following the path to an open door made of stained cedar, the space beyond lit by the soft glow of a Fire Affinity Shard suspended in a bell-shaped lantern.

"Ah, it's you," Birchwen said as she looked up at him. The yellow-eyed shardcrafter sat cross-legged atop a wide, embroidered cushion, her head wrapped in a familiar scarf, wrists jingling with charm-heavy bracelets. "The hero returns. How is the Tempest Fang?"

"It's doing well enough," Callum told her. "And thanks for trading it to me last time. It has definitely come in handy."

"Yet you have a new blade, a very good one as well," Birchwen said, her eyes glittered a bit. "I'm sure that came in handy last night. I heard the explosions. Sounded like fun."

Callum offered her a weary smile. "I've had better nights."

"Mmm. And worse, I imagine." She motioned to the cushion in front of her. "But nothing students from the Great College can't handle, especially with the instructors you have there."

"Yeah?" Callum asked as he took a seat on the thick cushion.

"They're the best, and everyone knows that. That's why the Soul Pythia is there. I always wanted to be one, you know. I studied at the Great College's campus in Karna. I tried many times to be accepted to one of the Pythia schools so I could someday be part of the Circle, but it never worked out."

<*Karna,*> Callum thought to Fen. <*Where have we heard that?*>

<*Draven is from there. His father is the Duke of Karna.*>

<*Right . . .*>

"To be expected," Birchwen said as she leaned in a bit, "it seems like every time I mention my origins to someone, they have to pause for a moment to consider it."

"It wasn't that. I was just confirming that one of my classmates is from Karna."

"Duke Blademark's son, yes? The warlock."

"Yes," Callum told her, "the warlock."

Birchwen's expression didn't shift, but something in her eyes cooled. "Anyway. You didn't come here to talk about Karna. Tell me what you need."

"I'm here for three Air Affinity Shards. Five Light Affinity. And Eight Empowerment of Deftness," Callum said, getting right down to it.

"Are you?" She pressed back, bracelets clinking softly. "And what exactly do you have to offer me in return?"

"I have seven Mana Affinity Shards, and six Empowerment—"

"I'm aware," she said, cutting him off. "I have access to the World Ledger, you know." Birchwen folded her hands, fingers steepled as she considered him. "Shame, really. What I *really* need right now are Death Shards. But you don't seem to have any."

Callum's brow furrowed. "I had a few but they've been handled."

"Handled?" she asked. "As in . . . ?"

"Destroyed." He kept his voice even. "Another shardcrafter took care of them."

Her eyes narrowed slightly. "*Took care of them.* That's very polite phrasing."

"I watched him do it."

"His name?"

"Te—"

<*Let's keep this information to ourselves,*> Fen said, interrupting. <*That part shouldn't matter to her.*>

<*Maybe you're right,*> Callum thought back. <*Telluride doesn't seem to like the Emporium very much.*> He looked back up at Birchwen. "That part doesn't matter. They're destroyed."

"Funny," she said after an uncomfortable pause. "Most shardcrafters I know wouldn't *dream* of wasting that kind of money."

"The Crown is paying for them, I'm aware."

"And with that money you could have easily purchased what you need. Not that your shards aren't useful, they are, but you would have made quite the savings. Instead of spending everything you have, you would have only spent two or three Death Affinity Shards. What was the shardcrafter's name again?"

"Like I said, that part doesn't matter," Callum said, echoing Fen's words.

She waved her hand as if brushing smoke away. "Fine. Secrets make the market spin, I suppose. But for the record—if he *did* keep them, he'd be sitting on a fortune. A dangerous one."

Callum remained silent, staring at her and waiting for the conversation to move on.

Eventually, Birchwen gave him an amused smile. "Now then, about those Air and Light shards . . ."

"And Deftness."

"Yes, eight Empowerment of Deftness Shards. You need a total of sixteen shards, but you only have thirteen to trade. And shards, as you should know by now, aren't always an even exchange. Certain shards go up in value and drop in value depending on a number of factors, such as an aetherstorm nearly destroying the city. So you're going to need more than what you have."

Fen appeared, the radiant fox flaring into existence. "We came here—"

"Ah, there you are, Radiant Fox. I was wondering if we would ever meet," Birchwen said. "Relax. Even though I would love to take a few of your Powercores off you, including the Onslaught of the Thunderhoof Shadowbull, and, if we're being honest, Inner Light, I'm not going to shake you down in that way. Not today, anyway. I will trade the sixteen shards you need for the thirteen that you have." Her yellow eyes settled on Callum. "But I need something from you."

"Yeah?" he asked, not sure what to make of the woman and the strange power she held over him.

"Where are you from again?" she asked.

"I never told you. I'm from Weatherby."

"Ah, out west, w*here the sky leans low and the wheat runs deep,* right? Not far from the Grimbald border." Birchwen gave him a knowing smile. "That explains it. You've got the farmboy look and a bit of that small-village softness around the edges. Don't worry. It's almost charming."

Fen stepped closer to her and the Fire Affinity Shard in her lantern flickered. "What are you trying to say?"

She cackled to herself. "Actually, it's pretty simple. There was a storm last night, as you likely recall, and it ruined the fence around my home. Normally, I wouldn't care, I'm only renting the flat. But that fence was the only thing between me and a road full of dust, carts, and drunks. So I need someone to fix it." She turned her attention back to Callum. "What do you say?"

Callum fought the grin rising to his face. <*A fence?*> he told Fen privately. <*I've been mending fences since I was six!*>

"Well?" Birchwen asked again. "Is that something you can handle? Today, preferably?"

"Thirteen shards and a fence repair in exchange for the sixteen I need for upgrades?" Callum reached across the table and she took his hand. "You've got yourself a deal."

CHAPTER 6

With each upgrade, the bond deepens. Power doesn't come from shards alone, but from the soul they reshape. Every new stage is a door.

—A quote from *On the Nature and Simplification of Mana Reserves* by Renova Dreagis, Mastress Shaper, Archona of Ridgebarrow, Soul Pythia

Two weeks later, Callum stood at the edge of a mountain ledge, breath fogging the air. The portal behind him shimmered like frosted glass, anchored by a rune-marked arch that crackled softly with ambient magic. He hadn't used this particular training space before, one of the many elemental domains the Great College had scattered across its sprawling grounds, but it suited him this morning.

Beyond, the mountains rose in jagged procession—tall, spire-thin peaks that seemed to defy the very shape of the world. Their ridges stretched like stone filaments into the clouds, their forms half-lost to veils of drifting snow and ice. Above it all, the sky gleamed pale, a crystalline blue that felt impossibly high, as if the air itself had thinned into light.

Callum rolled his shoulders and shook off the ache from his morning history class with Mastress Gilford. She had spent the entire hour tracing the timeline of the little-known Shardwar on the border between the Valestra Kingdom and the Geshwine Empire that ultimately resulted in the founding of the city of Karna. Though Callum respected her, she had a way of meandering like a river across too many valleys.

One hour to train before I need to meet Marcella and Quinn for lunch, he thought as he drew in a deep breath. *Time enough to sweat.*

Callum dropped into a low stance and began his drills, starting with bodyweight work: lunges, deep squats, core rotations. Each movement was anchored in breath and precision, his form sharpened by weeks of repetition. He felt the cold stone beneath his feet, the controlled tension of each hold, the slow burn waking in his thighs and shoulders. This was foundational work—muscle memory, posture control, the kind of discipline his Weaponcores demanded.

He transitioned into resistance training, pressing down as he held low stances and forced his arms through invisible strain. His body fought every movement. His shoulders ached. His balance wavered. His arms trembled. That was good. It meant something was changing—old limits stretching, new strength rooting itself in both muscle and mana.

When Callum finally summoned the Sunsteel Ram swords, they flared into his hands with a blaze of gold light. The twin blades curved outward like horned crescents, rippling with a heat that never cooled entirely. He spun them once to reset his balance, then dropped into a two-blade stance.

Master Cruedark's voice echoed in his memory: *Think of your new blades as a pair of twin knights trained from birth to fight alongside each other. One moves forward, the other guards. One creates pressure, the other punishes overreach. Lightning and thunder. Wind and weight. Never let them move in the same rhythm—make your opponent guess which half is coming next.*

Make your opponent guess, Callum thought as he slowed, left blade leading, right blade trailing. Slash, parry, pivot. Rotate the torso and use it as the pivot point of your strike. Lead with the shoulder, not the wrist. Move from the hips. Focus.

Two weapons can be deadlier than one but there is also more room for error, Master Cruedark had reminded him.

He practiced the moves again and sped up.

Soon, sweat beaded on his brow. The chill bit harder against his exposed arms. His boots slid across the snow-covered stone as he advanced, driving imaginary enemies toward the cliff's edge and pulling back before they could counter.

He stopped only when the edges of his breath felt electric.

Fen sat a few paces away, tail curled around his front paws, watching with bright, blinking interest.

"Ready to test your new ability?" Callum asked, not turning.

<*Always.*>

Fen rose and darted forward, leaping into the air.

A burst of gold light filled Callum's chest as the fox vanished, the familiar warmth of the meld washing over his limbs. His muscles tightened, strength flooding his frame with sudden, radiant clarity that came coupled with a powerful fresh breath of air that made it feel as if his lungs had expanded. Power surged to his core, light and fire coiling through his veins.

Callum exhaled once, slowly, then moved. He darted left—light bending behind him.

An afterimage burst into being at his flank, flickering like a reflection in broken glass. He shifted right, leaving a trail behind him, a glimmer of magic crackling in the air.

<*That's it!*> Fen said as Callum spun, slashed, and pivoted mid-step, causing three moving images to split from him, streaking outward like burning ghosts, each one perfectly echoing his motions with a slight delay.

They raced with him, moving alongside Callum as he performed a few more attacks. He stopped; the mirages flared and vanished like flames behind a speeding arrow.

To any observer, it would have looked like three versions of Callum had just crossed the mountain stone in a deadly dance, each one phasing into and out of existence like memory, light, and illusion rolled into one.

"I love this new power," he said.

<*The power to distract with mana clones will certainly help in a fight. We've already seen that with Cruedark's instruction. Plus, you're getting faster,*> Fen added, a note of approval threading through his voice.

"Thanks to you," Callum crouched. He checked his Soul Heart to view Fen's upgraded Aethercore.

Pact of the Radiant Fox
Type: *Pacted*
Grade: *Rare*
Infusion Requirements for Grade Increase:
0/15 Air Affinity Shards
0/15 Light Affinity Shards
0/10 Fire Affinity Shards
0/15 Deftness Shards
0/20 Might Shards
0/5 Resilience Shards
Mana Affinity Granted: *Air, Fire, Light*
Meldform Benefits:
Attributes:
+4 Might
+4 Deftness
+5 Vigor
+4 Regeneration

+4 Resilience

+1 Mind

Radiant Claws: *When melded with the Radiant Fox, the wielder gains powerful claws made of burning light, which can not only be used to attack its enemies, but also empower further, unleashing blazing slashes of fire and light a short distance before them.*

Radiant Inferno: *When melded with the Radiant Fox, channel pure radiant energy into flames that create a white-hot fire capable of melting through armor and dispelling darkness. The flames burn brighter than natural fire, blinding enemies with their intensity.*

Radiant Mirage: *When melded with the Radiant Fox, create afterimages of yourself made of flickering flame and light. These illusions trail your movements for a few seconds, confusing enemies and causing targeting spells to miss or strike the wrong image. While active, Deftness temporarily increases.*

"The upgrade was the way to go," he finally told Fen. "And I'm definitely getting a boost when I use Radiant Mirage."

<*Of course you are.*>

Callum cracked his knuckles. "Let's reset and try again. We only have about a half hour left before we need to get back."

Callum burst out of the portal at a sprint, boots hammering the stone path as he raced toward the eastern wing of the Great College. He reached the East Dining Hall and took the steps two at a time to the entrance, narrowly dodging a student balancing a tray with a steaming bread bowl.

"Sorry," he said as he spotted Marcella and Quinn already seated by the arched courtyard windows, mid-meal and mid-glare.

Marcella, as usual, stood out like a banner in a storm.

Her overcoat hung loose across her shoulders, designed more for ornament than warmth, and her hair was swept up into a polished knot, pinned in place by a jeweled comb featuring an intricate, leaping fish—its scales caught the light with every turn of her head, scales that matched the sequined material of her long skirt.

"You're late," she said, spearing a piece of melon. "Again."

Quinn raised a hand in mock greeting. "We took bets. I said ten minutes. I win."

"Sorry." Callum took the seat across from them and let out a deep breath. "I was working with Fen's new power."

"Oh?" Marcella ate a piece of melon. "Does it help with punctuality?"

"You could say that. It makes me a little faster."

"Well, let's see how fast you are at getting lunch." Marcella pierced another melon cube, nodding toward the slow-moving queue at the serving tables.

"I'll be right back." Callum stood just as Quinn finished shoveling food into his mouth.

"I'll join you," Quinn said, still chewing.

Marcella raised an eyebrow.

"I just want some fruit," Quinn told her.

She waved him off with a smirk. "I didn't say anything."

Soon, Callum returned to the table, his plate piled high with roasted vegetables, thick-sliced bread, sizzling bacon, and half a chicken.

Marcella wrinkled her nose. "You really need to add some color to your diet."

"There's color here," he said and he used his fork to pick through his plate. "Orange, white, brown, some green."

Marcella laughed. "Fruit, I'm talking about fruit. You and Quinn both eat like a pair of men preparing for a long winter."

Callum shrugged. "Old habits," he said as Quinn returned, his plate filled with anything but fruit.

"What?" Quinn asked after Marcella gave him a look. "I couldn't resist. I brought you your favorite rolls," he told her.

"I'll allow it." She plucked one of the buttery rolls off his plate and laughed. "What is your new power anyway?" she asked Callum. "You didn't tell us about it."

"It's called Radiant Mirage and it allows me to make copies of myself."

"Copies?"

Callum used Soul Heart and read the information aloud to her. "'When melded with the Radiant Fox, create afterimages of yourself made of flickering flame and light. These illusions trail your movements for a few seconds, confusing enemies and causing targeting spells to miss or strike the wrong image. While active, Deftness temporarily increases . . .'" He ate one of his carrots. "Copies."

Marcella looked like she was just about to say something clever when Rhea Whitecloak approached the table clutching a tablet of notes against her chest. "Hi," she said, bowing slightly to the three of them.

Callum stiffened just a little. Rhea had joined them on their last excursion, where she was able to use her pacted aethermouse, Jeronymo. She was a Soul Pythia–in-training, and she commanded an authority he couldn't quite place, even though she had always been kind to them.

"Hey, Rhea!" said Quinn, always the friendliest of the group. "How's Pythia life?"

She smiled, a little awkwardly, and joined their table. "Intense. They're setting things up for the trial, so everything's been—"

At the word "trial," the table fell quiet.

Marcella tilted her head. "Wait, wait, wait. Did you just say trial? What trial? I thought we were dealing with a tournament. Although, I guess if you're being pedantic, a tournament is a trial, but really, what trial?"

Rhea's eyes widened. "Oh—I'm not supposed to say. Sorry. I wasn't thinking."

"Well," Quinn said, unable to help himself, "it looks like the cat is out of the bag."

Right on cue, Tuck manifested on the edge of the table with a lazy shimmer. He sat, tail flicking, and fixed Rhea with his unblinking yellow eyes.

"Where's Jeronymo?" Tuck asked, licking his lips slowly.

That was enough to break the tension.

All four students laughed—Callum more than he expected to. Rhea looked momentarily flustered, then genuinely amused. "Jeronymo isn't afraid of cats," she said.

"Are you sure about that?" Tuck asked as he started to lick his paws. He vanished in a flash just as other students started to look over at their table.

Marcella leaned forward. "Come on, Rhea. At least give us something."

She hesitated, fingers tightening around her slate. Rhea glanced around and lowered her voice. "Here's all I can say. The tournament will play out in three parts."

"Three parts?" Callum asked. "Like . . . three rounds of fights?"

"Sorry, that's all I can tell you. But don't worry. You will find out soon. From what I've been told, the High Council will formally announce the tournament and . . ." Something flashed across her eyes. "The Crimson Sigil's delegation will be here for the announcement."

CHAPTER 7

Rivalry is just war with better manners.

—Combat Master Convoker Marius Kelthorn

Callum adjusted the collar of his freshly cleaned overcoat and stepped into the light. It was two days after Rhea had let a little information slip about the tournament, two days in which Callum and his friends had speculated what could possibly be in store for them in the tournament to come.

Now, he would find out.

The Vestige Arena stretched out before him, the arena impossibly vast. Callum had seen many impressive places since coming to the Great College, but this felt mythic. The arena was carved deep into the earth, its sunken foundation encircled by obsidian towers and stone pylons that shimmered faintly with leyline light. Every surface facing the battlefield gleamed with a dull, metallic sheen, like the whole structure had been forged rather than built.

"Ashglass," Quinn said beside him, running a hand along the railing. He knocked his fist against it. "That's what lines the inner bowl. Heard of it?"

"I can't say I have," Callum told him.

"It comes from the Sunless Peaks and is known for a few unique properties." He knocked his fist on it again. "It's hard and super expensive. Ashglass absorbs mana shockwaves. I can't imagine what the budget on this place must have been."

Marcella tilted her head, eyeing the crowd already filling in across the upper rings. "How expensive?"

"Oh, insanely," Quinn grinned. "My dad started his business working with it and got out as quickly as he got in."

"Why?" Marcella asked.

"It's difficult to mine and even harder to use for construction, but once it's in, it's basically indestructible."

As Marcella and Quinn continued discussing ashglass, Callum's gaze swept around the arena again. His eyes settled on the royal dais across the arena, where he spotted Princess Selene seated among the High Council, posture perfect as ever, sunlight catching the pale gold of her braid. She wore armor and had a golden necklace around her neck, one that pulsed with power.

"It's her," Callum said, pointing to the princess.

Marcella squinted. "Oh, that's definitely her." She waved, realized Selene likely wouldn't respond, and brought her hand back down. "When did she get here?" she asked, seeming suddenly flustered.

"She must have just arrived," Quinn said. "There's Sir Trindade."

Callum spotted the leader of her Legion Guard standing beside her. He bowed gracefully as another Legion Guard appeared, this one escorting someone who could only have been King Morninglade himself. Selene's father wore ceremonial armor that shimmered with divine light. No crown, Callum noticed; instead, a radiant golden wreath floated just above his brow like a living halo. From this distance, the king looked both untouchable and strangely human. There was power in his stillness, the kind that didn't need to speak to command a room.

Fen told Callum through their mental bond. <*Or something that Lisalen is doing. We need to ask the princess if I can speak to her father's pacted phoenix.*>

<*You mean ask her if we can speak to the king himself? I don't know.*>

<*I'm sure she wouldn't mind.*>

<*She's always so busy, though . . .*> Callum replied, watching as King Morninglade took one of the two thrones. He leaned in to speak to a man who had just arrived.

<*That must be the warlock's father, the Duke of Karna,*> Fen said with disdain as Draven appeared behind the man. Draven, draped in his usual dark armor with faint hints of fiery red mana, took his seat with that measured, effortless confidence that made Callum clench his fists. Draven's father, just as sharp-edged as his son, continued speaking with King Morninglade.

A moment later, Victrin Righexa arrived alongside a tall woman dressed in regal blue and silver. *His mother, the Duchess of Ontaria*, Callum thought, watching them approach.

The Duchess's emerald-green gown shimmered, each fold catching the light. Victrin's tunic and cloak matched her palette and bore the crest of House Ontaria stitched cleanly at the collar. He moved with practiced formality, his expression careful, almost neutral, like someone who knew exactly how many eyes were on him.

<Why isn't the princess sitting in the throne next to her father?> Callum asked Fen.

<I was wondering that myself...>

A deep, bone-rattling sound rolled out across the arena—not thunder, not music, but something older and elemental. The vibration pulsed through the stone benches and up their legs, coupled with an intense pressure and a sudden shift in the air, like the sky itself had thickened into something heavier, denser.

The buzz of the crowd faltered into silence and then there were gasps as the clouds split open above the Vestige Arena.

A fleet of floating vessels appeared with a subsonic boom, their hulls sharp as blades and draped in crimson and gold. Mist curled around them as if they carried their own weather, swallowing the light as they settled into place above the arena.

Callum shot to his feet, heart pounding, ready to take his meldform.

Quinn's hand caught his arm. "Not yet."

"It's the Geshwine Empire," Marcella said in a whisper.

Embarrassed, Callum quickly took his seat. "They have flying ships?"

"We have them too," Marcella told him, her voice on edge. "Sometimes they dock in Aveiro. Nothing like this though, nothing so violent looking."

"They're not even necessary," Quinn added, studious as ever. "They could simply open portals and come here from the Crimson Sigil that way. This is all for show."

The vessels were angular and predatory, their portholes pulsing with energy. From some angles, they resembled twisted beasts, all clawed curves and horned prows. From others, they looked entirely alien, as if they'd been carved from the bones of some other reality. Dark mist poured from their sides, veiling their descent like a slow-falling storm.

<Quinn's right, they're trying to intimidate us,> Fen said as the largest of the ships hovered directly above the king's dais, supported by wide, hissing pillars of magic-infused steam.

A stairwell unfurled from its underdeck, ornate and edged in platinum, descending with the precision of a blade. It extended through the air until it stopped in front of the dais.

Hushed whispers and murmurs spread over the crowd as everyone waited to see what would happen next. A quick look around told Callum that he wasn't the only one poised to strike. While Marcella, who had seen these ships before, was more relaxed, others like Lynnafer and

Godric, seemed ready to move into action. Even Draven's friends, Artur Filin, Theogar Desde, and Petyr Norwood, whom he had brought on the last excursion, seemed hesitant as they spoke quietly to one another. The upperclassmen looked equally disturbed, as did some of the teachers, most notably Master Cruedark who remained standing even as there were people seated behind him.

Finally, after leaving everyone waiting for a minute, the emperor of the Geshwine Empire stepped out onto the stairwell.

Draped in black robes, adorned with a necklace of shards and triangular amulets, the enemy king descended slowly and without any guards. A massive, jet-black cape trailed behind him, nearly twenty feet long. Magic held it aloft and it billowed perfectly as if carried by phantom hands.

Behind him came the Crimson Sigil's red-eyed warlock students, each one wearing tailored black military uniforms with short black capes held tight under golden epaulets. The warlocks stopped at the foot of the king's staircase and turned as one as they stepped into a line before the arena, facing the students of the Great College.

Their Soul Hearts all flared at once and aetherbeasts manifested.

Bursts of power crackled through the air as each prodigy summoned their bonded creature—shadowy silhouettes of impossible beasts, snarling and gleaming with corrupted elegance. Their magic rippled through the ashglass, warping the light as heat and pressure fizzled away.

For a heartbeat, it looked like they would attack. Even the aetheric columns flared, momentarily amplifying their defense runes.

But nothing happened.

The power settled, yet the tension lingered like static.

Callum remained frozen, trying to process the sudden shift when he noticed a tall, white-haired contender with long braids and a confident gait step slightly ahead of the others. The man turned his head, just enough for his blazing red eyes to meet Selene's gaze. Then, almost casually, he leaned in and said something to her.

She didn't reply. Didn't blink. Just stared over to where Callum was sitting.

Is she looking at me? he wondered as a new sound broke the silence.

A low, mechanical groan echoed through the arena as a gate rose from the arena floor. Thick stone plates peeled back in sequence, revealing a circular entry lift that cranked upward in deliberate increments, like the unlocking of an ancient vault.

The platform reached its full height and Masteress Lucerne, the Great College's Soul Pythia, stood at its center in flowing yellow robes. A silk veil was draped over her head, shadowing a face that seemed to change every time Callum blinked.

Mastress Lucerne hovered a few inches above the ground, perfectly still.

Behind her came twelve Soul Pythias-in-training, robes tailored with artful flair. The yellow fabric was stitched with circular mirrors that caught the sunlight at angles designed to impress, their hoods pulled back with precise uniformity. Callum spotted Rhea Whitecloak near the rear of the group walking with careful steps, her eyes straight ahead, and pointed her out to the others.

"I guess we'll see what she was hinting about two days ago," Marcella said, barely able to contain the nervousness in her voice.

The students circled the Soul Pythia in a slow, precise arc, forming a wide ring around her in the middle of the future battleground.

She raised her hands, and the amplifying wards laced her voice with power, casting it across the arena. "*We extend our warmest welcome to His Eternal Eminence, Imperion Rotharyn of the Bonded Flame and the rest of the Geshwine Empire for a tournament of the ages—one we hope will bring our people closer through challenge, resilience, and shared glory.*"

The tension in the stands eased, but no one relaxed.

"*The Great College receives the students of the Crimson Sigil in the spirit of academic camaraderie and sovereign goodwill. On behalf of King Morninglade, Princess Selene, and the High Council, we welcome each of you to our lovely campus, where you will be quartered in the recently renovated Dreagis Hall and its Vellor Commons. As agreed upon with the Crimson Sigil, you will all have individual portal access to your own college grounds, available at any time.*"

The Soul Pythia's hood tilted ever so slightly toward the Geshwinian emperor, who now sat in the empty chair beside King Morninglade.

"And now," she continued, "*the format. The tournament will proceed in three parts, each designed to test not only raw strength, but mastery, ingenuity, and the bond between soul and core. Phase one: the Culling Trials. All participants will be matched into rotating groups and assigned their trial windows. These trials will take place in Pythia-crafted survival zones—illusion-based worlds shaped to challenge every aspect of your training. You will be tested in integrated teams composed of students from the Great College and the Crimson Sigil, known as Concord Units.*"

Whispers stirred across the crowd as Fen spoke to Callum: <*They are going to make us team up with warlocks?*>

<*Apparently so,*> he thought back to Fen as he glanced to the other side of the arena, his eyes narrowing on the Crimson Sigil students. Yet

again, he focused his gaze on the white-haired student who seemed to have challenged Princess Selene.

"*Phase two: the Duelist Rounds, which will feature traditional eliminations. These one-on-one matches will take place here, in the Vestige Arena. Phase three will be kept secret until the champions of the former two rounds have met.*"

That drew more than a few sharp glances.

Mastress Lucerne seemed to smile beneath her veil. "*Each round will test the strength of your Soul Heart, your command of craft and cunning, and your ability to endure under pressure.*" She rose a little higher, her presence towering over the silent arena. "*The Culling Trials start tomorrow. May the finest among you rise beyond victory, soar to incredible heights, and carve your names into legend.*"

CHAPTER 8

Royal Decree: By unanimous vote of the Crown's advisory body and by royal assent, Duke Blademark of Karna is hereby elevated to Head of the High Council. Let his guidance serve the realm in these days of rising uncertainty.

—Edict of Appointed Order, Year 525

Students from the Great College lingered in loose clusters across the outer lawn of Dreagis Hall and along the garden walls of Vellor Commons, watching curiously as the Crimson Sigil delegation settled into its temporary quarters. Just as the Soul Pythia had said, the dorms had been renovated—Callum could see the fresh pale stone and darkwood along the walls, everything cleaner and sharper than the older buildings on campus. The arched windows gleamed in the morning light, glass so polished it almost looked enchanted.

Callum had only passed this part of campus a few times and never paid much attention to it. *Feels like I find a new building every other day*, he thought, eyes drifting back to the dorms. His gaze followed the clean lines of the architecture upward until they met the sharper, colder silhouettes of the pair of Crimson Sigil vessels hovering overhead, casting dark clouds onto campus.

Fen's voice appeared at the back of his head. <*These warlocks. Their mere presence tells me that the Valestra Kingdom is on the wrong path. As for the airships, I've seen similar things before. I'm certain of it.*>

<*You have?*>

<*Yes. The memory is vague, but I recall the Demon King having something similar. I don't remember there being as many though. There was only one.*>

"At least there are less of them now," Quinn said, as if he could hear what Callum and Fen were talking about. "Several left with the Geshwinian emperor's ship through that portal just after the speech. I don't know why these stayed behind. I can only imagine what New Albions must think."

"Does anyone even remember his name? Eternal-something-of-the-Flaming-I-don't-know." Marcella's breath escaped in a quiet huff. "But it only makes the last few days weirder. First, a literal aetherstorm—"

"Could have been a Beast Tide," Quinn said, interrupting her.

"What? No. They would have told us by now if it was. And all Beast Tides start as aetherstorms."

"Aware."

"As I was saying. First, a potential Beast Tide, then airships show up. It feels connected. But who am I?" Marcella glanced skyward again toward the airships. "Maybe they're for instructors."

"Actually, that would make sense," Quinn said.

"Their instructors won't stay in the halls?" Callum asked, squinting. The farmboy in him still struggled to imagine why anyone would need an airship when they had perfectly renovated rooms at the Great College. He had seen Princess Selene's suite; he assumed the Valestra Kingdom would provide something equally grand to visiting guests.

"Maybe they are picky about where they sleep," Marcella said. "That, or they're preparing for some kind of attack. Heh."

The three of them exchanged a look as Marcella laughed nervously.

"I don't think that would be wise," Quinn said after a beat. "We're in New Albion, the heart of the kingdom. It would be all-out war if they did anything aside from some posturing."

<*They did plenty of that earlier with their little mana flare display,*> Fen told Callum. <*I'm surprised everyone on the royal dais didn't immediately move to cover King Morninglade. Then again, he is pacted with Lisalen. Surely, she would have protected him.*>

"The chance for all-out war . . ." Marcella fidgeted with her bracelets. "That's an upsetting thought, more upsetting than the fact that we're partnering with them tomorrow. The idea of a Concord Unit feels terrible at best."

Quinn gave a noncommittal shrug. "The council must have a reason."

Marcella said nothing, which was rare enough that Callum glanced over to her. She was still looking at the ships, her jaw set tight. He knew her well enough to spot when she was dodging a thought.

The crowd around them shifted, drawing back as a group of Crimson Sigil students approached, two women and two men.

They moved in perfect formation, every step measured, their spacing unnaturally precise. The warlocks were still in their tailored black military uniforms, fabric crisp and unwrinkled, short black capes cinched tight beneath gleaming gold epaulets. Their sharp red eyes swept the area like predators taking stock. No idle chatter. No wasted motion. They weren't students arriving for a tournament; they were still on parade.

Callum recognized the guy at the center because of his braided white hair. *He's the one that was sitting near Princess Selene . . .*

The man shifted forward like someone trained in stillness, like every muscle waited for permission before moving. His eyes passed over them not with aggression, but with analytical weight. He stopped a few paces away. "I'm looking for something," he said in a quiet voice, every syllable precise.

Marcella waited for someone else to speak, and when no one did she stepped up. "Have you tried asking someone in your airships?"

The warlock looked up at them. "They are feats of mana engineering, aren't they? We were taught that Valestrans lost this kind of technology."

"You'd be wrong," she said.

"Oh?"

Callum watched him carefully. He didn't look entirely hostile, but there was something in the way he spoke, the way his gaze wandered slightly past their faces, as if measuring their auras instead of their words.

"We have similar ships in Aveiro," Marcella said.

"Aveiro?" The warlock repeated the word with a lazy grin. "I can't say I've heard of that village, I'm sure it's quaint, though. We were told your people trade shards in town. Where exactly?"

Marcella took a step closer to him, her tone a little too sharp this time: "We don't use Demoncores here."

A brief silence. Then, a faint curl of a smile on his lips. Not cruel, just aware. "That is quite apparent." He let this comment settle before continuing: "I suppose introductions are in order. I'm Laziel Thornhelm," he said, his tone almost absent, but not unfriendly. "Well?"

"Well?" Marcella asked Laziel.

"Aren't you going to introduce yourselves?"

"I don't know if that's necessary," Quinn said, smoothly stepping past Marcella to place himself between her and the Crimson Sigil delegation. "If we're paired in Concord Units tomorrow, we'll be formally introduced then." He offered a polite, almost apologetic smile. "No offense meant, of course, but you did arrive in floating battleships. I imagine if we'd descended on your school in armed vessels trailing mist and mana-vapors, it might have raised a few eyebrows too."

He let the words hang there just as Laziel had done moments ago.

"So this is how it will be?" Laziel finally asked.

"Nothing is ever how it was before," Quinn told him. "If you want to trade shards, the Emporium is your best bet. Top floor is where you'll get the best deals."

Callum nearly corrected his friend but stopped himself. *That's a lie*, he thought as Quinn continued speaking: "But, you might draw suspicion if all of you go at once."

"Because of our red eyes?" Laziel asked.

"They're . . . noticeable," Quinn said with a shrug.

Laziel studied him for a moment. "If I'm not mistaken, one of yours has red eyes as well. The man from Karna."

Callum tensed slightly.

"I imagine," Laziel said, voice cool and dry, "your kingdom will adjust to seeing more of us. Good luck tomorrow." He turned without waiting for a reply, his entourage trailing behind him like shadows.

As they disappeared behind the curve of Dreagis Hall, Marcella released her clenched fists and shook them out. "Well that wasn't weird or awkward or intimidating at all. Phew. I don't want to say that I'm going to hate them by the end of the tournament, but we certainly won't be visiting the winter markets with them."

"How did you bring this back to shopping?" Quinn asked, turning to her.

"Um, I didn't. I've never been to the winter markets they have here. I heard they have hot wine."

"Ah, that, yes, and plenty of it."

"And Quinn?"

"Yes?" he asked her.

"You handled yourself well back there. Good job."

"Agreed," Callum told him. "I still don't know what to make of these warlocks."

The two nodded in agreement. Marcella had the last word: "I don't like them. And trusting them would be plain stupid."

Later that night, Callum sat cross-legged on the floor of his dorm room, eyes closed, breath slow as he tried to tune out the cold fall drizzle outside his window.

Mana moved through him, steady, spiraling, and deliberate. His Soul Heart pulsed gently beneath his sternum, threads unwinding and reweaving as he guided energy along each channel. He could feel the air thicken just slightly, a low ambient resonance from the crazy day they'd had.

Draw in ambient mana.
Circulate.
Cleanse.

Callum tried to push thoughts of Laziel Thornhelm and the other Crimson Sigil students out of his mind, but the feeling their presence stirred wouldn't leave him alone. Especially when he could still see some of their airships from his bed.

That had been one of the reasons he had woken up, well past midnight, to do some cycling.

I'll be better at sleeping once I can upgrade Empowerment of Rejuvenation, he thought as he used Soul Sense to examine the Powercore.

Empowerment of Rejuvenation
Type: *Support*
Grade: *Legendary*
Infusion Requirements for Grade Increase:
1/30 Vigor Shards
0/40 Resilience Shards
0/10 Mind Shards
Effect: *When bound to one's Soul Heart, this core aids in rejuvenation and mana recovery with as little as one hour of sleep.*

He recalled the Core rankings—Common, Uncommon, Rare, Exalted, Sublime, Legendary, and Mythical—and remembered how Mastress Lucerne had explained that there was symmetry in the system and the way it corresponded to the seven classified stages for an archmage. Initiate, Conjurer, Wielder, Channeler, Shaper, Weaver, and Convoker.

So either I get a bunch of Attribute Shards or I move to the next Stage and gain better access to the Powercore naturally. There is always the hidden Powercores list. I can try for more of them, and sunder and fuse what I can. But when? He nearly laughed aloud at this thought. *When am I supposed to do that with the enemy right outside my window?*

A knock sounded at the door, pulling him away from his thoughts.

His heart picked up immediately.

It wasn't Marcella's knock. Hers was a staccato rattle, fast and impatient, always accompanied by a shout through the wood. This knock was soft, precise, and firm enough for Callum to know exactly who it was and that he'd better not leave her waiting.

He moved to the door quickly and opened it. The woman stepped in with haste, no hesitation, no announcement, just calculated movement.

"Hi," he told Princess Selene, who was wrapped in a storm-gray cloak, her blonde hair perfectly pinned, gold sigils tracing faintly across the cuffs of her sleeves. The rain still clung to her shoulders in pearl-sized droplets.

"I've missed you," she said, taking him by surprise.

And just like that, he couldn't breathe right. Not because it sounded romantic—it didn't. Not exactly. But because it might have been. *Was it?* Callum wondered. And by the time he was even processing that thought, she had circled past him, scanning his desk and the window, pacing like she owned the room and had something important to say but wasn't sure where to begin.

She finally stopped and gestured toward the airships glowing outside. "It's a terrible idea."

"Letting them dock here?" Callum asked.

"No, that has happened before. Not with their ships, but others. The Concord Units," she clarified. "Pairing us with Crimson Sigil students right from the start? What madness is this? I understand what Sir Trindade meant when he said, 'Better to put people together early, before rivalries calcify,'" she told Callum. "But still. This isn't Grimbald. Fifty years ago, *that* tournament ended in trade agreements and mutual pacts. But the Lands of Grimbald aren't the Geshwine Empire. Their loyalties and governments are totally different. The Flame Doctrine . . . you don't want me to get started on that one."

"I see what you're saying. They're not exactly our allies.".

"They're absolutely *not* our allies."

Fen shimmered into existence, curling onto the windowsill like he'd been there all along. "Do you think it will work?" the Radiant Fox asked her directly. "A tournament that can actually bring people together?"

Selene hesitated. "I don't know," she said quietly. "I really don't."

The princess turned toward them, her arms crossing under the weight of her cloak. "I've raised concerns. But the High Council seems to think it's a great idea."

"And who oversees the High Council?" Fen asked.

"Duke Blademark." She caught his expression before he could speak again. "I *know* what you're thinking. And I agree. There's something off about all of it."

Callum folded his arms. "Including Draven." The words came out a little too fast and a little too sharp. He tried to backpedal. "I mean, his involvement in all this."

Selene's gaze didn't waver. "Yes. But I don't know the extent of what that is. I've had people watching Draven and the duke for months. Sir Trindade has been helping me with it, discreetly, of course. My father wouldn't approve, he's old friends with the duke, so I've had to work around him."

Callum just stared at her for a moment. "Why are you telling me all this?"

She looked at him, long enough that he felt himself flush under her gaze. "Because . . ." She tried again, this time with more confidence. "Because it's nice to speak to someone."

"Why not Marcella?"

"Don't get me wrong, I like Marcella," Selene said. "But she's . . . loud. And loud people often don't mean to spill secrets, but they do." She paced once toward the desk and back again. "I'd speak to Quinn, but his family's merchant nobility. New money. Technically part of the Court, but . . ." She gave a slight, weary shrug. "It's considered improper. Like slipping ledgers to a rival guild before the auction bell."

"So . . ."

"So?" she asked.

"So that leaves me," Callum said, trying to smile. "The guy with a dorm room the size of a goat pen." He gestured around. "Actually, it's not that bad. Best room I've ever had to myself, if we're being honest. You're here, after all. So that leaves me for you to speak to."

"Yes," Selene said softly. "And no." She turned to face him again, the seriousness in her gaze catching him off guard. "No, you're not part of it—not directly. But yes, because none of this would be happening without your forefather. And I find that . . ." She paused, searching for the right word. "Intriguing. You're part of something older than all of us, Callum, and I can't help but feel like being here; speaking to you is part of what I'm meant to be doing." She stepped past him before he could respond. "I should go. I'll see you at the Culling Trials tomorrow. Try to get some sleep and . . ."

"Yeah?" he asked, caught in the moment.

Selene paused at the doorway, her voice quieter now. "Sorry for bothering you so late. It wasn't entirely proper." And then, she was gone.

CHAPTER 9

To understand a Crimson Sigil student, one must understand they were not raised to become individuals, but instruments. The Flame Doctrine does not cultivate mages. It forges weapons.

—A quote from *Comparative Studies in Soul Heart Philosophy* by Xander Callow, Master Channeler, Clergo

The rain had passed, but the ground still glistened, slick with shallow puddles that mirrored the gray morning sky. Water dripped steadily from the corners of rooftops and the curled tips of slate awnings, falling in soft, rhythmic taps against stone. Damp leaves clung to walkways and garden walls—russet, amber, and ocher, darkened by rain and fragrant with that earthy, sharp scent of fall.

Callum stood near a seating area, boots damp, his pressed overcoat catching the last of the morning mist. Around him, the rest of the first-year students clustered in loose formations casually murmuring as they adjusted their uniforms.

Before them all, rising like a monolith pulled from another age, stood the Aeternal Tabula, its core a towering slab of black stone polished to an unnatural sheen. It reflected the world around it like a mirror left out in moonlight, slightly distorting the campus grounds, like the images it caught weren't always from the present. Coiled around the stone was a spiraling outer frame of pale, gold-veined alloy, shaped like a shell or a helix, humming softly with dormant power.

This was where their Attribute Trials had been held. Callum remembered how much they had challenged him and how little he had known at the time. Now the building and the mysteries it held would serve another purpose.

But what? What could they possibly have in store for us? he wondered as he returned his focus to the students from the Geshwine Empire.

They stood in a perfect square grid across the courtyard. No talking. No shifting. Just rows of red-and-black uniforms, hands clasped neatly behind backs, expressions unreadable.

It had been startling at first, but seeing his own classmates relax had settled Callum somewhat. He knew better than to trust their stillness. *Some crops looked healthy right up until the root rot set in*, he remembered hearing in Weatherby. *The quietest animals*, his father often said, *were often the ones that kicked the hardest.*

He spotted Laziel Thornhelm in the front rank, the warlock tall and poised, his white braid slung over one shoulder. Laziel didn't make eye contact with Callum. He didn't need to. Every line of his body said the same thing it did when they had first met yesterday: *You're being watched.*

A hush rippled through the Great College students as Princess Selene approached from one of the distant archways, flanked by Sir Trindade and two other Legion Guards. She was dressed for both ceremony and cold: long-sleeves beneath her armor and a band of fur covering her ears. After she exchanged a few quiet words with Sir Trindade, he gave a nod and walked off to join the other instructors gathering nearby.

Princess Selene crossed the courtyard without pause, where she joined Callum, Marcella, and Quinn, her presence so composed it barely disturbed the rhythm of conversation—yet all three felt it.

"You're early," Marcella said, instinctively straightening her posture. "I mean, good morning!"

"Morning. Quinn, Callum," Selene said, her gaze already shifting past him as if she hadn't shown up unannounced to his room last night.

"Hi." Callum still had no idea what to make of her, or the strange trust she seemed to have put in him as evident in her visit last night. "I hope you, um, slept well."

"I did." Selene turned her attention to the far path, where Draven appeared.

His cloak was immaculate, boots dry, like the rain itself had been told not to touch him. He passed behind Callum with a low, amused voice, red eyes gleaming. "Misty day to be a farmboy," he said under his breath.

Callum didn't react.

<*Every time,*> Fen grumbled inside his head.

<*It's not worth it,*> Callum reminded the Radiant Fox. <*Hopefully he doesn't end up in my Concord Unit.*>

<*If he does, there are greater issues at play.*>

A low shifting sound followed, smooth and precise. Runes along the spiral edge of the Aeternal Tabula flared to life, and a circular panel folded open in tight, concentric rings.

Mastress Lucerne stepped into the light, the Soul Pythia in a sleek, oval-sheen material that shimmered with every slight turn of her head. Even beneath it, Callum could see the shifting of her features, the way her nose and brow reshaped subtly with each movement, eyes deepening, then lightening again.

Behind her came the Soul Pythia trainees, robes golden and flowing, steps synchronized and precise as they carried silk-covered pillows with bracelets arranged on them. Rhea Whitecloak was among them, calm and collected, her gaze sweeping once across the crowd before settling on some point in the distance.

A stranger joined the Soul Pythia, matching her composure but not her familiarity. The man was tall and razor-thin, with a sculpted face and a calm, unreadable expression. His robe mirrored Lucerne's in design but ended in a high black collar that framed his neck. His hands were clasped lightly at the wrist and, like the other warlocks, his eyes glowed red.

<*Crimson Sigil instructor,*> Fen noted.

Callum nodded slightly.

The Soul Pythia raised her hands, and without any magic, the campus around them quieted. The wind seemed to still, and even the calls of late fall birds dissolved into silence. "Good morning, all. I hope you were able to rest adequately and are ready to begin the Culling Trials. For today's trial, which is the qualifier for the Duelist Rounds, each of you will wear Culling Bracelets. These are linked to your Soul Heart and will ensure that you do not die."

"How exactly?" Quinn asked under his breath, a question that the Soul Pythia answered:

"The bracelets will force-extract you if you become unconscious, gravely injured, or if your Mana Reserves reach Hollowing. We do not want anyone Hollowing today. You may also use the bracelet to verbally submit by speaking into it. Now, before you take your bracelets, let us begin by forming your Concord Units. Callum Stross."

Me? First to be called? Callum felt his heart leap in his chest, by the time he stepped forward, the Soul Pythia had already moved onto the next student.

"Lynnafer Sunsouth." She watched as Lynnafer stepped forward and joined Callum.

"Hey," he told her quickly.

Lynnafer offered him a firm, but nervous smile.

"Sorcha Malvain," the Crimson Sigil instructor said, taking over from there.

A woman with yellow hair and a white streak running through it stepped up. She kept her red eyes locked on some point in the distance and didn't look at Callum or Lynnafer.

"Ryven Calesh," the Crimson instructor said next.

A brutish, bald man stepped forward, his neck thick with muscle and shoulders broad enough to fill the hallway. He tilted his head back slightly and flared his meldform.

"Therrin Vade," the Crimson instructor said.

<Two of us and three of them?> Fen asked as Callum turned to see a man with long dark hair and pockmarked cheeks come forward and join the others from his cohort.

<Looks like it...>

"Good," the Soul Pythia said, her voice quieting any of the murmurs from the Great College students. "The five of you will form the first Concord Unit. Please collect your bracelets and proceed into the Aeternal Tabula. You will be transported to a demonic battlefield—one drawn from the Great Demonswar. Succeed in your task, and all five of you advance. Fail, and all five are disqualified from the Dueling Rounds." She paused, her expression unreadable. "And for those of you still waiting... no, you haven't just learned what is to come. I'm afraid every trial will be different, every challenge unique."

CHAPTER 10

The Flame Doctrine teaches that all citizens are Embers of the Bonded Flame—a divine force not merely symbolized, but embodied by His Eternal Eminence, Imperion Rotharyn. His will is law, his vision infallible, and his soul the unbroken fire from which the Empire draws its strength. In Geshwinian culture and society, obedience is not a civic virtue—it is a sacred alignment. Power, whether magical or mundane, is sanctified only through unwavering service to the state. Individual desire is deviation; personal ambition, a contagion. Doubt is not weakness, it is heresy itself. And sentiment, unless expressed through useful action, is treated with suspicion. Loyalty must be proven through function, not affection. In the Flame Doctrine there is no self, only service.

—A quote from *Ember to Empire: Doctrinal Foundations of Geshwinian Supremacy*, 2nd Edition by Ines Meida, Mastress Weaver, Archona of Aveiro

Callum stepped into the Aeternal Tabula behind Lynnafer Sunsouth, the polished floor slick beneath their boots. The spiraling walls inside hummed with faint energy, casting reflections that shimmered with impossible depth.

The three Crimson Sigil students remained at the front, shoulders locked, their formation rigid. They didn't speak, didn't glance back, didn't fidget. Every movement was controlled and efficient. They weren't just standing tall, they were projecting authority, and they were very good at it.

Like the others, Callum now wore a Culling Bracelet, the silver and slate-black bands fitted tightly over his wrist, threaded with runes that glowed faintly. The bracelets pulsed in time with his heartbeats, a reminder that it was linked to his Soul Heart and that extraction would not be optional if things went wrong.

"What now?" Lynnafer asked, her eyes widening as she glanced at Callum.

"Your guess is as good as mine."

<*I'm sure it will all become clear soon enough,*> Fen told Callum. <*Let's just keep our focus on the warlocks; their continued silence is concerning me.*>

Lynnafer, whom Callum had only spoken to him a handful of times, moved closer to him so only Callum could hear. "We're outnumbered," she said.

He nodded a reply.

"You have a pacted fox, I have a badger. They have Demoncores and whatever they're pacted with. I'm going to go out on a limb and say it will be pretty nasty if a battle breaks out."

Once again, Callum nodded, lips tight, eyes facing forward.

"You don't think we need a strategy?"

"We need to know more about the challenge first," he told her, not harshly, but in a way that he hoped would stop her from asking more questions.

Callum couldn't help but have some doubts when seeing how the three Crimsons behaved versus his peers. They seemed more mature, but also less human in certain ways. No nervous glances or shifting weight, no whispered last-minute plans. Just silence and certainty, like they'd been trained to suppress doubt before it could form.

He thought of Quinn's crooked grin, Marcella's constant need to fill silence, the way Lynnafer now fidgeted with a ring she wore as the minutes dragged on. His peers were unpredictable, sometimes messy, but they were *people*. The Crimsons? They moved with the precision of machines and the conviction of zealots, and Callum didn't know yet if that would make them more dangerous, or more breakable.

Lynnafer eventually turned back to him. Before she could ask him anything else, a lotus of magic appeared, the sparkling flower forming into the Soul Pythia. It looked just like Mastress Lucerne, but Callum could immediately tell it wasn't her. The movements were too still. Too smooth.

A construct, he thought as her voice came rippling toward them, until it sounded nearly perfect. Callum remembered what Master Alpen had said in a recent Elemental Mana and its Principles class. Light mana, when properly channeled, could carry not just shape and sound, but intent. It could wrap around air and heat, reflect and refract like polished glass, trick the eye and mimic breath. This was how Radiant Mirage worked.

The Soul Pythia's construct was nearly tangible, flawless in posture and precise in speech. It was far beyond anything Callum could manage with his newly upgraded Aethercore. His own projections wavered shortly after they were cast. This one looked as though it could walk off the platform and leave footprints behind on a beach.

This was mastery, and it felt like the construct was actually watching them.

"Welcome, Concord Unit One," she said. "Please, this way." She turned and glided forward, the ends of her robes lightly brushing against the mirrored floor of the Aeternal Tabula.

The three Crimsons followed and Callum and Lynnafer quickly caught up. The hallway led into a podlike chamber carved from white marble, its walls curving inward like a collapsed dome. Stone inlays and warding lines were embedded throughout the surface, woven into the architecture. Five thick cushions were arranged in a wide ring on the floor, evenly spaced and facing one another.

The moment they entered, the temperature shifted. It instantly grew cooler, not cold, but still enough to feel the press of magic in the walls of the strange building. It was the kind of pressure that made the hair on Callum's arms rise.

"You will be transported shortly," the Soul Pythia construct said. "Take your seats and greet one another."

She vanished and the door slid closed behind, leaving the five students standing in the pod. Callum took the seat closest to the door. Lynnafer settled beside him, arms crossed, back straight, eyes flicking between the others with quiet intensity.

Across from them, the Crimson Sigil students moved as if preassigned. Not a word. Not a question. They sat without hesitation.

I might as well get this over with, Callum thought as he made his introduction. "I'm Callum Stross," he told the Crimsons. "Um, from Weatherby."

The only woman of the three Crimsons maintained her almost regal posture as her eyes traced over Callum. She was tall, sharp-featured, and looked older than she must have been. "Sorcha Malvain," she said simply.

"Ryven Calesh," The big man beside her grunted. His body language was soldier-born—elbows on knees, broad shoulders hunched forward like a charging animal waiting for the call. A scar cut along his jawline, healed clean but proudly visible.

Lynnafer cleared her throat. "I'm Lynnafer Sunsouth. Nice to . . . nice to meet you all. Wait. Were we supposed to say where we're from? I'm from Morefell."

The youngest of the three Crimsons looked up at Callum. He had a narrow frame and light bones, his long hair curled over the left side of his face. His voice, when it came, was quiet and without texture. "Therrin Vade."

Callum exchanged a glance with Lynnafer.

<*Maybe don't say anything else,*> Fen said. <*Let Lynnafer speak.*>

<*She's more nervous than she normally seems,*> Callum thought back to the fox. Lynnafer had been one of the first people he saw spar back when he had joined the Great College. She was a fierce fighter, nothing like the woman who now sat next to him.

<*They've already disrupted her rhythm,*> Fen replied. <*Let's not hand them ours as well.*>

A change took place in Lynnafer's voice as she spoke again: "We do not yet know our task, but if we fail this trial, all of us will be disqualified from the tournament."

"If we fail, it will not be because of us," Sorcha told her coldly. "We are Embers of the Bonded Flame."

"What's that even supposed to mean?" Lynnafer asked her.

"I believe what Sorcha is trying to say is that we will cooperate," Therrin said, "and any loss will be attributed to your lack of cooperation. The two of you are unforged saplings of the lenient Valestra Kingdom. You have had luck on your side in the past through certain actions from a legendary figure."

"You mean the Demonslayer?" Lynnafer asked, challenging him.

"I do."

<*So he is known there as well,*> Fen told Callum. <*Interesting. But I suppose that makes sense. This all used to be one kingdom.*>

She nodded to Callum. "That is his ancient relative."

"Callum Stross," Sorcha said. Something flickered behind her eyes, gone as quickly as it came.

"It doesn't matter who they are related to," Ryven told her bluntly. "There are legends in my caste as well but I have forgotten their names. The only thing that matters is obedience to Imperion Rotharyn, His Eternal Eminence."

"That is what it means to be an Ember of the Bonded Flame," Sorcha said, a self-correction.

Lynnafer glanced at Callum like he should say something. He did not.

Fen's voice came to him: <*Their conviction is clear. Whatever the Flame Doctrine is, or whatever it means to be an Ember of the Bonded Flame, we're not going to be able to reason with them.*>

<*Agreed.*>

<But we could use it to our advantage. What they aren't saying is that failure this early on would make them look weak to their peers. I doubt their emperor would even notice, the tournament has just started. But their peers will.>

<In other words, their desire to blend in and their strange beliefs might actually be to our benefit?>

<That's exactly what I'm saying. They may go above and beyond to ensure that we don't lose because losing would invalidate their very belief system.>

<Got it,> Callum told Fen as the air in the chamber tightened as a ring of magical symbols ignited around the outer wall, flaring once in amber light.

The walls didn't fall away so much as they disintegrated, peeling into threads of light. The floor lost its substance and Callum felt himself unmade, not falling, not flying, but unfolding, as if his body had been reduced to pure intent and flung across a distance too large to name.

The world slammed back into place with a jolt that rattled his breath. Sound returned first—a sharp rush of wind, the low crackle of distant thunder as snow flurries appeared in the air. Then weight, then gravity, then the ground beneath his boots.

The five of them now stood at the edge of a broken courtyard, facing a half-ruined monastery wreathed in stormlight and snow. The wind was cold and dry. Stone stretched out around them, the cracked flagstones scattered with old banners surrounding pockets of scorched gravel now covered in ice. Mountains loomed beyond the high ridgeline, where snow danced above slow-rising smoke.

The Soul Pythia construct reappeared beside a fallen pillar. "As you know, this illusion replicates a battlefield from the Great Demonswar," she gestured toward the monastery. "Now, your goal: Work together to defend the monastery for the next twenty minutes. Success will be determined by team cohesion, enemy suppression, and area retention. The trial begins now."

Her robes crumpled to the ground, the magic around her vanishing into a sudden gust of snow, blinding and bitterly cold, thick enough to swallow the edges of the courtyard.

They stood in silence, the battlefield beyond blanketed white.

CHAPTER 11

The monasteries built to safeguard fragments of the original Heart of Creation were not merely sanctuaries—they were batteries of civilization, each one pulsing with protective warding and sacred mana. As the Great Demonswar neared its final, bloody crescendo, these strongholds became targets. The Demon King's forces were relentless. Though most fell within days of their isolation, the final five resisted for weeks, their defenders burned into legend. Today, the ruins remain, weathered, haunted, and half-buried in moss and ash. And though their wards are long broken, the Valestra Kingdom honors their legacy.

—A quote from *The War That Shaped* by Sir Garrick Mormont, the Crown's Royal Tax Collector

The monastery Callum and the others needed to protect loomed behind them, half-buried in frost. Statues that might have once honored saints or heroes lay in broken heaps, some split in two by old impacts, others half-swallowed by snowdrifts and glacial ice. The main structure was weathered and cracked, its stone faded to bone-white after years of wind and cold. A frozen stillness clung to the place, the kind that whispered of long-abandoned prayers and battles no one had survived to remember.

It wouldn't stay that way for long.

Already, distant howls echoed across the valley, faint but rising—hunger carried on the wind.

"We should reinforce the front," Sorcha said, the Crimson Sigil student striding toward a cracked section of wall that overlooked the trail below. "The approach is narrow and forces a funnel. Defensible."

Ryven grunted a response, the big man ready to follow his peer's orders.

"We don't know they're coming from that front," Callum reminded them.

"I agree," Lynnafer told the Crimson students. "This isn't a siege. It's a trial. They want us to think tactically, not just dig in."

Sorcha didn't look at either of them. "It's the only logical approach."

"It's *not* the only logical approach," Lynnafer said, challenging her.

As the two started bickering, Callum took a quick jog around the monastery's perimeter. He circled the structure swiftly, moving between shattered garden walls and remnants of burned hedgerows, eyes scanning for distortions in the distance, anything that looked like a staging area for aetherbeasts.

Where will they come from? He glanced back toward the horizon which remained obscured by the snowstorm. Nothing yet. No signs of movement aside from the slight rumble and ominous sounds they had already heard.

<We've been given time to strategize or hang ourselves,> he thought to Fen.

<Agreed. What are you thinking? Sorcha isn't going to budge.>

<Maybe not. But maybe...> Callum took another look around. <Maybe this will work.> He returned to the others, breath puffing in visible clouds, to find the two women still arguing.

"Enough," he told them. "We have maybe two or three minutes to figure out how we are going to guard this thing. Question: Does anyone have a pacted beast that flies?"

The Crimson Sigil students glanced at each other. Ryven said nothing. Sorcha's jaw tightened. Therrin finally broke the silence, the thin man stepping forward, "The Doctrine cautions against revealing tactical strengths to those not yet proven in service to the Flame. I'm not sorry to tell you this."

Lynnafer snorted at this remark.

"In that case," Callum said, already a step ahead, "I will tell you what I have, and you can decide if you want to tell me what you have. I have a Radiant Fox. Lynnafer?"

"Stonehide Badger," she said dismissively toward the three Crimsons.

That got a small exhale from Ryven. Not quite a laugh, closer to a scoff of mild approval.

"We have to work together, for Imperion Rotharyn," Sorcha said, her tone making it clear she was speaking on behalf of all three. "I am pacted with a Seraph Python. Imagine a giant snake capable of..." A dark smile formed on her face. "Anything, really."

Ryven followed. "Spite-Tusk Juggerboar. Shadow and Earth."

"Paleburn Duskwret Bat," Therrin said at last, like it was being pried out of him.

Callum turned toward him. "So you have a bat. That means you can fly, right?"

"I can."

"Good. In that case . . ." Callum scanned the sky, winter flurries fluttering above. "Therrin, you're on overwatch. Stay mobile. If you see anything out of place, call it." He waited for pushback and there was none.

<Good intuition. It seems like their definition of order is being told what to do,> Fen told him. <That might not always be to our advantage, but it appears to be so here.>

<They could be testing us too. Maybe there's something in the Flame Doctrine about seeing how much an enemy reveals about themselves.>

<It would be helpful to know more about this Doctrine of theirs if we ever have to war with these people.>

<Let's hope that isn't the case.> Callum looked back at the others: "Here's what needs to happen: three of us should be stationed to hold ground, one mobile, one in the air. That's the only way this works. We could each defend a wall of the monastery and have Therrin keep to the air, but what if one of us is overwhelmed? This means that there will be a vulnerable position, but Therrin will be able to keep an eye on that and alert . . . me."

"You?" Sorcha asked.

Callum nodded toward the shrine. "Yeah. Foxes are fast. Quicker than a snake, a boar, or a badger. I'll move between fights."

Ryven cracked his knuckles. "Makes sense. In that case, I'll man the front."

Sorcha hesitated. "The Seraph Python is fast as well. But . . ." She glanced at Callum. "You're right. That role makes sense for your pact."

Callum turned to her. "Hold the rear entrance. Watch for movement through the ruins. Ryven, keep to the front. That's where I'm guessing the heaviest hit will come."

"Good," he grunted.

"Lynnafer, east flank. There's enough cover for you and your badger to make a stand. Therrin, stay in the sky. If the west side is hit, you and I will respond together."

Again, no protest, just movement as the students found their positions.

Callum took his place on the western front, where he would stay temporarily until the swarm began. He ignored the cold, aware that it was a figment of his imagination even though he could still see his breath. *Or is it?* he wondered for a beat, uncertain how the Soul Pythia was able to create a place like this.

Somewhere nearby, a crow cawed once and went silent.

It's happening soon . . . Callum thought, getting excited.

It was only a few moments later that the mana stirred beneath the frost-hardened ground beyond, like something old was waking beneath the ice.

Callum steadied his breath, eyes scanning the ridgeline. "Here they come!" he shouted as corrupted aetherbeasts spilled over the far slope like a broken tide.

"In front, too!" Ryven called back.

"All directions!" Therrin announced from above the monastery.

Callum watched the movement of jagged and unnatural silhouettes, the warped aetherbeasts loping across the ice-blasted terrain. Steam rose from their bodies as their tentacles beat in the air around them. Their howls were not loud, but they were wrong, the kind of sound that made the hair on his arms rise and tension gather tight in his chest.

Callum felt his strength and agility amplify as he took his meldform, the power of the Radiant Fox surging through him. His Armorcore flared with magic as it wrapped around him, giving Callum an extra layer of protection. He drew his double Ram swords just as the aetherbeasts neared them in a blur of claws and howling mana.

He rushed toward the western side of the monastery, Therrin overhead providing support. The first aetherbeast flashed toward him and Callum cut it down. He slashed his swords across another, landed, twisted, and conjured a blast of wind that took a pair of smaller aetherbeast mid-leap. A bolt of lightning courtesy of Therrin split a winged monster in half, sending it spiraling toward the ground.

Another down, Callum thought as he saw some monsters making a wide berth around the front of the monastery.

"I'm heading to the front!" Callum shouted up to Therrin. He dashed there and soon found Ryven stomping through the mud near the northern arch—his meldform hulking, mana tusks lit with molten cracks as the Juggerboar surged forward in a blast of earth and shadow.

Between tackles, Ryven spun with a massive, blocky Weaponcore crossbow trailing with shadow. He fired at close range, the shot slamming into another beast's skull, pinning it to a broken column.

<Looks like he's handling things!> Callum told Fen.

<For now. We'll check back!>

Callum saw two larger beasts break through the eastern side, moving straight for Lynnafer.

Their bodies shimmered with raw mana distortion, limbs stretched unevenly as if reshaped mid-scream. One dragged something behind it that looked like a chain, which sparked where it touched the ground. The other skittered low, its back split open to reveal twitching spines that pulsed with light, casting a sickly glow with every step. Their mouths were too wide, filled with teeth that looked more like giant splinters than fangs, gnashing in an erratic rhythm as they closed in.

Callum kicked off a stone covered in snow and launched himself forward. The Ram swords flared into his hands as he struck, first right, then left, catching the one with magic chains just before it leaped. The blade curved clean through corrupted flesh, splitting it in a flash of golden heat.

The second aetherbeast lunged for him; Callum dove to avoid it as Lynnafer stepped in, her goose-headed Weaponcore snapped out with terrifying speed, cleaving the beast across its side. It staggered; she drove the beak of her Weaponcore deeper into the monster and slammed it to the ground, splintering the ice, where she finished with a clean upward slash that snapped bone and scattered corrupted mana into the snowy wind.

Lynnafer's eyes darted past Callum, to an incoming aetherbeast.

Above them, Therrin's pale bat wings allowed him to slip through the air, ghostlike. He held a lantern Weaponcore, which he used to release distorted beams that split into hallucination-patterned strikes. One struck an aetherbeast mid-leap just behind Callum, sending it screaming back into the snow in a heap.

"Thanks!" Callum called up Therrin as he sprinted up a half-fallen statue, using its shattered arm as stepping stones. He jumped. Callum reached a wall and ran across the top of it as he charged up one of Fen's powers.

Radiant Inferno created several swells of fire that grew from the ground beneath four aetherbeasts surging in his direction. They were reduced to molten mana, the magic sparking in the air and fading.

<*That was not conserving power,*> Fen scolded.

<*It worked, didn't it?*>

<*It did.*>

<*I only wish we were getting shards for this,*> Callum said as he dropped down and landed near Sorcha.

The Crimson student was surrounded; her Seraph Python had coiled tightly around one enemy, crushing it, while another snapped at her heels. Sorcha spun a glaive with a jagged edge, moving it in calculated arcs, but not cutting fast enough. Her forehead glistened with sweat, every motion defiant, yet the fight was slipping from her grasp.

Callum leaped forward with Gale Pulse, sending a blast of pressurized wind that knocked two beasts off balance. He activated Onslaught of the

Thunderhoof Shadowbull, the spectral bull flaring behind him in a ripple of speed as he careened into the nearest creature with a shoulder-check and a bladed follow-through, the Ram sword splitting another beast cleanly down the back.

He heard a loud snap, then a yelp as Sorcha went down, one knee to the ground, a writhing tentacle around her throat.

Callum didn't hesitate.

He stepped in, slashing hard and fast, three cuts in less than a second. The tentacle dropped, sizzling. He turned back toward the aetherbeast, blocked its next tentacle attack by cutting through it, the monster turning to shadowy ash.

He extended a hand to her. "You good?"

Sorcha looked at his hand—but didn't take it.

Instead, she stood on her own, glanced away, and huffed, face taut with restrained fury. "Check the others," she said. "I've got it from here."

"Will do." Callum moved back toward the eastern wall. He sent his Ram swords away and summoned Tempest Fang, the wind twisting around him. He caught one creature mid-pounce and sent it tumbling in a wind-sheathed arc. Lynnafer slashed another down with her massive badger claws.

After clearing out the eastern side again, Callum moved to the front, where he found Ryven still going strong, his Juggerboar form seemingly energized by blood. Every attack slammed like a falling boulder. Every counterstrike seemed faster than the last. And then there was his Weapon-core crossbow, which he used to take out enemies from a range.

Ryven will be hard to stop in a one-on-one, Callum thought.

He rushed back toward Sorcha, only for her to snap, "I've got it!" To prove her point, she cleaved into an aetherbeast as large as a bear, its back covered in bristles. Her python twisted around its legs and brought it down, allowing her to deliver a finishing blow with her shadow-charged glaive.

Above, Therrin loosed another ripple of disorienting magic, causing a pair of aetherbeasts to stumble and attack each other.

Callum turned and saw them coming. *A final wave.* Dozens upon dozens, maybe more, surged over the ridge in a blur of limbs and snarling maws. The demonic aetherbeasts moved faster than the rest, unified in a terrible rhythm, like they could sense the last seconds bleeding away.

He braced for impact but it never came.

The beasts dissolved mid-charge, their bodies unraveling into tendrils of smoke and ash. One moment they were there—feral, thundering, inevitable—and the next, nothing. Only silence and the echo of what could have been.

The sky above them fractured as lines of light split the clouds.

A voice echoed through the air, unmistakable, resonant, and not entirely human. The construct of the Soul Pythia descended through the snow-choked sky, her face shifting behind the veil. "Congratulations on your survival. The five of you have passed this trial. Please step into the portal to begin your next and final challenge."

A bolt of magic ripped through the clouds above, slamming into the ground in front of them, causing Callum to stagger backward. Light flared outward on impact, unraveling into a wide, glowing portal that fizzled with energy.

Lynnafer stepped up beside him, eyes fixed on the light.

Callum didn't look away. "Ready for the next part?"

"Ready as I'll ever be."

The two Great College students stepped through together.

CHAPTER 12

A Portalstone is a stabilized arcane cipher etched onto aether-reactive stone, one that has been keyed to a precise spatial-mana resonance matrix. When paired with anchoring leylines connected to the Heart of Creation, the rune forms a fixed spatial bridge, allowing transit between two predetermined points. Due to their complexity and the unknown principles behind their original design, no new Portalstones have been successfully created in more than a century. There are archmages who can open portals, but this isn't the same as a portal from a fixed location. As such, each existing rune is considered a finite resource. Should the Crown or the Great College require a new portal site, an existing rune must be physically extracted from its housing by archmages specializing in leyline disentanglement.

—A quote from *Valestra Crown Infrastructure Ledger*,
Portal Appendix B, Revised Year 514

Callum, Lynnafer, and the three Crimson Sigil students appeared in the middle of an open field, ash swirling in lazy eddies above their heads.

"Not what I expected," Callum said as heat slammed into him—dry, suffocating, immediate. The air reeked of scorched wood and something harsher, like burnt metal and singed stone. The grass was long dead, the soil cracked and blackened. Off to the east, a line of trees and shrubs burned like matchsticks, flames leaping from branch to branch with frantic, greedy motions.

"It's literally hell," Lynnafer said beside him, voice low.

The Crimson Sigil students stepped forward, heads down, none of them saying anything after a brief exchange of looks, tension flickering in their silence. Sorcha remained at the front of the group, the de facto spokesperson, the look on her face unreadable.

<*The area reminds of Weatherby,*> Callum told Fen. <*Not far from the farm...*>

A wave of luminous distortion shimmered in front of them as the Soul Pythia construct reappeared, her robes untouched by the heat, her veil as glass-like as before. The construct's shifting face gave no indication of emotion as she looked the four students over. "Your final trial for today will challenge all of you in ways you have yet to anticipate," she said, her voice echoing oddly across the field. "You have less than fifteen minutes before the flames completely cover the area. If they do, and no one has claimed the Portalstone, you will all fail."

A lone point of light shimmered near the line of flames, sharp and steady like a star trying to pierce through smoke. It spun slowly, light glinting off it in an array of colors, flickering like a mirrored prism in the sun. The object continued spinning gently above a pedestal of polished marble, its base supported by clawed feet carved from the same stone.

"The Portalstone will allow only one of you to escape this trial," the construct told them. "It must be held in your hand for five uninterrupted minutes to fully charge. During that time, you will need to guard the stone, which will force you to either defend it against the others, or form an alliance. Only one of you can win this challenge, and that person, the victor of this Culling Trial, will move onto the Duelist Rounds."

Callum's stomach turned as what she had just said hit. *One person?*

"Good luck, students." The Soul Pythia construct vanished, but the fire encroaching on them didn't.

Callum felt his jaw tighten as the five stood there processing what they had just been told. He glanced toward Lynnafer, whose eyes were locked on the pedestal in the distance.

"I don't know," she said under her breath. "I really don't know."

The Crimson Sigil students still hadn't moved. But the change in their posture was visible—slight reorientations, a subtle shift of weight, Sorcha mere seconds from taking charge. They weren't relaxing; they were calculating, deciding how they would do this, considering there were three of them, but only one person could be the winner.

Fen had a theory: <*This goes against everything they've been taught. Their doctrine demands unity under imperial will, not rivalry among those who serve it.*>

<*They must have competed with each other before, just like we do here.*>

<*Certainly so. But they weren't expecting this, especially after the challenge we just went through in which we were forced to band together. They're just as hesitant as you are, especially with the fire on the horizon.*>

Seeing the flames in the distance stirred something in Callum, a memory he hadn't touched in years. It came rushing back, sudden and vivid, like a wound that had never fully closed.

Miss Barrowsly's farm. The west fields. That horrible snap when the fire line broke containment, and the line of destruction began its march toward her home. Callum had been maybe nine. His father had shouted for him to fetch water while Miss Barrowsly screamed behind them.

"Be careful!" the old woman had cried.

The buckets were too heavy for him, but Callum hadn't stopped. Even as the smoke clawed at his throat, thick and acrid, turning every breath into a cough, even as his muscles trembled under the strain, Callum had pressed on.

He had stumbled more than once on the path between the well and the fire line beyond Miss Barrowsly's farm, boots soaked as water sloshed over the rims and splashed across the packed earth. Each time he had thrown a bucketful at the flames, it had felt like he was falling behind, the flames growing higher. Still, he had pressed on, jaw clenched, eyes stinging, unwilling to quit.

Everywhere, the woods had burned, the crackling roar louder than any storm. Plumes of flame had leaped nearly ten feet high, devouring everything they touched. The smoke had soon turned the world black, pressing in from every side like a wall.

Still, he had gone back and forth. Again and again.

He had followed his father's voice, Rhane's shouts distant but anchoring, the sharp bark of orders through the chaos. That voice had given Callum's legs purpose, his fear somewhere to go.

He hadn't been able to think, had barely been able to breathe, but he had kept going.

Then a mounted guard had appeared from town, charging toward the farm with her head low and the wind gathering at her back. At the time, Callum hadn't understood what she had done, how she had rode in on a gust of wind strong enough to push the fire aside and drive it down a different path.

Now, he knew she had used a Powercore, some Air Affinity spell, similar to the ones he had.

He looked again at the pedestal, the rune flashing like a signal flare, the flames closing in, the overwhelming smoke.

"Go?" Lynnafer asked.

Callum didn't answer. He just *ran*.

The others did too.

Sorcha. Ryven. Therrin. Lynnafer at the rear. All five students sprinted toward the pedestal, the heat at their backs rising with every step as they took their meldforms.

For now, it wasn't about fighting. It was about getting there first.

The five students reached the pedestal together. They paused momentarily in front of the glowing Portalstone, which hovered above its base, spinning slowly in a radiant lattice of blue-white light that pulsed with layered wards, waiting for a victor.

For a heartbeat, no one moved.

Then all at once, the five summoned their Armorcores.

Callum felt the power of the Brightflame Falcon surge over him, a pair of wings forming on his back that provided additional protection but didn't allow him to fly, not like Therrin, who simply rushed forward with a single beat of his functional wings, where he grabbed the Portalstone and took to the air, his form shimmering as his meld completed.

It seemed like Therrin would get away too, like he would be able to fly high enough that no one could reach him. But then a shadow snapped out of Sorcha's open palm.

Her python! Callum thought as it coiled around Therrin's legs like a striking whip, and yanked, slamming the man to the ground with a hollow crack. His head bounced against the stone base of the pedestal and the Portalstone fell from his hands.

She killed him, Callum thought, only then remembering that all of this was taking place in some illusory realm, that none of it was real.

But that didn't mean there would be no consequences.

The four watched as the bracelet on Therrin's wrist lit up red, each pulse growing brighter. Before anyone could react, he vanished in a streak of light. They stood frozen, clearly stunned—no one had expected someone to be force-extracted that quickly.

<*Your sword,*> Fen said, breaking Callum's shock. <*Your sword!*>

Lynnafer moved first, the woman summoning her goose-headed blade. She charged, power gathering in her wake as energy from her meldform rippled around her. Now on all fours, Ryven met her halfway, his Juggerboar hooves cracking the dirt as he slammed into Lynnafer.

The ground shook as the two collided.

Lynnafer twisted to the right and came up with a sweeping slash. Ryven's tusks caught her weapon mid-swing and locked it. He craned his neck to the side and tossed the weapon away. Even as it fizzled out, the goose head managed to strike Ryven's armor before the two students went down again, badger against boar, earth mana flaring like sparks under each blow.

Tempest Fang now in hand, Callum turned toward Sorcha and activated Roots of the Willow Aethertree. Magic vines erupted from the ground around her, spiraling to bind, yet she sidestepped them, slipping through the attack with effortless grace, untouched.

<*Has to be some snake trait!*> Fen said as Callum fired a blast of wind at her from the tip of his sword.

Sorcha didn't even need to raise her forearm as her Armorcore pulsed into a fan-shaped ward where bracers should have been, dispersing the force outward.

It staggered her; Callum didn't waste the opening. His Radiant Claws flared to life and he darted forward, low and fast. He moved to strike as Fen shouted directions in his head.

<*Now! Radiant Mirage!*> Fen told him.

Light bloomed around him as four flickering afterimages peeled off Callum's form like reflections breaking away. They darted, weaving beside him as he moved. Sorcha slashed at one and missed. She tried for another—also a miss.

Callum lunged through the third mirage and landed a blow, claws slicing along her side only to be repelled by Sorcha's Armorcore, which discharged a wave of raw mana that blasted him off his feet.

Callum hit the ground hard, the impact knocking the breath from his lungs. He skidded across the dirt, rolled once, and forced himself upright on shaking legs. Even with his Armorcore active, pain radiated through his ribs. The fire was close now, maybe twenty feet away, tearing through the brush with a hungry roar. Heat pressed against his skin, and every breath pulled in dry, bitter soot.

<*Still alive,*> Fen said.

"Yep," Callum said, checking his mana reserves.

Steady.

He turned back to the Portalstone, which still hovered unclaimed. How long had it been since they reached the pedestal? *Two minutes? Three?*

Sorcha moved. Her aetherpython slithered low across the broken terrain, heading straight for Callum. He summoned his Ram sword and split it, bracing himself, prepared to cleave the python in half.

The serpent veered left at the last instant. It curved wide, gliding over the dust-choked ground in a blur of scaled muscle. Not toward him, but toward the figures still locked in brutal combat nearby.

Callum saw it happen a half-second too late.

The python wrapped itself around Lynnafer's legs. She twisted instinctively, claws slashing down, but the creature tightened just enough to disrupt her footing.

That was all Ryven needed.

The big man surged forward with a grunt of raw power and delivered a brutal headbutt, sending Lynnafer to the ground.

Ryven lifted her and slammed her down with enough force to crater the cracked earth. Dust and light flared around the impact as her eyes fluttered. Her bracelet flared red, its light growing with intensity. Lynnafer vanished only a few moments later.

The flames behind Callum surged higher, casting long shadows across the cracked field, smoke churning across the wind as Sorcha and Ryven turned to him. No words. No gloating. No questions.

Just a look between them followed by a single, silent decision as the two turned to Callum.

CHAPTER 13

Hollowing occurs when an awakened Soul Heart is depleted past the point of mana recovery. Symptoms include memory bleed, identity fragmentation, staggered breathing, and eventual Soul Heart collapse. Restoration is possible within roughly the first hour. After that . . . it's not the same person we're saving.

—Halwen Myric, Senior Medicus, Great College Infirmary

The first strike came without warning. Ryven barreled forward, his Juggerboar meldform burning away in a flash of mana-light as a new, even bulkier one appeared. Rather than a crossbow, he summoned an enormous Weaponcore hammer the size of a siege post, its head shaped like a snarling beast with twin tusks flaring outward from either side. Dark energy traced the haft in sharp, talon-shaped lines, giving the weapon the presence of something that had once stalked prey.

Callum rolled sideways just in time as the hammer slammed into the ground where he'd been standing, shattering the ground on impact.

A fissure tore through the ground, splitting the dirt wide and dragging up the blackened roots of grass and brush, stripping more from the field. He launched himself backward, drew his wind sword midair, and landed in a crouch.

<*Move fast, hit faster!*> Fen whispered in his head.

He didn't need the reminder.

Callum surged forward, blade trailing compressed air as he blasted back at Ryven with Zephyr Strike. The moment he crossed into Ryven's range, he twisted low, spun behind him, and cut upward. A burst of slicing wind followed the arc of the blade, catching Ryven across the side and buckling his posture.

Before Sorcha could close the distance, Callum jumped back and prepared for Radiant Inferno.

He swept his arm in a wide arc and unleashed a series of fiery mana flares. They burst outward in rapid succession, explosions licking around Sorcha as flames bit at the ends of her cape. She raised her arm-shield and stepped back, boots skidding over dirt and withered grass.

With a surge of effort, and ignoring Fen's warnings in his head, Callum triggered Radiant Mirage. Light split from his body, as several afterimages flickered and danced away in every direction.

Sorcha's python lashed out at one of his replicants; Ryven turned toward another, confused for a heartbeat too long.

<*You're using too much,*> Fen shouted, his voice finally breaking through. <*You can't sustain this!*>

<*What else am I supposed to do?*> Callum answered as the illusion broke and Ryven charged.

Callum met the brute head-on after tapping into his Thunderhoof Shadowbull Powercore. Mana surged through his limbs, heavy and tense, like something straining against the inside of his skin. The pressure built in his legs, his chest, his spine, the charge taking less than a second to ignite.

The two collided mid-run, the impact crackling the air like lightning.

Callum's shoulder drove into Ryven's chest. Magic exploded between them, the boar's spectral energy shattering into a ring of thunder. Ryven *flew* back, smashing through a line of debris, and skidding to a stop with a grunt.

The impact took Callum down as well, his knees hitting the dirt first, breath torn from his lungs. His Armorcore flared once, then burst, shattered by the recoil, mana scattering around him like hot sparks.

<*Get up!*> Fen said. <*Don't wait for them to reset. Get up now!*>

<*Should I get the Portalstone?*>

<*What? Wait ... yes! That's a brilliant idea. With your power levels, maybe it's better. Get it and get clear of them. We're running out of challenge time!*>

Callum stood. He was unsteady but up before Ryven, who lay on his side, blinking rapidly.

Sorcha stepped forward, her python already unfurling from her side, mouth open and ready to strike.

Rather than engage her again, Callum turned to the Portalstone, which still hovered above the pedestal, spinning slowly. He called upon the wind and a sharp gust tore across the field, not aimed at his enemies, but at the stone itself.

Just like the town guard years ago, he thought, *who turned a fire in a different direction with air!*

The wind caught the gem and moved it away from the pedestal. It also pushed the flames back, momentarily changing their trajectory. By this point, Callum was already sprinting toward the Portalstone and he was able to catch it.

The moment his fingers closed around the stone, the outer glyphs flared to life indicating the charge had started.

A hiss tore through the air just as Callum regained his footing.

To his left, Sorcha's serpent lunged—massive, fast, jaws wide enough to swallow his head whole. He didn't think. He thrust his free hand forward, Piercing Air Spear already coalescing. The moment it solidified, he fired.

The spear slammed into the python's open maw, driving deep before detonating with a sharp crack of air. The beast recoiled mid-lunge, its head snapping backward with a guttural screech. It hit the ground, twisted once in pain, then slithered back, coiling into a defensive knot.

Sorcha staggered as the feedback hit her, clutching her arm and cursing under her breath.

Callum didn't move, couldn't move. He stood with the Portalstone clenched in one hand, blood running warm down his temple, dripping onto the scorched dirt below. His mana flickered, stretched thin, on the verge of collapse.

His vision blurred at the edges, and his limbs shook with the effort of staying upright.

But he was still standing. Still in it. And for now, that was enough.

Ryven roared to life, the big man clearing the distance between them with a burst of speed and power. He slammed his great hammer into the ground again, its head cracking the earth like a meteor. A new fissure tore across the battlefield—this one arcing straight beneath Callum's feet.

Callum stumbled, thrown sideways as the ground pitched beneath him. The Portalstone flew from his hand, landing somewhere in the dirt with a soft thud.

Damn. He knew what that meant: he'd just reset the timer.

Sorcha's python lunged again, jaws wide and eyes locked on him. Callum hit the ground hard, the impact jarring through his already aching body. He rolled once, came up dizzy, head pounding, vision swimming. The firelight glinted off the Portalstone a few feet away.

He turned toward it, chest heaving, dust in his mouth.

Too far.

But not far enough to stop him.

<*I'm afraid we will need to deal with her first,*> Fen said as he took over some of Callum's motor functions, the fox able to help him dodge the

python's calculated strikes. Together, they hit the aetherpython with Radiant Claws, and Callum used the opening to sprint back toward Sorcha, who had just gotten her hands on the Portalstone.

He extended his palm and Gale Pulse burst from his fingers.

Sorcha flew back, thrown clean off her feet, the stone flying through the air.

<Go,> Callum told Fen. <Distract the python!>

<Will do!> Fen launched from Callum's shoulder in a streak of radiant fire. Light flared as his form unmelded midair, reshaping into the fox's full, glowing body. His fur shimmered with threads of golden mana and his tail burned like a comet's plume, long, fiery, and rippling with living light.

Fen landed in a blur, paws barely touching the scorched earth before he twisted sideways, darting through a whip-crack of shadow as the python's tail snapped toward him.

The serpent lunged, diverted for just a breath, giving Callum the moment he needed to dive forward and grab the Portalstone.

Callum felt his strength double as Fen returned to him, only to be struck hard from the side.

Ryven crashed into him with a brutal, shoulder-driven blow, driving them both toward the fire line. Callum held the stone tight to his chest with one hand, the other scrambling for balance as the world spun around him. Ash billowed around the two as they skidded to a stop near the scorched edge of the field.

"Give it to me!" Ryven reared up, hammer lifted.

Callum clenched his hand, conjuring magic roots from the dry soil, binding Ryven's legs just long enough to stop his attack.

With his free hand, Callum called on his wind sword, shifted his stance, and drove the blade forward in a clean, lunging cut. The strike caught Ryven just beneath the ribs, slicing deep through his Armorcore.

The brute's bracelet flared red and Ryven dropped, eyes wide with shock that he had actually lost. A second later, the bracelet began to glow steadily as the portal sequence initiated.

Callum backpedaled, gasping, surprised he had been able to bring Ryven down. "I can't believe..." Something caught his eye. Callum glanced down to see his own bracelet flashing red, glowing, indicating his mana reserves were at Low and that he would soon be force-extracted himself.

<You're out?> Fen asked.

Callum looked back toward Sorcha, already pushing herself upright, her giant python circling defensively. He only had seconds before he would disappear, leaving Sorcha to win this Culling Round.

"Not done yet." Callum raised his hand, magic sparking at his fingertips as his claws extended, glowing with raw intensity. He slipped them beneath the edge of the bracelet and tore it free.

The instant it left his wrist, the band collapsed inward with a sharp crack, folding into itself in a flash of red light before vanishing in a tight, silent implosion.

Callum turned to Sorcha.

"H-how?" She had seen everything, the woman dumbfounded by what he had just done. "That shouldn't be possible . . ." Her eyes narrowed with something that wasn't quite anger, something that became colder.

Sorcha didn't hesitate and neither did Callum.

They charged. Sorcha's python lunged, fangs open. Enhanced by Fen's power, Callum burst forward, Tempest Fang gleaming in his grip, wind howling around the tip of the sword.

He cut through the serpent in a single, blinding arc. The beast scattered into raw mana, howling as it collapsed.

Sorcha's eyes went wide. Callum closed the distance and struck, the blow shattering her Armorcore, cracks spiderwebbing across her chestplate before it exploded outward in a burst of force and fading light.

With a shocked look on her face, Sorcha staggered backward and vanished.

The field fell quiet, the fires burning even higher around Callum as he dropped his sword and fell to his knees.

The Portalstone warmed in his hands, flickering with light, glyphs glowing brighter. The world tilted and dimmed, yet Callum still held on, the Portalstone clutched to his chest, eyes closed, prepared for whatever would come.

CHAPTER 14

In one realm, the soul is a garden, tended yet allowed to bloom in curious shapes. In the other, it is a sword, sharpened from birth and sheathed only at command. Both can be beautiful. Only one remembers why it grew in the first place.

—A quote from *Soulcraft and State: A Dialogic Study* by Mastress Yelra Vindrel, Core Lectora of Ridgebarrow

Callum gasped as the world around him flooded with color and then reformed into the soft warmth of the pod chamber of the Aeternal Tabula, the curved ceiling still humming with residual light. He immediately sent his hands to the ground, anchoring himself until he realized he was seated, just as he had been before starting the Culling Trials.

Callum settled, his chest rising and falling in sharp bursts, for a few more seconds. He found the Culling Bracelet on his wrist and touched it with his other hand. It was still warm.

The others were already awake.

Therrin sat perfectly still, hands folded, gaze fixed on Callum with something between amusement and disdain for what he had done. Next to him, Lynnafer sat with her arms over her chest, a slight smirk on her face. Beside her, Ryven seemed out of place, the big man crushing his cushion, his brow hanging low. Then there was Sorcha, posture blade-straight, chin slightly lifted. Her gaze raked Callum with analytic disapproval.

"You were not supposed to take your bracelet off," Sorcha said, her voice clipped, offended.

"It's not like we knew that was a thing you could even do," Lynnafer replied, shrugging. "Callum improvised. I see nothing wrong with that."

Sorcha's mouth fell open. "We were *not* instructed to improvise," she said with absolute certainty, like a rule written in stone.

"Sure," Lynnafer told her, half-rising. "But breaking the bracelet wasn't against the rules, either."

"That's not the point. The structure of the trial was deliberate. The limitations define the test. Working outside them isn't innovation, it's disorder."

Callum could feel it now, too. The subtle pressure in the room keeping them from moving from their cushions. *Maybe it's a good thing*, he thought as he eyed the three Crimsons, all of whom were agitated.

Sorcha continued, her voice icy, "If we all begin choosing our own terms, the test collapses. What's left isn't competition. It's chaos."

Callum stayed quiet, his muscles still buzzing from the fight. Victory had been seconds away from slipping through his fingers. He knew if he had followed the rules, he would have lost.

Or worse ... I could have reached Hollowing, he thought, *which wouldn't have worked the same in the Soul Pythia's creation, but it has to be similar.*

Across from him, Therrin remained motionless, like a wolf watching the aftermath of a hunt it didn't join. Ryven leaned forward slightly, his broad hands resting on his knees, the quiet brute kept still by the magical tether rooting them all to their seats.

Only Lynnafer seemed willing to move against it, if only to pace. "Chaos?" she echoed, lifting an eyebrow in Sorcha's direction. "He didn't follow a script you were comfortable with. That's not chaos. You have a control issue."

Sorcha's posture didn't shift, but her lips thinned. "What I mean," she replied, with the calm certainty of someone reciting scripture, "is that structure exists for a reason. When a soldier breaks formation, people die. When a mage disregards limits—"

"You all use Demoncores," Lynnafer reminded her with a wave of her hand. "Any rules and structures were discarded long ago. Our two kingdoms are on the verge of war, and one of the reasons is your usage of corrupted magic."

"The Flame Doctrine teaches that only through constraint can we achieve clarity," Ryven told Lynnafer with a grunt.

"For real? And what happens when the structure breaks first? When the rules stop working in the middle of a fight? You freeze? Is that what you do when the rules don't conform to your expectations?"

"We adapt within parameters." Sorcha didn't raise her voice, but there was iron beneath the words. "Improvisation without command is rebellion."

Lynnafer rolled his eyes. "Callum didn't rebel. He *won*. He won because he understood his own power levels. You're just upset that he didn't play your game to do it."

A faint flicker crossed Sorcha's eyes. Irritation? Doubt?

"He circumvented the evaluation." Sorcha spoke now as if giving a report. "If we each create our own metrics, there is no measure. Only noise. We do not accept his victory."

Therrin and Ryven both nodded in approval.

"Whether you do or not, it was instinct." Callum finally looked up, just enough to meet her gaze. "Pure instinct. And for all we know, it worked."

"You don't know that yet," Sorcha said. "They haven't announced the results."

The words hung there, sharp and bright and unflinching. Callum closed his eyes. Not to avert her gaze, but to really decide what it was that inspired him to push it to the limits.

<Instinct,> Fen told him, as if the fox could read his thoughts. <Do not overthink your actions.>

Before their argument could continue, a hum of magic rippled through the chamber. It gathered in the ceiling, spiraling like smoke before folding back down in a stream of focused light. From that light, the hooded construct of the Soul Pythia emerged, tall, still, and impossible to ignore. She turned her head slowly, as if surveying the room not with eyes, but with something deeper.

"The Culling Trial has concluded," the Pythia construct said, her voice soft, yet carrying with it an unnatural clarity, as if it had been spoken inside his skull. "The challenge was not only of strength and survival, but of cohesion, judgment, and restraint. These qualities matter, especially when the line between unity and collapse is thinner than you think."

She raised one hand, a faint circle of light spinning at her palm.

"Congratulations, Callum Stross. You have won your Concord Unit's Culling Trial. You will now be recognized as a qualified participant in the Dueling Rounds. Because of the unique nature of your victory, Sorcha Malvain will also move to the next round."

"I . . . I will?" Sorcha asked.

"You are not the only Concord Unit to advance with two victors," the Soul Pythia said, seemingly interpreting her question, "one by technicality."

Sorcha's brow twitched. Even Ryven looked over in surprise.

Callum took the statement for what it was, proof that others had found ways to bend the rules. Maybe on purpose. Maybe not. For him, it hadn't been a plan. Just survival.

Therrin shifted, still seated. "I could have won it for all of us," he said. His words weren't sharp, but the aim was clear, directed at Sorcha.

She didn't reply, but she did glance over to him and offer a look that said everything.

The Soul Pythia construct flickered once and slowly started to fade. "You may now leave." Their bracelets all clicked at once. "Place the Culling Bracelets on your cushions and follow the lanterns." As she vanished, a set of glowing green lanterns flared to life in the hallway beyond the pod room, bobbing slowly in the air to form a path that would guide them out of the Aeternal Tabula.

The five rose to their feet, the pressure keeping them down suddenly gone. The Crimson Sigil students moved first, exiting without a word as they shouldered past Callum and Lynnafer. Once they were gone, Lynnafer turned to him. "You did it!"

"Yeah," he said as they began following the lanterns.

"That was crazy."

"I'm just glad it worked." He entered the hall and kept his eyes on the Crimson students ahead, assuming they would turn and say something like Draven and his friends would have done. They remained obediently stoic, the three soon stepping out of the Aeternal Tabula and through a side door, where they turned to go back to their housing.

"What are you going to do now?" Lynnafer asked Callum when they were outside as well.

"Probably wait for Quinn, Marcella, and Princess Selene." He exhaled and rolled his shoulders as his eyes drifted to the two airships above Dreagis Hall. It was afternoon now, which told him that time passed differently when they were in the trials. *But it only felt like an hour...*

"They're probably somewhere over there." Lynnafer gestured toward an outdoor seating area that was down a small hill. Callum spotted several Great College students from his cohort, standing and discussing their Culling Trials beneath a pergola. Marcella stood at the back facing away from everyone, while Quinn looked like he was trying to comfort her. "I'll come with you," Lynnafer told him, "I want to see how Godric did."

The meeting area outside the eastern wing of the Aeternal Tabula had stood for over a century—a quiet, open-air alcove framed by curved stone benches and an arching pergola of darkwood lattice. In warmer months, flowering silvervine covered it in lush green shade, but the vines had turned a brittle copper-brown now, their curling leaves falling with every breeze. The scent of last night's cold rain lingered in the stone, and though the storm had passed, the chill of autumn held fast, lending the space a quiet, reflective stillness.

As they approached, Lynnafer spotted Godric near the edge of the commons and peeled off after giving Callum a quick goodbye.

Callum moved through small clusters of students, exchanging brief hellos with Victrin and Demandra, before making his way to the back where Quinn and Marcella sat beneath a stretch of hanging vines. Quinn sat with a relaxed slouch, relief on his face. Marcella, by contrast, sat rigidly upright, her jaw tight and one foot tapping, like she was seconds from setting something on fire just to watch it burn.

"There you are," she said as Callum approached. "How did we finish before you?"

"No idea."

She pinched the bridge of her nose. "Right, right, time works differently in whatever realm the Soul Pythia sends us to. Ugh. You'd think Mastress Lucerne would give us a break."

"Why would she do that again?" Quinn asked.

"I'm just saying."

Quinn gave Callum a quick nod. "How did it go?"

"I won, if that's what you're asking."

"Of course you did," Marcella said, too fast, her voice tight before she caught herself. She blinked, glanced away, then back. "Sorry. That came out wrong. I'm not—jealous, not exactly. It's just . . . you know what? Never mind. You first. What happened? How'd you do it?"

Callum leaned back on his heels. "I broke my bracelet, that's how."

"You . . . what?" she asked.

Callum found a council stone and brought it over to them. He sat and began his explanation, starting with guarding the temple during a monster invasion. "The second trial was a Portalstone challenge. One victor, one rune, five minutes of uninterrupted control. It came down to me and a Crimson student—Sorcha Malvain. By the end, I was running on fumes and it was clear I wasn't going to hold out much longer. So instead of getting pulled, I shattered the bracelet."

There was a pause after that.

"And Fen?" Quinn asked.

<Tell them I approved, both at the time and in retrospect.>

Callum laughed. "He was fine with it. Or at least, he's now saying he was."

"You're a lunatic," Marcella said flatly.

"Probably. But it worked. It did result in a technicality. The Crimson woman I told you about, Sorcha, she's moving onto the next trial too. What about you two?" he asked.

Quinn gave Callum a pained expression. "If you want to go first . . ." he told Marcella.

"I lost. What else is there to say? My entire Concord Unit did in the first round. We were supposed to find statue pieces and reassemble them. Sounded easy, except each piece was guarded by demonic aetherbeasts. There was a time limit, and I said we should work together. Demandra and the Crimson students agreed. But freaking Artur didn't." Upon hearing this, Callum looked around again and noticed Artur wasn't with the students, same with Draven and anyone else he usually hung out with.

"It was Artur's fault," Quinn chimed in.

"Obviously," Marcella said. "He stormed off after the first one and got himself force-extracted. The rest of us did what we had agreed to do, only to arrive at the statue and find out that the guy who was supposed to go after its head was nowhere to be found. We had all of ten minutes left to find him and the head. Did I mention we were in a dense jungle? I'm talking vines, mosquitos, carnivorous plants, and crazy aethermonkeys. It was hot and humid, and I'm not talking the weather I'm used to dealing with in Aveiro, where it's hot, humid, *and* breezy. Anyway. Ugh. Long story short: we all ended up scattered trying to find the last piece and time ran out."

Callum shook his head. "And you learned about what happened after you returned to your pod and confronted Artur?"

"Exactly." She threw her head back and let out a deep, troubled breath. "We didn't even have a chance to reach the second part of the trial. Stupid Artur. Him and all his draff, gutterscrape friends."

"What about yours?" Callum asked Quinn.

He shrugged like it hadn't mattered, though the spark in his eye said otherwise. "Similar setup to yours. First half was a city defense. It looked a lot like New Albion during the storm, honestly, but it was a merger of several cities I've been too. New Albion, Ontaria, Ridgebarrow—"

"We know you've been everywhere," Marcella said. "Sorry. I'm still salty about losing so early on. Please, continue, Quinn."

"We were tasked with defending the city and surviving a Beast Tide with limited resources, and by limited I mean our power levels were all set at Steady."

"And the second part?" Callum asked him.

"Same Portalstone deal as yours, actually. Except everyone had one. And the person who ended with two and held them for three minutes won."

"And you won?"

"Hell yes, he won," Marcella said. "Do not underestimate the new noble with a pacted kitty cat."

Quinn gave her a crooked grin, one that bordered on grateful. "Thank you . . . I think. And it's true. I won because people often underestimated me. Tuck was quite helpful in that regard." His smile faded. "Overall, the Crimson Sigil dominated. Almost everyone from our Cohort lost. A few slipped through on technicalities, but . . . we didn't do so well."

"What about Draven?" Callum asked.

Marcella shook her head. "Haven't seen Karna's worst kept secret all day. But I did see Princess Selene."

Callum's pulse quickened just slightly. "And?"

"She won hers, of course."

"Good," Callum said, meaning it.

"Maybe, maybe not," Marcella replied, watching him closely. "You might have to fight her in the next round."

CHAPTER 15

The monument that now stands in the central plaza of the Great College was never meant for public display. It was originally the keystone of the Demonslayer's mausoleum—an edifice raised far from the eyes of court or campus or public. When the location of the tomb was lost to time, only the statue remained, moved to New Albion's Great College decades later in an effort to anchor memory to place. Even now, scholars debate whether the statue watches over us . . . or waits for its true home to be found.

—Xander Callow, Master Channeler, Clergo, and famed Demonswar Historian

Cycling mana is certainly a way to pass the time, Callum thought as he sat on the cushion in his room, envisioning the magic all around him. The power around him was real; he could feel it and sense it, but it was harder to see with his eyes open, especially the dormant variety, which didn't have an affinity and seemed to be the stuff that made everything in their world.

<*It's getting late . . .*> Fen reminded him.

<*She will come,*> he told the fox. <*At least I assume that is the case.*>

Callum wanted to know what Selene's trial was like, and what to expect going forward; he knew she wouldn't be able to tell him everything, but every little bit would help. From what he had pieced together from other students, most notably Victrin, who had told him that the Duelist Rounds would take a few days, they had time.

Time to improve. Time to figure out what I need to do next so I can . . .

Callum paused his train of thought. He wasn't as competitive as someone like Marcella, but he wanted to win. He wanted to do it for his father, for Weatherby, and for his family's legacy. In that regard, he also wanted to do it for Fen, who continued to put trust in him.

"I should go," he said, breaking his meditation.

"Where?" asked Fen, who sat curled up beside him.

"The Great Library."

"What for?"

"I want to better understand the Crimson students. There has to be a book that will give me insight into their Empire. To be completely honest, I don't know much about them. I know a lot more about the Lands of Grimbald because Weatherby is near the border."

"Yes, the neutral kingdom," the fox said. "It used to be part of Valestra, you know. I haven't really given it much thought, but I have wondered what happened."

"The War of Embers is what happened," Callum said as he got to his feet. "But that was two hundred years ago, and we've been allies since."

"So if you don't want to go to the library, and you're clearly putting on your father's cloak, where are you going exactly?" Fen asked as he joined Callum by the door.

"To see Princess Selene."

Fen gave him a funny look. "You intend to sneak into her suites?"

"I haven't thought that far ahead, but I know I need to talk to her. Besides," Callum said as he pulled the hood over his head, "I have you."

"You do, and I fail to see your point."

"Foxes are cunning. I'm sure we'll be able to get in there together, or you'll be able to reach her window in some way. Let's not worry too much about that. Let's just worry about getting out of here first."

"I suppose that will work for now," Fen said as he melded with him.

<Good.> Callum slipped out of the dormitory, moving with as much care as he could into the night. He took the long way to avoid a few open doors. If he ran into Marcella, it would ruin everything. He knew she'd demand an explanation or, worse, insist on joining.

Once he cleared the dormitories, Callum picked up his pace, heading toward the central courtyard and the path that curved around the outer towers.

A chilly wind stirred the fallen leaves as he passed beneath familiar archways. His boots echoed off the stone, each step drawing him deeper into the quiet stillness the Great College wore late at night.

<Stop there for a second,> Fen told him.

<You got it.> Callum paused for a moment in front of the Demonslayer Monument, a life-size statue of his forefather, the original Callum Stross, ringed by his five legendary pacted aetherbeasts.

Fen flashed into existence beside him, ears tilted, voice quiet but clear. "Rata," he said, nodding at the broad-shouldered wolf with sand-brushed fur, "the Sand Wolf of Aveiro. He could outrun lightning across the dunes." He took another step, lifting his head toward the rearing figure behind. "Killeas—the Gryphon Vanguard of Fates. Sharpest eyes of us all, even when the skies burned."

"I know, I know," Callum said, interpreting his tone, "we need to find Killeas now that I can get another Aethercore."

"That might be easier said than done, but you are correct." Fen turned to the phoenix, wings curved halfway open in sculpted fire. "Look at her. Lisalen, the Brightflame Phoenix. Always the first into the breach. Always so blinding that even I had to look away. And her wings. You should have seen them. Another thing we need to ask the princess about, considering Lisalen is pacted with her father."

"I still don't think we're close enough that she'll let me meet her father."

"You never know." Fen tilted his head up to the dragon curling around the back. "Astel, the Goddess of Dragons. Nearly strong enough to fight the Demon King alone." He stopped in front of the smallest shape, carved at the Demonslayer's side, a fox with a long tail and eyes filled with intensity. "And . . . me."

"I know," Callum said softly. "It's humbling."

Fen's tail drooped. "My size or . . . ?"

"No, not your size, to know what they did, what you did as well."

"I did some, but then I was locked away." Fen sat, his disposition souring. "Sometimes I feel like I didn't fully do my part. But now there's you, the Demonslayer's reincarnation, and maybe this was my part all along." Fen's ears flicked suddenly. Without warning, he turned and rushed back into Callum. *<Quick, hide behind the statue!>*

Callum didn't ask why. He moved to the side and crouched low at the base of the monument, pulling his cloak around himself.

Footsteps approached. Low voices. Boots on stone.

Callum stayed still, barely breathing as a group of students passed. Draven was at the lead, his stride as arrogant as ever.

He's . . . with them? It took Callum a moment to register what he was seeing as a group of Crimson Sigil students followed Draven. He immediately recognized Laziel Thornhelm, his braided white hair stark under the moonlight. Beside him, still carrying the scowl he had started to grow used to, was Sorcha Malvain.

Draven kept speaking, pointing out buildings though Callum was too focused on remaining absolutely still to hear him. The group cleared the Demonslayer Monument, and for a moment, Callum thought he was in the clear.

But then Sorcha slowed, her head turning just enough to scan the edge of the path. Her gaze lingered for a breath as she looked toward the statue.

"Let's keep moving," Laziel called back to her.

"Coming!"

The group of warlocks continued, heading toward Dreagis Hall, Draven still at the lead.

<*What is he up to?*> Callum asked. <*It's like he's one of them . . .*>

<*I don't know,*> Fen replied. <*But now I think it's imperative we speak to the princess.*>

Callum reached the outer edge of the Royal Quarters just as the last courtyard lamp was dimming. The suites that housed the princess and her entourage sat atop a gently sloped terrace, surrounded by high hedgerows, enchanted lanterns, and a perimeter of silent, silver-cloaked guards. The stone of the building was a deep violet-gray, veined with silver seams that pulsed faintly in the moonlight. Arched windows glowed softly with interior light and banners hung from the upper balconies—white silk adorned with the Morninglade emblem.

He crouched behind a hedge near the side path, breath tight in his chest.

This is a terrible plan, he thought.

Fen appeared beside him, flicking his tail with mild irritation. "Well?"

"I figured I'd send you ahead. You know, climb a wall, signal her somehow—maybe get a message through."

"To what end?"

"I didn't get that far."

Before Fen could respond, a quiet voice broke through the stillness.

"Callum Stross."

Callum flinched and turned.

Sir Trindade stood behind him at the edge of the hedgerow, flanked by two guards. He looked only faintly amused.

Callum rose slowly, brushing leaves from his cloak. "Sir Trindade, ahem. I was just—"

"Let me guess. You want to speak to the princess."

"If . . . that's possible," Callum told Selene's main Legion Guard.

The knight nodded once. "And normally, she comes to you."

"How did you—"

"Princess Selene is clever," Trindade said, stepping aside. "But not as clever as she thinks." He raised a hand and, with a subtle twist of his fingers, he opened a shimmering oval in the air, light rippling at its edges. A portal, cast with such casual ease that it almost looked like an afterthought.

Through the oval, Callum saw a cozy study lit with golden lamplight. The room had tall bookshelves, a woven rug, and a low table scattered with papers and glass spheres. Selene sat cross-legged on a floor cushion in a flowing nightgown of midnight blue, her hair loosely braided down her back. She looked up at the portal and smiled faintly.

She said something.

Callum heard nothing—only a faint pulse, like static across glass.

Sir Trindade tilted his head, then offered a half smile. "She asked what you're waiting for." He motioned to the open portal. "Join her. But not for long."

Callum took a breath and stepped through.

CHAPTER 16

Where Valestra prizes the strength that emerges from choice and self-direction, Geshwine exalts strength shaped through doctrine and duty. It is the difference between cultivating potential and manufacturing outcome—between curiosity and control. The question, always, is which survives longer beneath pressure.

—Katyrine Righexa, Duchess of Ontario

The first thing Callum noticed upon entering Princess Selene's study was the stack of books on her desk. Titles ranged from *The Flame Doctrine Exposed* to *Soulcraft and State: A Dialogic Study*, alongside a small, poorly bound roll of parchment labeled *The Great College During the Ember War*.

Selene sat near a stone fireplace, the crackling fire within adding an ambiance to the room that tied in nicely with the fur rugs and the gilded art. A lantern with a Fire Affinity Shard inside hung above the table, giving her plenty of light to read and take notes.

She gestured for him to take a seat. "Hi. Hello to Fen as well."

"Now this is studying," Fen said as he appeared.

The Radiant Fox greeted the princess with a graceful nod, then padded toward the fireplace. He skipped over a fur rug without so much as brushing it and landed lightly on the hearth. The flames, low and steady a moment before, flared in response to his presence, bending toward him as if drawn by instinct. Light danced across the stonework, casting flickers of gold and amber along the walls.

Callum pulled a chair out, careful not to disturb the expertly woven carpet beneath the table. "What are you reading?" he asked the princess, a question that echoed inside his head, making him instantly regret it. *Of all the things to ask her . . .*

"I was looking through books about the Geshwine Empire and a past tournament," she told him, a softness taking shape behind her eyes. "I've studied the Flame Doctrine enough by now and was hoping to find something a little off the beaten path." She removed a pair of glasses that Callum hadn't even noticed and set them on the table. He almost asked her if she wore glasses but stopped himself just in time.

"The Flame Doctrine," he said instead, getting control of himself. "They seem to always refer to it. At least the ones I've met did."

"I've read it several times now. I've read all these books, actually," she said, sweeping a hand over the table. "But information changes when you get closer to its source—what once felt abstract starts to take on weight." She paused. "What I'm saying is, I've met with Crimson officials. I've even been part of short diplomatic missions across the border. But I've never had to function beside them like this. Not day-to-day. Not like now."

"Through your Concord Unit."

"Exactly."

"What happened in yours?"

"Mine . . ." She leaned back slightly, her eyes lifting to the lantern above the table and returning to Callum. "The first part had us working together to build a dam before a great flood could hit a village, and no, Water Affinity didn't help. That was our initial plan, but we found that it had no effect on the gathering water. This left us having to find the parts for the dam using our aetherbeasts. Ecaris was helpful in that regard," she said, referring to her pacted bear. "So we found the pieces, dragged them back, completed the task, and then came the next challenge."

"Some sort of fight, right? Mine was about capturing and defending a Portalstone for a certain amount of time."

"Yes, I'm aware. I've already been briefed."

Now it was Callum's turn to lean back. He looked at her for a moment, watching a wry grin take shape on her face.

"There are advantages and disadvantages that come with my position as crown princess," she said matter-of-factly.

For some reason, Callum wanted to ask if she could use her position to nullify a future marriage with Draven but thought better of it. That wasn't his business. So instead he changed the subject to what she was studying.

"So, the Flame Doctrine. I was actually wondering more about it myself," he said, eyes drifting toward the fireplace, where Fen was now stretched luxuriously, his tails folding around him as the firelight deepened the gold in his fur. One ear twitched, but he didn't speak, content to bask near the flames.

"You want to know how it could help you in the Duelist Rounds?"

"They seem..." Callum didn't quite know the words to describe what he had seen from the three Crimson students that had been part of his Concord Unit. "Different. I've never met anyone like them."

"The Doctrine and their near-worship of Imperion Rotharyn has radicalized them, and prevents the Sigil students from thinking for themselves. That doesn't mean they are stupid. They are raised to be lethal, especially those that go into the academies. Mastress Yelra writes about that," she said, tapping the cover of *Soulcraft and State*. "She likens them to being 'bladeborn from birth and sheathed only at command.'"

"So dealing with them should be easy, right? We just outthink them."

"Easy? I wish it were that simple. I'm probably wasting my time going through these books again and again, but sometimes it helps me come up with something, a spark that can lead to great insight. It would be simple if we were presented with more Culling Trials in which we are able to outwit them. But that's not the case. The Duelist Rounds are exactly what you think they are."

"Fights against one another."

"Exactly. And the Crimsons have been raised to fight. Plus they're using Demoncores and demonic aetherbeasts."

"I seemed to hold my own against them in the trial," he said, perhaps being a bit too sure of himself.

The princess immediately picked up on this. "They weren't in their element. I've seen them spar. Believe me. They had a demonstration during every of the diplomatic missions I went on, which, if you're reading between the lines here, was a way to intimidate us. But I was with Beast Masters, and I wasn't too worried."

"Beast Masters," Callum said, remembering that the term referred to archmages that had broken past the typical bond between a pact. "You..."

"I what?" she asked.

"You've trained with them, haven't you? I don't want to step out of line, but I've seen you do things." He recalled a time at one of the abandoned campuses where she seemed to fully take the bear form. "It didn't look like a normal meld."

"That's right, it didn't," Selene said with a sly smile. "Moving on. I'm glad you came here, actually. I was about to send one of my notetakers for you."

"I thought you might come by my dorm and when you didn't, I figured I would visit you instead."

"I wanted to, believe me. But Sir Trindade gave me very clear instructions not to wander the campus while the Crimsons are still here." She smiled, the expression sly. "Will that stop me later? Probably not. But for now, I'm playing along." The princess's tone shifted as she stepped closer. "What we need to talk about is your new Stage. You've unlocked the ability to use another Aethercore."

"Yes, I'm at the Wielder Stage."

"Yes."

"Yes?"

"You can have another Aethercore now. Have you thought about that any?"

"I have. *We* have," Callum said, motioning to Fen, who looked up at him and gave a small nod.

The Radiant Fox leaped onto the table in a flicker of light, his paws landing with barely a sound. He sat between the scattered books and parchments, tails curling neatly around him as he looked to the princess. "We want to find Killeas. We may be outmatched in the Duelist Rounds without better or upgraded Powercores, shards, and a new Aethercore."

"Agreed. We as a student group are most certainly outmatched. Master Cruedark will speak more of this tomorrow. He'll also have an announcement about the tournament to come—"

"What announcement?" Fen asked.

The princess folded her hands together. "I'll let Master Cruedark take the explanation from there. But you're right to want to upgrade and evolve as quickly as possible. I don't know if it is possible to move to the next Stage," she said, looking at Callum, "especially this early on. It's not unheard of, but most students don't make it past the Wielder Stage in their first semester."

"You're a Wielder too, right?" Callum asked.

"I am, yes. It happened after our last excursion and to answer your question, I too am thinking heavily about my next Aethercore."

"Lisalen will know where Killeas is," Fen told her. "Your father's pacted phoenix. It once belonged to the Demonslayer."

"I'm aware."

"With that and mind, and with your permission, I would like to speak to her, Your Highness."

Selene didn't seem at all perturbed by this request. "I would say that is fine, but we may have to wait a day or so. My father is in Karna right now, and while I could portal to him, it might not be a good time for that. He's at the duke's residence."

"Speaking of Draven—" Callum began.

The princess cut him off. "And I don't want the duke knowing about you," she told Callum.

"What about me?"

"Because you're the Demonslayer's reincarnation," Fen told Callum.

"I wouldn't go that far—"

"No," Selene cut in. "He's not wrong. And the timing of all this?" She looked at him seriously. "It's not a coincidence. The duke may or may not know about you through Draven, so it's best I don't portal to my father to set up a meeting. I will speak to him about Lisalen, but only after he returns from Karna."

"Speaking of Draven, there's one more thing," Callum told her.

"Yes?"

"On my way over here, I saw him with the Crimson Sigil students, including a woman that was part of my Concord Unit and the guy that kept talking to you back at the tournament announcement."

Her eyes widened with shock. "He was with Laziel?"

"He was," Fen said. "There were six of them in total, and only Draven from the Great College. The fiends."

Princess Selene pushed forward and folded her hands together on the table. "Something is off about all of this. I'll see what I can find out, but in the meantime, you need to prepare for the Duelist Rounds and hopefully Lisalen will be able to help you find Killeas before the tournament starts again. Enjoy your excursion tomorrow."

The same portal Callum had just come through fizzled into existence behind him and Sir Trindade stepped through. "Will that be all, Your Highness?" he asked the princess.

"Yes, and thanks for visiting," she told Callum, her eyes remaining on him for just a beat too long.

"Are you joining us tomorrow?" Callum asked.

Selene put her glasses back on and focused on her books again. "That remains to be seen."

CHAPTER 17

Devonshire weeps in thundered breath; Each storm a name, each name a death.

—Khulan Roswaith, poet, *Devonshire Elegies*

The portal opened onto a wide clearing flanked by old stone ruins, where twisted trees grew along crumbled walls and shattered archways. Callum moved through with several of the first-year cohort, most of whom were commenting on the sudden shift in climate. The morning air was warmer here than in the capital and a steady breeze moved south through the dry grass, bringing the faint scent of pine and something older, maybe ash.

Quinn stepped up beside Callum, hands in his pockets as he scanned the ruins. "This is the Devonshire campus," he said, voice low but carrying. "Or what's left of it. They shut it down decades ago. It's too remote, and there were always aetherstorms coming from the Western Barren Steppe." He glanced at Callum. "We're not far from Weatherby, you know."

"I know," Callum said, the air here carrying a familiarity he hadn't realized he missed—dry, open, and touched with the same northern wind that swept through his home.

"A few hours north, give or take."

"There was once a town around here, right?" Callum asked.

"You're the expert, not us," Marcella said, who stood next to Quinn, eyeing the broken outer walls of the campus like they owed her an explanation.

"I swear there used to be a town," Callum told her. "My father took a few trips up here to help after one of the aetherstorms Quinn mentioned."

"There was. Devonshire." Quinn tapped his boot against a cracked stone tile half-swallowed by earth. "From what my father said, the place used to be for elemental specialization. Fire Affinity, mostly."

Ahead, Master Cruedark waved the lingering students forward. The towering combat instructor waited for them on the far side of the courtyard, hands behind his back. He looked more serious than usual, which was saying something.

The cohort gathered in a loose semicircle around him, murmurs trailing off as the combat master finally spoke. "I want you all to know," he said after a deep exhale, "I'm not disappointed."

A few students straightened, surprised.

Cruedark continued. "Yes, more Crimson Sigil students made it through the Culling Trials. But not as many as they think. And all of that is about to get more complicated."

"What do you mean?" Lynnafer asked. She stood near Marcella, both of them still carrying the weight of their losses.

Before Cruedark could answer, another portal shimmered into view. Princess Selene stepped through first, radiant even in her training robes, with Draven close behind. The warlock said something to her—probably a joke, judging by his smirk—but she ignored him entirely and moved quickly toward Callum, Marcella, and Quinn.

Cruedark watched them settle, then resumed. "I suppose it's best if we just get right down to it. There has been a change in the tournament structure for the Duelist Rounds. It won't affect all of you. At least not at first. But it *could* affect some of you later on."

A ripple of murmurs spread through the group.

"Let me explain," Cruedark said, his voice rising just enough to quiet the crowd. "And you should know, this wasn't our decision. Not the dean's, and certainly not any of the Great College faculty or anyone on the tournament council. The Crimsons pushed for this. Their instructors claim the format of the Culling Trials lacked structural fairness. They mentioned uneven team compositions, unclear expectations, and tests that didn't reflect direct ability. Even though they agreed to the terms beforehand. It goes without saying that I—*we*—disagree with their assessment. The team compositions were intentional, and the unpredictability was meant to test adaptability, not just raw power.

<*Surprise, surprise. Warlocks only want to play by their own rules,*> Fen said privately.

Cruedark went on. "They believe some of their students were eliminated unfairly. So they've demanded that *anyone* who failed in the Culling Trials be granted another opportunity."

"Seriously?" Victrin blurted out. He glanced at Demandra, then caught himself, softening his voice as her expression darkened. "But they didn't complete their trials." He didn't mention that she hadn't either. He didn't have to.

Cruedark gave a slow nod. "True. But the Crimson instructors have insisted. And, in the interest of keeping the tournament alive, we have agreed to a compromise." He paused to let that sink in. "So here's the change: anyone who was eliminated in the Culling Trials will now participate in the first phase of the Dueling Rounds. Those who succeed in that phase will advance . . . and eventually face off against those of you who won the Culling Trials."

Draven scoffed, his voice sharp. "So they get to skip ahead?"

"Is that how you interpreted that? No, they are not skipping," Cruedark replied, tone firm. "They're being given a second chance. You, and others like you, will sit out the first phase of the Dueling Rounds. Which, I might add, gives you a tactical advantage. If you're smart, you'll be watching, studying, learning."

Draven didn't respond. He looked like he wanted to argue, but he remained silent.

Quinn raised a hand slightly. "So those of us that completed the Culling Trials start competing in the second phase."

"Correct," Cruedark said. "You have one week to train. To gather shards, Powercores, and if you really work hard, move to the next Stage. The others have less time than that. The students competing in the first phase start in three days." He gestured behind him to the open paths stretching into the forest beyond the ruins. "Explore this campus. Venture into the woods or the abandoned town of Devonshire, which is a mile to the west. Or return to the Great College and visit another abandoned campus if you prefer. I brought you here to remind you of something important." Cruedark turned, clasping his hands behind his broad back as he looked at what was left of the campus. "It's time to reach deep down. To push harder than you think you can. And to show the Crimsons what you're really capable of."

Callum cleared his throat. "You said we have a week. Does that mean the Crimson Sigil students will be on campus that entire time?"

"They'll come and go," Cruedark asked without turning back to him. "They have access to their own college through separate portals. Their instructors may host lessons; we've agreed to some exchanges, but nothing sensitive," he added, "just histories, culture, basic coursework." He finally turned back to the cohort and looked them over one last time. "One week. Do as much with it as you can. It's a short window. But what you accomplish in that time could determine everything."

* * *

Most of the students splintered off after Cruedark's dismissal. Some formed loose clusters, already arguing about the direction they should go, or if they should return to campus and head through another portal to visit another location.

Marcella, Quinn, and Princess Selene stayed close, as always, waiting to see what the others did. Callum remained with them, his eyes locked on Draven.

Artur, Theogar, and Petyr orbited the warlock as always, the four men glancing over to Callum with snide looks on their faces. Draven gave the princess a mockingly formal nod and the four turned toward the heart of the abandoned Devonshire campus.

"Let's not go in whatever direction *they're* going," Marcella said.

"Agreed," Selene said.

"Should we head back to the Great College?" Quinn asked. "You know, go to another campus. There are places to explore in the Badlands that might prove fruitful."

Rather than answer, Selene reached into her overcoat and produced a folded sheet of parchment, the corners worn soft from repeated handling. The seal on the back, once royal, now faded, opened easily under her thumb. Her hidden Powercore list seemed to be custom-made, and it was clear based on the notes in the margin that she had been working on it.

"There are still seven cores that need to be claimed," Selene said as she examined the list. "Possibly more, if rumors are true."

"More?" Callum asked.

"There are a number of lists, one produced every year. Sometimes, there are known Powercores that are never found."

"And how do we get that list?" Quinn asked.

"I have access to it," the princess told him. "But I think it's better if we focus on this one for now. I already found the one I was most interested in, Armorcore of the Ironspine Panther. You now have the Weaponcore of the Sunsteel Ram, Callum. And then there's Draven."

"Ugh," Marcella said.

"Indeed. Draven recently acquired the Empowerment of Blightwing. I haven't seen the exact abilities yet, but I *have* seen a Weaponcore Blightwing before, and if it's anything like that, it's not good."

"What does it do?" Callum asked Selene.

"The Weaponcore version alters ambient mana around a target. Poisons it, essentially. It's a type of projectile sword, if you can imagine something like that, tethered to the hilt. If it strikes a person or an aetherbeast, it weakens them, not enough to kill, but enough to affect one's Soul Heart."

"Well that's just fantastic," Marcella said. "Callum already told us that he was hanging out with Crimsies last night. No? We're not calling them Crimsies?"

Quinn chuckled at the look on Selene's face. "I told you over breakfast that name wasn't going to stick."

"What can I say?" Marcella asked, flustered. "I thought giving them a nickname would help."

"Crimsies is too cute," Selene said as she handed her parchment to Callum, who carefully unfolded it, eyes trying to scan the information she had scribbled in the margins. <*What language is this?*> he thought to Fen.

<*I really couldn't tell you. Perhaps it is something the royals have developed for secret communication. It certainly isn't a script I have seen before, not to my recollection.*>

"Let's see what's still out there," Quinn said as he leaned in beside him, the two scanning the available cores:

Galeform of the Thunderhowl Wolf
Empowerment of Spiritfire
Antler Break of the Froststag
Armorcore of the Twilight Drake
Spiked Lunge of the Direwolf Stalker
Poison Hiss of the Ashen Viper
Lunar Sweep of the Shadowbound Crane

Marcella pointed to one of the entries before anyone else could speak. "Ooh, ooh! That's it. The one I've been eyeing, Antler Break of the Froststag. I saw Victrin's antler attack and I needed it bad. Like, real bad."

"You could just buy one," Quinn told her.

"Not all of us—"

Selene cut Marcella off before she could continue. "That's why we're here, Marcella."

She tilted her head to her. "It is? What do you mean?"

As she often did, the princess continued without answering the question. "Callum, you told me that Weatherby was hit by an aetherstorm. According to Royal Stormalogists, it originated from this region. It's one of the reasons that Master Cruedark brought us here. Which was luck on our part. I narrowed down the Antler Break to this region based on some information my notetakers uncovered about its Armorcore, which is also from here."

"Put a pin in that because I have a question," Quinn told the princess.

"Will do. If Master Cruedark had brought us somewhere else, I would have suggested we come here. So it's serendipitous in that way. Now, Quinn, you had a question?"

"Yes, does it often work that way, an Empowerment, Armor, and Weaponcore all in the same general area?"

"More often than not," Selene told him.

Marcella stepped past Quinn, her gaze softening with gratitude as she looked at the princess. "You really wanted to help me get the Powercore?"

"I did, and if you're interested in any, Quinn, let me know." Selene smiled at the three of them. "You are my friends." She turned slightly, chin lifting to face the west woods. Through the bare trees and rising hills, the edges of an old settlement peeked out, faint stone silhouettes lost to time. "Let's see what we can find in the heart of Devonshire."

CHAPTER 18

Pacting does not overwrite the soul—it adds a second dialect of power. Those who flourish are not the loudest, but the ones fluent in instinct.

—A quote from *Notes on Meldform Efficacy: A Treatise* by Pervus Sinbad, Master Convoker and Chief Combat Instructor of the Great College from Year 465–490

A fizzling shard flew into Callum's hand as he killed the aetherwisp he had been chasing for several minutes. It had gotten away from the pack and Callum had gone after it, leading him up a hill on the outskirts of Devonshire.

Empowerment of Regeneration Shard

"Nice," he said, stopping in front of what looked to have once been a barn, its roof half caved in, one wall missing entirely, and beams that were splintered and aetherscorched. All around him, the rest of Devonshire lay half swallowed by creeping weeds and brittle stone, the bones of the town choked by the lingering aftermath of storms.

So far, Callum had netted two Air and Shadow Affinity shards, one Light and Death Affinity shards, one Resilience, two Vigor, and three Might shards. There was also a Galeburst of the Murkat Powercore that he picked up near a collapsed water tower, something he planned to sunder with Telluride once he got back to the capitol.

He climbed atop some rubble and saw Marcella, Selene, and Quinn gathered at the bottom of a hill near an old water trough carved into stone, taking a quick break.

<There sure are a lot of aetherwisps here,> Callum told Fen. <But at least they're actually dropping shards.>

<Likely due to the storm that could have been the same one that brought us together. High-turbulence aetherstorms don't just damage land, they thin the veil, pulling everything out of place and sending lesser elements into our world. So it would make sense for the place to be active at the moment.>

<We always need shards,> Callum said as he made his way down the hill, his shard pouch noticeably heavier. <I would prefer more Powercores for sundering, but if we keep collecting shards like this, I might get enough to upgrade my wind sword.>

<Good plan. Using that one with Zephyr Strike is smart.>

Marcella spotted Callum and waved. "You get it?"

"I did," he said. "Regen Shard. Any luck on the hidden Powercore?"

"No," she said, brushing a curl from her eyes. "But the princess is going to try something."

Selene raised a hand to her chest and summoned a triangular flare of green mana, the same locator Powercore Callum had seen her use before. The shape hovered from her fingers, pulsed once, then floated into the air, spinning gently.

"It would have been nice to use that an hour ago," Quinn said.

Selene glanced at him. "It's not designed for shards. It reacts better to larger, more stable signatures. If there are Powercores here, this will root them out. And hopefully, we will find the one Marcella wants before it gets dark."

"I didn't bring anything for camping," Quinn said.

"We're definitely not camping," Selene told him. "I have dinner plans tonight with Victrin's mother."

"The Duchess of Ontario," Marcella added.

"That's right, and a few of her advisers. My father remains in Karna," she said, looking at Callum, "but he'll be back later this week, and I'm sure I'll have plenty to do once he arrives."

"That's also when the tournament starts," Marcella said.

"Exactly." Princess Selene turned as the triangle drafted west. "Let's see what we can find."

The group moved on, cutting through the overgrown street, stepping over broken carts and half-buried stonework, stained glass crunching underfoot. Weeds pushed through cracked flagstones, and old shop signs hung crooked from rusted chains. The triangle stopped in certain sections where the air had a strange charge to it, more than just ambient mana.

"Aftereffects of an aetherstorm," the princess said once she saw Marcella running her fingers through the nearly tangible magic in the air.

"Why don't we have these in New Albion?" Marcella asked.

"Because of the population. This is simply dormant mana; in a city like New Albion, it gets absorbed by everyone and the Heart of Creation. It lasts longer here."

"Or like that abandoned campus we went to," Quinn said, "the one that was hit by the Beast Tide."

"Exactly." Princess Selene paused as a trio of aetherwisps burst from the shadows near a collapsed staircase, swirling through the air like mist laced with knives.

They came together mid-flight, their forms fusing with a loud snap. The result was a tall, barely humanoid shape with shifting pustules over its body and two arms that ended in jagged, uneven blades. It lunged toward them, skipping ahead with a spring in its step.

Quinn reacted first, claws flashing to life. He dodged beneath its first strike and raked his claws across its side. As Callum stepped back and drew his Ram swords, Marcella took to the air. Her pacted heron flared around her, a streak of blue magic as she loosed a fan of spectral feathers like darts.

Each struck with force, staggering the amalgamation and collapsing it into a burst of magic-laced mist. A shard rushed toward her.

Quinn brushed some dust off his sleeves. "That escalated only to de-escalate. Maybe it's best if we ask Tuck and Fen to scout ahead. You could send Harold as well," he told Marcella as her glimmering wings faded away.

"Tuck and Fen are better prowlers," she said. "I'll keep Harold with me."

A soft light curled around Quinn's shoulders as the aethercat took shape, coalescing from shifting strands of silver mist. "Did someone call for exploration?" asked Tuck, his voice smooth and sly as his form fully settled. He gave Marcella a quick twitch of the tail, somewhere between a bow and a tease, and trotted ahead, paws silent on the cracked stone, ears flicking back and forth as he scanned the ruins for movement.

Fen unmelded from Callum a moment later, light flaring from Callum's chest as the Radiant Fox reformed. His tails fanned out as he landed lightly beside the cat, posture alert, golden eyes narrowed at the road ahead. He sniffed once, nose catching the edges of something old and unsettled, and fell into step beside Tuck without a word.

"Let's keep going," Selene said as the triangle drifted forward again.

The path ahead narrowed into tangled alleys and fractured homes, all empty, but not quiet.

"Why do I get the feeling that the Powercore isn't going to just be sitting there waiting for us?" Marcella asked.

"Because nothing ever works that way," Quinn told her jovially. "It would make this much easier."

"But it would also take away the challenge," the princess reminded him.

The ruins of Devonshire had proven worth the effort.

After another hour combing the wreckage, Callum had netted one Air Affinity Shard, one Water Affinity Shard, two Fire Affinity Shards, and another Empowerment of Might—a decent haul, all things considered. Fen and Tuck remained ahead, threading through collapsed granaries and root-tangled wells like two scouts on a silent mission.

The rest of the group trailed behind at a relaxed but ready pace, never fully lowering their guard.

"It has to be here somewhere," Selene said as they reached the far edge of town, her face illuminated by the floating triangle. The four stopped at a half-crumbled masonry site, massive boulders piled like forgotten pieces of siege equipment.

Her locator pulsed bright green and buzzed ahead.

"Huh," Quinn said as he looked around.

"The only thing we've encountered are those wisp amalgamations," Marcella said, glancing sideways. "Are you sure something is here?" she asked as she looked out at the piles of stone.

"It's usually right," Selene told her.

Tuck and Fen came streaking back. "It's one of the boulders!" Fen shouted mid-bound, diving straight into Callum in a burst of golden light.

"Boulder?" Quinn asked as he staggered backward from the sheer force of Tuck's jump.

Marcella straightened, her wings taking shape. "You mean it's in the ground?"

Selene's Weaponcore trident snapped into her hand, summoned in a flicker of magic. "Remember," she said, stepping forward, "Marcella needs the kill."

"I can't believe I'm getting this kind of special treatment," Marcella said.

The joke lasted just long enough for the stone to move.

The moss-covered boulder groaned and split, unfolding into a jagged creature twice the size of anything they'd faced in recent memory, a hunched mass of granite and raw magic, its back shrouded in fungal moss, and its single arm dragged along the ground as it rose. A slit of molten green opened across its chest like an eye, pulsing with corrupted energy. The earth shuddered beneath their feet as the creature began to move, each step heaving its monstrous bulk across the broken terrain with impossible weight.

Callum summoned his wind sword and fired a gale burst directly into its chest. The wind slid off its thick moss hide, barely staggering the creature. It lurched forward and swung its stone arm at Callum, who dodged it by jumping to the side.

Near him, Quinn leaped onto a broken foundation, charged up it, and threw himself straight onto the colossus, claws flaring. He dug into the moss, clawing at it wildly as the creature tried to buck him off.

"Quinn, get out of the way!" Marcella shouted, daggered feathers swirling around her.

"I'm *doing* something!" Quinn yelled. "The moss is covering the mana veins—Tuck spotted it!"

<*He's right!*> Fen told Callum, who could see it now, the glow beneath the mossy exterior of the monster.

Selene unmelded with her bear, allowing Ecaris to slam her massive body into the sentient boulder. It staggered only slightly, but the force created an opening for Callum to strike it with Radiant Claws, which cut away more of its moss.

"Target the magic veins!" Quinn called to them, still on the monster's back.

Callum produced roots from his hands to hold their opponent down. The colossus dragged them forward, its movements finally sending Quinn flying.

Like a cat, Quinn landed on all fours. Like a human thrown from the back of a giant boulder-monster, he subsequently faceplanted, fell to the side, and winced as he tried to get up and out of the way.

"Sorry!" Callum called over to him as Marcella struck next. Her magic feathers found purchase, slicing moss away in chunks and exposing more of the creature's magic veins.

Melded again, her form vibrant with power, Selene charged in, keeping the creature at bay. "Do it!" She shouted at Marcella, who swooped in with her Weaponcore dagger, stabbing the boulder directly into the exposed core beneath the moss.

Light surged from Marcella's dagger as it began to *drain* the creature's power, the line of energy connecting to Marcella as she rushed back.

Selene went in with her trident again, targeting the opposite shoulder. The colossus let out a sound like stones grinding together, an ancient, angry groan, as it dropped.

For a moment, it seemed like they had done it. Callum and Marcella even exchanged quick glances, a wild look in her eyes.

But then the beast convulsed, flaring back to life. The moss along its back ignited with a surge of emerald light, twisting upward into wild, snaring tendrils. They writhed across its body in a frenzy, weaving a desperate shell of living overgrowth. Marcella's blade disappeared into the tangled mass before it could strike again.

The colossus shuddered forward, surging with unstable power. Its seams split wider, leaking molten-green light with every breath, as if the magic holding it together was beginning to tear itself apart.

<*The moss is ripping it apart,*> Fen said in alarm. <*Tell Marcella—now! Use her new Aethercore ability!*>

"Marcella!" Callum shouted, dodging a hammering sweep of its stone arm. "Now! Use it!"

Marcella vanished, her body blurring into light and motion. One heartbeat she hovered above Callum and the next she burst past the boulder colossus, arm outstretched, fingers slicing the air like she'd just hurled a thread of lightning.

A sound like splitting stone followed, sharp and final. The mossy overgrowth shielding the beast unraveled in an instant, as if something had carved straight through it on a line too fast to see. It gave a final step, then its stone core cracked open and shards flew into Marcella's waiting hands.

"This is it," she said, showing them an orb.

There was a beat of silence.

Then Quinn started laughing. He started laughing so hard that he fell to his knees, Callum cracking up as well.

Marcella looked up just as a hunk of moss slid off her face and flopped to the ground.

Even Selene smiled. "Congratulations. That was thoroughly ridiculous."

"Never let it be said I don't make a scene," Marcella muttered, said herself off. "But this is what matters." She showed them the orb again. "The Antler Break of the Froststag. Another hidden Powercore off the list."

Selene turned toward the woods. "Then we've got what we came for." She hesitated, just long enough to betray the weight behind her words, then looked back at the others. "Let's get back to campus."

CHAPTER 19

We found claw marks along the interior halls that do not match any documented aetherbeast. Some were fused into the walls, stone and bone indistinguishable. Whatever hit the Silver Fang Academy . . . well, I'd rather not speculate.

—Mastress Weaver Emlee Sawbend, after-action notes from the expedition to the ruins of Silver Fang Academy

The portal closed behind Callum with a low hum, the shimmer of magic bleeding out like fog. It was the next day and Callum was once again working to prepare for the Duelist Rounds. He stood in a training ground of broken earth and pale sky, somewhere barren, a place where dry stone stretched for miles, sun-bleached and cracked, the only shade cast by jagged spines of blackened rock jutting from the hills and the occasional thornroot bush hardy enough to face the heat.

Fen appeared in a flash of radiant color that ran from the tip of his tail to his snout. "This is . . . unusual," he said as Master Cruedark took a lumbering step toward them, the heavy thud of his boots punctuated by silence. He looked at Callum and nodded him forward.

"Fen, Callum," Cruedark said as they approached. "Welcome to today's training ground."

"Where are we exactly?" Callum asked.

"A northern part of the Badlands, not far from Karna. Ever been to Karna?"

"No. Until I came to New Albion, I'd only ever been to Weatherby," Callum admitted. "Wait, that's not true. I went to the Grimbald border once or twice with my father for shards because our local shardcrafter wasn't available."

"Funny how that works, right?" Cruedark asked. "Get to the big city and the world opens up. Anyway, Karna, it's worth missing in my opinion. It's a cold northern desert city that looks . . ." He swept his hand at their surroundings and the stone spires in the distance. "It looks like this, actually. It certainly blends into the terrain. But we can have a geography lesson later, or more likely, never. Summon your Sunsteel Ram swords and split them."

Fen melded with Callum as the curved blade appeared in his hands. He split the weapon, forming two jagged scimitars bathed in power.

"Good," Cruedark said. "Let's begin."

As he had in their previous training sessions, Callum lunged for his combat teacher, who produced a bracer-shield to block his strike. Changing his stance, Callum moved in from a different angle, only to be repelled by Master Cruedark again. He kept this up until his chest heaved up and down.

"Already out of breath?" Cruedark asked.

"You know why," Callum said, referring to his instructor's bracers and the mana drain power they had. *Each strike is harder than the last*, he reminded himself, *and that's on purpose. I'm supposed to push through it.*

"Better to be pushed to the brink now than during the Duelist Rounds. And another note: your footing's sloppy," Cruedark added, circling. "Stop putting all your weight on your back leg. Double swords are useful for a cross-slash pattern, like I showed you, but you should only be bracing for the push off." Cruedark demonstrated what he meant. "Once you've launched yourself, stay with the power you have created. Try it."

Callum adjusted and tried again, but it still felt off.

Cruedark shook his head. "You're controlling space, not swinging farm tools. With twin blades, every movement creates risk. Miss your angle, and you're either wide open or cutting into your own momentum."

"Got it." Callum tried again. The Ram swords pulsed faintly, their curved blades humming with latent power as he went through several more attempts.

"Better," Cruedark said. "Keep it up!"

For a time, they trained in near silence, Callum maintaining a focus that seemed to have grown stronger since he had started cycling mana. Aside from focus, it was also his endurance, pushing himself to prepare for the upcoming fights.

I'm going to need all I can get, he thought as he continued his attacks, relying solely on his combat ability rather than any of his Powercores. It was the way he often trained with Cruedark and that, coupled with the muscle-building exercises the combat master had subscribed him, was starting to work.

Not only did Callum feel stronger, he looked stronger. He saw it whenever he caught a glimpse of himself in the mirror. He had always been strong from growing up on a farm, but constantly swinging weapons and being repelled by mana worked his muscles in ways that farmwork couldn't.

Eventually, Cruedark stood back, looked him over, and nodded. "You're getting better," the combat master finally said. "But it's not just power you need right now. The Duelist Rounds are going to be brutal."

Callum dismissed his swords in a flicker of light. "I can see the airships from my window. They are a constant reminder of what is to come."

"I can imagine that being a bit unsettling, especially if you've never seen them before now."

"I haven't."

Master Cruedark glanced toward the open sky. "I don't like the airships myself, grand and majestic as they are. Or the people who came in them. The Crimson instructors are as charming as granite. We've been asked to have communal meals with them. You ever eat in a room full of warlocks who think mercy is heresy?"

"No."

"Didn't think so. It's not great."

Callum half smiled. "You don't think the tournament was a good idea?"

"I wasn't asked," Cruedark said. "If I had been, I'd have told them we don't need a stage to prove what we already are and what we are capable of doing. I also question how a friendly competition is going to bring our kingdom and their empire together. I've been told it worked with the Lands of Grimbald in the distant past. But you're from that region, the people are different, aren't they?"

"They are. They're friendly. They always pass through Weatherby. So far, I've yet to meet a friendly warlock."

Cruedark laughed at this remark. "They aren't all bad, and the people of the Geshwine Empire aren't all bad, and they certainly aren't all warlocks. But that's what they have sent to this tournament, students from a school now specializing in Demoncores and warlock advancement. They could have sent students from a different campus, perhaps the Geshwine College, where students don't focus entirely on the darker aspects of mana and aetherbeasts. This is why it's crucial you continue to train and pay close attention to the first phase of matches. You also need another Aethercore. That will help too."

Callum straightened. "I am going to find Killeas."

"The Demonslayer's gryphon, huh?"

"Let's call him an old friend," Fen said as the fox took shape in a dazzling array of brightness. "We need to speak to Lisalen to do that."

That got a reaction from the big man. "You want to talk to King Morninglade's phoenix?"

"That's right," Callum told him.

"Princess Selene actually agreed to that?"

"She did. She said we could once they return."

"Eh, I guess I shouldn't be too surprised. It makes sense, given your legacy and the Stross family name. Still. I never thought one could just ask the princess to meet the king. Had I done that, I would've advised against the tournament altogether." Master Cruedark stopped himself. "What am I saying? I have no place in politics. But as for finding Killeas, I think that's a good plan. Two Aethercores are better than one. Three are better than two. You know what I mean. In that case . . . what else?"

Callum tilted his head. "What do you mean?"

"Surely you have more plans than *just* hunting an Aethercore. What about your current loadout? Shards? Powercores?"

"I've got one Powercore I need to sunder," Callum said. "I need more shards to upgrade."

Cruedark grunted. "And you plan to get that from one sundered Powercore? Unless it's Legendary, and I'd advise against sundering one of those, it won't be enough."

"I know. I barely have money. I sent part of my stipend to my father."

Cruedark's expression didn't change. "Good instinct. Bad timing. You've already found one off the hidden Powercore list."

"The Ram swords."

"And you obviously can't sunder them. Here's what I think." Cruedark stepped closer, lowering his voice slightly. "There are Portalstones all over this campus. Some are marked, common. Some aren't, like the one you found in the painting. Remember that cafeteria I sent you to during your first week, the one with food that instantly recharged your power levels?"

Callum nodded. "I do. I've wondered about that place."

"Same hallway. Go to the back of it. At the end, there is a pair of doors. The one on the right opens into a lecture hall that hasn't been used since I was a student because it's too small and possibly haunted. The other leads to an abandoned campus in the Badlands called the Silver Fang Academy. It's dangerous there, not quite suicidal, but you'll need to stay sharp."

"Should I go alone?"

"You'll get more that way, but that's really up to you. If you do go alone, don't stray too far from the portal. And don't get greedy." Cruedark turned and started walking. "Oh," he added, "and one more thing: if you find something dangerous enough to kill you, run. The tournament's no good to the dead."

CHAPTER 20

Weaponcores win the clash. Powercores shift the tide. But Armorcores? They're the reason you walk away at the end.

—A quote from *The Darker Aspects of Mana, 3rd Edition,* by Master Shaper Friedkin Oleksander

Callum stepped through the hidden portal that Master Cruedark had recommended to him.

Fine, yellow dust clung to the folds of his overcoat and boots the moment he arrived at the Silver Fang Academy. The air was dry, the sky a color blue he couldn't remember ever seeing, something between cerulean and turquoise. The courtyard stretched out before him, built from crumbling red stone baked brittle by sun and time. Jagged scars raked across the walls, as if something with claws had torn through it in a frenzy.

Something definitely came through here, Callum thought as wind moved across the Badlands in dry, restless waves.

Behind him, the portal shimmered softly inside the frame of a weatherworn arch, its surface like water with the sun hitting it at a perfect angle. The door he'd stepped through back at the Great College was also visible, though it now looked like it belonged to another world entirely.

Fen appeared beside Callum in a ripple of energy, the fox's nose twitching. "There's Corruption here," he said immediately.

"I see it," Callum said as he once again scanned the abandoned campus. The Silver Fang Academy had long since fallen into ruin. Thick stone walls had been burned bronze by years of exposure. What once might have been a library or dormitory now looked like a jagged cliff face, collapsed inward, its brickwork exposed and covered in the vines of dead succulents.

No vultures flew overhead and there was only the sound of the occasional gust of wind dragging across broken tiles.

Fen gave a short exhale and began to inhale the Corruption as Callum took a look around.

"It's hard to believe this used to be one of ours," Callum said.

"Not all things die loudly," Fen said. "Some just get quiet until they're forgotten. Let's keep moving. I'll absorb the Corruption as we come to it."

"Stay close."

The fox looked back at him. "I was about to tell you the same thing."

As he soon discovered, the academy's layout had a familiar symmetry to it: central quad, branching wings, a few long stretches that might have once been for demonstrations or dueling. Yet now everything felt distant, gone, a notion that reminded Callum how quickly civilization could pack up and move on.

He navigated a path that led around one of the crumbled buildings, thinking back to Mastress Lucerne's last Manavitality class, which had included a curious claim—that there was once an "alliance of knowledge" between the Geshwine Empire and the Valestra Kingdom, long after the kingdoms had split. This alliance included symposiums, joint expeditions, and even the exchange of students. Given its remote location in the Badlands, yet not far from the Geshwinian border, Callum suspected the Silver Fang Academy had once been part of that effort.

And now, judging by the edge in Princess Selene's voice whenever she mentioned the Geshwine Empire, the state of the crumbling campus mirrored the current relationship between the kingdoms: fractured, distant, and left to decay.

He tightened his hand around the pouch at his belt. "We really need to find some shards."

"We do," Fen agreed. "And Powercores to sunder. The first phase of the Duelist Rounds starts a day from now. Cruedark is right in suggesting that seeing the fights gives you an edge. I'm surprised the Crimson Sigil instructors didn't think this through in pushing for a rule change. The warlocks weren't thinking ahead."

"Strange."

"It is. Maybe it's their way of slipping more students into phase two and beyond," Fen said as they moved through an archway, entering a long, shadowed corridor where the heat folded in on itself like waves off a forge. The shade offered a little relief, but the air still clung thick to their skin.

Fen moved with purpose, tail flicking as he took the lead—always alert, always watching, as if the ancient walls themselves might shift around them.

Callum wiped his brow and kept walking, gaze trailing the fox until Fen stopped cold, his ears pinned flat.

"What is it?" he asked.

"This place isn't as dead as it looks."

"What are you sensing?" Callum asked Fen as he stepped into what might have once been a training circle.

Low stone walls ringed the space, broken in places but still forming a wide arena that was easily fifty feet across. There were shallow benches lining the perimeter, half-buried in sand that had overtaken everything, far more than any normal wind should have left behind. The surface inside the ring was scored with spirals, as if something had moved through it.

Fen jumped back toward Callum, instantly melding with him as the ground twisted without warning, the sand spiraling into mini typhoons of grit. The first cylinder of sand slammed into him, Callum staggering as he summoned his Armorcore.

Three figures spun out of the dust—thin, angular, and fast. Each was made entirely of compressed air, sand, and flickering magic, their forms pulsing with sharp-edged movement.

They twisted toward him, blades of translucent pressure forming where arms might be. No eyes. No mouths. Just rippling slits of force and intent.

<*Dervishes!*> Fen said as Callum summoned his Radiant Claws.

He caught the first dervish mid-strike with his wind sword, slashing a bright arc of light through its spinning torso. It split, but not cleanly; the two halves whipped past him, regrouping before it could fully dissipate.

"They're fast!" Callum said as he shifted to the next one.

<*I'm certain you can overpower them . . . just don't let them circle!*>

Callum dropped low and rolled left, avoiding a vertical slash from the second dervish. He came up spinning, wind lancing around his claws, and activated Zephyr Strike. The burst of speed carried him forward faster than expected; he bisected the first dervish cleanly this time, its edges blown apart by the power behind his cut as it exploded in a flash of diffused energy.

One down.

Fen separated from Callum and lunged toward the second dervish. He struck it from the side, his form a glowing blur of motion and flame. The dervish shrieked a burst of sand and wind as it pinwheeled into the wall. When it reformed, Fen was already past it, turning for another pass.

"You good?" Callum called to him.

<*They're quick but brittle. Let's finish them!*>

Callum hit the dervish with a blast of wind and then doubled down, using his Gale Pulse ability to send it flying across the training ring. The dervish bashed into the wall and more wind bore down onto it. It whirled apart, bursting into motes of scattered wind and corrupted mana.

Only one remained now.

It looped high, spinning with desperation, then dove hard toward Callum's chest, its wind-arm extending into a hooked edge.

Callum waited.

Waited.

Then moved at the last second. He dropped backward into a sweep, kicked up a cloud of dust, and activated Gale Pulse a second time. The concussive burst of wind slammed outward, smashing into the dervish and sending it spiraling into a broken column. This time, it didn't reform.

The wind settled around him as two shards rushed toward his open palm.

Air Affinity Shard
Air Affinity Shard

<*Not bad,*> Fen said. <*We get more of those and you'll be one step closer to upgrading your sword.*>

"I get the feeling they were a warm-up," Callum replied, scanning the next set of collapsed walls.

<*I get the feeling you're right.*>

The dervishes weren't difficult to fight once they appeared but spotting them was another matter. Callum moved carefully through the first few structures of the Silver Fang Academy, eyes sharp for any signs of spinning sand. They came at him in waves, some bursting out of the rubble, others swooping down from what was left of the building's structure.

Fighting dozens upon dozens of them netted exactly what Callum wanted as he finally reached what was once an atrium.

Empowerment of Might Shard
Empowerment of Regeneration Shard
Empowerment of Deftness Shard
Empowerment of Deftness Shard
Empowerment of Mind Shard

Air Affinity Shard
Shadow Affinity Shard
Earth Affinity Shard
Dervish Wisp Wind Powercore

He had even netted a Common Powercore from one of the larger dervishes, which looked to do the same thing as Zephyr Strike, giving him something to sunder later.

Fen appeared next to him, tense as ever. "I believe we have reached a good stopping point."

The abandoned atrium was wide and open to the sky, its roof long since collapsed. Torn strips of faded awning clung to a few skeletal beams, casting fractured shade over scorched tile that radiated residual heat.

A few stubborn cacti clung to life near the edges, tough, sharp-leaved things warped by stray mana. Most of the other planters lay barren, their stone basins cracked or melted at the rim, the soil long since blown away. Everything in this place bore scars—gouges, slashes, melted seams. Not just the erosion of time, but something more violent.

Half-buried in the sand, green shards of glass glinted in the light. They didn't belong to anything natural. They looked like the remains of something once enchanted, now broken and twisted. Scorch marks and deep gouges scored the tile, cutting through the pattern like claw marks.

There was Corruption everywhere, strong enough that Callum could physically see it.

<*Whatever calls this spot home isn't here yet, but it's close . . .*> Callum thought to Fen.

The fox turned to him. <*I think you're right. I'll absorb what I can before it returns.*>

Fen circled the edges of the ruined atrium, his movement silent against the burned-out tiles. His fur bristled as he drew in slow breaths, gathering the corrupted magic that clung to the edges of the space like soot. Golden wisps shimmered faintly around him, then vanished into his core.

Callum watched from a low wall near the far archway. He wiped more sweat away and blinked a few times to clear away the visible heat. The temperature was stifling. Not just from the desert sun, but something underneath it, like fire had scorched this place from the inside out and left the bones still simmering.

His hands tensed into fists as he scanned the area again.

Nothing moved.

Even so, he felt it. The wrongness in the tiles beneath him, the tension in the silence, the sense that he was just a little farther from the portal than he would like to be.

Maybe... Callum sat and let his pulse settle as Fen kept up his work.

<*The longer we stay here, the cleaner this place gets,*> Fen said. <*I'm pulling it in. The ambient mana's shifting.*>

<*Will that draw out whatever lives here?*>

<*Maybe. But that's to our advantage. If it is fueled by the dark power of this place, there will be less once I'm finished.*>

Callum closed his eyes and listened—really listened.

There was no wind now, only the sandpaper sound of dust shifting faintly. No birdsong, no distant creatures, just the crack of heat on tile and a steady, waiting stillness.

Then, a sound.

Not a roar, not a stomp, a scrape.

Stone on stone.

Callum's eyes snapped open.

Movement. From behind one of the collapsed archways near the edge of the atrium Heavy. Slow. Powerful. The soft rasp of brittle scales brushing through loose grit as something massive slithered out of the shadow, dragging heat and silence with it.

"Whoa," Callum whispered as the giant aetherlizard pulled itself over the lip of the atrium wall, its eyes burning beneath a ridge of blackened shale-like mana protrusions. Slabs of scale flaked away from its limbs as it crawled forward, low and coiled, smoke seething from its cracked third eye like breath from a furnace.

Callum didn't move.

He could feel the burn of its presence in the stone beneath him, in the heat behind his teeth.

<*I'm going in,*> he told Fen.

<*No reason to wait for it to say hello!*> Fen replied, voice taut with focus.

Callum stepped into their meld and the world sharpened, Fen's power surging through him. He summoned his Ram sword and split it into twin bursts of curved light, the blades flaring, hungry for movement.

Then he moved, dashing across the atrium in a single breath, intent on getting the opening strike.

<*Good!*> Fen shouted as Callum slashed across the reptilian beast's side, carving a deep line beneath its plated ribs. Dark magic hissed through the wound as the aetherlizard slammed its tail into the ground.

The shockwave was instant; an eruption of corrupted mana fractured the tiles in a wide arc, burning sandstone geysering upward like shattered glass.

Callum's Armorcore protected him as he took the blast with a grunt. He was thrown into a collapsed planter, then hit the ground, bounced up again, and was tossed into a bench.

<On your feet!>

Callum rolled to his feet, blades forming again as he spit some dirt out of his mouth. He hit the lizard with a blast of wind, followed by an intense gale, staggering it.

The aetherlizard compressed, shoulders tucking as it launched toward him.

<It's too fast!> Fen shouted as he vaulted the two of them to the side, smashing through more pottery.

The creature rushed forward in a spinning blur of molten stone and fury. It plowed through broken pillars, scattering shards like glass hail. Callum leaped just before it would have crushed him, but even the shockwave of its passing cracked his footing.

He hit the ground hard, sliding, coughing smoke as the monster skidded to a stop, dust and trails of corrupted mana curling off its back. It turned and reared up, shaking violently as ash exploded from its body.

The air turned black with ember-choked fog. It clung to Callum's skin, burned his throat. Soul Sense dimmed instantly. He couldn't see. Couldn't breathe.

He backed up instinctively, coughing, blades flickering—

The aetherlizard lunged through the smoke, its great maw open.

Callum dove to avoid it just as the creature clamped down onto him, cracking his Armorcore as fire surged through it. While he was protected from the teeth themselves, the heat still got through, Callum's skin blistering as he was flung away.

He crashed hard near the atrium wall, bringing down part of a standing structure that kicked more dust up into the air.

Everything blurred until Fen's voice cut through. <Get up, now!>

Callum forced himself upright in a blur of motion, arm dragging, side flaring with every breath. The Corruption from the lizard bite sizzled, his armor moments from shattering. He knew what that felt like now, the crack, the sense that the only thing stopping him from imminent death would soon vanish.

In that moment, he had a new thought, even as the aetherlizard circled, preparing to strike.

Another Armorcore . . . I need two . . .

Wind swirled as Callum once again summoned both swords, drew deeply from Fen's bond, and activated Radiant Mirage.

Three flickering afterimages broke from him as he ran—confusing the beast for just long enough to angle for a strike. The lizard snapped at one image, then another, and both vanished.

Callum leaped and summoned his magic roots, which tore out of the ground and wrapped around the lizard's legs. He sent his swords away and summoned his Piercing Air Spear, which he drove into an exposed part of its belly as it struggled to free itself from the roots.

The beast shrieked; flashes of golden fire flared from the cracks between its scales as the lizard's third eye bulged and then dimmed.

The monster reared back, one last time. Callum slipped under it and resummoned both his swords. He drove them forward, holding them there as the monster let out a final death rattle, ash churning in a spiral as its body crumbled inward.

Callum stepped back just as shards and a Powercore flew toward him.

Empowerment of Vigor Shard
Empowerment of Deftness Shard
Fire Affinity Shard
Fire Affinity Shard
Earth Affinity Shard
Cloak of the Ashcoil Tyrant Powercore

Cloak of the Ashcoil Tyrant Powercore
Type: *Ability*
Grade: *Uncommon*
Infusion Requirements for Grade Increase:
0/20 Fire Affinity Shards
0/15 Earth Affinity Shards
0/10 Vigor Shards
Affinity Requirements: *Earth or Fire*
Effect: *Release a thick cloud of charred and smoldering mana embers that can cling to anything it touches, choking and confusing enemies.*

That could be useful, Callum thought as he pressed the new Powercore into his chest. He took another look around and let out a deep breath. "I really need another Armorcore," he told Fen.

The Radiant Fox appeared beside him. "You do, a backup one in case the Brightflame shatters. And one more thing?"

"Yeah?"

"Next time, maybe don't wait until it bites you to finally kill the damn thing."

Callum smiled at the fox, a bit of blood in his teeth. "Next time, I'm bringing friends."

CHAPTER 21

Sometimes at the Emporium, what you need finds you.

—Said to be the motto of Old Grellin,
legendary shardcrafter

The next day, after classes, Callum parted ways with his friends, his mind already set on something else. He moved through New Albion with ease now, the city no longer a maze but a living map he could read by instinct. The districts made sense to him, how they wound like the spiral of a seashell away from the Heart of Creation, the landmark that everyone used to orient themselves.

"And after this, we'll visit Birchwen at the Emporium," he told Fen as he came to a cobblestone road, where he found Florence raking leaves she had swept from the main thoroughfare in front of a chicken pen.

"I was wondering when help would arrive," the teenage girl said as she leaned on her rake. Florence had been one of the first people Callum met when he arrived in the city in search of Telluride. She was a teenager who seemed fond of teasing him.

"Telluride has you dealing with the leaves now?" Callum asked, playing along.

"He wishes! My uncle owns the barn, remember?" she motioned to the old structure. "He asked me to deal with them because Telluride wouldn't or couldn't or won't. I can't remember the reasoning."

"Why wouldn't he?"

"Um, because he's a drunk? I'm kidding. Sort of. Odds are, Telluride is probably drunk at the moment. He joined his friend on a trip to Meadowglade."

"Kaelor."

"Kaelor?" she asked.

"He's Telluride's friend who often makes trips to Meadowglade. Or maybe it was Ridgebarrow."

"I like Ridgebarrow; they have wonderful bakeries," she said, a big smile on her face. "Have you been? It's outside of the King's Forest, between Meadowglade and Morefell. So Kaelor, if that is indeed his name—"

"It is, I rode in his wagon with him once."

Florence shrugged this statement off. "Well, that's where he is, somewhere between here and Morefell and probably at a bakery putting on the pounds for winter. Who knows? Maybe they're in Braga."

"Braga?"

"It's past Morefell, near the ocean," she said. "Anyway, did you come here to make a map or to help me?"

"I came here looking for Telluride."

"And I already told you, the kooky old shardcrafter isn't here. But I am, and I'm *tired* of raking leaves." She slumped her shoulders. "Please, big strong archmage-slash-farmboy, please help me."

"Actually . . ." Callum grinned at her. "Maybe I can help. Take a step back and keep the rake with you."

"Gladly!"

Once he was in position, Callum activated Gale Pulse, aiming to gather the leaves into a single pile. For a moment, it felt like a clever use of the Powercore—efficient, even. But the wind spun wilder than he expected, and instead of pulling the leaves together, the swirling current lifted and scattered them across the courtyard in a chaotic burst that had a few chickens running for cover.

He turned back to Florence, who now held her rake like she was going to attack him. "Sorry," Callum started to say.

"No, this is good." The annoyed look on her face soon morphed into a devious grin. "Blow all the leaves that way," she said, pointing to a particular fence. She made an effort of looking around to be sure they were in the clear. "Yeah, heh. Let's do it. That's Willgirth's property. He's always dumping things on my uncle's property, from slop that his pigs didn't eat to broken furniture. I'm surprised Telluride never mentioned him, but I'm also not surprised because Telluride doesn't do anything around here, really." She sighed. "I don't know why my uncle lets him stay here."

"I don't know if it's a good idea to send the leaves over there."

"I'm not paying you to think." Florence rubbed her hands together.

"You aren't paying me at all."

"Exactly. So finish, and we can be done with this, and I can go back to doing the stuff I wanted to do today."

<She certainly is bossy,> Fen said. <But...>

"If you don't do it, I'll cry. Right here in front of you." Florence started to sniffle. "I can cry on command, you know."

"Not necessary. I'll send the leaves over to Willgirth's place." Callum raised a hand and once again conjured a blast of wind. It swept the leaves past the barn, all of them ending up on the other side of a fence that he had once helped build. *So that's why Telluride insisted I put the fence there...* Callum thought as he finished up. He turned to Florence. "Happy?"

"Thanks!" After flashing two thumbs-up, Florence turned and skipped away, leaving the rake leaning against the front of the chicken pen.

<She's devious,> Fen said as Callum looked back to the barn.

"Agreed. Let's leave the Death Affinity Shard I have for Telluride alongside a note. I don't want to trade it to Birchwen, even if it's worth something."

<Clever. We can trust Telluride. Birchwen... I can't tell with her, but she's a good shardcrafter, and she'll likely have a solution to your Armorcore problem,> Fen said. <Namely, that you need another. And perhaps a shield.>

"Agreed." Callum circled behind the barn, to the place where Telluride left an extra key. "I'll make this quick."

The Emporium's multitiered structure was still bustling, even this late in the day. The usual chaos of trading chants and affinity readings drifted down from the upper levels, echoing off stone and glass. Callum paused for a moment, taking in the movement, the light, the hum of activity. Once he was situated, he stepped through one of the arched entrances and into the main corridor, where people wove between stalls.

He caught sight of Lynnafer Sunsouth, seated at a narrow iron table beside Godric Rush. She sipped from a cup of tea in small, exact movements, while Godric did most of the talking with wide gestures and flushed cheeks to a shardcrafter in a dark blue turban and matching charms dangling from his earrings.

Callum smiled faintly and stepped their way. "Good luck tomorrow," he called to Lynnafer.

She gave him a nod over her cup. "Thanks. And hopefully, I'll see you in phase two."

"You'll definitely make it to phase two," Godric assured her. "I can feel it in my bones."

"Let's *all* make it to the next part of the trial, whatever that may be, and call it even," Callum said before continuing on, weaving through the denser crowd toward the rear spiral staircase. He came to a stop when he spotted another familiar face. Laziel Thornhelm was joined by a couple of warlocks Callum didn't recognize, all of them locked in a deep negotiation with a shifty-looking shardcrafter concealing the bottom half of his face with a blackened cloth.

<*Perhaps we keep moving,*> Fen suggested once it was clear that Callum hadn't been spotted. <*It's probably better that way.*>

<*Agreed.*> Callum took the Radiant Fox's advice as he took the steps to the basement, the noise above dimming. The lighting grew darker. Any students in the basement seemed to negotiate with a lot less bravado than they seemed to have upstairs.

Soon, he pressed the beaded curtain aside and stepped into Birchwen's new space, which was dim and hazy with an incense that smelled vaguely of sandalwood. Hood over her head, the shardcrafter sat slouched over her desk, head tipped back in a posture of resigned exhaustion.

Callum shifted his weight, causing one of the old floorboards to squeal underfoot.

Birchwen snapped upright. "I definitely wasn't sleeping," she said instantly, blinking at him with her sharp yellow eyes. "Not even a little. Ah, it's you, the Stross heir! Please, sit. You're here to trade, right?" She yawned. "Sorry. Long night."

"The fence I made you isn't working?"

"No, it is, but the smell is terrible."

"The smell?"

"The drunks have made it their favorite pissing spot. Not only does it smell, but they're loud. So now I'll have to do something else to keep them away. You don't happen to have one of those big farm dogs they have out west, do you?"

"I don't."

She frowned. "Curses. Of course, you don't. I'll probably just sleep in the kitchen. I'm moving soon anyway." She peered at him for a moment. "Are you here to catch up or trade? Didn't I already ask you that?"

"Trade. I also want to see about another Armorcore."

Her eyes lit up a bit. "An Armorcore, you say?" Birchwen produced a couple of wooden boxes that were carved with images of dragons chasing their own tails. "Let's see what you're working with first," she said, once again looking up at him as he settled on the cushion in front of her. "Oh."

"Oh?" Callum asked.

"Still no Death Affinity."

"Nope, I haven't been able to nab any lately," he lied.

"It's too bad. These warlocks are fiends for the stuff. Whatever I said it was worth the last time we met, it's double or triple that now. But I see you have plenty of other things."

"Yep. And I have two Powercores to sunder," he said as he got out the Galeburst of the Murkat and the Dervish Wisp Wind Powercores. He placed them on a circular tray lined with jewels and she took them.

"I charge one Affinity Shard per sundering session. You can choose the shard, however. You seem to have quite a bit. And we can do it after, just so you don't end up giving me a shard you actually need. As for these two, I'll sunder them first and place the shards here," she said, gesturing to another circular tray. "You can decide what to do with them as we go. Understood?"

"Got it," Callum said as Fen appeared next to him.

"Why, hello," Birchwen told the fox, her eyes locking onto him. "You're here for the show, too?"

"Show?" Fen asked.

Birchwen's sundering wasn't much different from what Callum had seen with Telluride, at least in terms of outcome. But where Telluride was clinical and focused, Birchwen treated the process like a performance. She jangled her bracelets deliberately, each movement precise and practiced, and drew in a long, theatrical breath as if preparing to enter some trance state. Her eyes half-lidded, fingers sweeping through the air, she murmured something under her breath that might have been arcane, or more likely, was pure drama.

"Ta-da," she said with a wink, clearly pleased with herself once she had finished. "Six Air Affinity Shards, two Empowerment of Vigors, and one Empowerment of Might Shards." Birchwen said once she was finished. She placed these in the appropriate tray. "Now, what are you looking to do?"

"Upgrade my Tempest Fang."

"Ah, the one I gave you?" she asked Callum, a hint of fondness in her voice.

"Yes, it works well with one of the skills that came with Fen's Aethercore."

"Well it's pretty clear that you have enough Air Affinity to upgrade it now with twelve shards. You need five more Vigor Shards, and four Might."

"That's the thing," Callum said, "I'm part of the upcoming Duelist Rounds."

"And you're hoping to save some Attribute Shards. I assumed as much. It's all the talk of the city, you know. The public will be there. How's the Vestige Arena? I've never been."

"It's massive," he told her, spreading his hands apart to emphasize the scale.

"I might come for your outings. We'll see. It's awfully busy around here." She glanced up at the ceiling just as someone stepped overhead, causing a bit of dust to fall into her workspace. "I might need to change rooms in the future—ha, again—but that's beside the point. You're telling me you're part of the tournament in a way to suggest that you need Attribute Shards, right?"

"Correct."

"So you would like ten Might Shards and ten Vigor Shards from me. Also, an Armorcore. A good one."

"I didn't think of it that way exactly, but . . ."

"You're still new at this negotiating thing," Birchwen said, "which is why I like you. It's cute. And it's smart that Quinn introduced you to me rather than one of the sellers upstairs. They would eat you for lunch. I think we'll be able to work something out for the Attribute Shards. If you trade me all the Affinity you have, aside from the ten you need for the upgrade, I'll give you the Attribute Shards. That means all your Light, Fire, Shadow, Water, and Earth Affinity, plus the two Air Affinity Shards you'll have left after you fuse."

"Yeah?"

"It's a deal, trust me," Birchwen said with a quick wink. "You're trading twelve Affinity for twenty Empowerment. Do you want some parchment to do the math?"

"No, I see get you're saying." Callum looked at Fen. "What do you think?"

"I think it's fine. What about the Armorcore?" Fen asked her.

"That's a little trickier. You want to keep your Attribute Shards for the tournament," Birchwen told Callum, "and if you trade me all your available Affinity for Attributes necessary to upgrade, all you have left are Powercores. Well, and two Weaponcores and an Armorcore. So . . ."

"So?" Callum asked.

"Which one do you want to get rid of? You're going to have to make a sacrifice here, whether you like it or not."

CHAPTER 22

We tracked three separate aetherstorm signatures over five days, none originating from known routes. This confirms, yet again, what locals have said for years: the Western Barren Steppe doesn't attract storms, it makes them.

—A quote from Legion Guard Reconnaissance Report, Year 495

Armorcore of the Ironhide Pangolin
Type: Accessory
Grade: Rare Wearable
Infusion Requirements for Grade Increase:
0/20 Earth Affinity Shards
0/25 Light Affinity Shards
0/10 Resilience Shards
Requirements: Earth or Light
Effect: Summon layered, scalelike armor of hardened light mana that forms vambrace-shield plates on the forearms, allowing the wielder to deflect attacks and brace through impact-heavy strikes.

Callum hated having to trade Onslaught of the Thunderhoof Shadowbull, especially with the war he had waged to get the Powercore, but it was worth it for an Armorcore that also produced armguard shields. Still, the thought of getting rid of something with a Sublime Grade irked him as he made his way back to the Great College.

As if he could sense this, Fen eased his disappointment: <*You need armor more than you need to be able to charge at something. And it was smart on your end. The Pangolin Armorcore will change how you do battle, giving you more options for protection. The Cloak of the Ashcoil Tyrant is worth keeping because it will provide a distraction. Same with Gale Pulse, and your Root* ability. That has helped us in numerous battles. I can only remember us using Onslaught a handful of times.>

<You're right, and I know you're right. I just hate having to give a good core up.>

<Heh. I vaguely recall the Demonslayer saying something similar. It will be even better once we find Killeas. He specializes in Earth and Air Affinity.>

The towers of the Great College came into view as Callum crested a hill, the setting sun catching their fluted arches and narrow spires with a soft orange gleam. He slowed slightly as he approached one of the side gates. There they were again, the two Crimson Sigil airships hovering like birds of prey over Dreagis Hall.

<They haven't moved in three days,> he thought to Fen as he stared up at them, <not even to change formation.>

<It's like they're waiting for something. I don't like how still they are.>

Callum didn't either.

He reached the front door of his dormitory just as a woman about his age stepped in front of it. She wore the same overcoats as any other student, her cropped hair wind-tossed, yet she stood with calm authority, not quite smiling.

"Took you long enough," she said.

Callum peered at the woman for a moment. "Sorry, do I know you?"

She nodded toward the path. "The princess is ready to see you. I was sent to escort you there."

He straightened instinctively. "Wait, you're one of her notetakers, aren't you?"

"I am."

"Is everything okay?"

"I do not know Princess Selene's intentions." The woman turned on her heel. "But I do know the king has returned, maybe it has something to do with that."

"He's back?" Callum asked as he followed the notetaker across the campus grounds toward the princess's private suite, the graceful building nestled just off the main arc of the administrative halls. The path was quiet, but guards were everywhere, triple the usual number, stationed at the entry points and along the open porticoes. Most wore the polished armor of the royal guard, but a few . . .

Callum slowed slightly as they passed the central entry.

Standing on either side of the gilded door were two towering figures. At first glance, they looked like armored soldiers with strange cloaks.

But as he stepped closer, he realized those weren't cloaks at all. One had a pair of wings draped over his shoulders, leathery and scaled. The other wore a cape that barely covered his bulging muscles or the thick tufts of fur that scaled up his neck and the back of his head. Their armor didn't sit right either, the pieces shaped around forms that no human naturally had. Their eyes glinted with faint aetherlight, and the way they stood was off, predatory, even.

<*Are those what I think they are?*> he thought to Fen.

<*Beast Masters. Full pacts. Melded beyond recovery. What you're looking at is permanent. The elite of the elite pay a cost for the kind of power they wield.*>

<*I didn't see them with King Morninglade at the arena a few days back.*>

<*You probably did,*> Fen said. <*You just didn't know what to look for.*>

Callum tried not to stare as the notetaker pushed open the outer doors, leading him into a high-ceilinged corridor of pale stone and subtle detailing. The walls shimmered with soft wardlight and silk banners of the royal house hung at intervals stylized with morningglades on fields of gold and blue.

A small waiting room opened at the end, its arching doorway framed in amber glass, which was where Callum found Princess Selene alone on a cushioned dais, one arm resting against the curved edge of a throne carved from whitewood and polished obsidian.

The space was elegant and elevated, but not grandiose. The surrounding room was similarly refined, with no massive tapestries or jeweled murals, just the quiet gleam of power expressed with restraint. There were no other thrones or chairs near hers. He got the sense that this was not a room that was often shared.

Sir Trindade stood near the door, watching as Callum entered.

"You're here," Selene said, her tone dry. "Finally."

"I came as soon as I—"

"I'm teasing." She waved a hand to a chair against the far wall. "Have a seat if you like."

"There?"

"No, bring the chair here, in front of me. I imagine you noticed the extra guards. Some of them are . . . new."

"I noticed," Callum replied carefully as he set the wooden chair down. "Including the ones outside."

"Ah. The Beast Masters." Selene leaned her chin against her hand. "My father rarely travels without them anymore."

"Did he bring them to the Vestige Arena the other day?"

"He did. You just didn't see them," she said, confirming what Fen had suggested. "They're good at blending in when they want to. They're also good at standing out when need be."

Callum didn't reply, still absorbing that.

Selene sat back, fingers drumming softly on the armrest. "Lisalen remains with my father. She always does. He's eating in the next room with the Duke of Karna and some Geshwinian representative. Normally, I would be there, but I was asked to allow them privacy."

Callum raised an eyebrow.

Selene nodded, her lips parsed. "Trust me, I don't like it either. But to appease me, my father agreed to something." She glanced at Sir Trindade. "He promised to let Fen speak with Lisalen."

The knight bowed slightly and stepped toward the side door. He opened it with a motion, revealing a glimmering chamber beyond bisected by a long table. For just a moment, Callum caught a glimpse of the Duke of Karna sitting beside a long table, his profile unmistakably the same as Draven's—same angular jaw, same mouth—but his eyes were gray, not red.

<*He's not a warlock,*> Callum thought to Fen.

<*No. Apparently not.*>

Before Callum could study more or see the king's guest, the princess's throne room lit with a sudden burst of light. Sir Trindade shut the door as a flash of fire filled the space, hot and golden. It was followed by a wave of heat, one that radiated around Lisalen's wings once she landed on the perch beside Selene.

The phoenix settled, her brilliance fading just enough for Callum to catch a glimpse of her glowing orange eyes. "Hello, old friend," she said as Fen appeared in a shimmer of golden light at Callum's side.

For a moment, the two aetherbeasts simply stared at one another. Then, Fen lowered his head, bowing to the graceful phoenix, his tail lowering as well.

"It has been so long, Lisalen," he finally said.

"It has, Fen," she replied in a soft voice. "I never saw the Demonslayer so distraught."

Fen nodded his chin toward Callum. "This is his successor, his reincarnation. Meet the second coming of Callum Stross."

Lisalen tilted her head slightly as she took Callum in. "The second coming? You are certain?"

"I don't think I would be here if it weren't true," Fen told her.

"Then you know it is coming."

"I have sensed it, yes," Fen said vaguely.

"The Demon King will resurface if it continues," she warned, her feathers ruffling slightly, scattering radiant sparks of heat and brilliance into the air.

"I'm aware. We are trying to stop it. It seems like you would be more capable than I at the moment." Fen tilted his snout toward the other room.

"It has never been that simple. Humans do not always listen to reason."

"Surely..." Fen glanced from Lisalen to Princess Selene. "Are we allowed to speak freely?"

Sir Trindade, who stood near the door again, cleared his throat. "An audience with the king or one of his Aethercores is an honor. I needn't remind you that, but I'm doing so now before you say something that could get you dismissed."

"Sir Trindade," Selene began.

"I'm sorry, Your Highness, but it needs to be clear that this meeting is sanctioned by King Morninglade himself. In this case, his office takes precedence over yours. As we have experienced in negotiations in the past, this modifies the chain of command in certain ways with our relationship. I say all of this respectfully, but also, as a warning that certain things related to the High Council and the Crown are not to be discussed in this meeting." He turned his focus to Fen. "You came with a particular question in mind, did you not? A question regarding a location?"

Fen went for a different answer. "Certainly the sanctity of the Crown's power doesn't supersede the security of the kingdom. If I am back, it means we are on the brink of something that could rip the Valestra Kingdom apart, and you are suggesting we follow some lofty protocol that—"

"It is our way now," Lisalen told Fen, cutting him off. "The Kingdom has survived for five hundred years with this order in place. There is much more happening than you may be able to see from where you sit."

Fen stood on all fours and looked up at the phoenix. "I fail to see how the chance of a Second Demonswar would be anything but the topic everyone wants to solve."

"What do you think the tournament is? What do you think these negotiations are for?" Lisalen asked, tailfeathers flaring. "I don't wish to rush you, and it isn't my intention to be blunt, but what have you come here to discuss?"

Fen scoffed at her tone. "I am truly surprised that you would agree with the humans over what is happening before your very eyes. There are bloody warlocks on campus. There are forces on the High Council that could very well be in bed with the Geshwine Empire. Have you no thoughts on the matter?" he asked after a long, excruciating pause. "Surely, being as close to the king as you are, this is of the utmost concern."

"What have you come to ask me?"

Fen sighed miserably. "If you want me to get right down to it, I will. I am looking for the others."

"You won't find Rata easily due to the fact that the Sand Wolf of Aveiro died in the final battle of the Demonswar. Astel is with the other dragons, and I don't see her pacting again—"

"Killeas. I'm looking for Killeas."

"The Gryphon Vanguard of Fates?" Sir Trindade murmured from his position near the door.

"Where is Killeas?" Fen asked Lisalen "That's who I—*we*—are looking for."

"Killeas?" Lisalen's eyes flared, and the plumage along her neck lifted slightly before settling. "Gryphons are always hard to control, Killeas especially."

"That doesn't tell me what has happened to him," Fen said, barely hiding his agitation.

"Are you sure the young man you claim is the Stross heir is ready for Killeas?"

"You know exactly why he is here and so do I. Where is Killeas, Lisalen, please," Fen told her, "enough with the bird games."

"Bird games?"

"You know what I mean."

"Killeas vanished after the war," she said, eyes narrowing on him and shedding firelight. "Why do you care about Killeas?"

"That would be for me," Callum told the phoenix. "I reached the Wielder Stage. I would like another Aethercore."

Lisalen extended her feathers and tucked them back again. "Ah, for the Young Demonslayer, is it?"

Young Demonslayer? Callum thought.

"Sure," Fen said, "if that's what you would like to call him, that is why we need to find Killeas."

"Well, I wish I could help you more, but I know nothing of Killeas's whereabouts. He vanished after the final battle, resurfaced once, if I'm not mistaken, and hasn't been heard from again. You would have a better chance just lighting a sky lantern and seeing where it takes you."

Sir Trindade cleared his throat. "I have some information that may be of some help."

"You do?" Lisalen asked him.

"Please, tell us," Princess Selene told her Legion Guard.

"As you know, Your Highness, I was keenly interested in the Demonslayer as are many students who study to become Legion Guards. I spent a great deal of time studying the end of the Demonswar. I even wrote a paper on it, about the Lands of Grimbald and the border skirmishes that brought them into our Kingdom for several hundred years. I was especially—"

"Yes, I'm aware. You've told me before in our visits to the west."

Sir Trindade approached, the man now standing next to Callum. Rather than look at Callum or Fen, he kept his focus on Lisalen and Princess Selene. "For that research, I spent a great deal of time on the western border. It was the King's Scholarship that helped fund my journey, a scholarship which has been greatly reduced by—"

"Please, Sir Trindade, to the point," Selene said. "I only tell you this because I worry that my father might be finishing his meal soon, and Lisalen will be called back to him."

"Understood. What do you know about the Demonslayer statue at the Great College?" he asked the princess.

Callum answered before Selene could. "It came from his mausoleum."

"That's right," Sir Trindade said. "Which is hidden somewhere along the border between the Lands of Grimbald and our kingdom."

"Because it all used to be the Valestra Kingdom," Fen added.

"That would make sense," Lisalen said. "In that case, Sir Trindade, are you aware of its exact location? Because I am not. I was pacted with the royal family by that point."

He cleared his throat again. "That's the problem. I believe I was close, but I could never find it. There were a few books written about the subject, not on Killeas's disappearance, but his origins. The original Callum Stross encountered him out west."

"That's true," Fen said. "I know that part. But you think he's still there?"

"I think he was sealed in the Demonslayer's mausoleum."

Lisalen took it from there. "The Demonslayer wasn't entombed until nearly fifty years after his death by natural causes. His corpse remained on display, kept from deteriorating using Life Affinity."

"And during that time?" Sir Trindade asked her.

"During that time, Killeas roamed freely but he became erratic. And then he vanished."

"Around the time the Demonslayer was entombed, right?" he asked the phoenix.

"I can't say for certain, it was over four hundred years ago, but that would make sense. Killeas is a wild card, one of the hardest aetherbeasts to control, yet he listened to and respected the Demonslayer."

"How do we find it?" Callum asked Sir Trindade. "Do you have any idea where it could be?"

"I have an idea of its general location, north of Devonshire, in the Western Barren Steppe, past the border."

"That's..." Callum thought of just how vast the land north of Weatherby was. He steeled himself. "Then we will look for it, I guess."

Sir Trindade finally looked down at him. "We're talking about an area that spans hundreds of miles."

"Then I'll have to start sooner than later," Callum said.

Lisalen threw her head back and laughed, the sound rising like birdsong caught in the wind. A faint shimmer of heat rolled off her wings, casting a golden hue across the room. "He's more like him than I thought," she told Fen. "Willing to risk it all on hope alone."

"Yes, yes, he is," Fen said, looking at Callum with quiet fondness. "But sometimes, that's what it takes."

CHAPTER 23

Victory in pacted combat arises not from dominance, but resonance. Two souls moving as one will always overcome.

—A quote from *On the Bond Between* by Renova Dreagis, Mastress Shaper, Archona of Ridgebarrow, Soul Pythia

The next morning arrived, brittle and gray. Fen's mood hadn't shifted after his confrontation with Lisalen, the Radiant Fox pacing back and forth in front of Callum's bed.

"I can't believe it," he said, "Lisalen taking the side of the humans versus what we both know to be the truth. And who is Sir Trindade to step in and say anything?"

"He was helpful in the end," Callum reminded him. "We know where Killeas is now."

"Yes, somewhere between here, there, and the middle of nowhere. I'm sorry," Fen said as he sat with a huff. "I know you are from that region and I didn't mean it like that. I just hoped that we would be able to accomplish a bit more in our reunion, one nearly five hundred years in the making. We were both pacted with the Demonslayer. She was there when he buried my Aethercore deep beneath the East Manor. She *knew* why he did it. She definitely knows more than me about all of it, from the final battle to the Demonslayer's wishes in the end, but we could barely get anything out of her."

"Was she like that when you knew her?"

One of Fen's ears folded slightly. "You mean standoffish?"

"Yes. Or just . . . combative."

"Toward me, sometimes. Yes, I recall that. More now that I've seen her again. It's funny how that works. And she didn't like Killeas, I can tell you that."

"Another question."

"Yes?"

"If we find Killeas—"

"It might be impossible, but go on," Fen said.

"If we find Killeas, will there be two voices in my head?"

Fen actually started laughing. "Not what I was expecting, but to answer your question, yes, there will be. And I hope that's fine."

"And is Killeas really as wild as Lisalen said he would be?"

"Killeas is a different beast entirely. Have you ever met a gryphon?"

Callum gave Fen a funny look. "No. But I'd also never met a talking fox so I don't think that says anything."

"Perhaps you're right. Well, we need to find Killeas first, and before we do that, we have to start the Duelist Rounds."

"By start you mean *watch*."

"Yes," Fen said, "watch and learn how they fight and who makes it to your phase. Cruedark was right when he said this is good for us. Adding this round of people that didn't make it through the Culling Trials gives us a massive advantage. That and our new armor. It will be quite good, but you've yet to train with it."

"There hasn't been any time. I haven't even had a chance to upgrade my Tempest Fang," Callum told him."

"Do it now," Fen said, "just to be safe."

Callum found a small bowl carved from stone and lowered himself to the ground. He placed the Air Affinity Shards inside, then reached into his chest and drew out the Tempest Fang Weaponcore—its surface alive with sizzling magic. Holding the core steady, he pressed the shards into it one by one, just as Telluride had taught him.

Once he was finished, he used Soul Sense to check the upgraded weapon.

Weaponcore of the Tempest Fang
Type: *Accessory*
Grade: *Rare Weapon*
Infusion Requirements for Grade Increase:
0/20 Air Affinity Shards
0/15 Vigor Shards
0/15 Might Shards
Requirements: *Air*
Effect: *When bound to one's Soul Heart, this Weaponcore allows a mage to conjure a nearly invisible swirling wind sword capable of cutting through enemies.*

Callum pushed the orb back into his chest, feeling the subtle pulse of his Soul Heart's response.

He summoned the weapon and the wind sword bloomed to life in his hand. Air curled along its edge in tight, spiraling currents, each gust whispering against his skin. The pressure of it distorted the space around the tip, as if the blade refused to be seen in full, constantly shifting, alive with motion. It brimmed with power. Not just shaped wind, but something sharper, more precise. He had to squint to focus on the weapon's edge, as though the air itself wanted to turn it invisible.

"I would tell you to test Zephyr Strike, but we're still in your dorm room," Fen said as he approached. "It looks good, though. Powerful."

"Just what we need." Callum sent the weapon away.

"Yes, this, the Armorcore, and Killeas."

"Any idea how we will be able to find him?"

"Not just yet. We could visit the Archive of Destiny and see if the Demonslayer's construct knows anything. But first, the tournament."

Callum glanced out the window to the Crimson Sigil airships. "Let's hope our people clean up today."

Callum had never seen Vestige Arena this worked up into a frenzy.

The upper tiers of the arena were packed, citizens from every district of New Albion filling the stands alongside a delegation from the Geshwine Empire. The western seating, once reserved for Great College faculty and royal delegates, had been opened to the public. Families, students, and traders shouted encouragement for the Valestran contenders, while a steady wave of jeers and stomping rose each time a Crimson Sigil student stepped onto the arena floor.

The air flickered with ambient magic, charged and restless. Above, the walkways were lit by a midday sun that had pushed past the early morning gray and it looked like the obsidian ashglass shielding had been reinforced.

Twelve aetheric pylons pulsed faintly at the arena's edge, leylines bending toward them like whispering strings. These seemed to be connected somehow to huge tiles crossing the arena floor, which looked to be capable of replicating ecosystems. *Crazy*, Callum thought as they rearranged themselves into a new battleground of sandy dunes layered with broken stone, a setting meant to strain balance and footing.

From his seat near the competitors' platform, Callum could feel the tension more than he could hear it—a low hum that settled in his chest and refused to leave. He wore armor now. Actual armor, not borrowed or scavenged, but forged and fitted for him by the Great College's smiths. The weight of it grounded him and he was glad to have it on; he wanted to get used to it before he started his fights.

As he had when he first entered the arena, Callum found himself looking for Princess Selene. He expected her to be here, but the only people he had seen so far indicating her presence were her notetakers.

The first match began shortly after everyone settled.

Demandra of the Great College squared off against a Crimson duelist with a shadowblade and a pacted shade wolf. They traded bursts of power, shards flaring in tandem as the aetherbeasts clashed.

The ground shifted mid-fight—a ripple of magic that caused half the audience to gasp. A sudden incline beneath her heels caused Demandra to slip. The Crimson student closed in with a flash of speed and landed a vertical slash across her chestplate that sent her sprawling. Her Armorcore flared out in defeat as he delivered a finishing blow, one that was blocked by Demandra's aetherbeast but took her out of the fight for good.

No extraction. No bracelets like they had used in the Entry Duels. Just the old-fashioned pain of impact.

Callum remembered Cruedark's last words to his class, spoken after an hour of intense training: "This is the real deal. There are healers with pacted beasts attuned to Life Affinity, but there are attacks that can technically kill you. Will it happen in the Duelist Rounds? I don't think so. We haven't seen a fatality in over a hundred years. But injuries? Serious ones? Be prepared. This is a war of wits, power, and endurance now. Absolutely yield if your Armorcore is broken and it's clear you can't go on any longer."

The next name announced made Callum sit up straighter.

Marcella.

Quinn, who sat next to Callum, cheered for her as she took her place across from Therrin Vale, one of the Crimson Sigil students Callum had been teamed with during the Culling Trials.

"I wonder what he has," Quinn said.

"A pacted aetherbat," Callum told him.

"So we're about to witness something aerial, huh?"

Before Callum could answer, Marcella launched into the sky with her new Froststag weapon at her side. Therrin took off as well, circling around her as she went for her opening attack. She missed, but managed to hit him the next time, using the frost part of her antler weapon.

They clashed in the air, both weaving wind and power, wingbeats clapping through the open arena. Twice, the illusion of high-altitude wind forced them into a dive, disrupting their movement.

It's another feature of the arena, Callum thought as Marcella used the turbulence to her advantage, spiraling downward into a perfect aerial feint before striking with her new Weaponcore. Her attack slammed Therrin onto the ground, where she swooped down and pinned him. Before he could react, she sent her stagsword away and went for her blade, which she jammed into his Armorcore, shattering it.

The arena roared. Quinn leaped to his feet. "That's what I'm talking about!"

Callum joined him, cheering loudly for Marcella, who looked in their general direction and gave them a curt nod, one that indicated no one should have ever doubted her.

The applause was still echoing when Callum noticed motion to his right. Another wave of jeers echoed through the arena as a sleek group of Crimson Sigil students, led by Laziel Thornhelm, took their reserved section near the edge of the arena's upper tier. They sat with practiced poise, posture rigid, capes freshly pressed, hands folded across knees or resting flat on thighs.

And among them, Draven.

His expression was as arrogant as ever, but this time there was no mistaking the implication.

Draven had joined the other side.

Callum saw it not just in where he sat, but how he sat. Draven leaned toward one of the Crimson students and said something that made her smirk faintly. The others didn't bristle. They accepted him. Welcomed him, even.

<*He's not even pretending anymore.*>

<*Nope, he's making a move,*> Fen said, voice low in his mind. <*Aligning himself publicly with the Crimson delegation is more than just political posturing. He's consolidating influence. Resources. Access.*>

<*Access to what?*>

<*More Death Affinity, likely,*> Fen whispered. <*I'd bet my tail on it. He's trying to work the system—probably through off-campus trades or hidden shardcrafters.*>

<*But the Crown is collecting them . . .*>

<*The High Council's orders. And remember who leads the High Council? Draven's father, the Duke of Karna.*>

Draven leaned back with a smile, as if nothing about his presence should be questioned.

<*We still can't prove anything,*> Callum thought to Fen.

<*Not yet. But we will.*>

Lynnafer Sunsouth entered the arena, head held high. Her opponent wasn't from the Crimson Sigil, but from the Great College—proof that the duelist rounds weren't just school versus school. It was all random.

Theogar Desde stepped into the arena opposite her. He was a lesser noble from Karna and one of Draven's inner circle. With a sharp flick of his wrist, he summoned his pact—a massive, armor-plated porcupine that looked like it had never known a calm day in its life.

"Porcupine versus badger," Quinn said, arms crossed. "My money's on Lynnafer."

<Same,> Fen told Callum privately.

They were both right in the end. The fight was done in a matter of minutes, A flash of claws, a shockwave of earth mana, and then a shift in the terrain as a dust storm blew through. Once the match finished, Lynnafer stood victorious.

Once again, Callum got to his feet and cheered.

The matches continued for hours, dozens of students pushed through shifting terrain, elemental interference, and crowd noise that never ceased. Callum and Quinn, later joined by Marcella, watched every match. By the end, only about a third of their cohort would move on.

As dusk neared, the Soul Pythia returned to the arena, flanked by two Crimson Sigil advisors in matching black military uniforms. The crowd quieted as she entered, the hush spreading outward in ripples. Mana stirred faintly in her wake as she moved with ceremonial grace, each step deliberate until she came to a final stop.

"Phase one of the Duelist Rounds is now complete," she said, her voice echoed across the arena. "Those who succeeded will advance to phase two, which begins soon. Once it starts, there will be no rest between your matches. Due to the number of contenders . . . some of you may face up to three rounds."

"Three?" Callum asked, exchanging glances with Quinn.

<We should find a portal, now,> Fen said, already on edge as Callum looked back to where Draven was sitting, the warlock once again laughing with his new friends.

<A portal?> Callum asked. <Why?>

<We need to go through everything we have and make sure we're ready for tomorrow. Keep your armor on. Sleep in it if you have to. It's going to be a long night.>

CHAPTER 24

Every Aethercore you show is a card turned face-up. Show the right one too early, and all you're holding is regret.

—A quote from *My Time at the Great College: A Memoir* by Sir Gideon Coldwell, Master Channeler, Clergo

Callum hadn't expected the Veilchamber to be such a unique space. The walls, a marvel of magitek, shimmered with a mirrored sheen that faced the arena, reflecting back the crowd's roar and the flood of color from the stands. From the outside, nothing could be seen—but from within, the surface was clear as polished glass. Every detail of the tournament floor below was visible, allowing contestants to study their opponents and look out at the audience with perfect clarity.

Callum stepped closer, the enchanted wall gleaming inches from his face.

From here, it felt like he could reach out and touch the shifting tiles that made up the arena's main floor beyond. Up until now, he had only watched duels from the stands, from balconies, even from above.

But this was different.

Down here, beneath the arena's heart, the air felt knotted with tension and power, and seeing the packed crowd from this new perspective told him just how important people were taking the Dueling Rounds. The room carried no sound, only the low, restless hum of mana pulsing through its frame, all of which accumulated in a vertical flow of magic at the back of the room that would recharge him to optimum mana levels at the end of each fight.

Callum stood in his full armor among his peers, a subtle pulse moving through him with each breath. He had practiced late into the night, learning more about his new Armorcore and Powercore. The Ashcoil Cloak was going to be useful; he knew that now, and he was glad to have picked it up at the Silver Fang Academy. *And*, thought Callum of the Pangolin Armorcore, *that might come in handy in more than one fight.*

Beside him, Marcella stared at the arena's main battleground, quiet for once, the tall southern woman geared up and more focused than he could ever remember seeing. Quinn stood to his right, looking a bit awkward in his armor, yet confident nonetheless as he glanced over to Callum and offered him a short nod.

"This is it," Quinn said, a statement that turned out to be truer than he could have hoped when his name was called next.

"Good luck," a student named Silvia called to him.

Godric, Lynnafer, and Victrin did the same.

"Do it for Valestra," Marcella told Quinn as he approached the wall, which rippled momentarily, allowing Quinn to pass through it. It stitched back together the moment he was gone.

"I told you this room was crazy," Marcella told Callum, moving closer to him. "I've never seen magitek like this before."

"It really is," Callum said, watching as Quinn took his place in the center of the arena, his aethercat melding with him. Claws extended over his hands, and a cat's tail formed, a barb on the end.

One of the Veilchambers on the other side opened and Ryven stepped out, the Crimson student with the scarred face lumbering toward Quinn, his shoulders seemingly carrying him forward as he continued toward the center of the arena, the tiles around them shifting into boulders and angled rock formations.

Ryven was a full head taller than Quinn, and his red eyes flared as the fight began. Ryven's meld with the Juggerboar came instantly as his whole body was coated by a corrupted Armorcore, tusks of molten shadow curling around his forearms.

Quinn didn't flinch. His meldform with Tuck gave him speed and precision, and for the first few exchanges, Callum dared to hope.

"Come on," he said as Quinn avoided most of Ryven's first attempts and even managed to land a few blows.

<*Quinn is holding his own,*> Fen says. <*He could do it!*>

The fight sped up as Quinn used his twin claws like a whirlwind, dodging and redirecting Ryven's slams, striking from unexpected angles. Tuck snarled, unmelded at points, and delivered quick blows, forcing Ryven to constantly pivot. A burst of earthen mana followed, the ground shifting. Quinn jumped forward and delivered another devastating attack, the crowd gasping in unison as Ryven was knocked off-balance, the big man staggering backward.

"Let's go, Quinn!" Marcella said, her hands cupping her mouth, voice loud enough to startle some of the other Great College students in their Veilchamber. "What?" she asked some of them. "He can do this!"

<*He just needs to bring it home!*> Fen told Callum.

But then Ryven's attacks turned erratic. When Quinn finally missed an attempt, Ryven struck him down hard enough to crater the arena's tiled surface, causing it to ripple outward.

Quinn's Armorcore fizzled out. He pushed himself up, and Ryven struck him with a shadowy bolt from his Weaponcore crossbow. This attack yanked Quinn across the tiles, slamming him into a boulder that had formed at the start of their fight. Quinn got to his feet, took a final step forward, and collapsed.

"Argh!" Marcella punched her fist into the wall of the Veilchamber, causing it to flare with defense magic, forcing her back. She shook her hand out. "Dammit, I really wanted him to win."

"Me too," Callum said, fists clenching at the sight of Ryven, who stood there watching the medics rush the field.

A bell rang, the match over seemingly as quickly as it began.

Ryven's meld faded and he raised a hand in the direction of the Crimson Sigil students in the stands, who all stomped in celebration. The big man turned and walked off without so much as a glance back to Quinn's body, which shimmered as the extraction team helped him from the field, Quinn's head held upright but his mouth drawn in pain.

Callum was still stunned by the suddenness of Quinn's defeat a few fights later. The only thing able to snap him out of it was the announcement of his name, which caused a sudden murmur to trace through the crowd. He didn't know what to expect from the people that had come to watch the Duelist Rounds, but relative silence and amplified whispers from both sides told him that many were learning about his existence for the first time.

"Whoever it is, make it fast," Marcella said as he stepped forward, the Veilchamber's wall rippling away to allow him to enter the arena. "Do it for Quinn," she called after him as he stepped out. He turned one last time to look at her but only met his own reflection in the outer wall of the Veilchamber.

Callum took a deep breath in as he looked up to the stands, which were more filled than they had been during phase one. He could see Great College students in their overcoats, a sharp contrast with the Crimson Sigil students and their military uniforms and strict postures. Then there were the people of New Albion, all eyes on him, Callum feeling a new pressure he wasn't yet ready for.

<*They know who you are now,*> Fen told him. <*But I told you last night that would happen.*>

<*You did. I just didn't expect . . .*> Callum let a quick breath. <*I didn't expect for it to feel this way.*>

<*I can tell. Just focus on the fights, the first of up to three today.*>

<*Then let's make it fast, just like Marcella said.*>

They melded. Power rippled down Callum's shoulders as his Brightflame Falcon Armorcore flared to life. Silken bands of golden light streaking over his chest and arms, feathered with subtle fire that produced a pair of protective wings on his back. He quickly crushed two Might Shards and a Vigor Shard, his power instantly amplified.

Across from him, a Veilchamber opened and a Crimson Sigil woman with black hair tied in twin pigtails stepped out, her eyes red, her demeanor calm. She approached and bowed quickly without a word. Her aura ignited, wind and water peeling out from beneath her feet.

Behind her, the translucent shape of a dolphin flickered into form.

Callum dropped low, Tempest Fang in hand swirling in his hand, as the match began.

The moment the signal flared, she moved. Not fast, but fluid, her feet barely seeming to touch the ground. Her aetherdolphin pushed past her, shimmering into full form, sleek and pale blue, with fins edged in silvery wisps of corrupted magic. The arena shifted around them, reshaping into rolling hills thick with bramble and underbrush as the dolphin neared him.

Callum struck at it with a blast of wind. The aetherbeast circled back around and toward the woman, who melded with it and dove toward Callum.

He sidestepped her first attempt, only to find a slicing rush of water from the left. He parried with his wind sword, its edge catching the air and redirecting the watery force upward in a splash of corrupted darkness.

<*She's testing you!*> Fen said.

<*Then let's test her back!*> Callum darted forward, blade low, letting the wind guide him. She responded with a spinning flourish, energy spiraling around her and projecting a dome of compressed water-mana to repel his strike.

The barrier held.

Callum ducked beneath the rebound and rolled clear. As she reset, he summoned the Cloak of the Ashcoil Tyrant. In an instant, the arena changed. A cloud of blackness plumed across the field, pulling light and obscuring the rough terrain. The battlefield dimmed, visibility dropping.

Callum disappeared into the fog of ash, his full trust in Fen now as the Radiant Fox brought him directly to his opponent.

Callum struck from the side; she turned just in time to block, but the edge of his wind sword sliced her pauldron clean.

He vanished again, flickering through the dark haze, Fen taking the lead and helping him stay agile. His opponent turned defensively, trying to reposition, but Callum was already behind her. A gust-driven feint and a sweep of the blade sent her reeling.

Her dolphin moved to block with a huge tail fin, but Callum surged past it. He followed this up with a gale of wind that forced her down and blew some of the ash-ridden fog away.

Callum moved on her fast, where he was able to overpower her with a strike that had her Armorcore crackling.

"You're fast," she said at last, her voice husky with restrained hunger as she parried his strike with a jagged Weaponcore dagger. Sparks burst from the clash, illuminating her face and the wild grin splitting it.

Her red eyes had narrowed to pinpricks. There was nothing human in the way she surged forward, teeth bared, a snarl catching in her throat as something ancient and frenzied took hold.

Callum didn't have time to react as a force slammed into his chest and hurled him backward. He hit the uneven arena floor hard, the wind punched from his lungs with a rough grunt.

He rolled, coughing, trying to suck air back in as he pushed through the blur. When his eyes cleared, the water surrounding the Crimson Sigil duelist had gone deathly still—too still. The hiss and roar of battle had drained away, replaced by a silence that pressed against his ears like pressure at the bottom of a deep lake.

Then he felt it. A second pulse. Another presence.

<*Brace yourself,*> Fen warned, his voice taut inside Callum's mind as he scrambled to his feet. <*She has two pacted aetherbeasts.*>

A ripple of dark wind swept across the arena floor, bending the air around it with a low, unnatural hum. A second shape shimmered around the Crimson woman, massive and wreathed in corrupted mana. She surged toward Callum, her movement sudden and feral, a banshee-like scream tearing through the arena as she closed the distance.

Callum dodged a barbed tail, which forced him into the trajectory of another barbed tail, one he didn't see coming. It smacked into his

Armorcore, shattering it and sending him into some of the underbrush. Callum hit the stone hard, back skidding across the fractured terrain, overturned roots scraping against his physical armor as the corrupted aetherbeast's tail raked the air above him.

Callum forced himself to one knee and summoned the Ironhide Pangolin. Mana snapped through the space around him, sharp and immediate, answering his call as thick scales locked into place over his arms and torso, shield-fins flaring upward from his forearms like jagged ridges of forged bronze. His footing stabilized instantly, weight shifting differently now.

Denser. Grounded. Meant for brutal endurance.

The demonic aetherbeast shrieked again as the woman rushed forward in a blurred cloud of Corruption, barbed tail in the lead. Callum raised one armored arm and caught the blow mid-strike, the impact reverberating through his entire frame.

His opponent reared back, once again melded with her dolphin form, watery corrupted magic churning around her in violent waves.

Callum finally caught a clear glimpse of her second summon, the aetherbeast now unmelded, floating beside her as it sprouted more barbed tails. It looked like a monstrous jellyfish, bloated and translucent, its swollen bell pulsing with slow, deliberate malice. Dozens of yellow eyes blinked in eerie synchronization along its gelatinous body as it extruded more dark tendrils, each one slick with oily mana that hissed where it touched the air.

<*She wants to overwhelm me,*> Callum said. <*Two fronts.*>

<*Then divide them!*>

Callum triggered Radiant Mirage.

Light fractured around him in a sharp burst, splitting into five blinding afterimages that shot outward like shards of a broken soul. One veered left, another streaked right, two leaped skyward, and one charged directly toward the jellyfish horror. The corrupted aetherbeast recoiled, flinching in confusion, its barbed tendrils lashing at illusions that vanished the moment they were struck. Yellow eyes blinked furiously across its glistening bell, trying and failing to find the real threat.

Callum didn't wait.

He lunged through the chaos, boots slipping across scorched stone as he tore free from its kill zone. Mana surged at his fingertips. Behind him, the Crimson student snarled in frustration and gave chase.

He triggered another of Fen's powers.

Radiant Inferno erupted in his wake. Blinding flares of burning light burst one after another, each explosion cracking the air and washing the ground in white-hot brilliance. The pulses lit the arena like lightning caught in a bottle, tearing shadows from the walls and leaving scorched craters where his feet had been.

Still running, Callum risked a glance over his shoulder and caught a glimpse of the woman barreling through the blaze, eyes locked on him with unrelenting hunger.

The woman kept her pace as the ground shifted, crevices appearing. Water spiraled around her legs, launching her forward with speed that nearly blurred her form.

Callum jumped over some of the tangle, pivoted, and slid beneath her next strike. He swept his Tempest Fang up in a wind-laced arc, clipping her shoulder and knocking her sideways.

He didn't wait.

His Air Spear flared to life and hurled through the air right over her head. The corrupted aetherbeast shrieked, caught off-guard as it struck the monster and drove it into the ground in a crash of ash and stone.

The woman shrieked, her voice raw with desperation, and launched into a final charge. Water spiraled around her in a crashing vortex, wrapping her limbs in a sheath of liquid fury. Her Weaponcore dagger gleamed, jagged and wild, as she closed the distance with terrifying speed.

Callum's breath hitched. Mana roared through his Soul Heart.

He summoned his Ram swords, the twin curved blades manifesting in his grip with a flash of molten gold. He crossed them over his chest, bracing as her form neared him, and then tore the blades apart in a sweeping X-shaped strike.

The air screamed with impact.

The slash caught her mid-lunge. Her body twisted in the air as the blades struck.

She hurtled backward, limbs limp, crashing through the air until she slammed into an overturned tree trunk with a bone-jarring thud. Bark splintered. Her body bounced once, then dropped, rolling to a stop against the roots. For a heartbeat it looked like she might recover. But then her Armorcore flared, overcharged and cracking, before vanishing in a burst of white light.

She didn't rise.

Her arms lay sprawled in the dirt, her chin tilted at an unnatural angle, blood trailing from one lip. The water that had once obeyed her now soaked silently into the ground around her, no longer swirling, no longer hers.

Silence followed. Then thunder from the stands.

Callum stood panting, shoulders hunched, magic flaring from the rigid blades of his Ram swords. He staggered once, catching himself.

<*Good!*> Fen said, his voice sharp with approval.

Callum looked up at the stands, blinking against the light, heart still hammering.

One round down. Up to two more to go.

And that was only if he lasted.

CHAPTER 25

Valestra studies Death Affinity mana like it studies poison—cautiously, and always behind glass. Its psychological properties remain largely unexamined, yet every recorded instance suggests it reshapes more than just the body.

—A quote from *Unspoken Currents: A Survey of Rare Affinities* by Emilia Eadred, Mastress Weaver, Core Lectora

What a fight, Callum thought as he braced one hand against the edge of the Veilchamber's mana fountain, his breathing still uneven. The vertical stream of magic at its center pulsed with soft, golden light, the ambient power spiraling upward in a constant, twisting stream. As he touched it, his Soul Heart surged in recognition. Power rushed into him—not raw or chaotic, but clean, perfectly aligned, as though shaped to fill the exact cracks the last fight had left behind.

<*This is what proper restoration should feel like,*> Fen said, voice calm now, no longer tense from combat.

<*I could use one of these fountains in my dorm room.*>

<*I'll bet you could. Such advanced magitek,*> Fen said, <*clearly a deep leyline tap. The Demonslayer would be impressed and at the same time . . .*>

<*Yes?*>

<*Worried about what something like this could do in the wrong hands.*>

<*Heh. Wish I could take one home,*> Callum said, allowing himself a small smile.

Someone nudged him lightly on the shoulder. "Well done," Godric told Callum, nodding once. His hair was damp with sweat from a previous match. "I didn't expect the dolphin lady to have another pact. It makes me wonder how many of them have reached the Wielder Stage. Anyway, you handled it better than most would have."

Callum straightened. "Thanks. Still feels like I barely scraped by."

"I think that's the theme for today," Godric said, watching the next pair take the field. "Only gets harder from here. Ooh, Lynn's up."

Callum's attention shifted to the arena just in time to catch Lynnafer stepping out of the Veilchamber. She took her place in the center of the arena as her opponent did the same, Laziel Thornhelm moving like he already owned the floor, regal in motion, silent in presence. The stands fell nearly silent.

<I wonder what he is pacted with,> Callum told Fen.

<Maybe he will reveal it, maybe he won't.>

The match that followed was short and brutal.

Laziel moved like he had been born in shifting terrain. The arena transformed beneath them, the lush tangle of underbrush dissolving into a desolate moonscape cloaked in thick fog. Visibility dropped to nothing. The crowd leaned forward, but the mist swallowed everything except flashes of movement, the occasional flicker of mana, and a glimpse of Laziel's red eyes.

Callum strained to follow what he could, but Laziel was a ghost in the haze. He fought with surgical precision, never giving away his position, never offering a glimpse of the aetherbeast bound to him. Whatever he was pacted with, it moved in concert with him—fast, fluid, and utterly concealed.

For her part, Lynnafer fought like hell. Callum recognized the way she moved—focused, sharp, unyielding. Her badger darted through the mist at her side, a blur of low-slung motion and snarls. Her blades sang as she pressed the attack, trying to cut through the silence with sheer force.

Still, it wasn't enough.

A burst of light flared, followed by a concussive crack. The fog rippled outward. Through the veil, Callum saw Lynnafer stagger. A moment later, Laziel emerged behind her, just long enough for Callum to catch a glimpse of something towering, big enough to crush her.

A single, well-timed strike ended it.

Lynnafer crumpled, her Armorcore flashing once before it gave out, and she fell to the ground unconscious. The crowd hesitated, unsure if the match had truly ended, until Laziel's victory was announced in a voice that echoed with finality.

Whatever Aethercore Laziel was hiding, it wasn't just powerful. It was something he didn't want anyone to see.

"Is she . . .?" Godric asked as Lynnafer lay there, fog settling.

"No, she's fine," Marcella said, biting her nails now. "Or alive."

Lynnafer lifted an arm as the healers rushed the battlefield to help her off. Murmurs from the crowd rippled outward. Some students in the Veilchamber alongside Callum whispered, others looked at one another with wide eyes as Laziel walked casually to the Crimson Sigil's Veilchamber and stepped into the rippling wall.

Callum's jaw tightened. He'd known the man was dangerous, but that had been efficient and fast. *And what kind of aetherbeast does he have?* Callum wondered.

After the tile Laziel had disrupted was repaired, the field was reset. Princess Selene stepped out next from a private Veilchamber, the woman in silver-trimmed armor with the Morninglade crest on her chest. Her bear appeared with her, Ecaris calm, composed, and towering.

<She revealed it early,> Fen told Callum.

<Perhaps they already know what she has and it's a show of force.>

<Ah, that would make sense, especially with Ecaris, who looks larger every time I see her.>

The Crimson Sigil's Veilchamber shimmered open, and Sorcha emerged in full dueling gear, her expression unreadable, jaw clenched tight. The woman with the pacted aetherpython moved with coiled precision, every step deliberate as she crossed the arena floor. She came to a stop across from Princess Selene, who waited in regal silence, one hand resting lightly on her trident.

For a moment, the arena held its breath.

Then the signal rang out.

The ground quaked as Selene advanced, aetherbear melding instantly. She moved like a storm given form, each step carving divots into tiles as they morphed into a sandy beach. The crowd barely had time to register the motion before the two opponents collided.

Sorcha reacted fast, her python slithering up and over her shoulders in a blur of iridescent scales. It lunged with a snapping hiss, jaws wide and glowing with poisonous sheen. But Selene didn't flinch. She shifted her stance, unmelded, and drove her Weaponcore trident forward. Ecaris crashed through the snake's path a heartbeat later, swatting the aetherbeast aside with a shoulder that hit like a battering ram.

Selene pressed the advantage, weaving between strikes with elegant brutality. Every motion was honed, controlled. Ecaris circled behind Sorcha, cutting off any retreat while Selene handled the front. The python tried to rejoin the fight, but a single roar from the bear sent it skidding backward in a daze of disrupted mana.

The match ended in less than a minute.

Sorcha raised her arm to defend, and Selene swept her trident in a blazing arc, shattering her Armorcore and dropping her to the sand in a burst of cascading light. The silence that followed was broken by a thunderous cheer from the crowd.

Selene stood still in the center of it all, her chest rising with quiet intensity, gaze already turned away from her opponent as the medics approached. She didn't look to the stands. She didn't raise her weapon. She simply pivoted and walked off the field as if nothing had happened.

To Callum, that made it more intimidating than any victory celebration ever could.

Godric lost his bout just after midday, though not without a valiant effort. His opponent—a Crimson Sigil bruiser with a pacted aetherowl—had outpaced him with speed Callum didn't expect. The match ended when Godric was cornered at the edge of a terrain cliff, blasted down into a trench of summoned water.

Marcella, by contrast, won her next match.

Her opponent had wielded a demonic aetherturtle, a behemoth with iron-shell armor and glowing symbols running down its neck. Its defense had been nearly impenetrable, and for a while, the match had turned into a waiting game of attrition.

But Marcella had played it smart.

She used her Froststag Powercore to crack a seam in the Crimson's turtle-based Armorcore, then jammed her Life Blade of the Spring Ferret into the split. The moment the blade sapped enough of its mana, the armor shattered like brittle ice.

Watching her, Callum realized something he hadn't considered before.

The Crimson student had pacted with an aetherturtle, but also used a turtle-themed Armorcore. That synergy made the creature even more effective, more aligned. Fen hadn't said anything about it, but Callum could feel the connection. Like a puzzle clicking into place. *What if I had the same, a fox-aligned Weapon-, Armor-, or even Powercore?*

The thought lingered as he stepped to the wall of the Veilchamber, prepared for his next match.

As Callum entered the arena, the tiles shifted into a battlefield styled after the storm-wrecked cliffs of the northern coastline. Wind howled through broken rocks and Callum could even taste salt in the air as he activated his Brightflame Armorcore.

Once again, he reached for two Might Shards, feeling the familiar surge build in his limbs.

His Crimson opponent stepped into place across from him—a compact man with a shaved head and a long scar that traced from the corner of his eyebrow down past his ear. He moved with unsettling calm, sinking into a low stance, each motion measured, deliberate. Narrow shoulders, no real bulk to speak of, but something about the way he carried himself set Callum on edge.

Maybe I should add something else, Callum thought, already reaching for a Deftness Shard, then a Vigor. *Just in case.*

The fight started fast. Before Callum could move, he was airborne—thrown sideways without warning.

"What—?" he gasped, scrambling to stabilize himself.

<*Death Affinity mana!*> Fen snapped. <*He's not using force—he's affecting your body directly. Your nerves. Your bones. He has you on a string.*>

A string? Callum gritted his teeth and countered by summoning the Roots of the Willow Aethertree. Magic vines burst upward, wrapping around the enemy's ankles, throwing him off balance and nearly off the side of a cliff.

Callum reset his stance and breath, only to be struck by a shriek that seemed to come from all around him. He swiveled to find a demonic aetherscorpion, half-hidden behind one of the jagged stones. It lunged forward; Callum didn't move fast enough as a translucent stinger plunged directly into the center of his forehead.

No pain. Just pressure—a crushing force that folded in from all sides, swallowing sound, breath, thought. The world flickered out, and for an instant, Callum floated in a void where gravity meant nothing and time unspooled.

Did I lose? The thought came unmoored, drifting.

Then the world snapped back.

Flame and shadow reared up around him, the air thick with smoke and searing heat. He stood on scorched stone beneath a sky torn in half by firelight and falling stars. The roar of battle hit him like a tidal wave. Screams. Steel. Mana splitting the air like thunder.

And beside him—impossibly, undeniably—stood the Demonslayer.

"Now is our chance, lads! Go!" the legend bellowed, his voice crashing through the chaos.

He pointed toward the horizon, where demonic aetherbeasts writhed through the smoke. Around him, archmages surged forward, casting spells with desperate speed. Magic flared in every color, but it was the Demonslayer who commanded the field.

A spectral dragon coiled around him, its translucent form spiraling skyward like a cyclone of light and fury. The Demonslayer leaped, propelled by raw will and roaring magic, straight into the maw of a winged monstrosity descending from the clouds.

He struck it midair. Clawed hands tore into the beast's hide, ripping wings from its frame as the creature shrieked and disintegrated in a blast of scorched mana.

Callum stood frozen, the heat on his face, the weight of the illusion settling like armor on his shoulders.

This wasn't just any moment. This was the final battle.

And he was inside it.

The realization struck Callum as he watched the battle playout.

This isn't just an illusion . . . it's . . . it's a memory!

A hallucination. Real and unreal.

Callum turned just as a massive wolf thundered past him, coat static with magic. A gryphon swooped down from the clouds and latched onto a demonic aetherbeast, the two tumbling into a boulder.

"What are you waiting for, lad?" The Demonslayer called down to him. "Fate waits for no man!"

Callum summoned his wind sword and rushed into the fight. The blade shrieked with mana as he swung, arcs of compressed air slicing through the first demonic aetherbeast before it even turned. Black ichor sprayed as its limbs hit the ground, already dissolving.

Another lunged from the side. Callum pivoted low, driving the blade up through its underbelly in a burst of wind and light. The strike didn't just wound, it scattered the thing, breaking its corrupted form into flailing fragments that crumbled before they hit the earth.

It didn't matter how many came for him.

Callum surged forward, riding the storm that bloomed in his chest. Zephyr Strike cracked the air as he launched from one beast to the next, every movement honed, every blow laced with fury. For once, he wasn't surviving, he was *clearing* the field.

Callum looked up and saw the Demon King looming in the sky, the man draped in his infamous Bloodwoven Regalia, one arm transformed into a monstrous blade, veins pulsing with infernal energy. The yellow eye embedded in the Demon King's arm blinked, and focused on Callum.

It all felt so real.

Is this really what happened? he wondered, as the heat of battle, the roar of allies at his back, steeped Callum deeper into a memory he never lived.

<*Callum!*> Fen's voice tore through the illusion. <*It's not real! You've been stung. Pull it out! He's breaking you down from the inside!*>

Callum's breath caught. He looked down at his arms and, in that moment of clarity, he was finally able to break free.

He felt it. The weight of the thing latched onto him. A crawling pressure pressed against his skull, as if something heavy had anchored itself there, siphoning pieces of him away.

The scorpion's translucent stinger was still embedded in his forehead.

Callum hit the ground hard. The arena rushed back into focus—stone beneath him, blood in his mouth, mana burning hot through every limb.

Across the field, his opponent stood frozen, eyes wide with disbelief.

Callum didn't wait. He summoned the Piercing Air Spear into his hand, the weapon humming with pressure. And then he charged.

CHAPTER 26

Some say the eyes turn red to see the world as the Demoncore does. Others say it's not about vision at all, but about what the soul has begun to reflect.

—Hesa Sharron, Duchess of Ridgebarrow
and famed orator

Callum's breath came in ragged bursts, teeth clenched as he sprinted toward the Crimson student bound to the aetherscorpion, the same beast that had slipped into his mind and nearly broken him.

The scorpion struck at him again, its barbed tail a blur of venomous light as it skittered to the right. Callum pivoted hard, the stinger slicing through the air just inches from his face. The heat of it burned past him, close enough to raise the hairs on his neck.

He didn't slow.

Driving forward, Callum gathered every shred of speed and force he had from his meldform and channeled it into the Piercing Air Spear. He lunged and slammed the tip of his spear into his opponent's chest with brutal precision.

The Crimson duelist staggered as his Armorcore cracked down the center, the weakened core giving way in a blast of shattering light. Jagged ribbons of magic flared outward, snapping through the air.

The spear didn't stop.

It punched through the remnants of protection, carrying the force of Callum's fury straight through his opponent's stance. Callum held the man there, impaled and trembling, the spear's shaft still pressed against the ruined remains of his Armorcore and pushing in deeper. For one breathless instant, the battlefield froze. The scorpion hissed once, then recoiled, like its Aethercore had been severed.

Then the crowd from New Albion erupted. The roar came over the arena like a tidal wave. Across the stands, Crimson Sigil students—so often cold, composed, superior—shifted. Some stood. Others leaned in, lips moving, whispering furiously at the weight of what they were witnessing.

Callum stared into his opponent's eyes for one final second, saw the flicker of consciousness, the fear, the stunned realization. Then he ripped the spear free, blood trailing its tip as he tossed his opponent aside like refuse. The Crimson student hit the ground hard and didn't move.

The silence that followed was almost louder than the cheers.

Healers, the ends of their white overcoats trailing behind them, rushed the field, life magic already swirling from their hands.

Feeling savage and angry for some reason he couldn't quite place, Callum turned away before they carried his opponent off. He stormed through the cheers of the crowd and stepped into the Veilchamber again, the crowd's buzz dimming as the door closed behind him.

"Brutal," Marcella said, waiting in the shade of the stone arch. "But awesome. I thought you were going to push the spear all the way through." She paused as she registered the blank expression on Callum's face. "You . . . you weren't, right?"

Callum didn't answer the question. "I should have used an Empowerment of Mind Shard; it would have helped me with the psychological attack."

"Easy to say after the fact," she told him, still watching Callum cautiously. "I don't know what he was doing to you—"

"A vision trap; a distorted memory. How long did it last?"

"For a good minute," she replied. "You were standing there motionless like a statue. He tried to strike, but your Armorcore kept producing its wings to protect you."

This came as a revelation. "Really?" he asked, finally turning to her.

<*That would be my doing,*> Fen told Callum. <*I had some control; I tried to protect you and break you free from the illusion.*>

<*Thank you.*>

"Then *boom*," Marcella said, unaware of the conversation playing out in Callum's head. "You snapped out of it and ran your spear through his chest. Like right through. I honestly thought you killed him there for a minute. Pretty sure you shocked half the arena with that little move. But you know what?"

"Yeah?" he asked, not sure of what to think.

"They have had it coming for some time and I don't think it's going too far to say that this should be a lesson to them and their little flame pamphlet, whatever it's called. Valestra came to play."

Callum shook his head and moved to the fountain as the students around him all spoke quietly to themselves, murmuring about the Stross heir. Light flowed into him as Marcella continued to speak, replenishing his Mana Reserves. Even with the boost in energy, his thoughts still felt scattered. He couldn't quite shake the haze of that false battlefield, the memory of the Demonslayer's voice—of a time that wasn't his.

Callum barely registered the next match. Or the one after that, even though he should have been paying attention.

Draven entered the arena, squaring off against Victrin Righexa, yet Callum couldn't focus. He tried to watch, tried to care, but his thoughts kept slipping away, scattered by adrenaline and the aftermath of the powerful illusion he had just experienced.

I was right there with the Demonslayer, he thought. *Killeas was there as well, Rata too . . .* An image of the Demon King himself came to Callum and his weapon with the yellow eye on it. *What if I had tried to do something? What would have happened?*

By the time the fight ended, the crowd was already reacting. Draven was walking back to his private Veilchamber, victorious.

<*He won,*> Fen said quietly, the only one between them still paying attention. <*And you need to get it together. That stinger did more than mess with your vision. It rattled your senses.*>

<*I know, I know,*> Callum whispered. <*I'm trying. Maybe this will help.*>

He sat near the wall of the Veilchamber and cycled his mana. Slowly. Deliberately. Feeling each breath, each loop through his core. The edges of the false memory began to smooth, though the residue of it lingered.

Another match passed in a blur, and then Marcella's name was called.

"You've got this," Callum told her.

"For Quinn," she said, her voice steady as she stepped past him.

Callum walked with her to the edge of the Veilchamber, his racing heartbeat and rattled mind finally settled. He watched as the battlefield took shape—circular, flat, stripped of cover. Eerily open. It reminded him of a dueling ring used for executions, not trials.

When her opponent materialized, Callum's gut clenched.

Laziel.

Calm. Composed. The Crimson man stood with his hands folded before him, serene as a monk, his eyes half lidded as if already bored. No stance, no summons, no visible preparation, only quiet anticipation.

The signal sounded.

Marcella wasted no time. Her wings flared wide, antlered Weaponcore blazing with stored momentum. Mana rippled along her limbs as she shot forward, preparing to take the air.

But she never left the ground.

Something lashed out from the fog at the edge of the arena—a blur thick and coiling, like a tentacle or a monstrous serpent's tail. It wrapped around her waist mid-leap and yanked Marcella from the sky, slamming her into the stone floor hard enough to send fragments of tile spraying in every direction.

The crowd gasped.

Marcella let out a breathless cry, her body twisting in pain as she struggled to rise, but she never got the chance.

Laziel was already there.

He moved like water, no wasted effort. One strike to her shoulder with his bare fist and another to her chest. Callum heard the crack from where he stood. Marcella dropped without a sound, her limbs twitching once before going still.

Healers rushed the field. They knelt beside her, checking for consciousness, calling for stretchers. Callum saw Marcella's eyes flutter once before they rolled back. She didn't even hear the boos erupting from the New Albion stands, or the gleeful stomping from the Crimson Sigil students pounding their fists in mock applause.

For a moment, Callum couldn't breathe. He stood frozen, fists clenched, vision tunneling as Laziel calmly turned and walked away, his robes unwrinkled, his expression unchanged. Not even a glance back.

"Next round," Callum told Fen, voice low and flat as Marcella finally showed signs of life. "Laziel. Or Ryven. I don't care which. One of them is mine."

It came time for Callum's final match of the day.

The wall of the Veilchamber dissolved into light, and he stepped through, boots meeting sand and stone. The arena terrain lay quiet. Callum knew it could shift mid-match, but at the moment, it rested in its neutral state, the tiles flat and gleaming.

He looked toward the Crimson Sigil's Veilchamber, expecting his opponent to emerge from their ranks.

But nothing happened.

Instead, one of the private Veilchambers on the far side of the arena hissed open. Callum's breath caught as Draven stepped out onto the battlefield, shadow clinging to his frame. The warlock's crimson eyes burned brighter than ever, feral and cocky. His wings flared, longer now, broader than before, the mist trailing from his feathers dripping with corrupted magic.

It was a show of force, pure spectacle, exactly the kind of entrance Draven always used to remind everyone who he *thought* he was.

As the warlock approached, Callum activated his final two Might Shards, and another each of Vigor, Deftness, and Regeneration shards.

"Stross," Draven said, voice silk-wrapped venom as he took his place across from Callum. "Shame it took this long. I was beginning to think you'd fall before we ever met."

Callum stepped onto the field without answering. His Pangolin Armorcore ignited in bands of light, bracing his limbs with coiled mana plates as Fen's presence swelled inside him, steadying.

<*He's changed,*> Callum said silently to Fen.

<*That's no normal evolution. Those eyes . . . those wings . . . It has to be Death Affinity mana. Be careful.*>

The signal to start the fight was given and the tiles below them shifted with a grinding growl, polished stone giving way to ice. Snow howled in from a conjured wind, instantly dousing the arena in white as crystalline frost crawled across the ground, layering in sharp webs as the temperature plummeted.

Draven cursed as his wings were caught an icy crosscurrent. He tumbled into a snowbank, shards of ice splintering around him as he flipped one and landed on his side.

Callum moved fast downhill, each step cushioned by compacted snow. Wind tore past his ears. The cold bit into his face but he didn't slow.

He reached Draven just as the warlock twisted to his feet, rolling through the snow with practiced ease. In one smooth motion, Draven conjured a sword of writhing black mist, the blade hissing and shifting like it was alive. Shadows riled its edges, distorting the air around it.

<*Empowerment of Blightwing,*> Fen said. <*That has to be his new power. Selene called it a projectile sword that can poison you! Hurry!*>

<*On it!*> Callum brought his wind sword up to block Draven's strike before he could loose the weapon, their blades crashing together in a burst of pressure that kicked snow into the air.

"Farmboy!" Draven said through gritted teeth, his eyes blazing red.

The terrain shifted again, the chill giving way to an intense warmth. Sand poured like a tidal wave over the battlefield as the tundra cracked and bled gold beneath them. Desert heat rushed in, dry and sharp. Callum stumbled back just in time to see Draven flying at him full force.

Mana exploded from the warlock's eyes—a focused crimson beam of dark energy.

Callum caught the brunt of it with his pangolin vambrace-shield. The blast hit like a bolt of divine rage, shattering the hardened mana-plate in a single, thunderous impact.

He staggered, recovered, and leaped toward Draven as the warlock released a mist of violet-black fog.

<*Left! He's to your left!*> Fen cried.

Callum pivoted but it was too late.

Draven was already upon him, his palm pressed flat against Callum's chest as a pulse of dark mana surged outward—thick, soul-warping, impossible to block. It unraveled, the magic bypassing flesh and armor, striking something deeper, twisting into the core of his Soul Heart.

Callum dropped to one knee, choking on air that no longer reached his lungs. His armor shuddered, pangolin shards peeling off his shoulders in flakes of shattered mana.

Seconds later and Draven loomed above, his blackened sword humming with Corruption. "This is what they cheer for?" he spat. "A legacy built on backwater dirt and blind luck? You're nothing, farmboy!"

Callum's fingers twitched.

Before Draven could bring the blade down, Callum's hand shot forward. Mana surged as he conjured the Sunsteel Ram sword, but keeping it whole, forging a single gleaming edge.

He drove upward with all he had left, blade clashing against blade, the shockwave snapping through the air.

The warlock staggered back a step.

Callum rose, breath ragged, blood running in a hot line down his ribs. Ignoring the pain, he split the Ram blade into two and moved.

Draven raised his hand again, dark energy building behind his eyes—but Callum was already there. A feint. A twist. Then both blades tore across Draven's chest in a full-force cross-slash, one radiant, one sharp enough to cut shadow itself.

The impact burst outward, dark mana exploding in a wave of shrieks and whispers. Draven's sword flew from his grip and vanished. The warlock dropped to one knee, eyes wide with disbelief before he collapsed to the arena floor.

Callum stood over him, chest rising and falling, dust curling around his boots in tight spirals as silence gripped the arena.

Then the crowd erupted, cheers crashing down like a tide.

Callum didn't react at first. He let out a slow breath then turned his back on the fallen warlock and walked toward the Veilchamber.

It was over, for now.

CHAPTER 27

The Archive of Destiny predates the walls that house it. Every stone of the Great Library was laid with the crystal in place. Every renovation since has been made with that same silent permission. You don't move the Archive of Destiny; you just apologize to it and design your floor plan accordingly.

—Architect Talan Merund, during the planning
of the Great Library renovation, Year 487

That night, Callum sat cross-legged on the floor of his dorm room, his right palm pressed to his chest as he cycled the day's turbulence into something steadier. Mana moved slowly through him, no longer wild, no longer burning.

The room around him seemed stiller than usual, dim and unmoving. The only light came from the soft orange glow filtering through the narrow window slats, casting long shadows across the floor. Beyond his door, the rest of the dormitory was quiet—too quiet. All the other students had lost their matches and a sense of defeat lingered in the air, heavy and unspoken.

Marcella was fine. He'd seen her after the duel, awake and grumbling under the care of the healers. Quinn had found them both in the aftermath, bruised but grinning. Seeing them safe had taken some of the weight off Callum's shoulders. Not all, but enough.

Outside, a footstep broke the quiet.

Then came a knock—three precise taps, spaced evenly apart.

Callum blinked once, then rose. He crossed the room in a few strides and cracked the door, already knowing who it would be.

"Hey—"

Selene slipped in without a word, pushing past him, the princess cloaked in a layer of robes too fine to be mistaken for a common student.

She pulled the hood back, strands of her golden hair spilling free. Even like this, disguised and subdued, she carried a presence. Yet she didn't act like royalty, not in the way her shoulders relaxed, nor in the way she stood there for a moment, her expression one of utter relief upon seeing him.

"I wanted to come to you," Callum said instinctively, before catching himself. "I mean, I wanted to check in after, but we were told not to leave our rooms tonight."

"Too many eyes from the Geshwine delegation are still on campus. Most are gone now. Only a few remain. I was only able to slip out because Sir Trindade escorted me." She gave a small shrug. "He's downstairs. I told him I needed a moment."

Without waiting, she made her way to Callum's bed and sat, shifting her weight until she found a relaxed posture, legs angled, one arm braced behind her. Selene leaned back slightly, sighing like someone who'd been walking all day and had finally stopped pretending they weren't tired. "It's dark in here, Callum."

"I was cycling," he said as he lit a candle. A warm glow unfurled across the walls, Selene squinting for a moment as her eyes adjusted. The light caught on her face just enough for him to see a trace of fatigue.

"It's up to us now," she said softly, a hint of melancholy in her voice.

"What do you mean?"

She met his gaze. "You and me; Ryven and Laziel. We're the only ones advancing to the final round."

He sat down across from her. "Right, that." Callum let out a quick breath. "And I still don't know what Laziel is pacted with."

"Laziel? Easy. Well, not easy, but you know what I mean. He's pacted with a Cinder Mammoth," Selene said. "Volcanic-born. From the far western Badlands, past the mountains. It's corrupted, like most of theirs."

"Is that all he has?"

She gave a small shake of her head. "I'm not sure, and neither are my people. We know that he's a Wielder, but I haven't been able to uncover if he has a second Aethercore. Regardless, you need another."

"What about you?"

"Don't worry about me. I'm here to talk about you."

"I need to find Killeas," Callum said quietly. "But the only lead I have is what Sir Trindade told me. You remember."

"And? Nothing else? You haven't checked the Great Library?"

"Not yet, not with the tournament. What I really need is to visit the Archive of Destiny."

Selene tilted her head. "Why?"

Callum looked toward the window, where the pair of Crimson airships still hovered faintly in the distance, low on the horizon. "The Demonslayer left a construct there. It helped me once. It's how I got the Empowerment of Rejuvenation Powercore."

Selene absorbed this. "So what are you waiting for?"

"I already told you, there's been little time since the tournament started. And the campus is locked-down tonight."

"Right," she said. "About that. I could . . ." Something devious splashed across her eyes. "I could probably get you there. But that would draw attention to me."

"Because of Sir Trindade."

"Exactly."

"So . . . ?"

She finally grinned. "Easy. We smuggle you out."

Fen appeared in a flash. "Smuggle? Good evening, Your Highness, you performed well today. Better than well. Pleasantries aside, I don't know if smuggling is possible." He jumped to the window. "I suppose we could sneak down the side of the building here, but it could be risky, and I don't have wings, you know."

"You're not going to need wings for what I have in mind."

"Oh?" Fen asked her.

"Yes. There are Legion Guard stationed all over the campus. I'll have them deliver you to the Great Library."

"Deliver?" Callum stared at her. "What do you mean?"

"Yes, deliver. In a crate. It's a great idea, trust me. They're lifting movement restrictions tomorrow, and if you can visit the Archive now, that means you can get a headstart."

"What kind of crate?" Callum asked her.

"A wooden one. Unless you prefer a large treasure chest. Or a coffin. I suppose I could arrange that as well. Should it be padded? I'm joking, Callum, a wooden crate. They'll drop you off, you can head to the Archive of Destiny, and they'll return you to your dorm once you are finished. All kidding aside, you don't know how long it'll take to find Killeas. You need him, and we only have a few days until the finals."

"Tonight?" Callum asked.

"Yes, right now. In an hour or less."

He rubbed his face. "And tomorrow?"

"Tomorrow," she said calmly, "you wrap up anything that needs wrapping up here and head to Weatherby to begin your journey."

"Why Weatherby?" Callum asked. "I thought I'd portal to Devonshire and go from there if we're talking about the Steppe."

"To see your father."

He straightened at the mention of Rhane. "W-w-what does he have to do with any of this?"

The princess eyed him curiously. "Don't you miss him?"

"Of course, I do. But what does . . ." He bit his lip.

"It's a good gesture, think of it like that," Selene said firmly. "Don't make me order you to go. You can travel to the Western Barren Steppe from there. There's a caravan that heads toward the Lands of Grimbald. It passes Devonshire, you know."

"I know, I'm from there," Callum said, almost defensively.

She stood, pulling her hood back up. "Good, then I don't need to have a map drawn for you. Visiting your father is important, especially now. Especially with this tournament, your place in it, and what it means for our kingdom. Surely you would like to tell him about it."

"I was going to send a letter, but you're right, if possible, I should visit."

Fen hopped down and approached the bed. "Why do I get the feeling that there is more to this than you are letting on?" he asked as he looked up at her.

"Because there always is." The princess placed her hood over her head. "Now stay here. I'll have the crate delivered soon."

As a boy, Callum had imagined all sorts of covert missions while playing in the fields near the farm. A stick for a sword, mud on his face, darting between hay bales and pretending they were enemy watchtowers—that was a boy's life on a farm. He'd sneak through rows of wheat like they were shadowy war camps or scramble up the side of the crumbling stone fence pretending it was a castle wall. In his head, he was always slipping past guards under cover of night, a hood drawn low, his mission vital to the fate of the realm.

He hadn't, however, not even once, pictured being stuffed into a crate like stolen cargo.

<*Definitely a tight fit,*> he told Fen as the smell of oiled wood and stale breath came to him. His knees were jammed beneath his chin, his back pressed flat against a knot in the crate wall that refused to stop digging into his spine.

<*We should have gone the sneaking fox route, but it appears you'll do anything to appease the princess,*> Fen said dryly.

Callum rolled his shoulder to get the blood flowing. Cramped wasn't the right word; he could barely shift without bumping wood, and every movement sent a fresh ache down his spine.

A faint light shifted behind the crate's slats. He felt the pivot in the rhythm of the guards' steps, followed by a subtle tilt in the crate itself. The sound changed too, no longer the muffled echo of open hallways, but something tighter. Stone underfoot, but more hollow now.

It lasted for a good ten minutes.

This is brutal, he thought as sweat clung to his neck despite the chill creeping in. His legs were numb, his left foot fully asleep, and he couldn't tell if the thudding in his chest was nerves or claustrophobia.

Finally, the air cooled.

"Special delivery," said one of the Legion Guards. His tone was professional, but edged with boredom, like this wasn't even the strangest thing he'd done that day. "Authorized escort on Her Royal Highness's orders due to the campus lockdown."

"Crate?" a woman asked, her voice flat with disbelief, as if she'd just been pulled out of a particularly interesting passage.

"Yes, milady. With a student inside. Callum Stross."

There was a pause. Paper rustled. A ceramic cup clinked softly as it was set down with more force than necessary. "Do what, now?"

"We'll go ahead and open it up."

A long, weary sigh. "Very well," she said.

Moments later, the crate tilted, descended, and landed with a dull *thunk* on polished stone. The lid creaked open, and light poured in, stabbing straight into Callum's face. He squinted up from his cramped position he had settled in, blinking as a robed figure leaned into view.

"Ah. Callum Stross," the librarian said, without a shred of emotion. "One of today's champions."

"Good . . . evening." He unfolded from the box like a newborn deer. Fen chuckled somewhere inside him.

"Welcome, I suppose. This is very unorthodox, you know," she told the two Legion Guards, who didn't seem to care. "And why, may I ask, have you been delivered here in a crate?"

"Archive of Destiny," Callum told her as he rubbed the back of his neck.

"Well, then, you know the way," she motioned to the spiral staircase, a disturbed look on her face. "And careful down there. The assistants have returned to their dorms for the day."

Callum moved deeper into the Great Library, passing shelves that stretched from floor to vaulted ceiling, each one crammed with ancient tomes and dust-laced scrolls. For once, the space was empty. No murmuring students, no soft footfalls between aisles.

Silence pressed in around him, thick and absolute. Only the steady hum of a magical lamp above the spiraling central staircase broke the stillness, casting long, curved shadows across the recently polished stone floor.

He started down, floor after floor until he reached the basement, where he entered a chamber he remembered all too well.

The Archive of Destiny stood at its center, unchanged and unmoved. The massive mana shard pulsed faintly, runes scrawled across its faceted surface in ancient, burning script. It sat on a gold-etched pedestal that gleamed softly, its size, yet again, surprising him.

He paused for a moment to take it in. "Wow."

<Impressive every time,> Fen said in agreement.

Callum approached, then paused. He didn't reach for it, aware that doing so had forced him to pass out the last time around. Instead, he found the wooden bin tucked near the far wall and retrieved one of the meditation pillows. It was lumpy and slightly uneven, but better than nothing.

He carried it to the base of the shard and lowered himself into a seated position, folding his legs beneath him. For a long moment, he just sat there, watching the light spiral within the crystal, letting its glow wash over him like sun through water as he slowly transitioned off the pillow, so it was now beneath his head.

Light filled his vision. Warm at first—then searing.

In an instant, Callum was pulled elsewhere, the floor vanishing, the air breaking thin.

He floated. Or maybe stood. It was impossible to tell in the silence of the void.

Space folded in on itself, starless and endless, painted in hues that didn't exist in the real world. Time seemed to stretch as mist coiled into being, slowly at first, then faster. It circled him, tightening into a spiral, condensing. Shapes flickered in the haze, shadows of battles long past, shards of memories both his and not.

Then the mist snapped into place and a figure formed.

The Demonslayer . . .

The construct stood tall in the shifting light armor, gleaming like freshly forged steel, edges sharp with purpose. His expression was hidden but the weight of his gaze pressed into Callum's chest, radiating presence and power.

"You've returned," the Demonslayer said, his voice low, steady, and impossibly old. It sent a chill down Callum's spine. "Stronger than before."

Fen appeared. "He has grown much stronger, and at a time when strength looks to be increasingly necessary."

The Demonslayer looked Callum over. "I can see that. What has happened? Both of you seem . . . disturbed."

"The Geshwine Empire has brought their airships to campus under the guise of a tournament between the Great College and the Crimson Sigil," Fen said. "It's supposed to be for unity, games meant to bring the two kingdoms closer, but it all feels wrong. We have made it to the final round."

"You have?" the Demonslayer asked Callum. "Impressive."

"Yes," Callum said. "Along with Princess Selene and two of the Crimson Sigil's most powerful warlocks."

"But it's more than that," Fen told the Demonslayer. "Something is coming, and I know I'm not the only one that feels it."

Callum stepped forward. "We're here seeking your guidance because I need another pact. I need to find Killeas."

"The Gryphon Vanguard of Fates?" The construct asked after a long pause. "And you think you're ready?"

"I don't think I have a choice."

The Demonslayer loomed over Callum for a breath, as if measuring more than just strength. "Then listen closely. I might know a way you can find him."

CHAPTER 28

The Circle Masters hold no formal power under the Crown, yet their consensus determines the Soul Pythia. Their deliberations are closed, their authority presumed divine. The High Council considers them diplomatically sensitive.

—Classified addendum to *Valestra Governance and Magical Institutions*, Volume III

Callum now knew how to find the mausoleum, but he was going to need some Fire Affinity Shards to make it happen. He would have mentioned this to Princess Selene, but she wasn't there when he took the spiral staircase to the top of the Great Library. He found the librarian working on her notes again and the two Legion Guards obediently waiting.

"Back in the crate?" he asked the guards, who merely grunted a response.

Callum climbed back into the crate, and soon, following another strange and slightly excruciating journey that dragged longer than it should have, he was delivered back to his dormitory.

Once he was out, he started to thank the Legion Guards—but they looked thoroughly unimpressed with their assignment. One of them grunted, the other waved him off without a word.

"Fire Affinity," Callum said once he was in his room.

Fen unmelded and hopped onto the windowsill. "Ask around? Visit the Emporium and trade some Empowerments?"

"That, or I take a job. It just depends on when the lockdown ends."

Fen laughed. "You won't need to take a job. I'm sure Quinn or Marcella can spare some. Besides, they look like they could use some cheering up after their losses."

"They do, they really do." Callum dropped onto his bed, the same place Selene had sat when she came into his room. It felt like hours ago; he didn't know how much time had passed while he spoke to the Demonslayer's construct.

"Let's just see what the morning brings," Fen said as he moved into a relaxed position, his tail curled around him.

"Good call."

The next morning arrived with the announcement everyone had been waiting for—movement restrictions had been lifted. The official word had everyone buzzing, even though the campus had only been locked-down for one night.

Not what I expected, Callum thought as he entered the closest mess hall, which hummed with low conversation and restless movement.

The tournament wasn't over yet, but for most of the students inside, the real stakes had passed. There was a strange sort of quiet in the air—half relief, half bitterness. Only four contenders remained and only two of them were from New Albion.

Callum found Quinn and Marcella seated at their usual table, each staring blankly at untouched breakfast. Quinn poked at a flaky roll with the slow deliberation of a man in mourning. Marcella sipped her tea like it had personally offended her, the scowl on her face borderline permanent.

"Hey, guys," Callum said, sliding into the seat beside them.

"Callum," Marcella replied without looking at him.

Quinn glared down at his food. "Ryven is a monster. Just . . . *bam*." He clapped his hands for emphasis. "And I was done. It was pathetic. People were laughing."

"No one was laughing," Marcella told him.

"It sure felt like they were."

"That's just in your head."

Callum nodded sympathetically as he recalled his battle with the Crimson student in the Culling Rounds. It really could have gone either way. "Don't worry about it," he told Quinn. "Ryven's no joke and you did the best you could do."

"But you'll deal with him, right?" Quinn asked.

"I'll do my best."

Marcella huffed. "Come on, Demonslayer, Little Cal, you can do better than that. You're supposed to be the archmage in shining Armorcore here."

"Better than my best?" Callum asked her.

She finally locked eyes with him. "I want you to go in there and clean the floor with those Crimsons, Ryven and Laziel. Especially Laziel. But also Ryven, if you can swing it."

"And the princess?" Callum asked. "Where does she play into this?"

"Umm, well, I don't know about that part," she said. "Good luck. That's all I can tell you there. But honestly, if either one of you wins, I'll be happy. Or, at the very least, I'll be avenged. Just not those Crimson—"

A tray clattered to the floor nearby, cutting her off.

They turned. Godric Rush stood stiffly beside the mess, eyes wide, his mouth pinched like he'd bitten something sour. His shoulders hunched as he scrambled to gather bits of egg and toast with a too-small cloth, muttering apologies under his breath.

No one laughed. Lynnafer and Demandra, who had been seated together, moved to help him.

Callum watched until the three disappeared back toward the serving line, Lynnafer with her arm around Godric's shoulders. A silence settled, drawn thin by exhaustion and the weight of everything still ahead. All around, metal scraped, chairs shifted, voices hummed with soft tension, but their table held still.

Callum wiped the last of the yolk from his plate with a crust of bread and leaned forward slightly, elbows on the table. "I need a favor," he said quietly. "Do either of you have a Fire Affinity Shard?"

Marcella raised a brow. "What for?"

"I need to go somewhere."

"That doesn't answer my question."

Callum gave a small, exasperated laugh. "I'm at the Wielder Stage now—"

"That still doesn't answer my question, Callum."

"Look, I need another Aethercore," he said more plainly this time. "And I found the one I want."

Quinn's eyes narrowed in interest. "Really? Where?"

"What does that have to do with Fire Affinity?" Marcella asked.

"I'll get to that," Callum said, turning back to Quinn's question. "I believe Killeas's Aethercore is in the Demonslayer's mausoleum."

Marcella pressed back, expression skeptical. "And you know where it is?"

"I do, or at the very least, I know the mausoleum's general location. The Western Barren Steppe," Callum clarified. "That's where it's hidden, according to Sir Trindade."

"Ooh," Quinn said, disposition brightening. "Now there's a place I've wanted to visit for ages. Wait—" He frowned. "You were inviting us, right?"

"I don't know if I can invite you."

Marcella scoffed. "Of course, you can invite us. Come on, Callum, you're the Stross heir. Not only that, last I checked, we are your best pals. You can do whatever you want. And as for us, we have nothing else to do. Aside from going to our classes. Ugh. But who wants to do that?" She gestured around. "Everyone's moping. We lost the tournament. We're all officially losers." She cupped her hands around her mouth like she was going to say it louder and decided otherwise.

"You aren't losers," Callum told her.

"Just let us have this," Marcella cut in. "A little vacation never hurt anyone."

Callum hesitated. "I don't even know if you can go inside the mausoleum to find the Aethercore," he told her, repeating the words Fen was saying in his head. "But . . ."

"But?" both of them asked, leaning in.

"Fine, yes. Sure. You two can come with me."

Marcella pumped her fist silently to herself. "Good."

"But I'm going to Weatherby first," Callum added.

"To see your dad?" Quinn asked.

"How did you . . . ?" Callum trailed off, brow furrowing. Selene had suggested the detour for more than convenience—she wanted him to see his father. But the fastest route didn't actually require Weatherby. Still, he found himself nodding. "It's a great route. And I should see him."

Marcella reached for a piece of toast. "So . . . when do we leave?"

"Today. Soon now that the campus restrictions have been lifted. I was going to stop by Telluride's place first. He might have some Fire Affinity to spare."

"Right, that was your original request. Don't worry about Fire Affinity," Quinn said easily. "I got you covered. You're not the only one who's been hoarding shards for emergencies."

Callum smiled. "Thanks. I have some Attribute Shards I can trade."

"Keep them, really," Quinn told him. "You never know when they'll come in handy."

Marcella clapped her hands together. "So . . . we go now? Telluride then portal to Weatherby? Get this journey started? How are we portaling to Weatherby again? Should I pack an overnight bag?"

He glanced out the mess hall window in the direction of Princess Selene's private suite. "We'll have to ask Sir Trindade, but I think it'll be fine." Callum pushed away from the table. "Let's go."

Telluride's barn looked the same as ever—half stable, half abandoned apothecary. Near the entrance sat a pile of warped planks, some still studded with bent nails, and a bucket of sand that looked like it had been forgotten mid-task. A recently added wardrobe blocked part of the makeshift kitchen, wedged awkwardly into a space it clearly hadn't been built for.

Callum knocked politely on the doorframe for a second time. When that didn't work, he cleared his throat. "Tell—"

"I told you before," Telluride's voice called from inside, slightly muffled, "if you're here to sunder, I'm busy today! Unless you're a friend, in which case . . . bring tea. Really."

"Give me a moment," Callum told Quinn and Marcella as he stepped inside. He held a wrapped bundle of eggs that he had found outside under one arm, likely a delivery from Florence.

Callum stepped over a tangle of loose rope and around a broken chair whose back legs had given out sometime in the last thirty years and never been repaired. A scorch mark on the floor near the rear wall suggested something hadn't gone well and the air inside the barn smelled faintly of tea leaves and wet wood.

Fen appeared a beat later, leaping up onto a dusty worktable with a yawn. "Telluride, you old fool, how much did you drink last night?"

"Fen? Callum?" Telluride groaned as Callum stepped around an out-of-place wardrobe and found the shardcrafter lying with his back across the table. He sat up, squinted, and smiled. "Sorry, mates. It was my friend's birthday party last night."

"Are you sure it wasn't the night before too?" Fen asked as he hopped onto the table.

"It very well could have been!"

A pail by the door made a loud clanking sound as Quinn came into the barn. "Sorry," he said as he was joined by Marcella, who quickly elbowed him.

Telluride rolled off the table and tightened his robe. He offered them a painful smile as he frantically patted the pockets of his robe for the pipe. "Umm . . ."

"You look . . . alive," Marcella said, eyeing the attempt.

"Barely," Telluride muttered, rubbing his eyes.

"Sit, sit," Callum said, already unwrapping the bundle of eggs. "Let me cook something before you rub your eyebrows off."

"Don't mind if I do." Telluride groaned and lowered himself into a chair near the central table. "Ah, that's better. I should have sat in the first place. Eh. I usually use Life Affinity to clear a hangover, but I'm tapped out."

"I know what to do. Just give me a moment." Callum rummaged around in Telluride's seasoning drawer, which was filled with dried leaves and small tinctures of powder. "Pepperleaf," he said as he smelled the plant. Rather than take the leaves themselves, he broke the dry stems and was soon sizzling them in butter.

"What are you making over there?" Marcella asked, sniffing the air. "It smells . . ." She thought for a moment. "It smells."

"Eggs and pepperleaf stems. Clears your head quick," Callum said as he kept stirring the stems through the butter.

"So I've heard. And a clear head . . . I could use that," Telluride said as he leaned back and fluttered his eyes. "Rough night."

"It works, trust me," Callum replied, cracking an egg into a pan with practiced ease. "The eggs are from Florence, by the way."

"Oh, don't say that. Now I'm going to owe her again," Telluride said. He turned toward Marcella and Quinn. "So? I'm guessing the tournament's gone sideways for almost everyone."

"What makes you think that?" Quinn asked.

"I heard the people at the pub talking about it last night."

Marcella gave Telluride a wry nod. "We lost. The Crimson Sigil's Ryven and Laziel are in the finals, along with Callum and Princess Selene."

The shardcrafter puffed his cheeks out as he once again fished around in his pockets for his pipe. "Where did I leave that blasted thing? I guess it doesn't matter," he said. "And I'm sorry to hear you all didn't do as well as you would have liked. Warlocks are tricky. They're also bastards."

Callum brought the plate over and slid it in front of the shardcrafter. "Eat this."

Telluride grunted, poked at the eggs with his fork, and took a bite. "Mmm. That's good. You could run a tavern with this. Get them drunk at night, cure their hangovers in the morning."

"I'll keep that in mind if I survive the next few days."

"What's happening?" Telluride asked, pausing mid-chew. "They said the finals aren't for another few days."

"Killeas," Callum said. "That's what's happening."

"You're heading after . . . Killeas?"

"That's the plan."

"Is there a plan?" Telluride asked.

"There is the semblance of a plan," Marcella said with her thumbs up.

"And you all are going with him?" the shardcrafter asked her after finishing his bite.

"We are."

"Part of the way," Callum said.

"Well, don't think you're just going to walk in and pick up a myth. The mausoleum, if you can find it, will prove difficult. How do I know?" Telluride took another bite. "I just know."

"Do you think it's underground?" Quinn asked him.

"There's no telling, but I have been to a similar site once. Let's just say places like that aren't left lying around anymore for a reason. The Soul Pythia and her Circle Masters have made sure of it."

"Circle Masters?" Callum asked.

Quinn perked up. "You don't know about them? The Soul Pythia leads the Circle. Each campus or regional temple has its own Circle Master. Rhea might become one in the future, probably not a Pythia, though. Not that she's not skilled—she is—but it's a vote. A conclave, when the Soul Pythia dies or retires, another is chosen. Mastress Lucerne's not anywhere near retirement."

"Right," Telluride said after another bite. "So long story short: that mausoleum could be packed with unstable magic stitched up tight by Circle Masters that were around nearly five hundred years ago. Not your run-of-the-mill monster-hunting danger, but ancient, volatile, mind-rattling stuff. The kind they don't let loose on purpose. The kind the Demonslayer himself might have ordered sealed away." He burped. "Sorry."

"So . . . like Soul Pythia stuff?" Marcella asked, raising an eyebrow at him.

"Exactly that," Telluride said. "Exactly that. There's a real chance if you make it there, you'll be doing most of the dirty work, or clean work depending on what it is, inside your head. So be ready for anything and . . ." He squinted across the table at Callum and cracked another grin. "Who am I to tell you what you should do? You'll either find Killeas, or you won't. But be ready for a challenge, regardless."

CHAPTER 29

"I took the long way home thinking I'd changed. The gate still creaked the same."

—Phaedra Stoneshield, poet

Callum stepped forward, stopping just short of the wrought-iron gate that marked the entrance to Selene's residential suite. Two Legion Guards stood sentinel on either side, their expressions unreadable, their armor gleaming in the early light.

"Please let Sir Trindade know that we're here," Callum said, his voice steady as he exchanged quick glances with Quinn and Marcella. "We will all be going."

One of the guards gave a noncommittal sound, not quite a grunt but not quite an agreement. Callum couldn't say for certain if they were the same pair who'd carted him across campus in the crate the night before, but their level of enthusiasm felt identical.

With a sharp exhale and a curt hand gesture, the guard turned and led them into a private stone-paved seating area hemmed in by high hedges and warded walls. The space was quiet, the hum of protective enchantments, subtle but ever present. Benches had been carved from white-veined granite, and vines with late-fall orangeblood flowers curled up the western wall.

"Lovely," Quinn said as he took a seat and looked toward a couple of birds that had just landed in a tree. "It really is lovely. I do like a hidden garden."

Marcella laughed. "Of course, you do. In Aveiro, all the gardens are open so they can get all the sunlight they need for the flowers. There are huge communal flower gardens as well."

"I remember," he told her. "It is a lovely place, Aveiro."

About twenty minutes later, long enough for the three to start wondering if they were going to be portaling at all, Sir Trindade stepped through an arched doorway flanked by another set of guards. He gave them each a nod, his gesture making it clear he didn't intend to waste time.

"I can take you to Weatherby," he said. "But to come back, you will need to use the Devonshire portal. That's the nearest open channel to the Western Barren Steppe." He eyed them all warily. "I must say, I will be surprised if you pull this off—not because you aren't capable, the Steppe is just . . . well, you'll see. I wish you the best of luck, however. I do miss the adventures I took when I was a student here."

Sir Trindade handed a small leather pouch to Quinn.

"What's this?" Quinn began.

"There's a Portalstone receiver inside," Trindade told him briskly. "Do not lose it. That piece belongs to the royal family, and there are only a few in existence. This one is Princess Selene's, and she has personally approved of you borrowing it."

"A Portalstone receiver?" Quinn peered into the pouch, eyes curious. "How does it work exactly?"

"Easy," Trindade said. "To activate it, take it out, hold the receiver in your hand, and meld. It will trigger the return portal in front of the Devonshire campus. Once it forms, step through, and you'll exit here. That's it. Well, that's it, and you must return the receiver as soon as you are back on campus."

"So that's how that works," Marcella said. "I've always wondered about that."

"That," Sir Trindade replied, "or the ability to do *this*."

He snapped his fingers with a touch of showmanship and a crackle of energy flared in front of them. The air split open with a sharp hiss as a circular swirl of magic anchored into place rimmed with faint golden runes. Through the portal, the fields of Weatherby stretched out beneath a heavy gray sky.

Callum instantly recognized the lay of the land on the other side of the portal, the rows of tilled fieldstone, a low crest of hills near the far horizon. What surprised him most was the smell—the earthy scent of damp soil drifted through the open rift, immediate and real.

"Well," Trindade said, stepping back, "in you go. And another suggestion: Do not linger in the Western Barren Steppe. If you aren't able to locate Killeas, you can try again after the tournament. The princess wants you to have a second Aethercore, but, as I have explained to her, there is only so much time, and the final Duelist Rounds will begin shortly—with or without you. And one more thing?"

"Yes?" Callum asked, mere seconds from stepping through.

"We *won't* be sending a rescue party, at least not at the moment. Whatever you do, and whatever you encounter, do so smartly. Good luck."

Callum gave Sir Trindade a quick nod, and stepped through. The air changed immediately, cool and quiet in a different way. Not magical hush, but rural silence. Wind stirred the hedges, bringing the scent of turned earth and flowering ivy.

"So this is Weatherby," Marcella said as she stepped beside him. She pulled her overcoat tighter around her shoulders as she looked out across the farmland. "It's very ... rural."

"And flat." Quinn squinted toward the distant hills. "Well, at least until you reach that point."

Callum smiled. The tiredness from the last few days settled somewhere deeper, buried under something warmer. "It is. And my home isn't far from here." He pointed toward a cluster of chimneys peeked up over the tree line. "Come on."

They reached the edge of the Stross property just as the wind picked up, rustling through the line of oaks that framed the road. Leaves skittered across the gravel like small messengers, their colors muted in the gray light. The air smelled of woodsmoke, familiar in a way that hit Callum harder than expected.

He paused for a moment as he took it all in. The old fence still leaned at the same crooked angle, and Callum cursed himself for not fixing it before he left. One of the lantern poles had long since rusted through and lay half-buried in overgrown grass. Another thing he had wanted to handle before his departure. Nothing had changed. Not really.

"Almost there," he said as he led the way, boots crunching on the path that wound toward the front porch. The roof slanted a little more than he remembered, and the window above the kitchen still fogged from the warmth inside.

Callum stopped when the house came into full view. It looked smaller than he remembered. Not physically—he knew every beam, every rusty nail, and weathered panel by heart—but compared to the places he'd seen since joining the Great College, especially some of the mansions in the capital. Compared to them, the home seemed humble in a way that suddenly made him self-conscious.

So far away from the big city . . .

Marcella, turned in place, taking in the landscape with the keen eye of someone who'd grown up in the estates of nobles and still found peace in wild horizons. "It's bucolic, I'll give it that," she finally said. "I like it. I don't know if I'd want to live here, but I certainly would spend a few days here. There's something peaceful about the place. It reminds me of the sea."

"The sea?" Callum asked her.

She motioned to the hills in the distance. "There. That part. I can imagine the way it looks during a sunset."

"Ah, yes," Callum agreed, exhaling a quiet breath.

"And what's that building?" She pointed toward the East Manor, her brow raised.

"You don't want to know," Callum said flatly.

He took a breath and stepped toward the door, hesitating just long enough to realize that bursting in the way he used to would feel wrong now. Disrespectful somehow, and he didn't want to startle his father. He knocked instead.

Marcella laughed behind him. "You always knock?"

"I've never visited like this before," Callum replied as he knocked again, louder this time.

A muffled voice came from the other side. "I'm coming, I'm coming—"

The door creaked open. Rhane Stross stood in the doorway, blinking at the sight in front of him. He looked like he'd just come in from the fields with sleeves rolled to his elbows, tunic dusted with hay and frayed at the cuffs, hair tousled by the wind.

For a moment, he just stared, his brow furrowed.

"What happened to your cloak?" he asked at last, eyes drifting over the crisp, formal overcoat that marked Callum as a student of the Great College.

"My cloak? Father, it's me!" Callum said, half laughing, half exasperated.

Rhane came forward and gave him a firm, chest-thumping hug. "I can see that," he told Callum as he clapped him on the back. "And I can hardly believe it!" He stepped away and squinted at Quinn and Marcella. "You and your friends. All, ahem . . . Great College students. Welcome!"

Marcella offered a courteous bow of her head. "Marcella Faite, of Aveiro."

"Aveiro, huh?" Rhane said, his tone warming with curiosity. "I've only met one person from Aveiro, you know, a dockworker looking to retire to the countryside. I've always wanted to go there. And you?"

"Quinn Vendrick, of many places," said Quinn, who was currently crouched to pet one of the barn cats that had appeared at their feet.

Fen appeared beside them in a shimmer of warm light, stretching with a quiet huff before trotting up the porch steps.

"Ah, there he is, the famous Fen," Rhane said. "You've got quite the reputation around here, you know, even though no one saw you. I suppose that would be my doing. I might have . . ." bragged a little about your appearance and Cal's acceptance to the Great College."

Fen sat up proudly, frightening one of the cats, who scattered toward the barn.

Rhane smiled at all of them again. "Listen, Cal, um, Cal's friends. I'd invite you in but . . ." He looked around sheepishly. "It's a little less tidy than I'd like. Had I known you were coming—"

"It was a bit last minute," Quinn said. "My parents would hate it if I showed up without a two-week notice."

Marcella laughed. "Mine aren't far off."

"Good," Rhane said as he ran his hand through his hair. "In that case, how about we sit on the porch, then? I'll get some tea brewing."

"It's fine, Dad, really—" Callum began, but Rhane had already disappeared back inside.

"Take a seat," he called from somewhere within. "And grab one of the stools from around back. The cats will love the company. I'll only be a moment!"

They settled onto the porch. Quinn took a bench and coaxed another cat into his lap. Marcella pulled over an old stool and sat with her legs crossed while Fen relaxed, his head tucked over his paws.

Callum stayed standing until his father returned with a wide wooden tray balanced in one hand. A stone teapot steamed from the center, its sides engraved with winding patterns of flame and root. Mismatched teacups clinked as he set the tray down.

"So," Rhane said, pouring out the tea with practiced ease. "What brings you three to Weatherby? Aside from visiting me, of course. You're not planning to stay the night, are you?"

"We're heading north on the next caravan," Quinn said. "Toward Devonshire."

"North? Why? Devonshire is abandoned."

"We've got something we need to do for the College, Da," Callum added quickly, not wanting to derail the moment with talk of warlocks and corrupted mammoths. "Just a short detour from Devonshire."

"And where will you stay tonight?" his father asked. "If you wanted to run to town, we could borrow some cots but, the place would need to be swept as well and . . ."

"We'll use an inn somewhere along the way," Quinn assured him. "I have spent a lot of time on the road. There's always a tavern."

"There certainly is between here and Devonshire, which, as you said, son, is just a short detour." Rhane gave Callum a look like he didn't entirely believe that. "Well, I'm glad you're here. I'll say that. I didn't know when I'd see you again." He let out a sigh of relief. "The farm isn't the same without you, but don't let your old man with a touch of melancholy get you. I'm happy. I've taken a more active role in town and things . . . things are going well."

They spoke of Weatherby in the hour that followed, of the late rains and early frost, of the people who had bought Miss Barrowsly's farm and the price of rootwine in town, which had gone down with imports coming in from the Lands of Grimbald. For a while, it felt like nothing had changed.

They drank tea, and even Marcella looked oddly at home.

But as the sun dipped lower, Rhane grew quiet. His cup was half-raised when he finally said, "You're not visiting to talk about Weatherby, drink tea, and simply head on a little trip past Devonshire, are you?"

Callum looked down into his empty cup.

"A lot is going on, sir," Quinn said gently. "But we're doing our part. Your son is, too. New Albion was hit by an aetherstorm recently but it's fine. Some damage. Nothing serious."

"Anything else?" Rhane asked.

The three exchanged glances. "No," Marcella said. "Just classes and excursions, to be expected of First Years at the Great College. A small tournament, but nothing to worry about."

His eyes narrowed slightly, studying them in a way Callum knew too well. Rhane could tell something was off, that there was more to the story, but he didn't press it. "Well, if there are problems, King Morninglade and the High Council will handle them. I'm sure of it. That's what they're there for. Speaking of which, have you met anyone from the royal family?" he asked Callum.

"Actually," Marcella said with a grin, "he's friends with the princess."

Rhane sat up. "You . . . what? *The* princess?"

"And sometimes she visits him late at night," Marcella added cheerfully.

Rhane nearly dropped his cup.

"But not in the way you think," Marcella told him, clearly enjoying the moment. "They're friends. She visits me too. She's our friend, a First Year just like us. That's all."

Rhane leaned back in his rocking chair, letting out a low whistle. "What a world. My son, friends with Princess Morninglade. If this isn't a crazy time to be alive, I don't know what is."

CHAPTER 30

One lantern for the year that fed you; one for the ones you lost; and one for the hope that skies of tomorrow will still be clear.

—Traditional saying about the Harvest Festival, thought to have originated in Devonshire

The tavern smelled like roasted bread with a touch of hearth smoke. Morning light slanted through the warped shutters, catching the steam rising off their breakfast plates—scrambled eggs with wild onions, thick-sliced bread, and a jam Callum swore was closer to wine than fruit. The three had claimed the table near the window, and, for a brief moment, it felt like they weren't travelers headed toward something dangerous. Just students, friends, tired and full.

Quinn had unfolded a map on the table and was scanning it while eating with the focus of someone used to traveling. "So," he said, running a finger down one of the inked roads, "we don't actually get off at Devonshire, just as I suspected."

"What do you mean?" Callum asked.

"The caravan skips it entirely. You were there. It's dangerous near the academy. The closest we get is a trade bridge at the River Brack, along the border of the Lands of Grimbald. Expect shops, a grain mill, a couple of smiths—that's where we disembark."

Marcella leaned over the table, stabbing a sausage with her fork. "And from that point . . . ?" She looked directly at Callum.

"She's right," Quinn told Callum. "You haven't told us how we're finding this mausoleum, exactly."

Callum set his utensils down. "That's why I need the Fire Affinity. I also need some paper. Parchment, sticks, a knife for whittling . . ."

Marcella leaned back, folding her arms. "That explains absolutely nothing. You're getting good at leaving us in suspense, you know."

"To find the mausoleum," Callum said, lowering his voice a touch, "I was told to light a sky lantern and follow it."

"Light a sky lantern with Fire Affinity?" she asked.

"Exactly."

"Why didn't you buy a lantern back in Weatherby?"

"Because I know how to make one," Callum told her. "Harvest Festival is pretty popular in this area."

"That would make sense," Quinn said, his eyes still focused on the map, "considering it is the breadbasket of the kingdom."

Callum continued. "Everyone makes sky lanterns from whatever scraps you can find. Kids compete to see which one can fly the highest."

"Did you ever win?" Marcella asked.

"I never won, but I always came close."

She squinted at him. "And you think you can whip one together in a tavern, an hour before our caravan departs?"

"I'm certain of it," Callum told her. "Like I said, I just need a bit of parchment, some wood, a carving knife, a wick of sorts . . . I was planning on asking now."

Quinn finally looked up from his map and laughed. "This sounds like it'll need some testing."

"It'll be fine," Callum said confidently, rising from the bench.

He crossed the room to the bar, where the tavernkeep, a stocky woman with graying braids and yellow teeth, was wiping down a mug. She looked up as he approached. "Was there something else?"

"You wouldn't happen to have any parchment, would you?" Callum asked. "I could also use a bit of scrap wood and a knife."

She paused mid-swipe and gave him the once-over, like she was trying to decide if he was serious or just sleep-deprived. "What for?"

"A sky lantern."

"You missed the Harvest Celebration by several weeks."

"I know, I'm from Weatherby. It's for something else."

She set the mug down. "Well, if it's not for mischief, and you're from Weatherby, I suppose I've got some supplies in the back that you could use. Wait here." The tavernkeep disappeared through a swinging door, boots thudding on the boards. A moment later, the woman returned with a bundle tucked under her arm. "Parchment scraps, some softened pine slats, and a bit of cotton. There's some tweed twine, and a lid from an old tankard. I figured it would help. As for the knife, just use what I gave you for breakfast. It's sharp enough. There's oil on the table too."

"Thank you."

"Not a problem, deary," she said as she went back to her work.

Callum returned to their table and spread the materials out.

Marcella could barely hide the skepticism on her face. "You're serious about this."

"Watch and learn," he said, excited to prove that this was entirely in his wheelhouse.

Callum trimmed the parchment into four narrow panels, softening each with the back of his knife until the fibers flexed without cracking. He shaved the slats down into thin rods, then tied them into a frame using the twisted tweed thread. Panel by panel, he fastened the parchment to the frame, forming a loose barrel—uneven, but functional.

At the base, he fit a tankard lid as a makeshift shard-plate, securing it with a crisscross of tweed struts that held the structure taut. Callum soaked a twist of cotton in oil and coiled it through the center like a wick. The shard rested just above it, nestled in a shallow groove, ready to flare once lit.

"See?" Callum said, brushing off his hands. "It's not so hard."

"And you're sure it will work?" Quinn asked as Marcella offered him a slow, silent clap.

"I'm certain. I've been doing this all my life." Callum grinned at his two friends. "It's going to work. As to whether it will actually help us find the mausoleum, that's another thing entirely. But the lantern will do its job."

Later that day, the caravan dropped them off at the edge of the River Brack, where a long, arched bridge crossed the pale, rushing current.

Just as Quinn had said, shops clung to the banks of the River Brack, cobbled together in seemingly half-finished structures of sun-bleached stone and creaking wood. A smith's hammer rang in the distance, and the smell of cured meat drifted from a squat smokehouse nearby.

As Callum, Marcella, and Quinn dismounted from the caravan, the other passengers gave them long, sideways glances. One woman muttered something about students losing their way. Another man in a wide-brimmed hat just shook his head and snorted in response.

Marcella turned and offered the group of travelers a sharp smile and a four-finger wave. "We're from the Great College," she said sweetly. "We know what we're doing." She lowered her voice, her eyes darting to Callum. "Please wait until after they're long gone to light the lantern because I'm of the mind to get back on that caravan with them."

"It will work," he assured her again as they stepped away, moving northward into the dry winds of the Steppe, the land beyond wide and unforgiving. Scrubby grass clung to the sandy soil in patches, and twisted trees leaned into the wind like they were trying to escape the ground. The air shimmered with heat despite the season, and the occasional rocky outcrop jutted like old bones from the hills. The deeper they traveled, the more open and haunting the land became.

"It gets lusher closer to the border of the Lands of Grimbald," Quinn said. "When I was a kid, I used to study maps and books about this border. I really don't know why. I always wanted to travel, and it just seemed so far away from New Albion."

"Have you been to Grimbald before?" Callum asked.

"Once. By boat. I headed north to Braga, then took a ship from there. It was faster—only a day and a half to Braga, another two by water. The captain was using Wind Affinity, though," Quinn added, laughing nervously. "Not recommended. Tumultuous is a generous word for it."

Marcella frowned. "This would be much easier on horseback."

"But we can't exactly portal the horses back to the College," Quinn reminded her.

"Or can we?" she said thoughtfully.

"You can fly," Quinn reminded her.

"That's a long way to fly, and I can't carry anyone," Marcella said as they came over a low hill, the expanse beyond stretching wide and empty beneath the gray sky. There were no clear roads, no landmarks, just the open wilds between them and whatever ruins still stood out there. She shaded her eyes and scanned the horizon. "Even if I knew exactly where the place was, flying without true direction in this kind of terrain is a bad idea. Is it sky lantern time yet?"

Fen emerged in a swirl of low heat and light, padding beside them. "Yes," he said. "I'm curious to see what will happen as well."

Tuck leaped from Quinn and landed nimbly on a nearby rock, the Darkmoor Cat flaring with power as he stretched. "If he's coming out, I'm coming out too."

All eyes turned to Marcella. "As you know, Harold isn't as social as the rest of you," she said, referring to her pacted heron. "But he is offering words of encouragement."

"Then let's get on with it." Callum pulled the sky lantern from his pack, careful not to jostle the structure as he slotted the Fire Affinity Shard into place. The cotton wick caught first, a single bloom of flame flickering beneath the shard-plate as he held it.

The lantern wobbled a few times and finally hovered.

"Looking good . . ." Marcella said.

With a sudden whoosh courtesy of Fen, the lantern launched into the sky. Wind caught the parchment, tightening its shape until it looked almost too perfect, almost ethereal.

Fen surged into Callum, presence snapping into place with a rush of breath and clarity. *<There! Let's go!>*

Before Callum could so much as shift, wings erupted from Marcella's back as she took to the air. "Try to keep up!" she called down to them, already soaring after the lantern.

Callum and Quinn made eye contact, grinned, and started running.

The chase was on.

CHAPTER 31

Just because we've named the currents does not mean we've mapped the seas.

—Branscombe Joule, poet

The wind rushed past Callum's ears, whipping the ends of his overcoat behind him as he bounded over uneven grass and rocks. Quinn was a streak of motion beside him, a wild look on his face as he increased his speed.

The two ran in bursts, sometimes upright, other times low to the ground, melded with their pacted aetherbeasts. Fen's energy surged through Callum, sharpening his reflexes, steadying every stride and lunge with instinct that wasn't entirely his own. Overhead, the sky lantern floated, light and steady, tugged forward by something unseen.

"That's them!" Quinn shouted, breathless but exhilarated as he came to a stop. He pointed to the horizon, toward a thicket of trees rising like a wall of spears against the backdrop of the sky. "The Graywoods."

Callum felt a rush of awe as the forest came into view. He'd never seen trees so massive. From a distance, their leaves shimmered with layers of gray and deep violet, and their trunks were pale and streaked with a misty hue, branches stretched so high they nearly disappeared into the clouded canopy.

The sky lantern hovered for a moment, as if hesitant. Marcella lowered beside Quinn, her wings tucking back. "Um . . . what now?"

"No idea," Callum said as he watched the lantern hover at the edge of the woods. Callum took a look around, hoping for some sign as to where they should go next. His attention jumped back to the lantern once he heard Fen's voice in his head.

<*It's off again!*> Fen said as the lantern swooshed toward the forest a flash of gold, quickly vanishing above the tree line.

"I'll track it!" Marcella called, wings unfolding as she raced after it. She passed over the canopy in seconds, gone from sight.

Callum and Quinn remained at the forest's edge. Both of them leaned over, catching their breath—not winded, just feeling the weight of the run in their bones. Fen shimmered at Callum's shoulder, still partially melded, his fur reflecting the strange light of the trees.

"I've seen the leaves before," Callum said, eyes still on the treetops. "But never the trees themselves."

"The Graywood leaves?" Quinn asked. "Like in books?"

"No, back in Weatherby. Some have medicinal properties. People in town use them for winter decorations too. They make wreaths with them to decorate their windows."

"In winter?"

"After winter, actually. Well, after the worst of it."

"That's how long they take to get from here to there?"

"Uh . . ." Callum hesitated, not sure of what his friend was hinting at. "I never thought of it that way."

Quinn let out a low whistle. "That, my friend, is a business opportunity waiting to happen. Though . . . I don't think I'll go into the business of exporting leaves." He chuckled to himself. "Besides, my brother's the savvy one. I always preferred books and theoretical discussions over something as grounded as well, buy, ship, and sell."

A beat of wind swept through the trunks as Marcella landed with a huff near them. Her wings folded and her meldform faded. "Nope. I lost it."

"You lost it?" Quinn asked.

She shrugged. "What can I say? I tried to follow the lantern, but it was like the forest inhaled it or something. Just gone. I mean, the trees are massive here, but it was *above* them. I swear it should've kept going, but like I said, nope. Gone."

Quinn turned to Callum. "What now?"

Before he could answer, a shimmer moved across the canopy, subtle at first, like sunlight catching on dew.

Then it spread.

Clusters of treetops, spaced in pairs and trios, began to glow with soft golden light. The radiance pulsed gently, alive and unmistakable, each cluster illuminating the one beyond it. Together, they formed a winding trail that cut deep into the Graywoods, threading through the trees, a hidden artery finally revealed.

<The forest hasn't swallowed the lantern, it has marked the way,> Fen said. <How fortuitous!>

"Whoa..." Marcella breathed. "You think...?"

Callum nodded, already stepping forward. "Let's follow it."

The three moved on, walking now as golden leaves drifted through the wind. Each treetop that lit up dimmed after they passed, its brightness passed on to another tree deeper within the forest.

"This is crazy," Quinn said as he took it all in. "I know mana can change the environment, but I've never seen it do this."

"It's certainly put me on edge," Marcella told him with a shiver. "I think that's a good sign that we're close."

"I would certainly say so," Quinn said as the pattern pulsed forward in a slow, graceful chain, guiding them through the hushed woodland. The deeper they walked, the softer the world became, leaves whispering as they fell, birds singing high in the canopy, the sunlight dimming beneath the shifting hues of violet and gray foliage that surrounded their new path.

Eventually, the ground began to slope. The trees grew further apart. And then, the earth dropped away entirely.

Callum stopped at the edge of the gorge, the others halting beside him. A soft wind swirled by with gold and gray leaves drifting into the yawning abyss below.

"Insane," Callum finally said as he took it in.

The gorge stretched before them like the land had been pulled apart by ancient hands—so wide it made Callum's breath catch, so deep it seemed to swallow light itself. He had seen gorges before on his trip from Weatherby to New Albion, but nothing like this. This wasn't a simple break in the land; it was a vast chasm that defied comprehension, its far side barely visible through the shifting haze.

A cool fog coiled up from the depths, slow and ghostlike, too dense to see through. It drifted in layers, crawling over the jagged edges of the cliff walls and vanishing into the gray sky above. No bottom was visible. Not a hint of movement. No gleam of water. Just an endless void.

Did it fall forever? Was there anything down there at all?

He didn't know, and somehow, that made it worse.

The only sound was birdsong, carried across the chasm on faint currents of air. It echoed in odd, warbling tones along the stone walls, the cheerful notes twisted into something eerie by the sheer scale of the place.

A series of moss-covered stone pillars jutted upward like the remnants of a shattered bridge, forming what looked to be a natural, if not precarious, staircase. Each step emerged from the mist one by one, their edges softened by centuries of wind and rain. They rose unevenly, some closer than others, but together they hinted at a possible crossing. A dangerous one.

Marcella's wings formed around her. "Wait here; Harold and I will check it first." She swept down in a rush of air, landing neatly atop one of the pillars. With practiced grace, she leaped to the next, then another, her silhouette flickering in and out of view between curls of mist.

"What's going on?" Callum asked, leaning over the edge to watch her progress. He summoned his wind sword and kept it at his side.

"I can't tell," Quinn replied, eyes narrowing.

Tuck popped out of Quinn's shoulder in a soft ripple of mana. "We can't let her have all the fun," the cat said before leaping down into the mist, the darkened mana around him dissipating.

"He really does have a mind of his own," Quinn said.

Moments later, Marcella returned in a controlled glide, touching down beside them. "It's blocked," she told them simply. Her brow furrowed. Then she noticed Callum's weapons. "Why are you armed?"

Callum sent his Tempest Fang away. "We thought—"

"Something was wrong," Quinn said, finishing his sentence.

Marcella shook her head. "Nope, nothing. There's some sort of magic field stopping me from going even further. I couldn't even see through it. It's like trying to see through fogged glass."

Tuck returned a second later, the aethercat landing on a stone near Callum's feet. He flicked his tail toward the gorge, confirming what Marcella had just told them. "Some sort of invisible mana barrier. It won't let me through." He lifted a paw and began licking it.

<*It will let us enter,*> Fen said from within Callum.

<*You think?*>

<*Call it a hunch. But yes. I believe it will.*>

Callum looked down, gauging the distance to the first stone. "Let me give it a try."

"You sure you want to hop down there?" Marcella asked as the wind picked up, the mist below thickening between the ancient stone pillars.

He flexed his fingers twice. "Fen, think you can get me down in one piece?"

CHAPTER 32

Sealing corrupted mana is a viable containment method, particularly in field conditions. However, successful seals typically require an attuned Aethercore as the anchor—effectively sacrificing the core in exchange for stability.

—Excerpt from *Crisis Crafting and Emergency Containment*, Great College Field Manual

Callum stopped at the edge of the gorge, took a deep breath, and leaped down. Fen's mana raced through his limbs as he melded and landed on the first moss-covered pillar, knees bending slightly to absorb the force. The wind rushed past him, yet Callum kept his balance.

One step done, he thought as he looked ahead to the pillars rising from the mist. *A dozen more to go.*

Callum bounded to the next, then the next, Fen guiding the timing of each jump. A slip caused his foot to skid on damp stone, but he caught himself, arms thrown wide for balance, breath tight in his chest.

"Whew," Callum said.

<*We must be careful,*> Fen reminded him.

"Noted." Callum glanced down into the abyss. The gorge swallowed sound completely, leaving only the faint hiss of wind curling through the emptiness. He nudged a loose pebble with his boot, watched it tumble from the edge of the pillar, and leaned slightly forward, straining to hear any impact.

Nothing, just silence.

"Let's keep going," he said quietly.

Callum moved on, one stone pillar at a time, his boots scraping across timeworn stone. At the next crossing, he came to the pillar partially veiled by a shimmering curtain of magic. The barrier hovered in the air, semitransparent, rippling like heat haze and humming with a subtle, steady rhythm.

"Look," Callum said as he peered through the barrier.

Built into the far wall of the gorge was a massive structure—half temple, half tomb—embedded directly into the stone. Enormous statues flanked the sealed entrance: five beasts, each carved from the cliff face itself.

He recognized them instantly.

The Demonslayer's pacted aetherbeasts—Rata, the Sand Wolf of Aveiro; Killeas, the Gryphon Vanguard of Fates; Lisalen, the Brightflame Phoenix; Astel, the Goddess of Dragons; and Fen, the Radiant Fox . . .

"It's you," he told Fen as he pointed to the statue.

<*I see it . . .*>

The carvings were weathered now, camouflaged by moss and tangled with vines. Bird droppings streaked their once-proud visages. What had once been majestic now lay forgotten, as if the world had moved on and left its greatest champion buried in silence.

"They must have scaled down the cliffs to carve this," Callum whispered. "Or used Earth Affinity. This must have taken years."

<*I agree. Let's see what happens if you touch the barrier.*>

"Right." Callum reached out and pressed his hand through the barrier. It rippled, parting around his skin.

<*Just as I expected,*> Fen said, voice calm. <*Let's continue.*>

Callum stepped through and landed lightly on the final pillar, the surface damp beneath his boots, mist brushing his legs as he moved.

One more leap carried him to the platform at the base of the sealed stone doorway.

The moment his feet met the ancient rock, the runes carved into its surface flared to life, lines of gold lighting up one after the other, pulsing with sudden purpose. A slow light spilled out of the stone in ribbons, spreading from rune to rune in a chain of radiant connection. Each line ignited with a thrum, etching itself across the door like a quill, curling through letters and symbols older than anything Callum had ever seen.

<*Another good sign,*> Fen said.

"Can you read it?" Callum asked, heart racing.

<*I can't but . . .*> Fen appeared beside him, ears flicked forward, eyes locked on the door. As he stepped closer, the runes glowed even brighter. The light threaded outward, forming a five-pointed crest surrounded by ancient script that crumbled into the aether. "That seems to have done something."

The entrance began to move with a deep groan, dust lifting in clouds as stone slid against stone. The sealed doorway cracked, parted, and drew back into the cliff face with a thunderous hush.

Callum waited for it all to settle. He glanced down at Fen, his pulse steady, but tension buzzing just beneath the surface. "Let's see what's inside."

Callum stepped forward, the shift in temperature that followed as sudden as stepping into a cellar. The walls shimmered faintly within the mausoleum as thin lines of magic unfurled like growing vines, weaving across the stone in slow, deliberate motion. They twisted and branched like the roots of some ancient tree, etching fresh patterns over old carvings. No chiseling. No cracks. Just smooth, living movement.

The chamber was small. The ceiling hung just above his head, and the walls pressed close, six paces across at most. Every surface was etched and worn smooth by time, now threaded with growing veins of light. His boots made no echo, the stone seemingly drinking in the sound.

Callum took a breath and turned to Fen. "Head back. Let them know I got it open. I don't want them to worry."

"Are you certain?"

Callum gave Fen a silent nod and the fox darted away, tail flickering with every step.

He stood alone for a moment, letting the strange stillness settle over him like a thin veil. The mausoleum felt heavier without Fen's presence—quieter, but not silent. The glow of the runes had dimmed, their light faded to the point where the ancient script blurred into the stone. Dust lingered in the air, drifting through faint beams of light.

Fen returned less than a minute later, and the mausoleum brightened at once, the runes flaring back to life with renewed intensity. "They'll wait at the top," he said. "Tuck tried to follow me through, but the barrier kept him out."

"So, it really is just us. Interesting . . ."

"Which makes sense, if you think about it. Your heritage, the fact you're his reincarnation, and me. Let's keep going." Fen trotted ahead, his tail glowing softly. The passage bent slightly and then opened into a wider chamber, the floor smooth and undisturbed.

At the center rested a stone sarcophagus, shaped of the same gray stone as the chamber, its sides carved in bas-relief depictions of great battles. Through the swirl of demonic aetherbeasts, Callum could clearly make out his ancestor's pacts, from a dragon ripping through the clouds to a snarling wolf leaping into a horde of monsters.

Fen moved beside the sarcophagus and lifted his tail, casting golden light across the engravings. "There I am," he said, nose brushing one of the carvings—a swirling chaos of beasts and flame, with a spectral fox leaping beside it.

Callum walked slowly around the sarcophagus, every panel telling a story. He cleared his throat. "Uh, Killeas?"

Fen looked up to him, eyebrow raised. "Surely, that's not going to work."

"Killeas," Callum said again, as the magic threading through the chamber shifted.

It reeled inward, spiraling into a tight knot of light above the stone sarcophagus. Wind and shadow snapped together with sharp flickers of static, twisting faster, tighter, until they formed a brilliant orb of pale-blue flame.

Callum moved to summon his Weaponcore, but he didn't have time. The orb burst in a silent flash, swallowing everything as the mausoleum vanished.

In the space between one breath and the next, the stone floor gave way. Gravity buckled, and for a moment Callum felt completely suspended before the world slammed back into place.

"Where am I?" he asked, now standing on a plot of scorched earth, a battlefield devoured by fire. The air burned his lungs, ash shifting underfoot. Heat shimmered around him, both real and not.

The winds picked up, sweeping through fallen bodies and charred banners scattered across the battlefield. A sudden, shrieking wind rustled through the wreckage, nearly causing Callum to fly backward. He dropped into a crouch, summoned his Piercing Air Spear, and drove it into the ground. The weapon thrummed beneath his grip, anchoring him as a wild laugh echoed across the desolation.

"Who dares enter my crypt?"

The voice was jagged, too loud for the space, carrying both madness and mirth as the winds finally relented.

"Killeas?" Fen appeared at Callum's side in a flash, his mana-tinged fur flattened against his body. "What are you doing?"

"Fen?" the voice asked. *"Ah, Fen! Fen, old pal, how goes it?"*

Another gust blew past, scattering skeletons and sending soot spiraling into the air.

"Stop with the bloody winds, Killeas! What in the devil is wrong with you?"

"Wrong?" The voice cackled again. The winds folded in on themselves, replaced by shadows that swept across the land in a wave, smothering fire and wind alike. *"And who have you brought to me?"*

Everything went black.

Pitch black. Darker than anything Callum had ever known. Even a starless night would have felt bright by comparison. This darkness was complete, heavy, the kind that swallowed Fen's light whole and left nothing behind of the Radiant Fox.

"Can't you tell who this is?" Fen shouted into the dark. "You're guarding his forefather's mausoleum!"

"The Demonslayer's mausoleum?"

"Yes, that's where we are, yes?"

"You really think you reached the Demonslayer's mausoleum?" Killeas's voice was quieter now, but still laced with borderline madness. *"You really think that's what this place is?"*

"Killeas, no more games," Fen growled. "If not his mausoleum, then whose?"

"It is a place of sealed Corruption, Fen, something you should be all too familiar with!"

"Sealed Corruption? Speak sense! We saw the sarcophagus."

"What do you think is sealed inside?" Killeas's tone sharpened, lost its mockery. *"Well, aside from my Aethercore. Welcome to my crypt, fox!"*

"What?"

"Think, Fen! There's enough Corruption sealed inside the sarcophagus to spark an aetherstorm. Perhaps even tear open a rift to the Demonsrealm itself, if it morphs into a Beast Tide."

"Killeas, you aren't serious."

"I am dead serious." There was a pause, then a low sigh. *"But there is a way to free both of us."*

The agitation left Fen's voice. "How?"

"We clear the Corruption here—within this realm, within my crypt—and I join you. How about that?"

"Here?" Callum asked, peering into the black. Shapes seemed to shift just beyond visibility, forms without anchor or name. "Where is *here*, exactly?"

"Ah, so he can speak! It's a realm of shadow I created," Killeas said. *"An echo of memory, formed in part by me, in part by what clings to me, or something poetic like that. A mortal such as yourself should think of it like this: I imprisoned myself here with the Corruption so it wouldn't spread. It exists in the sarcophagus rather than the entirety of Western Valestra."*

"Like something the Soul Pythia would make," Callum said.

"I don't know who that is. But I know that now, now that our valiant Radiant Fox has arrived, we can end this. So what do you say, lads? Shall we get started?" A faint shimmer of movement passed through the

dark—something vast and slithering just beneath the shadow's skin. "*Or would you prefer to remain trapped here forever with me?*"

Fen shook out his fur, tail flaring with faint golden light. "Point us toward the Corruption," he said dryly, "and let's be done with this wretched place, Killeas."

CHAPTER 33

One Aethercore shows you what you are. The second shows you what you could be.

—A quote found on a tattered scratch of parchment in the Great Library, later attributed to Master Weaver Duke Vellor

Callum moved through a world that felt both weightless and burdened as he followed Killeas's voice, the shadows beneath his boots bending but never breaking. The sensation reminded him of running across water, if that were even possible, every step splashed without wetness, echoed without sound. He slowed just long enough to glance at Fen, who trotted beside him, light once again restored to his form.

Above, movement shimmered, slicing arcs of invisible force, the faint beat of wings catching in the strange air. Killeas was there, the gryphon never fully visible, but never wholly gone.

"*You really expected to find the Demonslayer's tomb?*" Killeas asked, his voice a breeze that brushed Callum's shoulders from behind.

"That's what the research told us," Fen replied, not breaking stride. "That you had been buried with him."

"*Buried with the Demonslayer? Ha! You academics,*" Killeas sighed, his tone half amusement, half pity. "*Always getting it wrong.*"

"I am not an academic," Fen snapped. "And we *did* find you, didn't we? That has to count for something."

Killeas's laughter shimmered through the air. "*It's everything, Fen. If you're here, it means it's time for my return.*" He released a sound somewhere between a war and a squawk. "*It has been so utterly boring here. I just hope we aren't too late.*"

"I don't know if we're too late or not. Warlocks are on the rise. The Geshwine Empire—what was once Eastern Valestra—has started using Demoncores."

The world around them fizzled and drew tight. A gust of fury spun up from the void-ground beneath their feet, shadows twisting violently overhead. The walls of darkness constricted, like lungs inhaling too deep. *"They what?"* Killeas boomed.

"Demoncores have been legalized there. They're binding corrupted aetherbeasts to students and turning them into warlocks," Fen said. "Everything seems to be lining up, racing toward a moment that the Demonslayer must have seen coming. From my first meeting with Callum until now—"

"Callum?" the gryphon repeated quietly. *"So that really is your name..."*

"How do you think I would even access a place like this without someone directly tied to the Stross lineage?" Fen asked. "This is Callum Stross, named after the Demonslayer, his famous ancestor who died nearly five hundred years ago. You are looking at his reincarnation."

The world seemed to stop around them, as if Killeas was now examining Callum. He could feel the gryphon's presence around him; yet again, Callum heard Killeas's wings.

"Reincarnation?" Killeas murmured, his voice closer than ever. *"You look nothing like him. Well, I take that back, he too had broad shoulders from his youth on the farm. Wait. Fen, did you say five hundred years? Has it been that long? I didn't know how long I'd be trapped. I'm sure you didn't either."*

"My entrapment wasn't like this," Fen said, tail flicking uneasily. "I don't remember much of anything, and certainly not some endless expanse."

"There were advancements," Killeas replied. *"Between when the Demonslayer sealed you away and when I chose this prison."*

"You *chose* this?" Fen asked, stopping for the first time.

"I did it to contain the last surge of Corruption spreading through Western Valestra. There was no other way to keep it from seeping further."

"There is no Western Valestra anymore," Fen said. "They call it the Lands of Grimbald now. I don't know why."

"Grimbald? Wasn't that a simple outpost not far from the River Brack? I suppose five hundred years will do that to a place. And my mausoleum," Killeas asked, wistful, *"still in the Graywoods?"*

"It is."

"On which side of the border?"

"To be determined."

"I hope it is the Valestra side, but I suppose that doesn't matter at the moment. Let's continue. The heart grows near!"

They pressed on until the air grew still. Callum squinted into the darkness to find a purple light crackling on the horizon.

It started small. A faint pulse. But each beat of its glow bent the space around it, a trembling oval ringed by rivulets of shadow and wind being consumed. The ground beneath it rippled and shards of color split off, vanishing as they were pulled into its center. The heart pulsed like a beacon dragged from the end of the world. Every beat of its glow pulled the world tighter, tugging at wind, shadow, even breath itself.

"*There*," Killeas whispered, his voice trembling—not with fear, but something closer to longing. "*That's the heart of the Corruption. Destroy it, and you will free us all. I wish I could help, but it's tied to me. As long as its influence holds, I can't strike at it without risking everything—this space, myself, maybe even the two of you.*"

Callum stepped forward, eyes fixed on the anomaly slowly unraveling what was left of reality.

"Let's remove the cancer!" Fen melded with Callum and his Pangolin Armorcore cascaded into place over his body. The twin Ram swords sparked into Callum's hands, their edges aching to cut as he neared the Corruption.

Callum lunged; the heart shimmered and vanished.

"What?" he growled, twisting in midair.

The heart reappeared several paces to his left, drifting backward, its surface warping with mocking grace. He rushed again and the heart blinked away again. Five more attempts, five more vanishing points.

<*Use your roots!*> Fen told him.

Callum summoned the Powercore and tendrils of spectral bark tore from the void-ground, clawing toward the heart and pinning it, if only for a breath.

He sprinted forward again, blades ready, but the heart of Corruption surged, snapping the roots apart with a convulsion of twisted light.

It expanded, drawing in more from the environment. Wind screamed around them, distant lightning spiraling through impossible clouds backlit by purple static and lime green lightning.

"It's . . . it's like an aetherstorm!" Fen shouted over the rising chaos.

"Fight fire with fire?" Callum asked.

"What do you mean?"

Callum didn't answer. He used his Gale Powercore, the powerful gust of wind surging forward and slamming into the heart of Corruption. It recoiled, its shape contorting in sudden resistance.

<*It felt that!*> Fen said.

Seizing the moment, Callum surged forward and broke through the heart's outer energy shell with his Ram swords. Purple flames burst in a spiraling wave as he hopped.

A sudden flash of pain came with it, the wrenching, soul-deep pull like his lungs had been inverted. His vision swam as he struggled to maintain his footing. "What—?" He staggered back. "What did it do?"

Fen sounded alarmed. *<Check your reserves!>*

Callum tried using Soul Sense and came up short. Before, he would merely think about it, and the information would come to him. *I lost access to it probably because . . . because I'm in Killeas's realm!*

"We need a distraction," he told Fen. Callum sent Radiant Mirage forward, his replicants sprinting across the field in all directions, confusing the heart as he ducked low. "Come on . . ." he said, trying to use Soul Sense yet again to no avail.

"*Finish it!*" Killeas's voice thundered through the wind. "*Before it overpowers you!*"

"That's what I'm trying to do," Callum told the gryphon.

Triggering his Ashcoil Powercore caused the air to erupt in smoke and embers, a spiraling inferno joining the shadows. Callum meant for it to only be another distraction while he got his bearings, yet the heart buckled inward as it took in the ash, acting as if it were choking.

"We're going in again," he told Fen as he dismissed his blades, summoned the Piercing Air Spear, and hurled it.

The spear tore into the heart's core with a howl, splitting the oval of corrupted energy. The piece broke into two puddles that splattered against the void-like floor.

The wind stopped and hints of color returned to the vast expanse of the realm.

Callum stood, chest heaving. "Did . . . did we do it?" he asked, eyes fixed on the two dark puddles where the Corruption had collapsed.

The pools shimmered, then stirred.

A hooded figure rose from each puddle, both draped in robes made of living shadow. Their limbs stretched unnaturally long, their movements too fluid, too quiet. No faces were visible beneath the hoods, only the pulsing glow of demonic light—red and writhing, like molten eyes burning through the dark.

Callum summoned his twin blades again. The Ram swords flickered into form, humming with restrained force, their tips trailing faint arcs of invisible pressure.

"*Do something!*" Killeas shouted, sounding increasingly crazed.

"Cruedark would say something about this," Callum said backpedaling from the advancing constructs. "*Pick one. Separate them. You're not a storm—you're a blade. Make them feel it.* Something like that."

<Then let's do that!> Fen told him.

Callum kicked off a platform of wind, twisting sideways in the air as one construct lashed through the spot he'd just vacated. The other followed, the dark construct's blades liquefying into sweeping arcs that curved midair.

Callum landed in a crouch and used Radiant Inferno to send flashes of fiery magic erupting in a wide ring around him. The explosion staggered both constructs, tearing loose portions of their shadow-formed cloaks. Their movements stuttered but only for a breath.

The pair resumed, arms contorting, the blades on their wrists morphing into fluid whips that crackled with cursed light.

Callum planted his feet and then surged forward. He ducked one whip of energy; the second tore through his shoulder plating, but he twisted with it, letting the momentum carry him into a spin. He blasted wind through his right blade and drove it into the gut of the closer construct, bringing it down.

Callum shifted focus just as the second construct lunged for him. *So much for taking on one at a time!* he thought as he slipped beneath the arc of another tendril of darkness, coming up with both swords crossed.

He slashed hard; dark mana split with a shriek only for the severed length to coil like a snake and lash around his ankle.

"It burns—!" Callum shouted, carving it away before it could dig deeper. He pivoted before the second construct rushed him again, its full body turning into a tendril that wrapped around his torso cracking through parts of his Pangolin armor.

Callum channeled everything he had and *burst* outward, activating the shield-fins on his Armorcore. His mana-forged bracers exploded wide, shattering the binding coil with a force that sent debris spiraling in every direction.

Back on the attack, Callum drove his Ram swords through the construct's core, unraveling its form into threads of corrupted light. "Absorb it—" Callum told Fen. "I'll manage the next one!"

<Are you sure?> Fen asked.

"Do it!"

Fen leaped from Callum's shoulder and landed on the downed construct, his form flickering silver as he unraveled the Corruption thread by thread.

Callum turned. The second dark construct reared up, its whip-blade arms twitching like a serpent preparing to strike.

The wind shifted, Killeas's voice booming from everywhere and nowhere. "*Yes, my power is returning! Prepare! Now, we have ourselves a little fun!*"

A tempestuous gale spiraled down from above, howling with power, and slammed into Callum. Shadow-wrapped force tore through him, flooding his limbs, fusing with his core.

Light flared as their meld locked into place and Killeas's voice appeared at the back of Callum's head. *<Let's finish this!>*

CHAPTER 34

The sky does not want us. It lets us visit, nothing more.

—Thalen Virest, the Bard of Ontaria

Wind tore through Callum's hair as he exploded upward, faster than any leap he could remember. The world became a blur, the shadows of Killeas's sealed realm shrinking below as he spiraled higher and higher into the dark. His arms flailed at first, more from instinct than panic.

<*What are you doing?*> Killeas's voice rang in his head, half thrill, half madness. <*Fly, lad! Soar like the storm!*>

"Fly?" Callum shouted as the wind whipped around him. "I don't know how to—"

<*Now's your chance to learn! I can do it for you, and I will. We're melded now. But you must be able to do it yourself as well. Tell me—can you swim?*>

"Of course, I can swim!" Callum shouted, barely able to orient himself as he pitched sideways through the intangible currents.

<*Excellent! Fun fact, the Demonslayer could not! Actually, I can tell you a hilarious story about the time I once—by accident, I assure you—landed us in a great body of water somewhere outside of New Albion. Care to hear it?*>

"Not now!" Callum clenched his jaw and kicked forward through the air as if diving into water. His arms tucked instinctively at his sides, and with a movement that didn't feel entirely his own, his shoulders pulled tight.

He surged forward. Only in that instant did he realize what had happened. Wings had formed behind him, not feathered but shaped from pure hardened, light-slicked shadow mana.

The world shifted and, with a silent whoop, Callum arced back toward the ground.

<*See?*> Killeas howled with delight. <*Flying is like swimming if you really think about it, especially if you have wings! Now crush the devil. Draw your sword and be done with it!*>

The final shadowy construct below reeled, rising in full menace as its tendrilled arms extended. It lashed upward to meet Callum just as he summoned his Tempest Fang, the Weaponcore's edge gleaming with rippling pressure.

Callum folded his wings, tucked into a dive, and unfurled them with a boom of force, dodging the first tendril with a fluid twist, then cleaving straight through the second. Power rushed around him as he struck the construct head-on, bisecting it in one clean pass.

The shattered remnant dissolved into Corruption and hit the void floor in chunks.

Callum landed hard next to it, boots skidding, knees bent.

A breath later, a pulse of light split the gloom as Killeas separated from him, a towering creature of radiant mana and shadowed grace, his eagle head fierce and crested with tufts of stormlight as he dropped in front of Callum.

"Ah, it feels good to be back!" Killeas folded his massive wings, their edges catching the light in streaks of gray and gold. His foreclaws flexed into the earth, talons sparking against stone. Behind him, leonine hind legs coiled with effortless power, tensed as if ready to leap skyward at any moment. His eyes—piercing, luminous, and unmistakably intelligent—fixed on Callum with a mix of pride and quiet curiosity.

"There you are," came Fen's voice, dry as ever. He took shape beside one of the shattered constructs, fragments of fading Corruption soon bleeding into his form. His ears twitched in irritation as a stray ember landed on his nose.

"It wasn't *me* who took forever to clean this mess up," Killeas said smugly, pacing beside him. "But together, we'll finish it quickly and then . . ."

"Then?" Callum asked, stepping forward.

Killeas didn't answer; instead, he worked alongside Fen, stripping the last strands of corrupted essence from the fractured battlefield. When the final thread faded, the two aetherbeasts turned to Callum and disappeared.

A heartbeat later, both voices echoed in unison inside his head:

<*Ready?*> Killeas asked.

<*We are both ready,*> Fen said.

<*In that case . . . let's get out of here!*>

Reality twisted, and light flared as the realm came undone. The ground beneath them cracked, splintering in every direction as the air folded inward, compressing into a single point of brilliance.

It exploded outward in a shockwave of searing magic.

For an instant, there was only light.

Then Callum staggered back into the crypt, boots scraping against cold stone. He nearly fell, the momentum of reentry jarring and violent.

The veins of magic etched into the chamber walls surged, blistering with volatile energy. The glow pulsed erratically, casting strobing shadows across the sarcophagus and broken floor.

The stone groaned beneath his feet, deep and guttural as dust poured down from the ceiling in slow streams.

<*The tomb is coming down!*> Fen shouted.

Callum didn't wait.

Wings tore from his back as Callum launched into motion. Around him, the crypt began to collapse in a roar of stone and fractured magic, the floor splitting apart as ancient supports gave way.

He twisted in midair, dodging a falling slab of stone, and shot through the opening just as the ceiling caved in, rockfall erupting in his wake. Wind slammed into his face, tearing at his coat as he burst through the mist and into open air, the gorge yawning wide beneath him.

The sensation hit all at once—freedom, weightlessness, speed.

He climbed hard, wings beating with raw, unfamiliar power. For a breathless moment, he was nothing but motion and sky, the broken earth shrinking behind him.

He reached a stopping point and looked down to see Quinn and Marcella waiting for him. Quinn waved both hands excitedly while Marcella grew her own pair of wings and prepared to join Callum.

<*And who is this?*> Killeas asked, his voice low and curious as Marcella approached.

<*One of his friends. She has a pacted heron,*> Fen replied briskly.

Moments later, Marcella glided into view, her wings catching the updraft with practiced ease. She joined Callum in the air without effort, hovering beside him above the gorge, the wind tugging at the ends of her overcoat, stirring her earrings with a soft clink of metal.

"So," she said, casting him a sidelong glance, "you can fly now."

Callum turned slightly, as if just noticing the wings stretched behind him. He dropped a few feet and caught himself. "Apparently so!"

Marcella did a quick circle around him. "Not bad. What affinities?"

"Shadow and Air."

"Nice." She turned back toward Quinn. "He's looking awfully lonely down there."

"We should probably join him."

"Or we could just fly to the portal . . ." Marcella laughed. "I'm kidding. We'll do this the civilized way."

<Is she implying flying is not civilized?> Killeas asked.

<Marcella has a way about her, a particular sense of humor.> Fen said, <She's from Aveiro.>

<That explains it! From what I remember, Aveiro is full of crusty sailors and dockside jades. Always has been.>

<Are you really calling her a dockside jade?> Fen asked.

<I'm merely saying that they are there!>

<Marcella is a noble. Aveiro, from what I understand, is a very affluent society these days.>

<What?> Killeas sounded genuinely alarmed. <Since when?>

Callum shook his head.

"What is it?" Marcella asked as she continued hovering beside him.

"Having two voices in my head is going to take some getting used to."

Callum, Marcella, and Quinn backtracked through the Graywoods, heading toward the Steppe with steady purpose. Above the treetops, Killeas and Harold soared in wide arcs, their light-filled bodies weaving between breaks in the canopy.

The journey gave Callum time to explain what had happened in the crypt, and to begin examining the new powers Killeas had unlocked. As they moved, he reached inward with Soul Sense, feeling out the changes, the subtle shifts now woven into his Soul Heart.

The first thing he examined was the Aethercore itself.

Pact of the Gryphon Vanguard of Fates
Type: *Pacted*
Grade: *Common*
Infusion Requirements for Grade Increase:
0/10 Shadow Affinity Shards
0/10 Air Affinity Shards
0/10 Deftness Shards
0/10 Vigor Shards
Mana Affinities Granted: *Air, Shadow*
Meldform Benefits:
Attributes:
+2 Might
+3 Deftness
+4 Vigor

+2 Regeneration
+2 Resilience
+1 Mind

Wings of the Shrouded Ascent: *When melded, the wielder gains a pair of wings laced with shadow. These allow for sustained flight and agile aerial maneuvering.*

The wings were something he wanted to test more, especially with the Powercore that Killeas came with, similar to the way Fen came with Inner Light and Zephyr Strike.

Empowerment of Keen Ascent
Type: *Ability*
Grade: *Common*
Infusion Requirements for Grade Increase:
0/10 Air Affinity Shards
0/5 Might Shards
0/5 Mind Shards
Affinity Requirements: *Air*
Effect: *When inserted into one's Soul Heart, this core gives heightened awareness during flight, making attacks more accurate and harder to counter.*

Shadowmark
Type: *Ability*
Grade: *Common*
Infusion Requirements for Grade Increase:
0/15 Shadow Affinity Shards
0/5 Vigor Shards
0/10 Mind Shards
Affinity Requirements: *Shadow*
Effect: *When inserted into one's Soul Heart, this core allows the user to apply a Shadowmark to a target. While the mark is active, the target takes increased damage from the user's abilities.*

"That sounds very useful," Quinn said after Callum explained how Shadowmark worked. "And increasing damage?" A pained expression traced across his face. "I really, *really,* need to reach the Wielder Stage."

"You'd better pact with something that can fly," Marcella told Quinn as they hiked toward Devonshire. "We can't keep walking everywhere like peasants."

Quinn laughed. "Maybe I'll get Tuck a pair of wings. You think he'd mind?"

"Doubt it," Marcella said dryly. "Callum's got a gryphon now, so why not a flying cat?" She glanced skyward at Harold and Killeas. "Anyway, it shouldn't be much longer now."

Quinn frowned. "What do you mean? We're at least five hours out."

"I'm trying to manifest a shorter hike, Quinn. Let me have this."

They made it in just under four hours thanks to a Weatherby-bound caravan that gave them a ride after the driver recognized Callum.

Before they left the main road, they stopped briefly near a thicket of low redleaf shrubs growing in the shade of a stone ridge. Callum knelt, brushing a few leaves aside to reveal a patch of small, knotted berries with a faint silvery sheen. "We call these frostknots," he said. "They grow wild this time of year. Bitter at first, but they'll wake you up." He bit into one and winced at the bitterness. "Definitely wake you up." Both Quinn and Marcella declined to try the herb.

By the time they reached the collapsed gates of the abandoned Devonshire campus, Quinn already had the Portalstone receiver in hand. He activated it just as Sir Trindade had instructed, triggering a shimmer of magic. The return portal to the Great College flickered into existence, crackling with steady energy.

Quinn stepped aside and nodded toward the opening. "You first."

Callum turned to Marcella, gesturing for her to go ahead.

She waved him off. "No, Little Cal, you can go. I want one more moment of bucolic splendor before we're thrust back into city life."

"Thanks for coming with me," Callum told the two of them. "Really. And I'm glad we were able to visit Weatherby."

Quinn gave a one-shouldered shrug, the corner of his mouth lifting. "You kidding? This was the fun part."

"Even waiting there in the middle of nowhere while I dealt with the mausoleum?"

<Crypt,> Killeas corrected him. <The Demonslayer's mausoleum is still hidden.>

"Eh, it was only about thirty minutes or so," Quinn assured Callum.

"Not long enough for us to abandon you, if that's what you were worried about," Marcella added, "but close. Another thirty minutes, and we might have turned around. I'm joking. And really, it has been nice. I can only imagine the pressure on campus right now with the finals of the Duelist Rounds coming and the fact that Geshwinian airships are hovering above the Great College, ominous as ever. Ugh. Is it weird for me to say I don't want to go back?"

"Not really," Quinn told her. "Travel often ends that way."

She motioned toward the distant line of the Graywoods. "There just seems like so much to explore out west. But I guess . . . we have a duty. And that duty is to get good marks and for you to win the Duelist Rounds," Marcella said, fixing Callum with a look. "Obviously, don't tell Her Highness I'm rooting for you."

"I won't."

"And seriously." Marcella took a step closer to him. "No pressure. Ignore the fact that saying 'no pressure' *definitely* implies pressure. The Great College needs this win. The whole kingdom needs the Geshwine Empire to understand that warlocks and whatever Demoncore sorcery they're dabbling in isn't the future." She gave a small, crooked smile. "So yeah. No pressure, like I said."

CHAPTER 35

Peace endures not through strength alone, but through the willingness to set strength aside when the realm needs stillness more than triumph.

—King Morninglade in his address to the Wounded Legion, Year 494

The last thing Callum expected was to find an entourage waiting for him back at the Great College. He stepped through the portal and came to an abrupt halt when he was greeted by a full squad of Legion Guards standing in formation, their polished armor catching the glowing lamps around campus as they formed a tight semicircle around the princess. Selene stood at the center, hands folded, her expression unreadable. Sir Trindade was just behind her, his stance unyielding, his gaze fixed and unwavering.

"I'm glad you returned safely," Sir Trindade said once Quinn and Marcella joined him. "But there's a matter we must address, as per His Majesty's orders."

"Hello to you as well," Marcella said, instantly perturbed by their appearance.

"Before we do that," Sir Trindade said, continuing as though without interruption, "the Portalstone receiver."

Quinn handed it over. "Hi, princess," he told Selene, who merely nodded at his presence.

<You didn't tell me we would be welcomed by a royal entourage!> Killeas said privately to Fen. <You told me he was a poor farmboy.>

<I didn't say that,> Fen said. <And this isn't his entourage. It's hers. She's the princess and Lisalen is pacted with her father.>

<Ah, that makes more sense. What a devilish phoenix! I never did like her as much as Rata and Astel. Did I ever tell you that?>

Callum tuned back into Sir Trindade just as he delivered the devastating news: "Callum Stross, it has been decided by the High Council that Princess Selene will forfeit her match against you in the coming finals. This has been decided for her safety."

"Safety?" Marcella took a furious step forward. "Are you *crazy*? They're our only chance to win this thing!" She motioned between Callum and Selene. "One of them has to do it. If she's out, that cuts our chances in half."

"I would mind my tongue if I were you," Sir Trindade told her. "Neither you nor your family are on the High Council. You do not have a say in the matter."

Marcella crossed her arms and turned to Selene. "You can't seriously be dropping out. I know you. You've been anticipating this for weeks. You . . . you told me."

Selene, as composed as ever, held her gaze. "The decision came from my father and the High Council. It will be announced at the start of the match." She paused, then added, more quietly, "In the end, only one of us can really compete. This just moves that part along."

"I don't follow," Quinn said, frowning.

"The brackets were finalized last night, while the three of you were out west," Selene explained. "Laziel and Ryven will fight first, after which, Callum and I will face each other. This is to make it so the final match of the day will be between one Great College student and one Crimson Sigil student. So by bowing out, I'm making it easier for Callum to beat whoever wins between Laziel and Ryven."

"But this is only the second leg of the overall tournament, right?" Quinn asked, his brows furrowing. "If the first was the Culling Trials, and the second is the Duelist Rounds—"

"The third phase," Sir Trindade cut in, "will be announced." The way he said it made everyone pause. His tone remained hard as steel, and his eyes locked on Quinn like he was daring him to ask another question. Callum could feel something unspoken churning beneath the surface, something even Selene wasn't saying.

<Ha! So these jacked up jesters are in charge of the kingdom?> Killeas snorted inside Callum's mind. <No wonder the warlocks are back. And who are we kidding? You would've crushed the princess anyway. You have me now, remember? She looks frail at best.>

<Princess Selene is incredibly powerful and she has a pacted aetherbear,> Fen replied sharply. <Perhaps now isn't the time to gloat, Killeas, especially with your limited knowledge of these people.>

<*Oh, it's exactly the time to gloat if you ask me!*> Killeas said, his tone positively delighted. <*I've been sealed in a tomb for hundreds of years, and now I get front-row seats to court drama and magical tournaments? Count me in!*>

Selene stepped closer to Callum, her voice low now, like it was only for him. "As Sir Trindade said, I will forfeit at the start of the match. Not before then. It is important we keep this quiet." She looked to Quinn and Marcella. "That all of us keep this quiet."

Callum shook his head. "I still don't—"

"It is equally important that you do everything you can to prepare for your victory," Selene said. "You have two days before the final round. Cruedark has agreed to meet with you tomorrow."

"I . . ." Callum looked away from the weight of her gaze. "Got it. As you wish."

She studied him for a moment. "What else do you need?"

Callum hesitated, eyes narrowing slightly as he glanced over her—not assessing, just thinking. "What do I need?" he echoed, as if tasting the words. "Good question."

"You have a new Aethercore, right?" she asked, tone brisk now. "Killeas?"

"Yes."

<*Gryphon Vanguard of Fates!*> Killeas bellowed in Callum's head. <*Do not make me show myself and force these mortals to bow to my magnitude!*>

Callum pressed his lips together, choosing not to respond out loud this time. Fen was already sighing through their bond.

"Good, so you have your second pact. In that case, you and I are going shopping," Selene told Callum.

"Princess—" Sir Trindade began but stopped when she raised one eyebrow. He cleared his throat and adjusted the cuffs of his coat. "I suppose that makes sense. We do want to put our best foot forward."

"To the Emporium?" Callum asked.

"Not exactly," the princess told him. "Tomorrow night. I'll send someone for you." Her grin, while still measured, hinted at mischief. "Same time, same place as always. Until then, stay vigilant, work with your new powers, and do what you can to prepare."

Callum gave a slight bow. "I will."

"Good." Selene turned to Quinn and Marcella. "It was nice to see both of you." And with that, the princess turned away.

Callum watched as Selene disappeared down the stone corridor, flanked by Sir Trindade and her guards. She carried herself with the same regal composure, yet something was different. Beneath the polished exterior, he caught it: the faint drag in her step, the way her shoulders sat just a little heavier. She hadn't said a word about it, but the weight was there, pressing down on her all the same.

<Shopping with a princess?> Killeas asked. <I can hardly wait!>

The next morning was cooler than expected. A gusty breeze swept through the upper courtyards of the Great College, carrying with it a swirl of yellow and brown leaves. Callum had just grabbed an egg sandwich from the main hall and was making his way toward his Manavitality class when Marcella intercepted him like a hawk spotting prey.

She didn't speak; Marcella just grabbed his arm and turned him down a different path.

"Where are we going?" Callum asked as he chewed a bite of his sandwich. "I need to get to class."

"You have the most important fight of your life in two days. You're *not* going to class. Finish your sandwich."

"I'm pretty sure they'll notice if I skip," he told Marcella, mouth full.

"I can't believe I have to even suggest that. When do you meet Cruedark?"

"We usually meet before lunch, and sometimes—"

"I know," Marcella cut in as they passed beneath the shadow of the Demonslayer statue. "Your training runs long."

<Hey, stop. I said stop! That's me!> Killeas announced gleefully in Callum's head as they passed the famed statue. <Who carved this? Fen, are you seeing how poor this work is? Were they an artist, or a drunk? They clearly never saw how majestic I am. They got my feet wrong!>

<Your feet?> Fen asked, bemused.

<Bird talons in front, claws in the back. What an absolute idiot! Whoever sculpted this shardforsaken monstrosity has it the other way around. We need to register an official complaint and likely hire a team to fix it. Who is in charge around here? The princess? We're meeting her later for shopping. We can ask about it then.>

<You are absurd,> Fen told Killeas.

<I am passionate about art!>

<Let's not mess with the statue right now,> Callum thought tightly. <And let's leave any official complaints for another day.>

"Are you listening to me?" Marcella asked, exasperated.

Callum finished his egg sandwich as the two aetherbeasts continued to argue. "I now have two voices in my head. It's distracting."

"Two voices? Right, that," she said as they neared the open-air portal just behind Dreagis Hall, the temporary home of the Crimson Sigil cohort.

Several Crimson students were outside, not training or dueling but standing in perfect rows as a tall, thin student with a hooked nose paced in front of them. Whatever he was saying, it had the cadence of a command and the clipped precision of indoctrination.

<Warlocks . . .> Killeas growled. <We could start our training here.>

<Here?> Callum replied warily.

<Fen, be a good fox and tell me how many we could take out before the administration intervenes. Ten? Fifteen?>

Before any more bloodthirsty plans could take root, Marcella grabbed Callum's wrist and pulled him through the portal and into the training ground, the sunlit clearing encircled by chalk-drawn boundaries and set with elevation platforms for sparring. The air smelled of dust and mana-scorched wood.

Marcella stepped in front of Callum and turned back to him. "I've been flying a lot longer than you, and if you're going to fight Laziel or Ryven, you're going to need more than Killeas's pep talks and instinct. Lesson one starts now."

She summoned her wings and rose smoothly into the sky, graceful as a brushstroke. "You probably already intuited some of this," she called down, "but trust me, wingbeat discipline matters more than instinct."

<Wingbeat discipline?> Killeas asked. <What the devil is she saying?>

<Just let her help him,> Fen told the gryphon. <She might actually show him something and he should be able to do it better himself.>

Callum took his meldform and opened his wings, the magical appendages unfurling like dark banners behind him. The moment he took flight he could tell his rhythm was off. His wings beat too hard at first, then not enough. He bobbed in the air like a paper boat in rough water.

"See?" Marcella asked dryly as she hovered next to him, her wingbeats smooth and graceful. "Erratic. You're fighting the air. I noticed it back in the Graywoods."

"I thought I was flying."

"You were, or Killeas was, sure; but I'd describe it closer to flailing. Feel the sky's pulse, not just your own."

<Ha! Such fancy words!> Killeas told Callum. <If ever you need me to fly for you, say the word, lad. This isn't a poetry lesson. We are pacted now. If you need to run on all fours and jump through a flaming log, you call upon the fox. For flight, just say the word and we will take to the sky.>

Callum ignored Killeas as he circled Marcella at mid-height, her posture loose and in control while he worked just to keep altitude. She pointed at the ways his legs dipped slightly. "Find the rhythm in it. If you force your wingbeats against it, you're wasting energy. Chest up. Sync with the natural flow of mana, and you'll fly twice as far using half the strength."

Callum tried again, timing his wingbeats to the faint push he felt on his left side. He glided longer before needing to flap, his movements smoothing out.

"Better," she said. "Next," she gestured toward a patch of earth ringed with fallen leaves and pale dust, "let's try a silent descent." Marcella folded her wings tight and dropped, only flaring them at the last second to coast into the clearing without disturbing a single blade of grass. Callum followed suit, aiming to do the same.

He landed with a gust and kicked up a spray of pebbles and twigs.

"Subtle," Marcella said. "But it's a start."

"That felt great to me," Callum replied as he scratched the back of his head.

She laughed. "It sounded like an airship fell out of the sky. Try again."

They repeated the exercise until Callum could drop into the clearing with a whisper instead of a blast.

"And so we continue." Marcella led him to the training field's edge where a steep rift cut into the hill, a natural chute funneling wind straight up.

"Thermals," Marcella said, spreading her wings and banking into a wide turn. "Warm air rising off the ground. You don't have to fight it; just catch it and let it lift you. Tilt into it like a hawk would. No flapping unless you have to."

She angled slightly, letting the invisible current do the work. Her ascent looked effortless.

Callum followed her lead, adjusting his wings. Almost instantly, the rising air caught him. He began to climb, lifted by the current with barely any effort. The forest fell away beneath them as they spiraled higher, leveling out in smooth flight above the trees.

"One thing I've learned—you can't muscle your way through an aetherstorm," she said. "What I'm trying to say is the thicker the flow of magic, the more you have to read it like underwater currents. Keep your wings tight, your senses wider. Let the flow carry you."

"Understood," Callum said, though the wind was rushing past fast enough to tear the words from his mouth.

Marcella glanced back at him. "Now, spiral dodge. Watch." She twisted sharply, spiraling downward in a tight corkscrew, her wings folding and unfurling in rhythmic bursts.

Callum mirrored her as best he could, his spiral a wobbling blur. "I'll get it!" he shouted as his spin grew tighter than he intended.

"You're going to crash. Careful!"

Callum nearly clipped a tree, skimmed the ground, then surged upward with a burst of magic. Seconds later, he landed shakily on one of the sparring platforms.

Marcella touched down beside him, laughing. "Not bad for your first try."

"I'm alive," Callum said, catching his breath. "That counts for something, right?"

"It does. Let's try it again, and smoother this time. Fly like a dancer, not a farmboy."

CHAPTER 36

Keep a core in the dark and you control the next move.

—A quote from *Unspoken Edges: Tactics Volume IV* by Combat Master Twillo Voss

Callum waited beneath the pergola outside Master Cruedark's office, in a quiet stretch of campus where vines coiled up painted stone columns. The pergola stood in the shadow of an old statue of an austere figure in sweeping robes, a pacted monkey perched on his shoulder and a book in his hand. Callum had passed it dozens of times before and still hadn't read the plaque, which had weathered over time. Dean Everholt? Evermire? He wasn't sure. He told himself he'd check next time.

Cruedark emerged from his office as silent as usual, the broad-shouldered man's cloak catching the sun like a falling shadow. "Come," was all he said, motioning for Callum to follow.

They moved into one of the nearby administrative buildings, the kind with echoing stone floors and narrow staircases that twisted deeper than they had any right to. Callum had assumed this was a storage complex or an archive, maybe both. It turned out to be something else entirely as they passed a series of arched entries that opened onto nondescript halls, with no markings at all.

Cruedark laid his palm against the stone next to one of these arches and the door hissed open. A portal flickered to life inside, Callum's noticing the Portalstone above it as the piece activated.

"Do you remember how to get here?" Master Cruedark asked.

"Not really."

"This is a portal often used by upperclassmen, not that you can't use it. Instructors use it as well." He cracked his knuckles. "Just because we're now teachers doesn't mean we don't need to be ready for anything." Cruedark glanced around. "There's not a window in here, but if there was, I'd point to the Geshwinian airships as proof of what I'm telling you. Anyway, follow me."

They stepped through the portal and Callum was instantly met by a humid rush of air thrumming with ambient power. "This way," Cruedark said as he led Callum to the edge of a sunken glade with a fountain pouring a curtain of light into a pool below. It wasn't water—it was mana, streaming in constant threads from the sky like a waterfall fed from the world's magic itself.

"Do you know why I've brought you here?" Masker Cruedark asked as he turned to Callum.

"To train?"

"To train and recover," Cruedark corrected. "You'll need both. I'm going to push you past your limit today, so you can spend all of tomorrow doing the opposite—cycling mana, resting, getting your mind right. Picture the win. *Own* it before it happens. That's tomorrow's job. But today?" He stepped forward, eyes sharp. "Today, we go beyond what you thought you could handle."

"Selene's meeting me later, something about shard shopping. As long as I'm back for that."

"So I've been told. And yes, you'll be back before that," Cruedark said. "I'm also aware she intends to forfeit. Which is why today is crucial. You'll face either Ryven or Laziel. One has a pacted boar. The other, a Cinder Mammoth. Today, we prepare for the elephant considering you've already fought Ryven in the Culling Trials. I want you to be ready to face something that can run you down and flatten you into dust."

Callum's mind flashed back to the aetherstorm that had torn through New Albion, and the moment he'd seen the horns burst from Cruedark's head. He still didn't know what the combat master was pacted with. "What exactly do you want me to fight?"

"We'll get to that. First," Cruedark gestured, "let me see Killeas."

"Gladly!" Killeas burst from Callum's Soul Heart in a surge of silvery mana, wings flaring wide, head held high. His leonine haunches flexed with power and his talons gleamed as he struck a pose worthy of a statue, or at the very least, a dramatic tapestry. His feathers ruffled in a self-summoned gust, and a halo of wind and shadow coiled around him like a stage curtain drawing back. "Behold the Gryphon Vanguard of Fates!" he boomed, his voice echoing across the training ground. "The skies tremble at my cry. The winds bend to my will. Let all present bear witness to my majestic arrival!"

<*He's insufferable,*> Fen said with a sigh in Callum's mind.

Cruedark remained unfazed by Killeas's boasting. "I believe this new pact will serve you well," he said with a firm nod.

"Of course, I will serve him well. Wait—no! We serve each other." Killeas snapped his beak. "I like to think of us as cocaptains on a skyborne ship destined for eternal greatness."

"That may be so," Cruedark said. "But the fight ahead will test even you, Gryphon Vanguard of Fates. Not because you lack the strength, but because he's still learning, and there are many unknowns going into this fight." He nodded at Callum. "Please step back. Both of you. Better yet, meld."

Killeas gave a mock bow before vanishing in a burst of light.

<*Miss me?*> he asked Fen.

<*Just let us pay attention to the lesson.*>

Cruedark took a breath, set his stance, and focused again on Callum. "Have you heard of Beast Masters?"

"I've seen them. Some serve the princess."

"I could have become one," Cruedark told him, an absent look in his eyes. "And perhaps I will, if war returns. I'm telling you this because what you see next might unsettle you. Like the Crimson student named Laziel, I too have a pacted War Elephant. These are quite rare, and have only made appearances in the Lands of Grimbald. That's where I got mine. I spent some time there, you know, but that feels like a lifetime ago."

Callum thought of the map of the three kingdoms, Valestra in between Grimbald and the Geshwine Empire. *The only way to get there without passing through all of Valestra would be by boat, portal, or airship,* he surmised. "How would someone like Laziel get a pact like that?"

"Money. His family's line is deep-pocketed, aligned with the Geshwine Empire and Imperion Rotharyn, though not directly—just enough distance to dodge suspicion." Cruedark rolled his shoulders. "I'm telling you this because what matters now is the form I'm about to take. It may shock you."

"I'm ready," Callum said.

"Then come forward," Cruedark said, his voice deepening.

The transformation was grotesque and regal all at once. Cruedark's muscles bulged, tusks split from either side of his jaw—real, not magical. His skin grayed and thickened. His feet crashed into the ground with a tremor, cracking stones. The air around him pulsed with raw, earthen mana that gave a magnetic force to the soil, one that pulled at Callum.

"Let's go!" Cruedark bellowed, voice like thunder as tusks broke free from his jawline. "Show me what you've got, Stross!"

The second Callum activated his Brightflame Falcon Armorcore, a rush of radiant heat swept over him. His armor shimmered to life with feathered crests of gold and ember orange, the pauldrons shifting into swept-back wings, thin but dense with pressure.

He barely had time to step back before Cruedark was on him.

The combat master's blow landed center-mass, a single, forward step and a punch so heavy it cracked the light. Callum's armor shattered with a bright, birdlike screech, fragments dissolving into smoke around him as he flew backward across the field.

He hit the ground hard. Rolled. Groaned.

"That all you've got?" Cruedark called, shaking out his massive hand.

Callum gritted his teeth and spawned his Pangolin armor.

The second Armorcore crawled across his limbs in plates and scaled over his back and shoulders, raising the finlike vambrace shields with a satisfying hiss of power. The air warped around him.

Yet again, Cruedark acted before Callum could summon a Weaponcore.

The combat master slammed his fists onto the ground, releasing a shockwave shaped like a massive charging beast, more blast than magic. The ground peeled apart and soil buckled. Earth fractured and surged outward like a trampled field beneath a stampede.

Callum was hurled back again.

<*Do I have to do everything myself?*> Killeas asked as he took the lead.

Wings burst from Callum's back, formed of shadowy mana shaped like feathers cut from stormlight. He snapped them wide, catching himself in a soaring arc. His blood surged with momentum and magic.

Cruedark looked up with a grin, cupped his hands around his tusked mouth, and bellowed. The sound ripped through the sky, the shockwave warping the air with raw force. It tore at the wind, stole it, turned everything inside out.

Callum felt the mana drain from his limbs as if something had sunk hooks into him and pulled him down. His wings faltered. He spiraled, losing altitude fast, caught in the invisible drag of Cruedark's war cry as Killeas took over. Callum rushed higher into the sky, only for Cruedark to leap toward him and seize Callum by the legs.

"Let's bring you back down to earth!" he said before Callum or Killeas could pry free from his grip.

The slam into the ground rattled his vision and shattered his armor.

"Again," Cruedark said, looming over him as he offered Callum his hands. "Refill your reserves, summon your Armorcores. Let's go."

Callum's vision spun as he looked up at the hulking man, whose meldform seemed to radiate an intensity that bordered on dangerous. "How am I supposed to—?"

"Up you go," Master Cruedark said as he turned away. "We don't have all day."

Callum stumbled to his feet and shuffled toward the stream of cascading magic to recharge. The flow washed through him like ice-laced fire, not painful but full of motion—unstoppable, primal. He took deep breaths as his reserves climbed.

<*We need to dive-bomb him. Rip his heart out!*> Killeas yelled inside his head.

<*He's trying to help us,*> Fen reminded the gryphon.

<*What's gotten into you over the last five hundred years? Where is the fox that once took on an entire squadron of demonic bunnies?*>

<*What?*> Callum asked.

<*Demonic bunnies?*> Fen echoed. <*They were much bigger than rabbits, damn you!*>

<*Ha! I remember them being quite small. But where is that fox? The one worthy of his title?*>

<*You'd better watch what you say to me, Killeas!*>

<*Relax, both of you.*> Callum told the two of them. <*We're still in training.*> He strode back into position, Pangolin armor snapped back over him. He summoned his Ram swords.

When Cruedark charged this time, Callum didn't meet him head-on. He leaped back and let the impact crater the ground.

Callum soared into the sky, wings bristling with wind, where he pivoted, aimed, and dove toward his teacher, blades glowing, aiming for a clean cross-slash. Cruedark raised a single massive arm and blocked, but this time the hit landed with weight.

The old warrior staggered back a half step.

<*Shadowmark him!*> Killeas shouted.

Callum conjured a dark disc that spun like a moon and landed square against Cruedark's chest. A pulse of energy rippled across the man's form.

"Good!" Cruedark barked. "You're learning!"

Callum swept wide and used Radiant Mirage, sending four shimmering clones darting in different directions. Cruedark didn't flinch. He charged straight at the real Callum, ignoring the illusions entirely.

Callum zipped away and countered with Radiant Inferno, sending explosive bursts of fire and light all around. They flared hot against

Cruedark's tusked face—but the combat master plowed through them with a growl.

He caught Callum mid-flight and swatted him out of the air like a fly. Callum crashed, tumbled, rolled nearly thirty feet, and stood again, vision doubling. Pain bloomed down his spine.

Cruedark slammed both fists into the earth again, triggering a mana-borne gravity shift. The world lurched and the air pulled. Callum felt himself being dragged toward the impact crater, his boots scraping against fractured stone.

<*Let's go!*> Killeas shouted as he launched Callum upward, wings spread. Callum pulled his Tempest Fang into his hand. He let it charge, then released a volley of slicing wind blasts one after another. Each hit staggered Cruedark, the last forcing him to one knee.

But Cruedark wasn't done. He punched the earth again, and a pillar of stone erupted from below, catching Callum across the chest and launching him skyward so fast that he wasn't able to stop himself from plummeting toward the ground.

When the dust cleared, Cruedark was standing over him with a hand extended yet again, the big man's shoulders moving up and down. "Do you see now?" he asked, panting.

Callum took the hand, wincing as he got to his feet.

"Your only real advantage is in the air. Use it. They won't be able to handle you if you're fast, focused, and above them."

"You seemed to handle me . . ."

"I'm different. I've been doing this longer than you've been alive," Cruedark said. "As for the Gryphon Vanguard of Fates. That's your secret, your edge. Do not reveal Killeas too soon."

"How?"

"How? What do you mean?" Cruedark asked.

"A shardcrafter can see our loadout; they have access to the World Ledger. Why wouldn't the Crimsons know what we have? Why don't we know what they have?"

"Ah, yes, that. Well, for one, the arena is protected by wards that prevent this sort of spying. And the World Ledger as you know it isn't truly a *world* ledger, it's Valestra's ledger; only people from our kingdom have access to it. But you do bring up a good point. Have you visited any shardcrafters since you found Killeas's Aethercore?"

"I haven't."

"Good. Only visit ones you trust." Cruedark let out a short grunt. "Now, recharge and reset. We need to get going."

Callum turned to the mana fountain. "I see why you want me to rest tomorrow."

"Exactly," Cruedark said, his voice low and gravel-edged. "It's going to be a long day." He paused. "And I'm afraid what comes next will make this look easy."

CHAPTER 37

There are vaults even the Crown cannot name, places where the realm hides what it dares not use but refuses to destroy. Their locations, contents, and access protocols remain so classified that not even the High Council holds full records. Power this concentrated is protected from everyone—especially from those who believe they already own it.

—Vensil Darrow, former royal archivist

<You call this focus?> Killeas asked. <Ha!>

<Give the lad a chance,> Fen told the gryphon as Callum did everything in his power to ignore the voices in his head so he could cycle mana.

His arms were draped over his knees, eyes half-lidded in focus. Even in the quiet of his dorm room, with his Soul Heart pulsing gently, and his mana cycling as cleanly as he could manage, soreness radiated from the base of his spine up through his shoulders. Callum's legs still felt like bricks, and his core throbbed from the powerful strikes Cruedark had launched at him hours before.

He rotated his shoulders with a wince. Empowerment of Rejuvenation hadn't been enough to dull the aftermath of that training session; that alone told him how serious today had been.

"Just give me a moment," he told Fen and Killeas.

Then came a knock, soft, barely more than the brush of fingers against wood.

"Sounds like she's here," Callum said as he stood with some effort, his muscles complaining every inch of the way as he approached the door. He opened it to find the same woman he'd seen once before, Princess Selene's notetaker in a nondescript overcoat with eyes that didn't invite questions.

"Evening," she said simply, then turned. She stopped halfway down the hallway. "Aren't you going to come with me?"

"Give me a moment." Callum didn't ask where they were going. By now, he'd learned not to bother asking when it came to Princess Selene.

After he slipped into his boots, the two crossed the Great College quad in silence, lanterns flickering above the walkways as twilight bled into deeper blue. She led him toward a part of campus he'd passed countless times before, one near the heart of the grounds.

Unsurprisingly, Callum had never registered the tower until now. It rose, narrow and tall, more spire than full keep, its smooth stonework etched in concentric rings up its surface. A cluster of Legion Guards stood motionless out front, their expressions blank but alert.

They let him pass. Inside, Callum stepped into a round chamber lined entirely with mirrored walls aside from a spiral staircase to his left and a single door to his right that appeared to lead down.

<*You look like hell,*> Killeas said.

<*Is it that bad?*> Callum ran his hand through his messy, dirty blond hair, hoping to fix it. His own reflection stared back at him from every angle, infinite and unblinking. He touched his chin, noticing the slight beard stubble and instantly corrected his posture.

<*You're meeting the princess. You should have tidied up.*>

Callum smirked at the gryphon's comment. <*I'll keep that in mind,*> he thought as he noticed Sir Trindade suddenly standing there.

He wasn't in here before . . . Callum looked the Legion Guard over again. *Maybe he came through a portal.*

"Good," Sir Trindade said before he could ask. "You're here. Follow me."

Callum's gaze drifted to the nearby spiral staircase, and then to the heavy wooden door beneath it, assuming Sir Trindade would lead him in one of the two directions.

Instead, Trindade stepped directly *through* one of the mirrors.

His form rippled across the surface like water disturbed by wind, then passed through entirely, vanishing without a sound. No swirl of magic, no flare of light, just a silent, seamless disappearance. For a heartbeat, the glass went still.

Callum stared.

His own reflection flickered briefly across the mirror's face, warped and trailing, the surface now shimmering faintly in the torchlight, as if remembering the shape that had passed through.

Then the mirror stirred again.

Trindade's face reappeared on the other side, framed in soft silver distortion. "Well?" he asked, his voice perfectly clear as he pressed one gloved hand outward, palm open inside the glass. "Are you coming?"

A portal. Callum reached his hand out to the mirrored surface, which filtered away at his touch, the sensation not cold or slick but soft and pliable.

He moved into light and warmth; not the glow of day, but of flickering hearths, distant sconces, the dull luster of rich tapestries lining the walls. The room was circular, tall, and hushed. Velvet drapes hung in folds across high windows, filtering starlight into silver veils. The floors gleamed with polished maroon marble broken apart by white veining, some sections so smooth and dark that they mirrored the room itself, a second world beneath his boots.

Callum had the vague sensation of having entered a castle, but he couldn't tell where he was. The air smelled faintly of old parchment and rare oils, like incense burned in sacred places, the scent not matching the ostentatious look of the space.

Princess Selene stood across from him, hands tucked behind her back. She wore a long, dark cloak lined with pale thread, subtle embroidery shimmering with movement. It was the quietest he'd ever seen her.

Beside her, a man with a somber expression on his face sat on a big red cushion in full royal attire, long robes of deep indigo traced with gold. He was barefoot and cross-legged, hands resting on his knees. A blindfold of fine black silk was tied over his eyes, embroidered with the faint crest of the Morninglade family. Before him was an ancient shardcrafter table, one carved out of stone and marked by ancient petroglyphs, its top surface porous.

Callum stepped forward and hesitated. The blindfold. The stillness of the place. It resembled the start of some sort of ritual.

"This is Sir Gregor Avenid," Selene said, her voice low but clear as she gestured to the seated man, "personal shardcrafter to the Crown, to my family. He will be assisting you tonight."

Gregor inclined his head, lips curved in the faintest smile. "Please, sit, Stross heir." He gestured gracefully to the space before him, where there were two red cushions next to one another.

Callum swallowed and lowered himself onto the mat across from the man.

"Let's begin," he said, though his blindfolded gaze never turned, it remained focused on a point just beyond Callum's shoulder.

"Wait." Selene sat next to Callum.

"Your Highness," Sir Trindade began.

"It's fine," she told him softly. "Callum and I are friends; besides, I am allowed to sit wherever I'd like."

"Where are we exactly?" Callum asked, fumbling the first words to come out of his mouth. He couldn't remember a time when she'd been so close to him, Callum practically able to see his own reflection in her eyes.

"If I told you, I'd have to kill you." The princess let this statement stand for a good twenty seconds before she laughed lightly to herself. "I'm kidding. But I still can't tell you where we are. I don't know myself. It's a location in the Valestra Kingdom, I can tell you that, but I've never been outside of these walls. And that is for good measure. The crown holds much of its wealth here. The people that work and live here have relinquished their command over sight due to the secrecy needed in this role."

<Is that the royal way to say someone has been blinded by the Crown?> Killeas asked. <Seems unnecessary. If you put the right kind of people in charge of defense, you wouldn't need to do something so cruel. Ha! Who am I kidding? The poor fellow in front of you probably begged for this honor. You humans are all the same, always looking for your next master.>

<Is that what you have taken from the human experience?> Fen asked. <Perhaps we let them operate in the way they so choose rather than comment on everything they do, be it good or bad.>

Killeas continued to laugh as Callum tuned back in to Princess Selene's words.

"So, to answer your question," she said, "I, myself, really don't know where we are. I only know how to get here."

Callum considered asking if *anyone* knew but held the question back. He didn't want to sound completely lost.

The blindfolded Gregor nodded slowly. "Let's begin with your new Aethercore. Please provide it to me now."

Callum withdrew Killeas's core from his chest and noticed how it shook violently with power. It sprouted a pair of shadowy wings and slapped into Gregor's open hands. "Ah," he said, the energy washing over him, "it truly is an honor, Gryphon Vanguard of Fates." This seemed to calm the Aethercore down. Gregor released it and let it hover before him as he spoke again. "I will first bring the gryphon to the Uncommon Grade. This will take ten Air and ten Shadow Affinity shards, as well as ten Deftness and ten Vigor shards."

The shardcrafter reached his hand into a small pouch. His actions took Callum off guard once the man's entire hand fit into a pouch that should have only fit up to his knuckles. He put it in deeper and slowly tilted his head back.

"Ten, ten, ten, ten," he whispered. Gregor produced the shards and placed them on the table. He gathered Killeas's Aethercore again and slotted all the shards in. A smile formed on his face. "And with it, comes a new power. I will let you discover that in a moment though. Now, and before you thank me, we must bring it up to the Rare Grade to better align with your Stage. It will take twenty Shadow Affinity Shards, ten Air, fifteen Deftness, five Might, and ten Vigor shards. Are you ready?"

Callum exchanged a quick glance with the princess. "Yes, and thank you."

"You don't have to thank me yet," Gregor told him. "And really, you should be thanking her."

"Thank you, prin—"

"Selene," she told Callum, "and it's the least I can do considering you will be representing the Great College's first year students, and for that matter, the Valestra Kingdom, in the match to come. This is something we have done before in games like this, and we suspect that the Geshwine Empire will be doing the same. Please continue, Sir Gregor."

"With pleasure," the shardcrafter said as he released Killeas's Aethercore, which once again buzzed with excitement.

<*I really wish he would behave himself,*> Fen told Callum. <*He's too eager.*>

<*It's fine,*> Callum thought to Fen as Gregor retrieved the shards necessary to upgrade Killeas once again.

"Twenty, ten, fifteen, five, ten," he said quietly as he placed the shards in the grooves on the crafting table. He took the Aethercore gently and pressed each shard into it. Once he was finished, he sent the orb floating back to Callum, who pushed it into his chest.

Pact of the Gryphon Vanguard of Fates
Type: *Pacted*
Grade: *Rare*
Infusion Requirements for Grade Increase:
0/25 Shadow Affinity Shards
0/20 Air Affinity Shards
0/20 Deftness Shards
0/10 Might Shards
0/15 Vigor Shards
Mana Affinities Granted: *Air, Shadow*
Meldform Benefits:
Attributes:

+3 Might
+3 Deftness
+4 Vigor
+2 Regeneration
+3 Resilience
+2 Mind

Wings of the Shrouded Ascent: *When melded, the wielder gains a pair of wings laced with shadow. These allow for sustained flight and agile aerial maneuvering.*

Windstep: *Melding allows the wielder to create bursts of compressed air beneath their feet, granting short-range aerial steps and sudden directional strikes.*

Noct Thread: *Upon melding, trails of shadow mana thread along the user's Weaponcore, enhancing reach and impact with every attack.*

"We're not done," Gregor said before Callum could even consider his new powers. "First, we will focus on the powers that I believe came with your Gryphon. Empowerment of Keen Ascent and Shadowmark, hmmm?"

"That's right," Callum said.

"Well?" Gregor asked after a pause. "Are you going to let me upgrade them?"

Callum accessed both Powercores and sent them over to Gregor. He started with Empowerment of Keen Ascent. "Ten Air Affinity, five Might, and five Mind shards coming right up." He placed his hand in the pouch and fused the shards. "Again?" he said, mostly to himself. "Sure. Fifteen Air Affinity, ten Might, and ten Mind shards."

<I've never seen someone so enthusiastic about shardcrafting,> Killeas said.

<How many shardcrafters have you met?> Fen asked him.

<Enough to know that this one really likes his job. Why, he's practically humming to himself!>

Sir Gregor fused the shards and sent the Powercore back to Callum, who used Soul Sense to check it before putting the core away.

Empowerment of Keen Ascent
Type: *Ability*
Grade: *Rare*
Infusion Requirements for Grade Increase:
0/20 Air Affinity Shards
0/15 Might Shards

0/15 Mind Shards
Affinity Requirements: Air
Effect: *When inserted into one's Soul Heart, this core gives heightened awareness during flight, making attacks more accurate and harder to counter.*

The shardcrafter did the same with the Shadowmark Powercore. As he had before, Sir Gregor went through each upgrade individually, listing the shards necessary to change the Grade from Common to Rare.

Shadowmark
Type: *Ability*
Grade: *Rare*
Infusion Requirements for Grade Increase:
0/30 Shadow Affinity Shards
0/15 Vigor Shards
0/25 Mind Shards
Affinity Requirements: *Shadow*
Effect: *When inserted into one's Soul Heart, this core allows the user to apply a Shadowmark to a target. While the mark is active, the target takes increased damage from the user's abilities.*

"Now, let's see what else we can do," Gregor said as he looked at Selene. "Princess, you told me I am able to upgrade his Aethercore and any cores that came with it. What else am I allowed to do?" The shardcrafter tilted his chin back as if he were giving Callum the once over. "He has several Weaponcores, two Armorcores, and a handful of other Powercores. One is Legendary, one is Exalted, the rest are Rare and Uncommon. He has fourteen in total, and at the Wielder stage he can have fifteen. One more core is in order."

"Anything that is Uncommon, upgrade to Rare," she said. "As for the Fifteenth Powercore, we will head to the armory next and let him select one."

Gregor grinned. "I like the sound of that! Give me your Piercing Air Spear, Gale Pulse of the Skyrend Screech, and Cloak of the Ashcoil Tyrant Powercores and I will get to work," the shardcrafter told Callum.

By the time Gregor had finished, the three Powercores were all upgraded.

Piercing Air Spear
Type: *Accessory*
Grade: *Rare Weapon*

Infusion Requirements for Grade Increase:
0/20 Air Affinity Shards
0/20 Vigor Shards
Affinity Requirements: *Air*
Effect: *Conjure a spear made of air capable of both piercing your opponent and blowing them off their feet*

Gale Pulse of the Skyrend Screech
Type: *Ability*
Grade: *Rare*
Infusion Requirements for Grade Increase:
0/25 Air Affinity Shards
0/20 Might Shards
0/15 Resilience Shards
Affinity Requirements: *Air*
Effect: *Unleashes a concussive burst of wind in all directions, knocking enemies back and interrupting spellcasting or movement.*

Cloak of the Ashcoil Tyrant Powercore
Type: *Ability*
Grade: *Rare*
Infusion Requirements for Grade Increase:
0/30 Fire Affinity Shards
0/20 Earth Affinity Shards
0/15 Vigor Shards
Affinity Requirements: *Earth or Fire*
Effect: *Release a thick cloud of charred and smoldering mana embers that can cling to anything it touches, choking and confusing enemies.*

"Wonderful," Princess Selene told the two of them. "Let's grab a new core for you as well." She smiled at Sir Gregor. "And thank you. Your expertise is always appreciated."

CHAPTER 38

Aveiro is much more than an old sailor's haunt.

—Serra Dalin, poet, *Verses from the Vale of Blue*

Selene didn't speak at first; she only gestured for Callum to follow as she slipped through a side door behind the chamber where the royal shardcrafter sat, the blindfolded man still with a big grin on his face.

<Well? What are you waiting for?> Killeas asked Callum.

Callum got to his feet, thanked the shardcrafter again, and joined the princess.

"This shouldn't take long," she said as she guided him into the next room, Sir Trindade close behind them. "But it will be worth it. You'll see."

They traveled down a short hallway, its walls etched with faded sigils and half-worn reliefs of long-forgotten battles. Old sconces lined the passage in uneven intervals, their holders shaped like open dragon claws.

At the end, the three stepped into a new chamber, one filled with an eerie quiet that pressed against the ears. The curved walls were lined with stone alcoves, each holding a suspended orb enclosed in a transparent, smoky casing. The cores inside hovered just above their pedestals, casting soft glows in shades of violet, gold, and green. Light leaked through the haze around them, flickering as if reacting to the air.

Callum took a step closer to one, his reflection warping across the casing's curved surface. "What are these?"

"They're core containers made of ashglass," Selene said as she joined him.

"Ah, Quinn told me about that stuff. It's the same material used to make the pillars in the Vestige Arena."

"Yes, but this is much, much thinner." She tapped a knuckle gently against one of the container's shells. It made a muted, hollow sound.

"There are so many," Callum said as he took them in again, in awe of the Crown's wealth. It seemed like there were hundreds, and that was just in this room. He could see more through an arched doorway beyond, and even more through another doorway after that.

"You wouldn't believe how many nobles tried to pocket these during the last century," the princess said, "but they're all accounted for here, and listed on the World Ledger."

<Which isn't exactly a World Ledger,> Killeas reminded Callum, <because it only covers the Valestra Kingdom. If we had a true World Ledger, we'd be able to better understand what our enemies are hiding.>

<The Demoncores and their pacts,> Fen added.

<I really think it would have been different had I been around the last five hundred years. I have a way with humans, you know.>

<Killeas, your presence wouldn't have changed any of this.>

<Says you. Remember, I wasn't trapped as long as you, my vulpine friend, I have more connections than you may think. I could have been like Lisalen if I hadn't been burdened with Corruption.>

<You want to be a royal pet?>

Killeas laughed. <Now there is the Fen I like, the one with the biting tongue!>

Callum shook his head and focused on what Princess Selene was saying.

"This is only one vault." She turned slowly, motioning toward another room. "One of several for each affinity. The Royal Depository of Powercores is ancient. Older than this campus. Some of these cores were drawn from sealed vaults in fallen cities. Others were donated by Great Houses or recovered from corrupted beasts."

Callum didn't know what to say. So he simply took it all in again, aware that he was in a place most of the people in the kingdom would never see.

"We don't have much longer, Your Highness," Trindade said without looking at them.

Selene glanced toward Sir Trindade, now stationed quietly near the door. "Actually, we do," she answered calmly. "There's little to gain from another meeting with the Duke of Karna, and if I never saw Draven again, my life would be significantly better." Then, as if dismissing the matter entirely, she returned her attention to the glowing orbs. "Now, Callum, you have Light, Air, Fire, and Shadow affinities, yes?"

"How did you know?"

She didn't look at him when she answered. "How do you think I knew?"

"Fair," he said as she stepped onto a golden-threaded carpet that led into another chamber, this one bathed in a brighter, almost blinding glow. The orbs here pulsed within their casings in hues of white, gold, and pale amber, their light so intense it made the edges of the room blur. Callum squinted, eyes struggling to adjust, the radiance pressing in like heat without warmth.

"In that case," she said, "Light or Shadow? That seems right, considering your new pact. The Shadow Affinity room is next."

"Light," Callum answered before he could think.

<*What? After everything we've been through?*> Killeas grumbled.

<*It was the first response to come to mind,*> Callum shot back.

The princess stepped forward. "Then we have come to the right place." Selene shielded her eyes as she turned back to Callum. "I don't suppose you want a Weaponcore or Armorcore, do you?" she asked as she moved ahead of him.

"I have—"

"Three Weaponcores and two Armorcores," she said smoothly. "I'm aware."

Callum hesitated. "Then . . . I guess I don't need one."

<*Perhaps let the princess pick one,*> Fen suggested gently. <*She's forfeiting her match to you. She believes in you; surely, she will pick something helpful.*>

"You can pick," Callum said quietly. "If that's alright."

"In that case, I'll find something that I think suits you best. Just give me a moment." Selene studied the wall in silence, her expression calm but focused. She moved slowly, touching each ashglass case. Callum remained still, resisting the urge to fidget. He could feel the weight of it, of what this meant to have access to such power.

Eventually, her fingers came to rest on the edge of an orb bathed in soft, radiant silver. Light bent subtly around it, warping like a lens as if the air itself responded to its presence. She paused for just a moment, then lifted the case. The glow inside stirred gently, casting pale reflections across her robes as though recognizing her touch. "I think this one will do," she said, holding it out to him.

Callum stared at the orb in its strange shell. He didn't know what it was. Not yet. But his pulse quickened as he reached out and took it from her hands.

Callum had been told to do nothing the following day. That was the order. Rest, cycle mana, stay off his feet. But it was hard to take it easy when his entire body still throbbed from the final training session with Master Cruedark and his mind was circling the battle ahead. The biggest match of his life was less than a day away, a fight that would pit him against either Ryven, who he had faced before, or Laziel, who might be the strongest contender from the Crimson Sigil. Despite everything he'd done to prepare, the pressure was mounting, especially after what the Crown had just done for him in advancing his cores.

Callum lay on his bed, blinds drawn, the filtered sunlight barely brushing his brow as he thought about what would come. His legs ached. His breath came a little too fast when he thought about the crowd, the arena, the expectation.

I still need to test the new Powercore the princess gave me, he thought. *But . . . I can do that later. I should definitely do that. Maybe her Legion Guards can smuggle me out again?* He smiled at the ridiculous thought as he heard a familiar knock at the door, one that pulled him out of his trance.

"It's open," he called out.

Marcella stepped into his dorm, her heeled boots light on the floor. She placed her hands on her hips, a knowing look on her face as she looked down at Callum. "Preparing for your big fight by taking a nap?"

"Not exactly," he told her as he sat up. "It's what Cruedark said I'm supposed to do."

"You're also supposed to eat breakfast, though, right?"

"Yes, but . . . I haven't gotten around to it."

"In that case, I know just the place."

"Eh—"

"Please?" Marcella asked, voice strained. "I know you're supposed to be preparing, but you've earned this. And Quinn and I just so happen to have a very special connection."

"A what?"

She held something behind her back, her expression sly. "Can I blindfold you?"

Callum instantly remembered Sir Gregor the shardcrafter. ". . . No?"

<*No? Yes! This sounds like a great plan,*> Killeas declared. <*It's been a boring morning thus far; we are due for a surprise. There had better be cake!*>

"Will there be cake?" Callum asked.

"Not to my knowledge."

"I don't know . . ."

Marcella pouted dramatically. "Come on, Little Cal, it'll be more fun that way!" With a dramatic flick of her wrist, she pulled a silken blue scarf from behind her back, the deep blue fabric embroidered with tiny silver threads. "You trust me, right?"

Callum gave her a long look, head tilted slightly. "Am I going to regret this?"

Marcella grinned. "Do you regret fun? Because that's what this is. Pure, unfiltered fun. No danger at all. Probably. Now stop whining and hold still. Sit up, turn around, and let me blindfold you."

Moments later, blindfolded and very unsure of himself, Callum allowed Marcella to lead him down the dormitory stairs, her hand firmly gripping his elbow.

"This is ridiculous," Callum said out loud.

"No, it'll be worth it. Trust me. We're almost there. I wanted you to see and enjoy something."

"See? I'm blindfolded."

"Details to follow," she said as they stepped outside, a cold rush of wind meeting his face. "It's only a few minutes' walk from here. And don't worry, it's not like everyone is staring at us wondering what tomorrow's champion is doing walking around campus in a blindfold. Hey!" Marcella shouted to someone. "Why don't you find someone else to look at? Stupid," she whispered to Callum. "Careful, steps coming up!"

Killeas roared with laughter inside Callum's head. *<This is great!>*

They descended more steps, and paused on a stone platform, where Callum heard the faint buzz of a portal. Before he could ask where they were going, Marcella shoved him through the portal.

The temperature shifted instantly.

Warm, damp air wrapped around him, heavy with the scent of salt and something briny, almost metallic. He heard the distant cry of gulls, the crash of waves against the shore. Sand crunched faintly underfoot as the breeze pressed in from all sides, carrying the whisper of the sea.

"You actually blindfolded him?" Quinn's voice asked with a laugh.

"I thought it'd be fun!" Marcella answered. "And it's a surprise . . ." She yanked the blindfold free in one swift motion, revealing the scene in front of him.

"Where . . . ?" he began.

"We're in Aveiro!"

Callum squinted at the sudden rush of sunlight.

They stood on a private stretch of beach tucked inside a lush grotto, shielded by steep cliffs and swaying palms that rustled softly in the breeze. The sand underfoot was pale gold, warm and fine, and the air smelled faintly of salt and blooming starfruit. Just ahead, the water sparkled like liquid crystal, each small wave catching the light as it lapped gently at the curved shoreline. Smooth stones ringed a shallow tide pool to one side, where bright yellow fish darted between strands of seagrass.

High above, floating almost lazily at the edge of the horizon, a cluster of sleek airships drifted like silver leaves on the wind, their hulls bearing the Valestran crest in glinting relief. A low hum from their propulsion cores barely touched the tranquil hush of the cove.

"Nice, right?" Quinn said, gesturing to them with a grin.

"I told you we have airships too," Marcella added.

She led him toward a shaded pavilion of woven fronds and thin stone supports. Beneath it waited a whitewashed table set for three, draped in fine linens and already covered with food—fresh-cut fruit, honeyed pastries, smoked fish on flatbread, herb-baked crab claws with lemon zest, eggs poached in saffron, and a cake with pink icing.

"No sand cookies," Marcella said. "But we have pretty much everything else."

<*This is what we needed!*> Killeas said. <*Even Fen is excited, the old devil.*>

"I have to admit," Fen said as he appeared next to Callum, "this is quite the surprise."

"Cat's out of the bag," Tuck said as he padded forward, Quinn's pacted aethercat now fully visible.

A sudden gust of wind swept through the clearing as Killeas took shape—larger, sharper, and far more imposing. The gryphon's appearance startled Tuck, who arched his back and let out a low growl.

"Ah, hello, feline friend!" Killeas said cheerfully. "I would call you brother, but my brother had a beak."

He snapped his own with a sharp *click* for emphasis.

Tuck hissed and backed away, tail lashing the ground, ears flattened in clear agitation.

Unbothered, Killeas stretched his wings and launched into the air, powerful strokes kicking up a flurry of sand. A moment later, Harold the aetherheron rose to join him, the two sweeping out over the water, their movements elegant as they twisted in slow, synchronized arcs above the cove.

"You did all this for me?" Callum finally asked as he took in the spread of food again, his mouth watering.

"Well, Selene helped," Marcella said as she sat. "Tomorrow's an incredibly important day. And we know you need to relax today."

Quinn nodded. "And what better place to cycle mana than by the sea?"

Callum looked out at the surf, the warmth of sunlight on his face, the smell of salt and spice in the air.

"If you want to go into town and shop after, we can do that . . ." Marcella offered.

Callum smiled, overwhelmed in the best possible way. "I think . . . I think I'll be happiest just staying here. Besides, I have the new Powercore Selene gave me to test out."

After a lazy seaside meal, one in which Callum, Quinn, and Marcella shared plenty of laughs, Callum sat by the ocean and began cycling mana. Somewhere behind him, Quinn rested on his back, staring up at the pale blue sky while Tuck and Fen roamed about.

Marcella had left for Aveiro to do some shopping, promising to return in a few hours. She took Harold with her, but that didn't stop Killeas from enjoying himself. The gryphon wheeled through the sky with gleeful abandon, diving in and out of the water in wide, sweeping arcs. He let out a proud cry and flipped once in midair before diving in again.

<*Are you sure you want to remain pacted with him?*> Fen asked, breaking Callum's focus.

Callum laughed. <*You're joking.*>

<*You can change Aethercores, you know. Perhaps we find something more agreeable, more peaceful. I'm kidding, you know. This is me joking with you.*>

"Noted," Callum said as Killeas landed in front of him, magic sizzling off his dark wings.

"They, and by *they*, I mean *you*, Stross Two, never let me fly like this on campus," the gryphon announced.

"You can just call me Callum, and we're not supposed to have our pacts out. It's sort of an unwritten rule."

Killeas sat and tilted his beak up. "Then what are we fighting for?"

"What?" Callum asked.

The gryphon snorted. "We haven't visited the Geshwine Empire, so I may be speaking out of turn here. But if they're allowed to have their aetherbeasts out all the time, it might be a step up. I'm kidding," he said as Fen took shape, ready to disagree. "Nobody hates warlocks more than us. That's what you were coming out here to say, right?" Killeas asked the fox.

"Actually . . ." Fen looked up at Callum. "Maybe we should test your new Powercore."

"Good idea." Callum got to his feet and stepped into the sand, where he used Soul Sense to read the details of his new power:

Empowerment of Haloedge
Type: *Ability*
Grade: *Legendary*
**Infusion Requirements for Grade Increase:*

0/50 Light Affinity Shards
0/35 Might Shards
0/30 Deftness Shards
0/10 Mind Shards
Affinity Requirements: *Light*
Effect: *Grants the ability to summon and control radiant phantom blades, which orbit the user defensively or can be launched toward enemies at range.*

"This should be interesting," he said as he prepared to test it.

Quinn called over to him, the other student now lying on his side. "Is it Powercore testing time?"

"It sure is!"

"Ooh, sounds like fun." Quinn got to his bare feet and Tuck melded with him as he approached. "Let's see what it does. Also . . ." He raised an eyebrow as he looked Callum over. "Question: Have you ever been to the beach before?"

"I haven't. I've been to lakes out west, but nothing like this."

"Then you should take your boots off."

"My boots?" Callum looked down.

"Yes."

"Right, because I'm at the beach." Callum smiled at Quinn. "That's what you're supposed to do, isn't it?"

"Not always, and certainly not if it's a rocky beach," Quinn told Callum as he began removing his boots. "But one like this, with perfect sand and an even nicer breeze. It's great."

"Wow," Callum said as curled his bare toes into the sand. "Not . . . not at all what I was expecting."

"Good, right?" Quinn flashed him a grin. "Now let's see this new Powercore."

Callum took a breath and cast Haloedge.

Three swords of shimmering light bloomed into the air above his head—long, slightly curved, and hovering with precise elegance. Each blade vibrated with quiet power, mana rippling in harmony with the surrounding light. The swords rotated slowly in a triangle formation, casting gold-tinged reflections on the sand.

Killeas rose into the air, wings outstretched. <*Now that is a fancy trick! Let's see how good it is. See if you can hit me.*>

Callum focused on the leading sword, then gestured, barely more than a flick of his wrist.

The nearest blade zipped toward the gryphon like a bolt of sunfire.

Killeas banked to dodge, then curved in with a playful shriek. "Come now, surely you can do better than—" He flared wide to avoid the second blade. "Hey!"

Fen laughed. "Careful up there!"

"Quiet, fox," Killeas said as he looped back. "What happens if I actually hit one?"

"Let's find out." Callum called up to him.

Killeas dove, talons extended, wings folding into a controlled plummet. Just before impact, Callum guided the sword down and—

Whomp! It clashed against Killeas's energy, then sizzled out in a flash of energy.

"That's brilliant!" Fen said. "They break when they're used?"

"Disposable guardians. You clever little blades!" Killeas called down to Callum.

Quinn let out a low whistle. "That is going to be really useful. Tuck thinks so too."

"It's what I was expecting," Callum said, eyes still on the last sword hovering protectively overhead. "But also . . . not what I was expecting."

"That's the best kind of surprise." Quinn glanced toward the winding path Marcella had taken into town. A breeze rolled in off the sea, warm and salty, brushing over the quiet cove. Palms rustled gently above them, and the sun cast long golden streaks across the sand. "How long do you think until she returns?"

"No telling." Callum stepped toward the surf, the last lightblade still hovering above him. The water foamed over his feet, cool and welcoming. "But . . ." he lifted his arms and inhaled the ocean air, "I think I'll take a swim."

"You should." Quinn smiled, eyes reflecting the sea's glint. "Enjoy yourself, Cal. You've earned that."

CHAPTER 39

Victory is never certain. But belief can make your next step feel like the first one that matters.

—Tensan Faire, Master Convoker, Archon of New Albion

The day of the tournament came faster than Callum would have liked, especially after his nice daytrip to the beach in Aveiro, which had definitely cleared his head.

He woke early that morning, his body finally recovered from his intense training with Master Cruedark. *First things first*, he thought as he got out of bed and sat cross-legged beneath the open window of his room, which continued to provide an ominous view of the two Geshwinian airships parked sky outside.

Callum ignored them as he focused on absorbing the radiant mana all around him, bringing the power that coursed through his world into his Soul Heart. A knock at the door pulled him out of his meditation. He opened it to find a wooden box with the Morninglade crest branded into it.

"A gift from the princess?" Fen asked as he appeared beside Callum.

"Looks like it." Callum lifted the box and brought it to the foot of his bed, not bothering to shut the door behind him. Inside, armor lay folded with meticulous care, each piece wrapped in deep navy cloth threaded with silver filigree. The plating gleamed with a tempered finish, compact and refined, designed not just for function but for agility. Every joint, every edge, looked custom forged. "It's so light," he told Fen, referring to the box that it came in. "I didn't actually think there was armor inside."

Fen sat near the armor and stared at it for a moment, appreciation on his face.

Killeas said something, but Callum ignored the gryphon as he continued to examine one of the pieces, a vambrace thin enough to fit under his overcoat. He placed it on his bed and went for the chestplate, which was etched in subtle silver relief with the Morninglade crest—the same insignia he'd seen on Sir Trindade's shoulder.

"She's really putting her faith in you," Fen said.

"The whole kingdom is!" Killeas reminded Callum, the gryphon finally appearing. He stretched like a cat and resettled on the ground, front claws folded over one another. "Well, there is another match, but yours is especially important."

"You keep telling me that." Callum fastened the armor into place, feeling the balanced weight settle over him like a second skin. *The only time I wore armor before joining the Great College was during militia training in Weatherby, and that armor was nothing like this,* he thought as he examined it once again.

"Is something the matter?" Killeas asked with a yawn.

"No."

"Can I take a quick flight around the campus and perhaps stir up trouble for the warlocks' airships?"

"Also, no."

"It would be easy, you know," the gryphon assured him. "The ships are powered by mana. I could disrupt something like that faster than you would think."

"Could you?" Callum asked.

"I could. Ask Fen!"

"He's not lying," the fox said, "but I don't think now is the time for an act of war, because that is exactly what that would be."

"A war is what this place needs," Killeas said. "A war—" His attention snapped to the door as Marcella stepped in with Quinn behind her, both carrying woven containers filled with breakfast, the scent instantly reaching him.

"Everything you like," Marcella announced, already scanning the room for a place to set it down. She closed the box that the armor came in and placed it there. "Hi, Fen, Killeas."

"Greetings, human friends," Killeas said.

"Umm, that's one way to say it." Marcella showed Callum the containers of food again. "What are we waiting for? Let's dig in." She opened one of them to reveal a plate filled with thick slabs of bacon, fire-roasted root vegetables, and round seedcakes smeared with berry jam.

"Don't forget this," Quinn said, producing a folded cloth filled with chunks of savory egg pie. He glanced around for a surface. The only one in sight was Callum's study desk, currently buried under open books and a half-written parchment meant for his father.

"We'll just do it on the floor, like we're shardcrafters," Quinn declared. "Actually . . ." He spotted the polished wooden box that had held the armor. "We'll use that for the table. And for a tablecloth . . ." He snatched Callum's cloak and laid it over the lid. "Perfect. Wait, are you okay with this?"

"It works," Callum said.

"I always wondered why shardcrafters set up that way," Marcella said as they gathered around the food.

"Couldn't tell you." Quinn took a bite of egg tart and was talking with his mouth full. "But I can ask around."

"Hey, save some of those for the champ," Marcella teased.

They laughed. And for a few minutes, it felt like a stolen moment from a simpler life. No impending duel. No title. Just three students sharing a morning meal.

Callum ate less than usual—nerves dulled his appetite—but the familiarity of it all, the closeness, the comfort, grounded him. He didn't need to speak it aloud. They were with him. That was enough.

When they finished, they cleaned up in silence, and headed out, the cheers from the Vestige Arena already rising. Overhead, the clouds had thickened and dropped lower, their edges smudged and heavy. Callum glanced up, noting the shift in the wind and the scent on the air.

Rain is coming, maybe not today, but soon, he thought as they found Master Cruedark waiting for them outside the staging entrance, the combat master fully armored in dark silver scale with tusked pauldrons and a battle-worn coat of arms draped from his hip.

<Maybe it's a sign of respect,> Fen offered, sounding unsure. <Or maybe he knows something we don't. He's never worn that much gear before.>

"You're early," Cruedark said to Callum, nodding once. "Good." Callum opened his mouth to speak, but the combat master held up a hand. "And I want to say it now, there's no 'remember what I taught you' nonsense here, no pep talk. You'll remember what you remember. Just fight smart and be sure to power up when necessary."

He handed Callum a worn leather pouch. Inside were more than a dozen shards. "Seriously?" Callum asked as he looked inside to find four Might, two Vigor, two Resilience, two Deftness, two Mind, and three Regeneration shards.

"I'd give you more, but it won't matter at your current Stage," Cruedark said. "That's enough to get through what's ahead. Use them willingly, not sparingly. Understand? Willingly, not sparingly."

"Understood, and thank you," Callum said, sealing the pouch and clipping it to his belt.

"Do well today," Cruedark said as he motioned the three of them toward the Vestige Arena. "I'll be cheering for you from the stands."

Callum and his friends moved on, continuing along the stone path that led toward the heart of the arena. The sound of the crowd grew with every step—distant at first, then thunderous.

The passage opened onto a long walkway flanked by towering flagpoles, each bearing a banner of the Great College, its divisions, the Valestra Kingdom, the Morninglade Crest, or the sigils of past champions. The flags snapped and rippled in the wind, a tunnel of color and history that led straight to the inner gate.

Just as they neared the threshold, two Legion Guards stepped forward, halting Marcella and Quinn with an outstretched arm.

"And who are you?" one of the guards asked, leaning forward slightly to get a better look.

"Students," Quinn replied quickly.

"His *trainers*," Marcella added without missing a beat. She elbowed Quinn in the ribs.

"Ahem, right," Quinn said, straightening. "You should see what we've done with his footwork."

The guard arched a brow. Marcella, ever committed, slipped behind Callum and began massaging his shoulders. Unfortunately, the gesture lost all effectiveness given the armor and thick overcoat. She smiled in her effortless way—charming, confident, just flirtatious enough to disarm without trying too hard.

The guards exchanged a look. One gave a grunt. They stepped aside.

<I can't believe that actually worked,> Fen said as they moved past and into the Veilchamber, where the fountain at the center glowed with a soft, steady light, casting shifting hues across the walls, just as Callum remembered.

The roar of the crowd pressed through the stone, muffled but steady, a constant pressure that sent faint tremors through the patched floor beneath their feet. Cheers, drums, and the occasional chant rose and fell above the din. The energy in the arena was unmistakable and still rising.

"It's going to be crazy out there," Quinn said, stepping up beside Callum at the slotted viewing wall. They both leaned in, peering out into the arena.

Vestige Arena had never looked more alive. The stands overflowed with spectators, every tier packed to the edge. On the far right, a sea of crimson and black marked the Geshwinian delegation—dignitaries and nobles seated in rigid rows, their armor polished, their ceremonial sashes gleaming in the light.

Callum's gaze lifted toward the central balcony nestled above the highest tier, the one marked by golden banners and a protective ward shimmering faintly around its edge. He saw King Morninglade, unmistakable in his golden regalia. To his right sat the Imperion Rotharyn, silent and still, robed in muted crimson. To the king's left was the Duke of Karna, broad-shouldered and severe, his expression unreadable. There was no sign of Draven.

Even from a distance, the king's seat was fully exposed to the arena, elevated for visibility—and, Callum couldn't help but notice, only a light barrier ward separating it from the open air.

Callum exhaled, nerves flickering through him.

Marcella sidled up beside. "It's better this way."

He glanced at her. "What do you mean?"

"You're nervous. That's good. You should be. But you're not up first up, remember."

"Right, Ryven and Laziel will face each other first," Callum said.

"Which is to your benefit," Marcella said, eyes focused on the shifting tiles in the arena beyond. "You might as well study your enemy while you wait. Ooh, it looks like it's starting."

They watched as the Soul Pythia floated into the center of the Vestige Arena beneath a cascade of horizontal banners moving like the tide Callum had watched in Aveiro. Standing beside her, robed in crimson garb and draped in the unmistakable golden threads of the Geshwine Empire, was her counterpart, a severe man whose expression was as unyielding as the iron staff he bore.

"Today," the Soul Pythia announced, voice magnified by magic, face everchanging, "the Duelist Rounds draw to their natural conclusion. First, Ryven Calesh and Laziel Thornhelm."

A rumble of whispers broke across the arena. The announcement rolled through the stands as the Crimson Sigil students began stomping their feet.

"Following their match," she added with ceremonial poise, "will be the bout between Princess Selene Morninglade and Callum Stross. For the final match of the First Year Duelist Rounds, the victors from each institution will face one another to close this portion of the tournament between the Crimson Sigil and the Great College."

The murmurs from the crowd turned to a great clamor. Callum barely registered the rising noise, his attention now locked on the two figures walking from opposite ends of the Vestige Arena.

Ryven came forward first, thickset and low to the ground, his arms swinging loose like he was already halfway melded. Across from him, Laziel stood taller, lean but massive, his stride casual and red eyes unreadable beneath a blank facial expression offset by the startling white of his hair.

The two didn't exchange words. They simply faced one another as the crowd behind them roared to life. Stomping began from the Crimson side, slow at first, then growing in force and rhythm. Dozens of boots in perfect cadence, building pressure with every beat.

On the Valestran side, the booing came swift and sharp, voices rising in defiance, trying to drown out the stomped rhythm with sheer volume.

"This might be one for the ages," Quinn said, wrapped up in it all as the match began. "But let's hope they beat each so thoroughly that—"

Mana crackled around Ryven as his body bulged outward, tusks forming, hooves thudding hard against the shifting arena tiles as he melded forward. The tiled ground itself trembled with his charge, yet Laziel didn't flinch.

As Ryven closed the distance, Laziel leaped, clearing the rampaging boar-man by a full body's length.

The arena floor shifted in real time, tiles groaning as they transformed. Flat stone fractured and rose, reshaping into jagged ridges and uneven outcroppings causing Ryven to jump to the side. Dry riverbeds snaked through the terrain, their cracked surfaces spiderwebbed with age and heat.

"Look!" Marcella said as cacti jutted up from the ground in irregular clusters, their spines glinting under the harsh, conjured mana-sun overhead as dust whipped along the shifting ground in short, sharp gusts of ancient dust. The temperature rose noticeably, the air brittle and dry, and the distant walls of the arena shimmered with heat distortion, making it feel as if they had stepped into the heart of a scorched wasteland.

Ryven turned with a roar and fired a bolt from his crossbow Weaponcore, the arrow hissing with shadowy magic. To avoid it, Laziel slid across a flat bit of stone with unnatural speed. He jumped over a cactus as it exploded into bits courtesy of Ryven's next arrow.

<*That's more than just heightened agility,*> Fen said. <*He must be using Attribute Shards. Has to be!*>

<*Powercore?*> Callum thought back to the fox.

<*Or another Aethercore,*> Killeas said, more serious than usual. <*Something is off about the pony-tailed one. Too smooth. Too fast. It's not a Powercore.*>

<*I think you're right,*> Fen told him.

<*I know I'm right, fox!*>

Ryven roared and charged just as Laziel's form blurred. A mist of shadow spilled across the arena from his feet, and he vanished into it.

Suddenly, he was above Ryven flying down toward him in his meldform. A trunk of raw magic slammed into the brute, the impact ringing out like a thunderstrike. Ryven hurtled into the ashglass barrier protecting the crowd. It shuddered but held.

He dropped back to the arena floor, groaning, but was back on his feet in a matter of moments. He dug deep channels into the stone with his hooves as he rooted the tiles, forcing thick spikes of earth upward as he rushed toward Laziel.

His opponent didn't slow.

Laziel crashed straight through the earthen barricade, scattering grit in every direction as he swept one arm forward. A surge of molten mana spilled from his palm. The glowing torrent hissed and cracked as it cut across Ryven's path, forcing the boar-man to backpedal hard.

Both duelists separated from their Aethercores in near-unison, and with a flash of light, the battlefield grew wilder still.

Laziel's Cinder Mammoth materialized in full, its hide streaked with glowing orange cracks. Ryven's Juggerboar bellowed in response, a wall of shadowy fur and muscle, tusks like scythes and eyes blazing with fury.

They met in a thunderous collision.

The ground shuddered beneath them as meldform tusk met meldform tusk. The Mammoth reared, stomping down with enough force to crater the stone; the Juggerboar answered with a brutal headbutt that sent a shockwave through the arena.

Magic flared with every strike as shockwaves rippled outward, shaking the protective barrier around the spectators, who gasped and cheered as the field shimmered from the force.

Laziel turned his trunk into a sweeping arc of charged power, knocking Ryven off-balance. Ryven countered with a shockwave stomp that broke the tile around Laziel's feet, yet Laziel didn't stop. He spun, slammed his tusks forward, and sent Ryven skidding across the arena with an epic punch.

Ryven pushed to his feet, face now covered in blood. He spat red as Laziel, still pacted, darted forward in a riveting charge, speed unnatural for something so massive. He caught Ryven mid-step and slammed him into the stone with such force the entire arena fell silent.

Laziel stood there, heaving, shoulders rising and falling as Ryven tried to rise. Unable to make it to his feet, Ryven stumbled and dropped to one knee before finally collapsing.

Healers rushed in, but Laziel stopped them with a raised hand, his meldform fading away in a swirl of embers. He stepped forward and offered Ryven his hand, pulling the big man to his feet.

Once Ryven stood, the two locked eyes and leaned in, foreheads touching in a silent gesture of respect, Ryven's covered in blood, Laziel's white hair a mess. Ryven accepted the outcome with quiet dignity as he took a knee.

The Geshwinians stomped with approval as Laziel returned to his Veilchamber.

"What just happened?" Marcella asked.

"Which part?" Quinn asked her as they watched Laziel turn back to his Veilchamber.

Marcella shook her head. "It doesn't matter, you've got this, Callum."

"Yeah," he said, steeling himself.

<Eh, we could have handled either of them,> Killeas told Callum. <If I'm being honest, I'm less worried than before.>

Marcella placed her arm around Callum's shoulder and gave him a quick side hug. "You good?"

"I'm good," Callum said, his mind still processing the fight he had just witnessed.

"Smash Laziel's in like he did his friend out there. I'd say something way darker but it would upset Quinn. Rip him a new one? How about that? Start with his long white braid. Just yank it off his head, take control, and be done with it."

<She's not wrong,> Killeas said. <And I'm not opposed to pulling hair.>

"The match will be over sooner than you think," Quinn added. "Just don't let him get control early. If Laziel starts pounding, you're doomed." A hesitant grin stretched across his face. "Huh. I guess we really are your trainers."

Callum looked out across the arena again. *Trainers and witnesses*, he thought as the tiles reset, his name moments away from being called.

CHAPTER 40

You can dress a Morninglade in silk and crown her with light, but you can't stop her from ramming her head through the nearest stone wall if she's made up her mind.

—Overheard from Nan Elsy, Queen Viandralis Morninglade's night attendant

The Veilchamber dissolved before Callum in a shimmer of light that allowed him to pass through. The moment felt slower than it should have, his thoughts narrow, his breath tight as he stepped out into the arena prepared for Selene to forfeit. The change in temperature hit Callum first, followed by a surprising round of jeers from the Geshwinian side of the arena. The Valestran crowd remained curiously silent, which Callum expected considering he would be facing the princess.

They're definitely not going to be cheering for me in a match against the crown princess, he thought as he glanced up toward the royal dais, where King Morninglade sat flanked by the Duke of Karna and High Council, Imperion Rotharyn, and a ring of other attendants. The king was too far away for Callum to make out his expression, but he somehow imagined there was a hardened expression on his face with what was about to happen.

His head bowed slightly, Callum moved forward onto the reformed arena tiles, which were now flat, neutral. His gaze flicked up to the far side of the Vestige Arena where one of the private Veilchambers pulsed. As the shell of magic peeled away, Princess Selene emerged in full armor with a deep blue sheen, portions accented in gold and silver filigree. A flared metal tasset encircled her hips, swaying with each step. The crest of her house was emblazoned across her chestplate and her hair was braided tight along the sides of her head, pulled into a precise bun at the back.

Callum offered the princess a quick smile as she approached.

<*Isn't she supposed to forfeit?*> Killeas asked.

<*She will,*> Callum assured the gryphon.

<*It doesn't look like it to me. It looks like she came to fight.*>

<*It would make sense for her to be wearing armor,*> Fen told Killeas. <*She's playing a part, remember?*>

<*It looks like she's doing more than that . . .*> Killeas said as Princess Selene lifted her hand and the Valestran crowd erupted in a frenzy of adoration. Cheers rolled across the arena. Everywhere, hands clutched hearts, eyes shone, and the sound swelled louder than a thousand voices raised into battle.

<*Now would be the time for a signal,*> Fen said as Selene took a step closer to Callum. <*Or at least a dramatic show of retreat.*>

Callum nodded to himself. *Maybe this is part of the act*, he thought and he half raised a hand to wave, just enough to show good faith and to question what it was he was supposed to be doing. *She didn't say I should take a knee or anything. And if I did that, wouldn't that be forfeiting myself?*

Selene stopped a dozen feet from him, her eyes burning with readiness, posture balanced, feet grounded like a knight preparing for war.

The tension thickened with the roar of the crowd.

"Selene?" Callum asked, brows drawing together. "What's going on?"

She opened her mouth, hesitated, and finally spoke: "I'm sorry, Callum."

The words were so quiet, so measured, they were nearly swallowed by the sudden blast of sound that marked the start of the match.

The arena shifted at once.

Tiles flipped, sank, and reformed with mechanical precision, transforming the battleground beneath them. A glacial expanse spread outward in every direction, jagged with ice ridges and glinting frost. What had been smooth beige tile was now buried beneath brittle, uneven snow, hard-packed and crusted-over frozen earth that cracked beneath their steps.

Flecks of snow drifted lazily through the air, swirling in dry, unpredictable currents as the wind turned sharp. Visibility began to dip as frost clouds fell low to the ground and distant spires of ice rose around them like flags being erected. The arena, now sculpted by cold magic, had fully formed into a bleak and vast tundra.

<*She's really going to fight us?*> Killeas asked, his voice a half laugh, half growl of disbelief. <*In that case, yes! Yes! I accept this fight!*>

<*No!*> Callum shouted internally, immediately breaking into a run to avoid the ground shifting beneath him. <*She's going to fight Fen and me. I can't reveal you. We agreed on this!*>

<*That was before we were challenged by the princess! Let's take to the air, Lad, and be done with this before she can even get a hit in!*>

<*No, just Fen,*> Callum told the gryphon as Selene took her meldform in a burst of golden-white mana. A veil of fur-lined frost armor rippled into existence across her shoulders and gauntlets, as she dropped to all fours and took off after him.

Callum moved to advance on her when a sense of fear came over him. "Damn it," Callum said, ducking behind a rising shard of ice as he conjured his Ram sword.

<*Hiding was not the plan,*> Killeas said as Callum split the weapon in two.

<*Clearly!*> Callum's Pangolin Armorcore formed around him as he continued to fight for some distance.

<*Focus! Why are you running?*> Killeas asked.

<*Let us both focus, Killeas,*> Fen told the gryphon as Selene tore after Callum through the snow, the princess now melded with Ecaris.

She lunged, twisting midair as she conjured her Weaponcore trident in a sweeping arc meant to skewer him mid-dodge. His foxlike reflexes took over as Callum met her blow with crossed Ram swords, the clash sending out a crack of power that blasted snow outward in a ring.

Selene landed cleanly, crouched, lunged again, and immediately swept her trident low, taking out Callum's legs. He hit the ground, shoulder-first, and rolled as her second impact slammed into the snowy tile he'd just vacated.

<*I can handle her!*> Killeas crowed, his voice a storm in Callum's skull. <*Stubbornness will get you nowhere!*>

<*I've told you once already, we've got this!*> Fen appeared beside Callum in a flicker of light. The fox sprinted with him, aiding his acceleration as Callum surged across the battlefield, boots crunching snow and lungs heaving through the frozen air.

With a glance over his shoulder and a flick of his hand, Callum cast Radiant Inferno. Bursts of blinding flame and sharp-edged light detonated behind him in staggered flashes, shredding through the snow and forcing the princess to veer left. One of the explosions caught her in her side, disrupting her momentum.

<*How about Haloedge?*> Fen asked.

<*I think . . . I think I should save it!*> Callum dismissed the Ram swords and conjured his Tempest Fang, the wind-forged blade humming with volatile promise. He raised the blade and fired, the slices of air spiraling across the arena, carving divots in the frost and kicking up snow.

Selene bolted forward, tanking through two of the strikes in her bear form. The third gust of wind struck her dead on, forcing her to stagger as the battlefield changed again.

The snow beneath their feet hissed into vapor, vanishing in curling ribbons of mist as heat rushed over the arena.

In an instant, the tundra was gone, replaced by a searing, golden expanse. Sand erupted upward, dry and restless, shaping itself into steep ridges, red hoodoos, and sweeping dunes. The air shimmered with distortion; Callum found himself standing atop one of the newly formed dunes, the loose earth shifting under his boots.

Overhead, the artificial sun blazed mercilessly, its light refracting off the heat-haze, casting coronas across his vision; the halos of brightness blurred the edges of the arena until it seemed like the sky itself was burning.

Below him, Selene stood in the trough between dunes, her stance steady, her gaze as unreadable as ever.

The moment Callum's eyes locked with hers, something shifted. A wave of pressure rolled through him, tightening his chest, prickling the back of his neck, the same creeping primal dread that he'd felt before. His breath caught, muscles tensed.

No.

Callum forced it down. Pushed back against the instinct to freeze, to retreat, to hit the stands and climb out of the arena, forfeiting the match.

He called forth a burst of tangled roots. They erupted upward in a twisting mass, wrapping around Selene's legs and halting her ascent before she could gain higher ground.

For a brief second, he saw hesitation in her eyes, which was quickly replaced by a sudden fury as flames spiraled along her arms, then coalesced into burning blades from wrist to elbow. With two savage slashes, she tore through the roots and leaped toward the dune.

<*Where did she get fire?*> Fen asked, but Callum was already on the move as he jumped down toward her, Tempest Fang raised high.

He never saw the flash of light coming.

It tore upward, like a spectral bear's strike, and hit him full in the chest, flinging him sideways and shattering his Pangolin Armorcore. He spiraled once, twice, then hit the slope hard, Callum sliding, scraping, half tumbling as the sand gave way beneath him in uneven bursts.

He finally crash-landed in a patch of brittle brush, the stalks snapping under his weight. Groaning, Callum pushed himself upright. Grit filled his mouth and heat tore at his skin as the world turned sideways.

And that was when he understood.

<It's her Aethercore,> Callum told Fen and Killeas, panting now. <Ecaris . . . fear. I've felt like I'm going to die this whole time, but it's not just the stakes. It's her bear's power. I remember it from our last fights!>

<Right,> Fen confirmed. <She doesn't even need to activate it. The aura alone is enough.>

<What is there to be afraid of?> Killeas asked, unimpressed. <Add me to this fight and it will be over before you can wet your pants again.>

Back on his feet, Callum cast Ashcoil. The battlefield erupted in smoke, swirling with charred black embers and drifting cinders that scattered like burning leaves, visibility dropping instantly.

The terrain shifted beneath his boots again. The sand dunes disappeared, smoothing into a vast stretch of rolling plains. Tall golden stalks now covered the ground in every direction, their dry husks hissing in the wind. The field seemed endless—flat, open, and deceptively empty.

Like . . . Weatherby, Callum thought, taken back by what he was seeing.

The grasses bent and rippled with each gust, breaking up lines of sight, masking movement.

<Perfect cover,> Fen said. <Get low!>

Callum did as instructed, moving low and quiet, his breath shallow as he summoned his second Armorcore. He conjured the Piercing Air Spear and stepped back as Selene leaped through the smoke, claws wide.

He slammed her with the haft of his spear. She twisted and stumbled, but kept coming. Another lunge; this time, he met her clean. The Piercing Air Spear struck center mass, cracking her Armorcore in a burst of splintering light. The impact drove her backward, boots skidding across fertile soil.

Selene reeled back, rolling once before digging into the earth with clawed feet. She formed a second Armorcore as she came up, the chitinous pieces snapping into place one by one with sharp, insectile clicks.

Selene slammed into Callum with the full force of her bear-melded form. The two of them tumbled, grappling, crashing through the tall golden grass until they hit a small ledge.

"Wait—!" Callum shouted as the two went off the ledge and landed in a pool of water, the impact and rush of it all deep and sudden.

Callum broke the surface of the pond, gasping for air.

Selene's clawed hand clamped around his ankle and yanked him under, water swallowing him whole.

He twisted and kicked as he fought against her grip, but the strength of her meldform was overwhelming. Ecaris wasn't just a bear; she was a towering beast, all muscle and will. And underwater, that will became an anchor, dragging Callum deeper and deeper with relentless force.

<I can get us out of here!> Killeas called.

<No!> Callum snapped back. *<Not yet!>*

Bubbles exploded around him as he thrashed, lungs screaming, pressure building in his skull. The weight of the water crushed in from all sides, cold and endless, each movement slower, heavier.

He kicked hard, straining toward the surface, but Selene was still on him.

She moved with grim purpose, slicing through the water. Her trident flashed in the dim light; Callum barely twisted out of the way, shoving off her shoulder to spin free, limbs burning as he fought to stay conscious.

He finally broke the surface to suck in some air only to be dragged under again.

They collided in the murky dark, limbs tangling, kicks and claws scraping past each other in a blur of violence as both Fen and Killeas shouted in Callum's head. Mana flared around him, brief flashes of light in the pond's deep gloom.

Her eyes met his. Blue. Intense. Not cold, not cruel. Something else flickered there. A warning?

Before Callum could process it, the entire arena buckled.

The water around them twisted unnaturally, drawn upward by unseen force. A vortex formed, then collapsed, the lake vanishing as gravity reasserted itself.

They dropped and the ground caught them hard.

Tiles slammed together beneath their feet with a grinding snarl of stone and pressure. A new platform rose beneath them—wide, fractured, and jutting high into the open air like a solitary mountain peak.

Soaked, breathless, and reeling, they faced one another again. No more water. No more cover.

Selene charged; Callum blasted her with a surge of wind, the sweeping arc lifting her off her feet and hurling her over the side of the plateau, the crowd gasping, the arena still for a moment.

Callum stood there alone, chest heaving, magic crackling around him as he stared out across the transformed arena, blinking in disbelief.

Did I do it? he started to wonder, yet again having to swallow a growing sense of fear.

The wind shifted and heat bloomed. From below, a flare of brilliant orange lit across the edge of the plateau. Fire rose through it and Selene ascended in a rush of brilliance, her arms wide, her trident gripped tight as enormous wings spread open behind her. Not wings of feather, nor of scale, but of pure flame, fiery red orange with golden tips, each beat scorching the sky as they lifted her gracefully into view above the cliff.

Callum's eyes widened, heart skipping.

<*Those are Lisalen's wings,*> Fen said, his voice rising with intensity. <*She's pacted with the phoenix!*>

CHAPTER 41

Lisalen was no falcon. The Brightflame Phoenix, singular and sovereign, pacted to the Demonslayer and, later, to the Royal Family. The first and only one of her kind. The aetherfalcons that bear her name are elegant imitations. Powerful, yes, but nothing like the flame that once answered only to the Demonslayer.

—Henry Evo, Master Convoker, Clergo and former Chief Historian of the Great Library

She pacted with Lisalen? Callum thought as he peered up, Selene's ascent hidden in a ring of smoke and flame, far above the screaming crowd and shifting tiles. She landed amid the smog and pointed her trident at Callum as a crown of light formed around her head. "Why aren't you fighting me?" she demanded.

A pulse of flames surged outward from her phoenix wings, widening the veil of smoke that cloaked them from the stands.

"You were supposed to—"

"You're not answering me," Selene cut in as she raised her weapon. "Why? Where is Killeas? Lisalen demands to speak to him."

<*And I will speak to the wretched Brightflame Pigeon! Let me show her what a real pair of wings looks like!*> Killeas yelled in Callum's head.

<*No,*> he told the gryphon as he focused on the princess, feeling betrayed and confused, which didn't mix well with the adrenaline racing through him. "I can't reveal my other Aethercore. I was told by Master Cruedark to save it for the fight to come."

"The fight you might no longer get to. Use your ash again," she said as the smoke started to clear. "I want to settle this now."

Callum released a cloud of charred mana, thick and smoldering, which drew more annoyance from the crowd as they struggled to see what was happening on the battlefield. The princess flared her wings again to make it look like something was happening.

"We only have a moment before the tiles shift again," Selene said, her voice low and urgent. "Callum, I need to prove to myself, and to everyone else, that I can do this. I don't want to forfeit this fight. I never wanted to. This is my choice, it is my choice to face you for the challenge and for the kingdom, for everyone to see and understand what I'm capable of. You understand that, right? I don't care what Sir Trindade, what my father—"

"You're going against your father's will?"

"Not exactly." She looked at him, the fire in her eyes mirrored in the ember-glow of her phoenix wings. "He gave me Lisalen as a second pact."

"What? Why?"

<I want to talk to the phoenix,> Killeas growled. <I want to talk to her now!>

<No,> Fen replied sharply. <We still need to keep you under wraps. This is all wrong.>

<They're young. They're passionate. I'm sure there are other ways for them to work through their urges than in the middle of a fight! We can take the phoenix, Fen. Are you afraid? I would think not! Ha! Did you hear when I called her Brightflame Pigeon? She always hated that.>

<I'm sure she did.>

<I have bested her before, you know. The others were there. She pushed me or I pushed her. I can't remember the details of our disagreement, only that we had one and it was serious.>

"Callum," Selene stepped forward, ignoring the swirl of fire that licked off her wings, "I need this. I need to show the kingdom, and the Duke of Karna, that I'm more than just a title, a prize, a gift to be given for some hastily decided diplomacy to keep our borders secure. What I'm saying here is I need them to know I am not someone to be overlooked or controlled."

"I'm sure they don't think that. Your father gave you Lisalen . . ."

She shook her head in disbelief. "He only gave her to me because the Duke of Karna told him to. He encouraged me to fight. They both did."

"Wait, really? I thought their plan—"

"Plans change."

"Why didn't you tell me? And why would he do that? Does the duke want your father to consider a demonic Aethercore?"

"I . . . I don't know. But he insisted, last night." Selene's gaze sharpened. "He's the king, and I am both his daughter and his subject. And as the crown princess, you are my subject. Do I make myself clear? I hate to say it like this," she told him, "But Callum Stross, I am ordering you to fight me. Not only that, I'm ordering you to fight me to the best of your ability."

The smoke around them began to thin. Shifting winds curled across the arena tiles, parting the veil of ash and heat. Light broke through in fractured shafts revealing the crowd around them, brimming with anticipation. Cheers erupted, rising in waves that pounded against the arena walls.

"I won't use Killeas," Callum told her hastily.

"Are you sure?"

"I need to save him for later, in case I make it to the next round."

"Then so be it." Selene stepped back, fire coiling along her limbs as her wings flared wide.

The tiles started to lower beneath them, revealing a scorched battlefield. Jagged stone jutted up from the arena floor in uneven spires, red-hot cracks hissing steam into the air. Lava flowed in slow, glutinous streams through deep trenches as geysers of molten rock burst upward around the edges of the arena, casting a rush of heat and smoke across the arena that had the crowd gasping.

<We need to power up,> Fen said. <If we're going to do this, we need to do it to the utmost of our ability!>

<Agreed.> Callum dashed back, skidding over cracked stone. He reached into his pouch and crushed three Attribute Shards in one swift motion—Vigor, Regeneration, and Might—feeling their energy ripple through his body in a sudden burst of vitality.

Across the field, Selene soared upward, her phoenix wings catching the rising thermals. Each beat scattered embers, heat warping the air in her wake. Fire streamed from her trident, casting streaks of gold and red across the sky. She circled above with precision and purpose, less like royalty and more like a predator claiming her territory. Her gaze locked on him from above, unwavering, regal, and relentless.

<We're going to have to try something new,> Callum told Fen. He focused and cast Haloedge.

Three blades of radiant light spun into existence above his shoulders, orbiting in a slow, glowing spiral. Just as he finished using his newest Powercore, Selene swept her wings forward, hurling a burning cyclone of flame in his direction. One of the lightblades snapped into action, lancing it down and shattering the inferno midair.

Before he could counter, Selene dove, twisting midflight and slamming into Callum with the haft of her trident. The blow sent him flying across the lava-streaked field. He hit a jagged stone outcropping hard enough to cause his Armorcore to flicker and cut out.

He rolled instinctively, narrowly avoiding a jet of lava that hissed up from a nearby fissure. As he scrambled to his feet again, his Brightflame Armorcore flared back to life, coating him in protective flame-forged plates. Without pause, Callum hurled the two remaining Haloedge blades toward the princess.

She deflected the first with a burst of heat from her wings. The second struck, forcing her to veer hard and lose altitude.

<*Go!*> Killeas shouted.

Callum surged forward, heat roaring at his back as he leaped across a narrow stream of lava. The molten flow hissed and sizzled beneath him, then erupted in a burst of fire, spitting glowing embers past his boots. His wind sword manifested in his hand as he met Selene. Their weapons clashed in a barrage of force and heat, trident against storm-forged blade.

They both landed; Callum jumped back as Selene's armor shifted and twisted, her body expanding, her eyes burning brighter. A low hum of magic vibrated the air around her as fur pushed through silver plating, her arms thickening, shoulders haunching. Her face remained, just barely, as something deeper had taken hold.

<*What's this?*> Killeas asked as her trident burst with energy as she let out a roar that wasn't entirely human.

<*A beastmeld!*> Fen said.

<*At her age? How is it possible?*> Killeas asked.

<*She's been training all her life,*> Fen told the gryphon as Callum staggered backward.

"No . . ." he whispered, once again feeling that instinctual, bone-deep fear return, the kind he couldn't shake no matter how hard he tried, made even worse now as the princess continued to transform.

<*Say the word and I will join,*> Killeas pleaded with Callum, who remained entirely focused on Selene now. He had seen her in a partial beastmeld before, but this was far worse. Flame coiled around her arms as her Armorcore peeled into her skin and fused with it, claws growing, layered with hardened mana. She produced bearlike fangs at the same time wings of fiery feathers roared outward from her back, growing vast and terrible.

<*That's not just a meld, that's almost a complete fusion!*> Fen said as the crowd went silent for a heartbeat, watching this burning colossus rise against the smoke-streaked sky.

Selene charged, a streak of fire and fury, her new form thundering across the scorched arena. The tiles cracked beneath her paws. She launched fire with every wingbeat, her movements sharper, heavier, carrying the will of something else.

Callum's heart jolted in his chest as Selene speared toward him.

He raised his arms and caught her first swipe on the reinforced wings of his Brightflame Armorcore. Sparks and heat flared on impact. She struck again and he staggered, blocking another. They skidded through molten dust, the scent of burning magic thick in the air.

"Selene!" he called out, hoping something in her heard him. "Be careful!"

There was no response, just another charge. Her claws tore through the air, trailing fire. Mana flared wild across her limbs, heat bleeding from every strike.

Callum gritted his teeth, falling back into stance. He had to fight her. But he also had to bring her back. Hoping to break whatever spell had come over her, he flicked his wrist and summoned Haloedge once again.

The trio of glowing swords flared into being and shot toward her. Two struck her flaming side, fizzling into nothing. The third found a gap in her guard, struck her arm, and vanished without slowing her.

A scream ripped from her throat, raw and not entirely human.

It wasn't a scream of pain, it was something worse, one of possession. Callum was now fully certain that Selene knew she had melded too far, that she couldn't control it.

She came at him like a crazed beast and slammed into Callum with raw weight, her claws digging deep into his Armorcore. He felt his defenses nearly break yet he still managed to roll, hopeful that he would get out of the way. She landed on him again, pummeling him down into the fractured stone.

"Selene!" he yelled as she continued to strike him.

<*I will handle this!*> Killeas roared.

<*No!*> Callum told him as Selene pinned his chest. Another paw reared back, trembling as she fought the madness.

Callum didn't even need to check his Mana Reserves; he could sense he was approaching Low, that the fear he kept fighting off had become a serious drain on his power.

"C-Callum?" she asked, her voice not her own.

Something snapped over her. Selene reared back with another snarl, ready to finish the fight.

With a sudden breath of desperation, Callum pressed his attack, planted his boots beneath her chest, and launched a burst of wind from his back, one that he knew after he had done it had been augmented by Killeas. The force sent him upward, and Selene tumbling backward.

He landed hard, rolling through dust and soot, limbs shaking.

<*Up! Up!*> Killeas said as Callum forced himself to his feet.

Selene swayed across from him, her massive melded form smoldering, fire dripping from her wings. Her body twitched, pulsing with unstable magic as she fought through what looked like a seizure. The flame-wings beat out of sync, one guttering at the edges. Her shoulders spasmed, arcs of mana flaring and snapping down her spine.

She launched upward in a desperate bid for flight, but her balance gave out mid-rise. She crashed hard, her fiery wings folding in on themselves like broken fans, scattering ash across the stone.

<*She's losing control,*> Fen said. <*She can't maintain the beastmeld and phoenix merge. Not both!*>

<*Hit her with everything you have. Now, Lad, be done with this or I will bloody do it myself!*> Killeas said.

Callum didn't wait.

With one final surge of strength, he summoned his Ram swords, mana blazing along their light-ridged edges. He charged, feet pounding across cracked stone and ash. Selene raised her trident too slowly, her body jerking with every motion, as if caught between two instincts.

Callum avoided her attempt to defend and came down with all the power he could muster, the blades connecting with force and light that broke her armor and sent her to the ground. She grabbed his ankle as she fell, yanking him down onto the stone.

He landed on his shoulder but didn't let go of his two swords. Gathering what little wind he could in the span of a heartbeat, Callum blasted her point-blank, sending her reeling, twisting across the ground. Then, pushing past the fire in his limbs and the weight of fatigue crushing his chest, he lunged for the crown princess, both blades overhead to deliver one final strike, his whole body behind it.

The swords came down in a cross-cut, crashing onto her flaming back, exploding in a burst of air and light.

Selene shuddered. She let out a gasp, the sound instantly making Callum realize what he had just done.

The light in her body flickered. Her wings dissolved into ash and cinders. Her arms shrank, fur retreating, claws receding as her armor cracked and vanished in glints of falling flame.

The princess fell to her knees, her breath shuddering as she looked up at him, no longer melded.

Silence followed as Callum staggered back, his swords vanishing into motes of exhausted nothingness.

The crowd remained stunned, the realization only now catching up to them.

Selene Morninglade, the crown princess of Valestra, had lost. Not because she was weak. No one would ever say that, not after how she just performed, but because her power had consumed her.

And Callum Stross, the Demonslayer's distant heir, bruised, battered, and very nearly broken, held on just long enough to eke out what already felt like a Pyrrhic victory.

CHAPTER 42

A century ago, the Geshwine Empire did not merely revise history, they incinerated it. Historians were dragged from their archives and burned at the stake, their bones turned to ash, their names struck from every ledger. It is said that the copy of the Flame Doctrine owned by Imperion Rotharyn is written in ink darkened by their remains. What the Empire teaches is not memory. It is mythology, forged in fire and silence.

—A quote from *Ash Ink and Empty Shelves: A Summary of Geshwinian History* by Magistor Elric Tane

Callum paused in front of the stream of mana in the Veilchamber, barely feeling his feet under him. His body ached, the echoes of fire and utter shock he had just experienced still clinging to his skin like soot, his mind a blur of movement and confusion.

Selene.

He looked back to the slotted exit of the chamber, to the Vestige Arena's battlefield beyond, just as the princess moved toward her own Veilchamber. She did so on her own will, limping past any of the healers that came to her, shame on her face, defiance in her gait. She lifted her fist in the air one last time and the Valestran crowd cheered for her.

"I can't believe what just happened," Callum said, oblivious to Marcella and Quinn, who hovered around him, speaking rapidly. His hand found the smooth curve of the mana fountain's edge and he turned, sitting with his back to it, the same way he would sit if he were cycling mana.

Tunnel vision narrowed his view, the Veilchamber closing in around him. Everything else—the voices, the crowd, even the chamber's ambient hum—blurred to background noise.

Marcella's voice finally broke through the fog. "Callum, are you there?" She crouched in front of him, her hands gripping his shoulders. "Little Cal? Does that help?" She gave him a firm shake. "Please don't make me smack your cheek a few times. The fight isn't over, you know."

He finally met her eyes, his wavering, hers steady and filled with kindness. "Yeah," he said. "That was just . . . unexpected. Add Ecaris's fear power and it's going to take me a moment to fully recover." A sense of terror washed over him and he willed it away. "I've never been subjected to it for so long."

Fen appeared beside the fountain, the Radiant Fox pacing with his tail rigid. Killeas materialized near him with far more flair, the gryphon's talons tapping the stone, wings fluffing from the residual magic.

"You should be proud," Killeas told Callum as he puffed his chest out. "You beat Her Highness and the royal Brightflame Pigeon without my help! Obviously, had you actually utilized my talents aside from the power you take from our meld, we would have won much earlier, but we've still done well."

"Pigeon? What happened?" Quinn asked, coming to Callum's other side. "She was supposed to forfeit. What did she say? You two were hidden from us for a minute or two on that half mountain or whatever."

"Plateau," Marcella said.

"That. Yes, that. What did she say? What did Selene say?"

Callum blinked again. "She said it was her choice. Her father gave her Lisalen . . . the Demonslayer's phoenix. She wanted to fight me at my full capacity. She wanted to prove herself."

"What?" Marcella's tone turned sharp. "Why would King Morninglade give Lisalen to her?"

"She didn't really know. She said something about the Duke of Karna recommending it."

Quinn frowned. "That doesn't seem right."

"It seems strange as hell." Marcella stood and walked to the edge of the Veilchamber's slatted wall. She looked out at the glowing, translucent curtain that hid the crowd.

"We should get armor," she said abruptly. "I know that might sound a bit odd but . . ." She turned back to them. "We have this saying in Aveiro, 'A fish that doubts the currents doesn't last long.' Anyway, actual armor. Plus our Armorcores, of course. I think that would be best."

"What for?" Quinn asked, looking over to her.

"I don't know. Maybe I'm overreacting." She returned and leaned against the fountain, her gaze distant. "But I'd feel much better if we were prepared for anything."

Fen moved in front of Callum and looked up at him. "What you did was smart. You maintained your composure, and the warlocks still don't know about your second pact. That was the goal, wasn't it?"

Callum nodded. "It was."

"Personally, I'm *so* ready," Killeas said, flexing his wings. "*So* ready to put a warlock in the ground. But . . ." his voice dropped, "I agree with the seawoman."

"Is that what you're calling me?" Marcella asked him.

Killeas continued, "Something is definitely off about the entire affair, and I don't just mean the princess challenging us. Of course she would. Power has been handed to her simply due to the womb from which she came, and now she has to prove she deserves it. That's how authority works. If she doesn't assert it, what's the point of having it at all? I'm not finished, fox," he added before Fen could cut in. He looked at Marcella and Quinn. "You two *should* be ready for something to happen. There are a lot of guards here. They should be able to control the crowd when Callum wins, but if not, I can foresee a stampede."

"A stampede? That's what you're worried about?" Fen asked him flatly. "I thought you were more concerned about the princess pacting?"

"My only thought about that is we beat her anyway, even with Lisalen at her side. No, I'm thinking more about what happens after we win. You and I both know humans do crazy things when they're struck by grief or loss, when they sense they are absolutely going to lose," the gryphon said. "I don't know if there will be riots, but I expect something, and we should all be ready. Armor, not just Armorcores, is a good thing."

Fen's gaze shifted to Marcella and Quinn. "Do you think you can get armor before the match starts?

"They have some down below the stands," Quinn said. "I saw people turning in their sets when they lost earlier. We can grab something."

"Good call," Fen said. "What are Tuck and Harold telling you?"

"I can speak for myself," Tuck announced as he spiraled into visibility in a swirl of green and violet. The aethercat stretched, yawned, and arched his back dramatically. "And I agree."

"Harold agrees as well," Marcella added, tapping on her temple. "We're going to go. We'll try to hurry. If we're not back before you are called, good luck." She smiled down at Callum. "But if we're being honest, I don't know how much luck you're going to need. The princess was the strongest in our class, and you beat her without your second Aethercore."

"I did," Callum said slowly. "But that was also because of her beastmeld. She couldn't control it. I was way closer to Hollowing than I'd like to admit. If it had gone on any longer—"

"Take the compliment," Marcella said, offering her hand.

He took her hand, and she pulled him to his feet.

"We'll be back," Quinn added as they turned to go. Their footsteps faded, leaving Callum alone with Fen and Killeas in the Veilchamber. In the distance, the crowd's volume spiked as the final match was announced.

This was it. All the upgrades, the training, even finding Killeas's Aethercore—every step had led to this moment.

Fen hopped up onto the edge of the found, his fur lit faintly by the glow of magic. "We have one more obstacle to get through today," he said quietly, "but it may be the start of something we can't even fathom."

"You worry too much, fox. We saw the warlock fight," Killeas said as he approached. "Together, we will defeat him quickly, I'm sure of it. Once again, the seawoman was right. That last fight was likely harder. One, because I wasn't able to participate. And two, because you have a relationship with the princess."

"A relationship? She's my friend," Callum cut in, not looking at the gryphon.

"Ha, *friend*. That's not what your heart tells me when you see her." Killeas gave his wings a shake. "But I'm no matchmaker, I'm the Gryphon Vanguard of Fates!" He strutted forward, placing one talon on the edge of the fountain as he turned his head to Fen with a dramatic flair. "And the fate I see today is one of total victory for us and embarrassing defeat for our enemies."

Callum wished his father was there. As he stood in front of the mirrored walls of the Veilchamber, waiting for them to thin, he cursed himself for not figuring out a way to bring Rhane to New Albion.

I have access to portals now. I could have called in a favor with the princess. I could have . . . He closed his eyes and took a deep breath in, trying to silence the voice of doubt at the back of his head. It was a reaction to what was about to happen, his nerves, the tenseness he felt knowing that so many people were counting on him to win the fight. *But maybe . . .*

Callum glanced up toward the seats of the Vestige Arena, his eyes scanning across the royal dais. King Morninglade was seated at its center, flanked on one side by Imperion Rotharyn and on the other by the Duke of Karna. The three appeared composed and distant now, watching from their elevated perch.

Callum let his vision blur ever-so-slightly as he imagined his father there watching him. *You've got this, Cal*, his father would say, his voice somehow heard over the crowd, over the thrumming energy of the arena, over the clamor of New Albion itself. *Make us all proud.*

He nodded.

<Ready?> Fen asked carefully.

<I am. You?>

<Ready.>

<You know I'm ready!> Killeas growled. <The faster the better. Let's not let the warlock overwhelm us with his puny aethermammoth.>

<Yes,> Fen said, agreeing with Killeas for once. <We must do it fast and smart.>

The Veilchamber thinned as Callum's name was announced.

The magical tiles of the arena hissed beneath his boots, steam still curling from the last fight, heat shimmering in the air. Callum still didn't know how the arena's magitek worked, but he understood enough to know it could twist reality beneath his feet. And in the coming minutes, it likely would do things for this final match that he could only hope to have prepared for.

Taking his time, Callum moved toward the center, listening as the crowd swelled around him, louder now, back to how it had been before his match against the princess. He reached the middle and paused, drawing a slow breath, grounding himself.

Across the arena, the opposing Veilchamber opened.

Laziel Thornhelm stepped out, once again the picture of composed brutality. Not a strand of his long white hair was out of place, each braid immaculate, his uniform crisp and untouched, like the fight against Ryven had only sharpened him.

The crowd didn't cheer. Instead, the Geshwine delegation began their slow, rhythmic stomping that echoed across the Vestige Arena, the sound of a war march, low and ominous, the energy in the air thickening with corrupted anticipation.

Like Callum, Laziel didn't rush.

He moved with the unhurried, assured pace of someone convinced of their own victory. He wore no smirk, no arrogance, only stillness and weight behind his glowing red eyes. As he approached, he locked onto Callum, chin tilting back just slightly, gaze cast down his nose.

<Any slower and the match'll end before it starts!> Killeas snapped, voice flaring inside Callum's mind.

Callum ignored the gryphon, his gaze fixed forward, body loose, senses sharp.

Laziel came to a stop six feet away, then finally spoke, his voice carrying over, calm and dark. "Are you ready for this?" he asked with a slight sneer.

"Are you?" Callum replied.

Laziel let out a breath, almost like a sigh of pity. "We have yet to face each other, but I've heard about your unique fighting style. You gave the others a good challenge. And the princess"—he smiled, slight and thin—"well, she tried. Beastmelding. That was bold. Foolish, but bold."

Callum said nothing.

"I don't think I'll be doing anything quite so reckless," Laziel continued, his eyes beginning to flare with unnatural crimson light. "I won't need to. It'll be enough to beat you as I am. And it will be . . . interesting, won't it? To see how New Albion reacts when the Stross heir falls."

Callum's gaze sharpened. "You sound pretty sure of yourself."

"I am." Laziel tilted his head a few hairs higher. "You see, your distant relative, the one your nation calls the Demonslayer, the one they practically worship, is quite famous in the Geshwine Empire as well. A hero, even. But he's also famous for something else."

"What do you mean?"

"He was one of us," Laziel said, voice low and lethal. "The original Callum Stross was a warlock."

<*What?!*> Killeas bellowed, a gale of outrage flaring through Callum's core. <*Lies!*>

<*It must be something they're force-fed,*> Fen said, unsettled. <*Some perversion of history. Ignore it!*>

But Callum couldn't ignore it. He stared at Laziel, chest tightening. "Yeah?" he asked quietly. "Where did you learn that?"

"The Flame Doctrine teaches it." Laziel bared his teeth in what might have once been a smile. "The Lost Verses. They were written by the Demonslayer himself."

CHAPTER 43

Perhaps the greatest act of revision was not what the Geshwine Empire added to the Flame Doctrine—but what someone else asked to have removed.

—A quote from *Margins of Fire: Doctrine and the Forgotten Pen* by Duchess Arolina Mez of Aveiro

Laziel's revelation startled Callum to the point that he had to take a step back. "What?" he asked, not believing what he had just heard.

<Such a foul statement!> Killeas roared. <The Demonslayer had nothing to do with any Flame Doctrine, nothing! I . . . I wasn't there all the way up to the end, but I can assure you, he would never stoop to such a low. He was never a warlock either. They have warped the truth to accommodate their unique brand of deception.>

<It can't possibly be true,> Fen said. <The Demonslayer? Codifying iniquity? Codifying worship? The Flame Doctrine can't be that old. I'm sure there is more to this, but why would we ever believe someone who has been brought up to see the benefits of Demoncores? Focus on the fight ahead, Callum, not the warlock's clear and apparent lies.>

Callum braced himself, aware that the signal to start the fight was mere seconds away from sounding. He summoned his Brightflame Armorcore, noticing Laziel remained completely relaxed, hands clasped in front of his body.

"You're nervous," Laziel said just as the signal to start the fight sounded. "I can tell."

Callum gritted his teeth as the arena shifted, stone tiles vanishing beneath a wash of projected illusion. A lush valley unfolded around them. Arched rock formations loomed overhead, draped in moss and curling vines. Flowering trees swayed in a wind that wasn't real, sunlight filtering through the clouds above, warm and golden. Somewhere, birdsong echoed.

It was beautiful. Too beautiful.

Then it cracked wide open.

Callum burst into the air with a gale-charged leap, Windstep flaring beneath his boots. His wings shimmered out, slicing through mist and bloom. He reached a high arc above the canopy when a molten mammoth trunk whipped through the vines and latched onto his leg.

Before Callum could react, he was yanked downward, the trunk constricting like a vise as the trees caught fire around him.

<*I've got it!*> Killeas said. The gryphon's talons materialized through their pact, slashing down and cleaving the red-hot trunk in half. Callum flipped midair and pushed forward again, mere seconds away from colliding with a cluster of sharp succulents.

<*Your spear!*> Killeas shouted.

<*On it!*> As his Piercing Air Spear formed, tendrils of shadow mana snaked down Callum's arm, Noct Thread thickening and strengthening the Weaponcore. The spear nearly doubled in length, the tip glistening with a deadly black glimmer. He thrust it downward as gravity took him, cleaving the last remnants of the trunk into smoky trails.

<*That's how we do it!*> Killeas shouted, delight crackling in his tone. <*Shadowmark next! We get him before he finds his feet. Fox, I'm counting on you after this!*>

<*I'll be ready,*> Fen said. <*Just get me to solid ground!*>

A black orb burst from Callum's fingers, compressed Shadowmark flickering at the core. It slammed into Laziel's chest. The moment it struck, a blast of inky light exploded outward in a pulse, latching onto Laziel's form and marking him.

<*Good!*> Killeas encouraged. <*His defenses are weaker now. Go!*>

Callum dove, twisting through the air. The twin Ram swords split from his back and dropped clean into his hands. In one motion, he crossed them over his chest and released a blast of force. Wind and pressure surged forward in a wide X-pattern, tearing through the air with brutal speed.

He landed hard and looked back. Laziel's hulking silhouette was still coming, mammoth and man fused together, stampeding through the mist.

Just as Callum started to move again, the terrain responded.

Vines exploded from the moss-covered ground, thick and barbed, their movement too fast to track. One lashed around his forearm and yanked him sideways, throwing off his balance.

Another coiled around Callum's ankle and dragged. He tried to cut free, but the ground shifted beneath him, slick with blooming roots.

Blossoms burst open around him. Their petals curled back to reveal rows of needlelike thorns. One snapped shut on his shoulder, somehow puncturing his Armorcore, electric pain jolting through his nerves. Another struck his thigh; he cried out, staggering as his vision blurred.

<*Hold on, lad!*> Killeas surged to life in a blur of light and wings, slicing through the tendrils and freeing Callum. <*It looks like the arena is attacking too,*> the gryphon told Callum as he took to the air again, only to be snatched from it once more.

Laziel's molten trunk whipped out, wrapped around Callum, and flung him sideways like a discarded wine bottle. He crashed through one of the stone arches, the impact sending chunks of rock exploding in every direction.

Debris rained down as Callum spiraled through the air, slammed into a second formation, and struggled against a curtain of ravenous vines clawing for his limbs and trying to bite him yet again. He slid down the sloped edge, wheezing, every breath scraping his throat.

His boots had barely hit the moss when the air flashed bright.

A blast of lava hissed toward him. Callum dove aside, the heat licking at his back, the stench of scorched greenery and sulfur curling into his nose like smoke through a chimney.

Laziel caught him mid-recovery and slammed down with a weighted fist. Callum's Armorcore wings snapped forward just in time to block the next strike, the hit sending him to one knee.

Laziel pressed in, both fists glowing. Mana surged around his fists as he pummeled forward with Weaponcore knuckle enhancers, forged for brute force and close-quarters destruction.

The third blow came fast, but Fen was faster.

The fox surged into Callum's limbs, forcing him to roll as Laziel's punch smashed the ground where Callum had just been, splitting the stone. Debris rained down as Callum twisted to his feet. He lashed out with a desperate slash, claws catching Laziel's cheek, then vaulted upward, wind twisting behind him.

The pillar crumbled beneath his feet, cascading dust and rock as Callum found a position overhead that gave him a vantage point over his opponent.

Laziel rose from the haze, bleeding from his face, his Armorcore flickering at the joints. A flurry of vines came toward him and he cut them away with a molten chop.

He stepped back, momentarily obscured by the smoke as Callum remained above.

The roar of the crowd rose, his name echoing from every direction, shouted by strangers. *I have to do this*, he thought as stomps thundered from the Crimson stands. *Finish this*, he told himself, the building pressure, feeding the moment with heat and weight.

Callum turned back toward the smoke, toward where he had last seen Laziel.

<That was just the first round,> Fen said.

<Eh, we're still here,> Killeas added.

Callum summoned his spear, eyes fixed on the shifting curtain of debris as shadow threaded down the weapon again, strengthening it, sharpening and lengthening his wind spear's tip. There was a synergy he noticed, one that he now knew was tied to affinity.

He sent it hurtling down at Laziel the moment the warlock appeared, wind pulsing from the tip of his spear in sharp, concussive bursts, each one tearing across the battlefield like a blade of force.

Just as Callum began conjuring another spear, a fresh shimmer of mana flared below as Laziel summoned a second Armorcore, this one darker, sleeker, layered in bands of segmented plating that wrapped across his arms and chest. The armor thickened his frame, adding weight and bulk with a dense, almost scaled finish.

Whatever it was, it wasn't just for protection. The mana pouring off it was heavy, aggressive, designed for close-quarters domination.

Laziel was gearing up to finish this. The warlock dropped, striking the ground with both fists, pounding down with enough force to send ripples through the air. A shockwave followed, bursting from the impact point, one that caught Callum mid-flight.

His wings twisted violently as the air buckled beneath him.

<Hold on!> Killeas said as Callum spiraled, barely managing to adjust his trajectory before the battlefield transformed.

Water rushed in from the sides, brackish and brown, choked with algae and thick sludgy moss that instantly covered the tiles. Callum landed and his boots sank into the muck, water rushing past his shins, the smell earthy and rotting. Tree limbs loomed overhead. Mosquitoes buzzed. Shadows slid beneath the surface and a faint mist lingered.

<A swamp? Blah! This cursed battlefield,> Killeas said.

<Focus on the warlock,> Fen said just as Laziel broke through the haze ahead.

Callum thrust a palm forward and released a gale-force burst. The blast hit Laziel mid-charge, lifting muck and debris as it slammed into his chest. The warlock dropped low, scrambling forward on all fours, but the wind had done its work, his charge slowed, his footing off.

Above Callum, three swords of radiant light formed in a tight orbit, humming with restrained power. They spun slowly, casting pale illumination across the field as Callum leveled a hand.

The first sword snapped forward. It struck Laziel clean in the chest, forcing him to a stop.

Laziel growled, then threw his arms wide and let out a bellow that shook the air.

The mammoth's roar was more than just sound, it was pressure. Callum was flung backward, skidding through the water as trees bowed and swampgrass flattened from the sonic force. He rose, coughing, just in time to see Laziel hurl his massive trunk at him.

The second lightsword flared to life and intercepted the trunk with a burst of radiant feedback.

Laziel twisted, his entire body spinning with terrifying grace; Callum responded, sending the third sword hurtling toward him. It struck Laziel, sending him into a deeper stretch of the swamp, the Crimson duelist instantly engulfed by the water.

<*Go for it!*> Fen said, and Callum seized the opportunity.

Vines erupted from the water, thick tendrils slithering through the swamp. They wrapped around Laziel, pulled tight, and dragged the warlock beneath the surface. Froth churned for a moment and then went still after a few final bubbles.

The crowd roared in anticipation.

Callum stood motionless in the shallows, soaked, chest heaving as he summoned his Ram swords, their edge steaming in the cool air. He didn't smile. Didn't celebrate.

This wasn't over.

The water shattered as Laziel burst free, landing hard on all fours in the muck, his body and face now smeared with swamp sludge.

Laziel had changed.

Slate-gray texture rippled across his skin, almost scaled. Translucent wings unfolded from his back, wide and undulating like a stingray's, edged in faint violet light. Mana pulsed through them, crackling with corrupted energy. A long tail uncurled behind him, sinuous and twitching, tipped with a jagged stinger.

<*His second pact,*> Killeas growled. <*It looks to be . . .*>

Laziel staggered forward, water lapping at his shins as his body swayed, his consciousness hanging by a thread.

Then, the tail struck.

The stinger arched behind him and plunged into Laziel's own back, punching clean through just beneath the sternum.

Laziel gasped, his red eyes going wide as he threw his head back, blood spilling from his mouth. Magic detonated around him in a pulse of searing purple light. His entire body jolted as wings expanded, newfound power flooding through him.

<*He stabbed himself,*> Fen said, stunned. <*That's not a summon. That's . . . augmentation.*>

<*Self-harm to amplify force,*> Killeas said, low. <*A Demoncore power if there ever was one.*>

The wound sealed around the stinger with a hiss of magic. Laziel stood taller now, mana pulsing violently through his body as he hovered into the air.

CHAPTER 44

Where battles end, consequences begin.

—Caison Biterolf, poet

Laziel threw his head back, blood flecking his lips, his grin split too wide to be sane.

The stinger continued to hold him up, the barb jutting out of his torso. Blood dripped steadily down his torso, pooling in the swampwater below, but Laziel didn't seem to notice.

If anything, he looked stronger.

Hardened mana ran in cords along his torso and arms, flickering faintly with a sickly blue sheen. His body flexed; Laziel twisted as the stinger twitched, the image like a hovering puppet on strings. Thin, magic blades slid down his arms, curling along his forearms and forming into twin sickles as the tips of his boots grazed against the top of the water.

Better now than never, Callum thought as he quickly crushed the rest of his Empowerment of Might Shards, his power instantly amplifying. He used a Vigor Shard as well, mere seconds before Laziel lunged at him, the warlock's entire form blurred into a spin, blades akimbo as he whipped through the swamp like a scythe caught up in an aetherstorm. Callum tried to leap back, but there wasn't enough space. Not enough time.

The first blade rang off the shoulder of his Pangolin Armorcore. The second skimmed low, throwing sparks as it carved through the layered plates of his Armorcore. Pain burst across his side. He landed hard, boots sliding across wet roots and slick stone.

<*One more attack like that and this is over!*> Killeas bellowed, wings flaring in Callum's mind. <*You must reposition—now!*>

<*Smoke, Radiant Inferno, and replicants,*> Fen said, voice sharp as ever. <*Get us out of the open. Now, move!*>

Callum didn't hesitate. He summoned everything he had, spreading thickened smoke through the sludgy swamp around him. Smog rolled low across the battlefield, thick as tar, domed explosions of fire taking shape everywhere he looked. He followed Radiant Inferno up with illusions, which shimmered to life, four illusory Callums sprinting in different directions, each flickering just long enough to create a distraction.

Laziel cut through one of them with his armblades, then wheeled toward the real Callum, red eyes burning with unhinged focus.

Callum met him head-on, raking a strike across Laziel's side with his claws, the hit powered by a sudden burst from Killeas's wings. The force carried him upward, each wingbeat straining as he climbed higher into the haze. He angled for space, just enough breathing room to draw mana back into his limbs and reset his stance.

Below, the swamp warped and bled away into something worse—a terrain of crumbling stone and sinking ground. Massive slabs buckled and collapsed into the depths, sending up bursts of dust and shards. Others heaved upward in sudden, violent shifts, the motion scattering debris and gouging fresh craters into the earth. Every change sent ripples of instability across the battlefield, promising to swallow anything that lingered too long in one place.

Still pierced by his own stinger, Laziel rose to meet him, his eyes halfway shut, chin tilted down. Once again, it became clear that whatever relationship he had with the demonic stingray, Laziel was no longer in control.

Is this how a true Demoncore works? Callum thought quickly. *How do I use this to my advantage?*

The stingray swept to the side and sent a gust of lightning-laced wind in his direction. Fen blocked it; the fox appeared midair, pivoted right, and sent a concentrated blast of a fiery mana right back at Laziel with his tail.

<*And they say foxes can't fly!*> Killeas told Fen once he had melded with Callum again.

<*I'm giving the lad a moment to think!*> Fen said. <*What are you doing?*>

<*Keeping him afloat!*>

<*The stingray is in control,*> Callum thought to them both as he rushed back toward the ground, landing for a brief moment, eyes on a pillar of stone that would soon collapse. <*How do we use this? How much do you think it understands the terrain?*>

<*What do you mean?*> Fen asked.

<*You want to try to crush it. Is that what you're saying?*> Killeas asked Callum.

<*I think that might be the only way!*> Callum told him.

<*Unconventional, but smart! I love the lad's way of thinking. Let's do this!*>

The stingray drifted Laziel closer, his broken silhouette haloed in mist and firelight.

Callum braced, then blasted upward with a burst of wind. The arc of force cracked through the swamp, catching the stingray's flank and pushing it sideways, straight toward the jagged pillar of stone now rising just ahead.

A new magic-laced stinger burst from the ground behind him, cracking stone and reaching straight for the small of his back. Callum twisted aside at the last second, breath catching as the stinger speared the space he'd just vacated, the impact strong enough to splinter stone.

No room for error, he thought as he rushed back, hoping to get a clear shot.

Above, Laziel's form flickered, twitching in the air as a weapon snapped into place in his hands. The Weaponcore blade was long and ridged like a ceremonial banner pole, dripping black fluid from its cloth-wrapped hilt, unmistakably corrupted, a brushstroke painting with a mind of its own.

Laziel slammed the Weaponcore down, the sword quadrupling in length mid-swing. It cracked into the shifting tile below and the ground split beneath it, shockwaves tearing through the terrain and bringing down more of the stone pillars.

Callum windstepped sideways; the force lifted him clean off his feet and hurled him into the side of a crumbling platform. He hit hard, his armor cracking on impact.

<*Ready? Let's bring the pillar of stone down onto him!*> Killeas shouted.

<*Can you?*> Callum asked, coughing once, eyes still on Laziel.

<*Gladly!*>

Callum's eyes darted from Laziel to the large slab of stone. <*Go. Fen, draw him. Make it count.*>

He felt their connection pull as both pacts released at once. The moment it happened, something inside Callum went quiet. Not empty, but lighter. Less stable.

Killeas launched left, talons glowing, while Fen streaked right across the debris-strewn field.

For added protection, Callum triggered his Brightflame Armorcore. Sparks raced over his limbs, a golden glow tracing the lines of his armor. It was a shadow of its full strength without his pacts, but it would have to be enough.

He moved into a position that was too open, too obvious, vulnerable by design.

Laziel took the bait.

The possessed warlock snarled with delight, pivoting toward Callum with his Weaponcore raised, focus locked.

Fen lunged from midair, teeth bared, and released a concentrated blast of wind that slammed into Laziel's flank, knocking him just off balance.

Killeas hit the pillar a heartbeat later. Stone and tile cracked with a deafening groan, then gave way entirely.

The pillar came down in a roaring cascade, slabs breaking mid-fall, chunks shearing off and spinning through the air. Dust exploded upward in choking waves as the mass of rubble crashed down on Laziel's position. The sound was deafening, an impact that rattled the ground beneath through the soles of Callum's boots.

Through the haze, he was certain he saw the flash of Laziel's wings fold in, then vanish beneath the wreckage. The dust boiled up too thick to confirm as shards of tile and fractured stone clattered and slid into the settling heap.

No movement. No sound but the slow rumble of debris shifting into place.

Callum summoned his Ram swords, eyes fixed on the mound. The weight of it was enough to crush a fortress wall.

Killeas and Fen returned to him a heartbeat later, their shared power sealing in place with a sharp rush of augmentation. Callum pushed forward, haggardly split his blade and stepped over the fractured terrain, where he reached the mound of stone. He looked down, prepared to jump back, to deliver a finishing blow if need be. Dust and blood marked the edge, the battlefield still.

<*We got the warlock!*> Killeas crowed with delight.

<*You may have actually killed him,*> Fen told Callum, his voice carrying something quieter now.

Callum didn't answer. He turned slightly as a pair of healers approached, their steps quick but cautious. Beyond them, the arena crowd watched in silence, thousands holding their breath to see if the fallen combatant would rise.

His eyes went wide as a sharp, echoing rupture tore through the air. Then another. From the far side of the arena, the Geshwine spectator stands lit in flashes of crimson and black, sparks racing in jagged bursts as screams broke out.

Callum spun toward the noise, swords drawn.

CHAPTER 45

You can break the walls and scatter the people. But if the Heart still beats, we've not yet lost.

—Traditional Valestran saying, origin unknown

Madness overtook the crowd, just as Marcella had predicted. Still reeling from his fight against Laziel, Callum turned toward the royal dais, where he caught flickers of motion, figures rushing amid a burst of red light.

He staggered backward, processing it all.

For a moment, he thought it could be a hallucination. Surely, this wasn't happening. Had Laziel hit him with some mind-distorting attack, similar to the Crimson student pacted with the aetherscorpion? Was it really all coming down?

"It can't be . . ." Callum said, his mouth dry, heart racing as the calamity continued to unfold in the stands above.

The swell of the crowd drew his broken attention again as Crimson Sigil students were locked in combat with Great College defenders. Two professors were already down, slumped near the edge of the pathway above one of the veilchambers. An explosion sent limbs and gore into the air; one of the warlocks unleashed a gout of acidic flame into the rows behind him. Callum saw students scattering, some rushing toward the fight, others away from it.

<*Snap out of it, Lad,*> Killeas said. <*It's an ambush!*>

A Geshwinian airship blinked into existence overhead, tearing free from the sky as if the clouds themselves had been ripped open. Black metal caught the light in cold flashes, its hull slick with strange reflections. Lines of runes Callum didn't recognize pulsed along its flanks, flaring brighter as the vessel settled into position above the Vestige Arena.

A bolt of black lightning erupted from its prow, a thunderclap so violent it rattled the arena's stone foundations. The flash burned across Callum's vision as it struck the royal dais, the world fracturing into motion: guards rushing, spells firing wildly, people screaming as the shockwave rolled through the stands.

Even from his vantage point, Callum knew the king had been hit.

He saw the bolt connect, saw the figures on the dais recoil. And he had felt it, the crowd's fervor twisting in an instant into a single, collective gasp at the Geshwine Empire's calculated strike.

A second bolt of black lightning fired from the airship, tearing out a section of the Vestige Arena and bringing the collective pillars down with it. This was followed by a bright flash above the royal dais as Imperion Rotharyn beamed upward into the waiting airship, the enemy emperor vanishing in a column of white-gold light licked with traces of red.

<They've been waiting for this,> Fen said tightly. <Surely the High Council must have seen this coming!>

A shape burst forward from the Great College section. Master Cruedark vaulted over the stair rail, launched into the air, and slammed down near the High Council in a crouch. The impact cratered the platform and threw several Crimson Sigil fighters off their feet.

A moment later, Selene's Veilchamber exploded open in a wave of royal blue light as the princess emerged in full meldform, her silhouette trailing ursine radiance. She headed straight into the calamity without hesitation, fiery wings erupting out of her back as she took to the air.

Behind her came Quinn and Marcella, both in armor.

Once melded, Quinn intercepted a pair of enemy warlocks, ripping through them. Marcella soared overhead, wings unfurling as she ascended into the smoke above the arena.

Callum gritted his teeth and sprinted forward to join the fight, his Ram swords tight in his grip.

<That's it!> Killeas said. <We shall bring wrath upon our enemies!>

Imps and blade-wing dervishes poured down amid streaks of red lightning, screeching as they dove toward the crowd. Mana fire sizzled as it hit columns of water, the elements clashing as Great College defenders rallied to meet them, but Callum could see they were already being overrun.

Callum ducked under a falling imp, slashed twice, and kept moving, stone cracking beneath his boots. A dervish landed and twisted toward him, tendrils lifting off its back. Callum cut through them, reached the creature, and drove his swords into it.

He took another quick glance at the stands and nearly started toward it. Yet the arena floor was already crawling with bodies and demonic aetherbeasts.

<This is just the start!> he told Fen and Killeas as a shadowy imp landed in front of him. Callum swept low and cut its legs clean through, pivoting before the body hit the ground as two more dropped in. He met them head-on, driving one back with a feint, then parrying the second and slamming it to the dirt with a flare of wind from his left gauntlet.

<You're not going to make it up there like this,> Fen said. <There are too many of them!>

<We're going to cut a path,> Callum said, his only response to the overwhelming despair and anger he was starting to feel as the reality of what was happening continued to play out.

<They are opening a Demonstorm,> Killeas said. <The sooner we drive them back, the better.>

<A Demonstorm?> Fen shot back. <They can't possibly do that without...>

Callum tuned them out, his eyes fixing on the point where Selene had disappeared into the melee, to the place where he was certain King Morninglade had fallen.

A hiss cut through the roar of battle. Scales slammed against his chest, wrapping tight, locking his arms to his sides. The pressure crushed the air from his lungs. One of his Ram swords slipped from his grip, dissolving before it hit the ground. The other was knocked free a moment later, booted from his hand as Sorcha drove into him from behind, the Crimson woman's aetherpython winding around his torso in a tightening coil.

They crashed hard. Stone bit into his back. The serpent's grip constricted, each spasm of muscle threatening to snap his ribs.

Callum gritted his teeth, heat and power surging through his limbs as he twisted hard, fighting for a gap. He caught one and shoved his weight sideways, forcing the coils to slide just enough for him to wrench himself free.

He rolled, boots scraping until they caught. Air gathered under him, and he launched upward in a burst of wind, breaking free of the aetherpython's reach.

Mid-flight, his spear shimmered into existence, solid and bright in his grip. He leveled the tip at Sorcha, sighting her through the smoke, and aimed straight for center mass.

Sorcha hesitated. It was barely a flicker—just the way her foot slipped half a step back, how her lips parted before her jaw tensed.

<Now!> Killeas shouted after she'd been marked.

Callum hurled the spear toward her. It punched clean through her snake's body, pinning it to a sparking fragment of tile that lit up with arcane feedback. Callum landed, his hand closing around his Tempest Fang as it formed in his grip, blade gleaming, wind tracing along its edges.

"You don't have to do this," he told Sorcha, breathing heavily his presence pressing toward her.

"The Flame Doctrine says . . ." Her voice cracked, but she caught it. "It is what must be done."

She summoned a shield-blade Weaponcore, the piece flaring once with dark light that fizzled at the edges. The aetherpython dissolved and remelded into her body, pain visibly surging through her as she drove the weapon down onto the tile.

A pulse of scalding magic exploded outward.

Callum flew backward. He barely registered the blur of wings before Killeas caught him midair, Callum spared from a rib-jarring impact that would have followed.

<*Do I have to do everything myself?*> Killeas growled.

Callum twisted around and surged up and over, where he dropped down behind Sorcha. He cast Radiant Mirage. Afterimages split from his form, each flaring with false light and moving fast.

Sorcha turned as Callum and his replicants closed in. She took one down, then another, blade sweeping wide.

Yet the third struck.

Radiant Claws flashed as Callum's strike cut through her Armorcore, splintering it on impact. Sorcha staggered, falling to one knee. Her aetherpython lashed out one final time, jaws clamping onto Callum's neck.

His hand rose, glowing with mana as he ripped it away.

The python dropped first, dissolving as it hit the stone. Sorcha fell a breath later after Callum's next strike, her shield-blade slipping from her fingers and dissolving.

She didn't rise.

Callum stood over Sorcha, chest heaving, blood trickling from his collar. The battlefield noise surged back into focus—the screams, the shouts, the chaos still tearing through the royal dais. Above it all, the crimson sky churned, filling with the shapes of demonic aetherbeasts spilling into the city.

<*We need to help the princess.*> Callum's gaze lifted beyond the Vestige Arena—and froze. His breath caught, a cold weight settling in his gut.

<*Wait . . .*>

<*It . . . it can't be!*> Killeas said.

Fen's voice followed, low and heavy. <*This . . . this is a two-pronged attack!*>

"The Heart," Callum said, forcing the word past dry lips.

Callum could see the Heart of Creation through the opening in the Vestige Arena's shattered flank. The towering obelisk stood, yet the structure that had protected the capital for centuries now pulsed unevenly, shuddering with each beat. A darkness spread from its base, climbing up the obelisk jagged, creeping lines.

Above it, a different airship hung in the air, tethered to the Heart as if the ship was feeding on it. The wards surrounding the obelisk flared weakly, then dimmed again, unable to push the Corruption back.

For the first time, Callum understood what he was looking at.

If the Heart falls, more storms will come, and the gate to the Demonsrealm could be split wide open . . . he thought as everything he had learned, everything he had experienced came to him in that moment. Callum not only understood his destiny, but the calamity that was set to befall his kingdom. The Heart of Creation flashed again, its light weaker, its pulse slower. Magic warped and shimmered around its midsection in jagged, uneven waves as Corruption continued to climb from its base.

<*Let's go there now!*> Killeas said.

Callum crushed two Empowerment of Deftness Shards and the last of his Vigor Shards. The rush hit instantly, mana pouring through his limbs and sharpening every movement. His muscles felt lighter, his focus tighter. He banked toward the broken incline, clearing the shattered edge of the stadium with his blades leaving bright trails in the air.

Yet the lift in his strength came with a hollow edge. He had expended a lot of mana; each beat of his wings felt like it drained more than it should.

Spells from Valestran archmages lit the air above the arena, striking down fresh waves of aetherbeasts. But more monsters pushed through as fire spread along the crowd's edge, eating through the stands.

Killeas boosted Callum's ascent until he soared free of the arena, wind slamming into his face. A second shape joined him midair, rising from the side in a flash of crimson and gold.

"I see it!" Marcella shouted before Callum could even point. "We need to get to the Heart!"

The pair climbed higher, dodging through tangled smoke and a flurry of small, winged horrors that burst from the red clouds above, demonic things with distended jaws and serrated talons.

Callum cut one down mid-flight, spun through the wreckage, sliced through another, and rose again.

Beside him, Marcella barreled ahead, wings flared wide, streaking light across the broken sky. "There's a tether anchoring the airship to the Heart!"

Callum caught it again, the unsteady beam of dark magic stretching between the ship's undercarriage and the Heart's crown. The line twitched in uneven intervals, threads of violet lightning crawling along its length, leaving a faint shudder in the Heart's glow.

He spotted movement on the ship's upper deck just as a bolt of dark mana screamed past his ear, close enough to scorch the air.

<*It's Ryven,*> Fen said as Callum rolled aside from another shot.

The brute gripped a massive Weaponcore crossbow, braced against his shoulder like a siege cannon, eyes locked on Callum.

Callum tensed, ready to counter, ready to move.

Something hit him first.

The world pitched sideways, the sky tearing away as his body spun. Air rushed past Callum, pain ripped through his side, and a flash of gold cut across his vision. Then the ground surged up to meet him.

CHAPTER 46

Demoncores unravel power—twisting function into hunger, purpose into impulse. No two behave the same, but all lead to the same end: more power than you can bear and less self than you remember.

—A quote from *Fragments from the Edge of Use and the Price of Potential* by Emilia Eadred, Mastress Weaver, Core Lectora

Callum canted midair, his eyes slamming open as Killeas caught him just in time. The gryphon spread their shared wings with a snap before Callum could smash through a rooftop. He banked hard and eventually leveled into a low flight.

"Damn," Callum gasped.

<*Damn is right! The seawoman nearly took us out!*>

A blur of motion pulled up beside him. Wings outstretched, Marcella grabbed his forearm, stabilizing them both. "Sorry for the hit," she said quickly. "That beef-headed Crimson was aiming right at you."

"You knocked me out of the sky!"

"He would've shot you—"

"I was going to dodge it," Callum said. "He missed the first time."

Marcella rolled her eyes even as she released his arm, letting Callum fly on his own. "You got lucky the first time. Dodge a shadow bolt? Nah, it's better this way. We're beneath the airship and he won't be able to shoot us just yet. Let's get up there and deal with him."

Callum looked back to the bloodred sky. Ripples of bright hot mana fractured across the clouds, every flash of it feeding something that howled far beyond the wind. Lesser aetherbeasts swarmed over New Albion, demonic, tentacled things twisted by Corruption. Some flew and a few seemed to crawl through the air itself, scraping at it with their mangled claws. Others just fell, shrieking until they hit the stone below.

Callum focused on the ship again, which seemed to cut through the stormlit sky—enormous, jagged along the edges, its hull layered in blackened plates and still tethered to the Heart. It wasn't flying so much as anchored in the air, a blight suspended over the city.

"And the ship?" he finally asked, his focus flashing back to Marcella. "We bring it down, right?"

<Of course, we do!> Killeas said.

"There's nothing I want more in the world right now than to bring that piece of shit to the ground." Marcella raised her right arm, and her Weaponcore flared, an antlered blade of jagged ice curving into place. "The faster, the better. But first, we need to deal with someone. I'll see you up there." She launched higher, wings slicing through the rising heat, arcing toward the vessel looming above.

<We can do something like that too,> Killeas said. <Let me handle it!>

Their bond flared as Callum gave over control, his arms going light. His legs rebalanced as Killeas whipped him upward with brutal precision, arcing above the ship's towerdeck.

Below them, Ryven stood at the prow, his boar-thick muscles hunkering his frame like armor. His Weaponcore crossbow hung at his side, already reloading with another bolt of spiraling shadow.

Crewmembers scrambled across the deck of the airship as Callum dove toward Ryven, magic flowing around him as he summoned Haloedge, three swords flaring into place overhead. Ryven charged. Callum's boots hit the wood. He sidestepped and launched one of the floating swords into the brute's shoulder, knocking him off-balance.

Callum followed this up with a blast of wind, staggering Ryven, whose boots skidding across the deck toward the far rail.

<He can't fly!> Killeas shouted. <Use that to your advantage and send the boorish man overboard. Ha!>

Callum surged toward Ryven, intent on finishing the fight right there by throwing him off the ship and letting the storm and the distance to the ground handle the rest.

Ryven dropped to a knee and summoned his hammer as Marcella streaked across the air and struck him with her frostblade, which cracked against the haft of his weapon, sending a pulse of freezing energy up Ryven's arm. Ice spread fast; his fingers locked around the weapon for a half second too long before it vanished.

He hopped back and shook his hand out; Callum surged in again and the two traded hits, Callum pressing fast with Tempest Fang, Haloedge ready for any openings. Ryven batted one of the flying blades away and caught Callum in the ribs with a flat-handed shove that sent him stumbling.

The second floating sword intercepted Ryven's next strike. Callum ducked another blow and jumped back.

How . . . Callum thought. *I used shards. My power levels seem—*

As if Fen could intuit what he was thinking, the fox summed up what was happening: <*You're running low. You didn't recharge after Laziel.*>

As Marcella moved in again, Callum slipped behind a collapsed mast housing, cursing himself for not briefly visiting the mana fountain when he had the chance.

<*It's not your fault,*> Killeas told him. <*We should have said something.*>

<*He's right,*> Fen said. <*It is our duty to steward you and the shock of the attack left us all scrambling.*>

<*We'll figure it out,*> Callum said as he watched Marcella switch to her Weaponcore dagger and drive it straight into one of Ryven's trapezii, the blade flickering as it broke through the big man's Armorcore and started siphoning power.

Ryven roared with pain.

He twisted, trying to grab her, but Marcella locked her legs around his torso and held tight, dragging him back even as he staggered.

Their fight spiraled across the deck, raw and close to the edge, right where Callum wanted Ryven. Below, parts of the New Albion were ablaze, the buildings crumbling, streets choked with smoke, and flags torn from their poles fluttering as they burned midair. The wind carried the ashes upward in glowing spirals, banners of a fallen calm.

A fall like this will kill him . . .

Just as he was about to move, just as Callum was about to push forward with everything he could muster and send Ryven overboard, another impact instantly drew his attention.

Draven landed hard on the rear walkway.

The warlock swept the ends of his overcoat aside as his black crow wings folded back in tight, controlled angles. His Armorcore formed in a surge of rippling dark magic, layering over him in jagged, angular plates shaped like twisted iron feathers and ridged with flared lines.

Draven took Callum in with a twisted grin. "Well," he said, voice smooth and cruel. "Isn't this familiar?"

"What are you doing?" Callum asked, even though he already knew.

He had seen Draven with the Crimson students. His hometown was on the border with the Geshwine Empire. *Everyone should have seen this coming*, Callum thought as Draven spoke again.

"It's always you, isn't it, farmboy? Every time something matters, it's you standing in my way, the Stross heir, the thatched welp from Weatherby. But not today. No, not today. Today, you, and the rest of the kingdom," Draven said as he motioned to the Heart of Creation, "will come to understand the true power of Demoncores, the Flame Doctrine, and . . . and it's fitting, considering your lineage, considering the Lost Verses. The Stross family lineage isn't as innocent as it thinks."

Callum straightened, Tempest Fang drawn, ash stinging the back of his throat.

Draven smiled. "You seem surprised?"

"No," Callum finally said. "Just disappointed."

He burst forward, catching Draven's thin rapier-like Weaponcore on the flat of Tempest Fang, the impact ringing through his bones.

<*He's stronger now!*> Fen said. <*Attribute Shards and Death Affinity.*>

<*Let me help!*> Killeas said, extending his influence forward. Callum's next strike would have beaten Draven down had it not been for a sudden burst of magic from Draven's red eyes, the concentrated beam, singing through Callum's Armorcore, the sting instant.

Draven followed this up with a torrent of concentrated darkness, so strong that it sent Callum skidding across the deck, planks splintering beneath his feet. He gave ground, then ducked low and fired a burst of wind at Draven's center mass.

Draven summoned a black shield Armorcore mid-stride as Callum's attack slammed into him, doing little to disrupt Draven's advance.

Callum pushed forward again in a flash, rage sharpening his step as their blades met in a vicious grind of power.

Draven pushed back and released a sphere of dark magic, which exploded outward from his palm. It caught Callum full in the chest, lifted him off his feet, and hurled him backward. He smashed through a bulkhead wall, splinters flying as he crashed through wood and iron braces, landing hard inside a corridor that ran beneath the deck.

Boards creaked and fell toward him. Fen rolled Callum's body out of the way just in time.

<*Thanks!*> Callum said, pain flashing through him as he got back to his feet.

Above, Draven was already in motion, jumping down after him, Armorcore shield raised.

Callum dodged and managed to sweep Draven's legs out from beneath him. Instinct took over as Callum grabbed a jagged length of broken pipe and slammed it against the ground, narrowly missing Draven as he used his wings to right himself once again.

He burst into the air above the vessel, wings snapping wide.

<*Let's go!*> Killeas said. Callum dropped the pipe and raced up to meet Draven, the two above the airship now, circling as storm winds howled between them.

Callum summoned his Ram sword, cracked it open, and rushed toward Draven. He struck hard enough to shatter Draven's shield; the warlock advanced again with a new Weaponcore flail, the end of which fizzled with corrupted magic.

A flash of silver below caught Callum's eyes as Marcella hit the side of the ship with enough force to dent the plating.

Draven moved.

He slammed his flail into Callum, the blow cracking through his Armorcore in a burst of splintered light. Pain stole his breath as the force hurled him downward. Callum crashed through broken planks, hit hard, and rolled, each impact stripping away more of his remaining strength.

<*Don't give up!*> Killeas urged.

"I'm not . . . done yet . . ." Callum rasped, forcing himself upright.

Draven hovered above, his gaze sliding past Callum. Mana flared behind his red eyes as he fixed on Marcella's position.

CHAPTER 47

Of all the portal types, skybound constructs are the most temperamental. The surrounding mana lattice can collapse inward, drawing matter, light, and intention into a single fixed point until either stability is reestablished or the anchor burns out.

—Oliven Ladas, Master Convoker, Magistor of the Fire Wyrm, and Dean of the Great College from Year 400–431

Draven locked onto Marcella, mana flaring behind his eyes.

There was no time for Callum to think.

<*I've got you!*> Killeas said as he poured power into Callum, the sudden surge of energy ripping through Callum's limbs. He launched upward, wings clipping into the air. Callum collided with Draven shoulder-first, knocking the warlock off-balance mid-cast.

A bolt of corrupted energy fired anyway, searing past where Marcella had been a moment earlier and carving a black scar across the front of the ship.

Callum and Draven twisted through the air, wings tangled, hands locked in a vicious grapple. Callum slammed a fist into Draven's jaw, but the hit threw his balance off. They spun apart, and in that instant, something began to take shape in the space behind the warlock.

It started as a pinprick of blackness, spinning in place. The edges pulsed, widening with each beat, layers peeling back to reveal more of the void beyond. Rings of shadow rippled outward, overlapping in jagged waves until the shape deepened and curved, forming a gaping rift over New Albion. Power bled from it in visible currents, distorting the air, the whole construct flexing like it might collapse, or explode, at any moment.

<*A portal to the Empire!*> Fen said. <*The airship is trying to leave!*>

The massive portal churned ahead, growing with each second that passed, its light cold and hostile. It swelled rapidly, the drag in the air growing stronger with every second.

Below, Marcella was still locked in combat with Ryven, her frostblade flashing.

Too far. No angle to reach her, Callum thought as he fought the sudden pull of the portal.

Draven rushed him again, their bodies slamming together midair, wings flaring wide. "You're coming with me!" he snarled, eyes burning. "You're going to see how this ends!"

His arms locked around Callum, muscles straining as he drove them both backward, straight toward the open portal with an explosion of dark energy.

Callum managed to slam his elbow into Draven's side. He twisted and kicked, but Draven held on.

A burst of dark mana surged through Draven's arm as the warlock conjured a knife-shaped Weaponcore, its edge humming with venomous energy. He drove it hard toward Callum's neck.

The point never broke skin.

Instead, the instant the blade made contact, a shock of raw, corrupt mana tore through Callum. It was like a hook sinking into his Soul Heart and ripping it out. His body locked, breath hitching in his chest. Callum expected pain, something sharp, something bloody, but what came was almost worse.

Exhaustion spilled over him, his arms suddenly heavy, muscles refusing every command. The strength bled out of his wings in an instant. His vision blurred at the edges, colors smearing, depth tilting. Suddenly, Callum couldn't tell where the sky ended and the portal began.

"I thought you might like that!" Draven said as his grip tightened around Callum, dragging him close again. Callum tried to push back, to twist free, but all of his attempts fell flat.

The portal ahead swelled, its shadow spilling outward until it loomed over the Heart of Creation. Layers of shifting black and violet churned within its depths, each ripple distorting the world around it. It pulled at the scarlet-threaded clouds, drawing them into its core and devouring their light as its edges twisted and warped.

Draven drove them straight toward it, each beat of his wings pounding in Callum's ears.

Through the haze, Callum caught flashes of what lay beyond the portal, the Geshwine Empire's angled towers dark and jagged, rising into a lightless expanse. Gothic stonework gleamed under the weight of red banners that hung heavy in the wind. Gargoyles clung to the upper ledges, their stone eyes glinting in the stormlight, wings half-spread as if ready to leap. Far off, storms clawed at the horizon, lightning spilling across numerous spires that speared upward from the ground.

<*I'm on it!*> Fen said as he unmelded in midair, and latched onto Draven's back with his claws. He ripped into the warlock, fiery tail lashing, body glowing. Draven screamed and lost his grip as they continued through the portal to the Geshwine Empire.

Callum's body went slack, the poison from Draven's Weaponcore knife drowning every signal his mind tried to send. His grip on reality slipped and his sight dimmed, sound warped, and his limbs still refusing to answer.

The wind tore past him in a constant, punishing rush, spinning him end over end. Sky and ground traded places in a dizzying blur, each rotation striking another nail of nausea into his gut as whatever poison Draven had used continued to play with Callum's mind. He tried to catch hold of something—anything—but there was nothing but air and the distant echo of battle.

Then, through the pounding in his head, a voice finally reached him.

<*Not today, lad!*> Killeas said, the gryphon extending their shared wings and driving upward, away from Geshwinian soil, away from the Empire's gothic spires. They looped back toward the portal's mouth, toward the airship burning over New Albion, toward the Heart of Creation.

The pull behind them was relentless. Magic-riddled air dragged at their wings in an attempt to pull them back into the Empire. Every beat felt heavier, each stroke met with invisible resistance. Callum could feel it gnawing at their speed, at their momentum.

For a moment, everything went white, Callum pushed to the brink and fighting his way back as he realized that something was wrong. His thoughts scattered; he did everything he could to cling to the sensation of flight, of staying alive as the pressure mounted.

<*Fen . . . !*> he thought, barely conscious.

<*The fox is buying us time,*> Killeas said, his voice a steady anchor in the chaos. <*He'll make it!*>

But Callum could feel the absence where Fen should have been, an emptiness along their bond that gnawed at him worse than the portal's pull. The gryphon cut through the current, wings tilting as he pitched into a turn and forced them through the warped air pressing in from all sides.

They had nearly cleared the threshold of the portal when Fen vaulted toward them in a burst of fiery light, fire trailing in his wake as he surged back toward Callum, pulled by the force of their bond.

Callum gasped, the rush of Fen's presence reigniting inside him. Killeas stayed locked in control, wings steady, the gryphon angling them toward the airship.

<We have to destroy it!> Killeas growled.

<Marcella . . .> Callum thought, dazed, his vision swimming.

<Yes, we will destroy it and make sure she's fine as well. Attribute Shards. As many as you can. Now!> Killeas told Callum as he hung in the air for a moment.

Callum sent a shaky hand into his pouch and crushed all he had left of what Master Cruedark had given him, the Mind, Resilience, and Regeneration shards instantly igniting his senses. They flared to life the instant they broke, flooding him with clarity. Heat surged through his chest, pushing back the fog in his head. His pulse steadied, his thoughts snapped into focus, and the weight in his limbs eased just enough to move.

He hit the deck hard, boots skidding across blood-slick planks. His vision, once singed at the edges, snapped into clarity.

Ahead, Ryven stood tall, that massive crossbow braced against his shoulder, aimed skyward. Callum followed the line of sight to find Marcella.

She hovered above the ship, wings laboring with every beat. One arm hung limp at her side, her armor scorched and torn. Blood ran from a cut at her forehead in a thin, steady line. Her other hand still gripped the frostblade, the antlered weapon flickering with failing frostlight.

Ryven adjusted his aim and Callum moved, no hesitation, no thought, just forward.

He raised his hand and a gust of wind tore across the deck, hammering Ryven from behind as he pulled the trigger. The shadow-bolt veered off course, screeching across the sky and vanishing.

Ryven turned, hit the deck, and charged toward Callum, who summoned his wind sword, aimed it at Ryven, and unleashed another compressed gale that struck the warlock mid-charge. The Crimson brute flew backward, crashing against the central rigging.

The ship groaned, still floating but unstable, its frame shuddering. Callum could feel it now, a pitch in the balance.

<Something is happening!> Fen said.

The ship yawed beneath Callum, the deck tilting hard. Ryven rose, his crossbow hissing as it locked into place, aimed squarely at Callum's chest.

Marcella dropped from above, landing on top of the big man. Her frostblade drove down in a clean, brutal strike, piercing between Ryven's shoulders with a crack of antlered ice, the blade punching through armor and into bone.

Ryven howled once as she twisted her weapon, Marcella's power amplified by a sudden flourish of her wings.

Frost erupted from the wound, racing across Ryven's back in jagged pulses. It surged up his neck, over his jaw, across his cheekbones. His eyes froze mid-blink, pale blue and sightless, just before his body dropped to the deck with a dull thud.

Marcella yanked her frostblade free and turned to Callum, the savage look on her face shifting to surprise as the airship locked into a new position. "What's happening—?"

A blistering discharge of black lightning exploded from the vessel's mouth, cutting a jagged line through the red sky as it traveled along the tether it had formed with the Heart of Creation. The air trembled; wards across the cityscape lit up in panicked succession, flaring brightly just before the blast reached its mark.

The strike landed, leaving both Callum and Marcella to cover their eyes as light and shadow collided in a blinding flash. A shockwave followed, fast and circular, ripping through the air with a deafening crack accompanied by a bone-deep roar that tore across New Albion.

The Heart flared once, brighter than the sun, its veins glowing with unstable mana.

Lines spidered across its surface, cracks deepening as a wave of corrupted energy rippled outward, warping the air. For a breathless second, the Valestra Kingdom held still. Then the Heart of Creation fractured and collapsed, exploding into a storm surge of light, stone, and stored magic. The shockwave leveled the nearest buildings as arcs of uncontrolled power tore through the sky, the protective wards buckling, more towers collapsing.

"No," Marcella said, her voice barely audible. "No . . ."

<*It can't . . . It can't be,*> Fen said as the airship tilted toward the portal.

New Albion's ancient safeguard was gone, demolished, and it was clear at that moment, without a shadow of a doubt, that the Valestra Kingdom would never be the same.

CHAPTER 48

A kingdom is only as strong as those willing to rebuild it.

—Hugo Thirdson, Duke of Aveiro and famed orator

Smoke filled the sky, stained red by the Demonstorm still bleeding overhead. Lesser aetherbeasts swarmed the airship, crawling over the rails, dropping from above, their shapes twisted and unstable—too many legs, too many mouths, or not enough form at all.

"I've got this one," Marcella said as a serpent with dragonfly wings and a gnashing, bone-split muzzle darted toward them. She stepped into its path and gracefully cleaved it clean in half with her frostblade, the ice-crack of her strike loud against the rising wind.

Callum pivoted behind her, slicing a horned crawler that had just leaped onto the deck. It burst apart in a spray of sizzling black magic. Another dropped from above, the spined, centipede-like thing clinging to the rigging. He took it down with a blast of wind, where Marcella finished it off before the tentacles on its back could attack them.

A trio of winged aetherbeasts buzzed toward them, shrieking in harmonics that stabbed at the nerves. Marcella spun and slashed upward, her blade trailing a spiral of cold that froze one mid-flight. Callum caught the next with his Radiant Claws, smashing it into the deck.

"Too many," Marcella said, panting. Her breath steamed from her lips as she reached into her pouch and crushed a few shards. "Better. Do you still have any?"

"I'm out," Callum said.

"I just took—"

"It's fine," he told her. "We have to stop the ship," Callum managed, voice thin. "If it gets through the portal . . ."

"Leave that to me!" Killeas appeared beside them in a rush of wind, wings spread low for balance, his talons gouging deep furrows into the shifting deck. Smoke and embers clung to his feathers, and his chest rose and fell with slow, deliberate breaths, every line of his body shimmering with raw mana. "I will bring the ship down," he assured the two. "She can take you; let me do my work here."

Marcella turned sharply. "Me? Take him? How?"

"You always struck me as clever; just make it work!" Killeas launched down into the heart of the airship before she could argue, magic flashing from the tip of his tail.

She turned to Callum, eyes scanning him. "Okay, we can do this. Harold says I can carry you. At least for a little while. Um . . ." She spread her arms and gestured abruptly for Callum to approach. "I guess we do it this way?"

"Do . . . what?"

"Don't make this awkward. You can't go on my back, that's where my wings are."

He couldn't hide the skepticism on his face. "You want to . . . cradle me?"

"As opposed to, what, hugging you or holding onto your wrists? Now is *not* the time to debate this, Callum!" she snapped, slicing another beast in half without looking. "Your crazed gryphon is about to bring this ship down; that, or, it's going to disappear into the portal that I'm already starting to feel. Now or never. Do you trust me?"

<She's right,> Fen said. <We have to get off this airship. We should already be off it by now.>

<And you think Killeas can actually do it?> Callum thought back to the fox.

<I know he can, but don't tell him I told you so.>

"Okay," Callum said, half wincing as he approached Marcella. "I trust you. Let's do this—"

Marcella scooped him up before he could finish. "Ugh, you're so much heavier than I thought," she grunted, one arm under his legs, the other behind his back. "It has to be your diet. Way too much starch. And you don't stretch, do you?"

"Maybe don't critique me *while* flying," he muttered.

"Then maybe don't weigh as much as a collapsed statue. And we haven't started flying yet. Let's do that now!" Her wings snapped wide. They launched skyward with a powerful beat, only for gravity to instantly punish them. Marcella lurched sideways with a startled curse, nearly dropping him.

"You okay?" Callum asked, trying not to flail.

"Stop squirming—you're messing up my balance!" she said, adjusting her grip.

Another beat of her wings steadied them, wind cutting past their ears. Below, the airship groaned as mana fire licked across the deck. The storm wasn't waiting. Neither could they.

The moment her wings beat into the air, gravity bit hard. Marcella lurched sideways, almost dropping him.

Callum's fingers curled. "Are you sure about this?"

"No!" she said as they dove under a section of broken mast and emerged into open red sky, clearing the edge of the airship. They dipped lower, barely keeping altitude as a flurry of tiny aetherbeasts rushed toward them, snapping at Marcella's heels.

<*I'll deal with them!*> Fen leaped into Callum's lap, the Radiant Fox launching fiery bolts of wind at the smaller monsters swarming below.

"That's one way to do it!" Marcella growled, wings flaring as she streaked downward, cutting through smoke and shadow.

Then the world behind them erupted as the airship detonated in a pulse of unbearable heat and staggering thunder. Mana fire spewed from the heart of the blast, spiraling into the sky in columns of black and red. Shattered metal screamed as it tore itself apart, jagged chunks of shrapnel spinning outward.

<*Killeas did it!*> Fen said.

The shockwave that followed hit hard and fast, flattening clouds and tossing debris in every direction as the sky folded around it.

Marcella jerked sideways mid-flight. "Whoa—!" One of her wings snapped in the wrong direction, torque ripping across her back. The other caught a surge of displaced magic and flared wide, sending her into a violent spiral.

Smoke swallowed them, sparks flying past their eyes. Callum's shoulder slammed into her ribs as they tumbled. "I got you!" Marcella said she clutched him tighter, trying to correct until a hunk of burning wreckage clipped her wingtip.

Callum tore from her grip, body spinning through open air, wind shrieking past his ears. Gravity seized him like a falling anvil, dragging him down fast. His stomach lurched. Every joint felt like it was trying to separate.

Then, at what felt like the very last moment, a moment in which Callum did what little he could to prepare for impact, hands caught him. Arms locked around his shoulders and hauled upward with brute force. The momentum snapped against his frame, knocking the breath from his lungs, his boots kicking at empty space.

Marcella had him again. Her breath rasped near his ear, wings shuddering with strain. "I . . . guess . . . we could have . . . done it . . . this way," she managed, her voice shaking but alive.

Fen gasped. *<I can't believe . . .>*

A surge of wind slammed into them as Killeas burst from the wreckage above, wings outstretched. He arced downward, meeting them midair.

"I've got it from here!" he told Marcella as he melded with Callum, wings taking shape.

<Guess who's back!> the gryphon howled, wild and triumphant. *<Ah, and just like that, the warlock's little airship is finished. I told you I could do it!>*

<You bloody did it!> Fen said, celebrating.

<Did you ever doubt me, fox?>

Buildings outside of the Heart of Creation's cratered epicenter rose fast. "That should work!" Callum said as he spotted a flat rooftop ahead, and angled his body toward it, Killeas adjusting their descent.

Callum landed, legs nearly folding from the impact, but Killeas caught him with a surge of stabilizing force before Fen took over. Together, they kept moving across the rooftop, each step faster than the last as roof tiles broke beneath him.

Callum leaped for the ground as the airship's wreckage twisted overhead, burning as it spun end over end. It slammed down near the outer ruins of the Heart of Creation. A sound like a cathedral tearing itself apart echoed through the city, deep and final.

He stopped beside a shattered fountain, where water spilled from jagged cracks in the stone.

Crazy, he thought as he took in his surroundings. Chaos reigned all around him. Screams echoed from the plaza, civilians fleeing in every direction and archmages shouting spells as they tried to hold the line. Bodies lay scattered across the broken walkway, too many of them still.

Marcella touched down next to him, her brow furrowed, eyes scanning the chaos. "We have to keep moving," she said, gaze locking onto the Great College. The airship above the Vestige Arena was gone, but the sky still burned red, a few monsters still falling from it.

"I probably shouldn't fly anymore," Callum said, feeling the strain in his Soul Heart as he summoned his Ram sword but didn't split it. "But we're not far."

"We'll stick to the ground, then." Marcella started toward the Heart of Creation, then froze. "I still can't believe it," she said quietly. "And the king . . ."

The words hung there, heavy and raw.

For a moment, they didn't move.

New Albion groaned around them—distant steel clashing, voices crying out, the low hum of lingering wards flickering across fractured stone. Smoke drifted between the ruins, clinging to the broken arches and charred walls. Somewhere nearby, a man called out for someone who no longer answered.

Marcella's gaze swept over the wreckage. "Everything's changed," she finally said.

Callum didn't speak. He couldn't.

"I . . . let's just keep going," she said at last, straightening her grip on the frostblade.

They moved toward the Great College. As they rounded a bend, a bipedal aetherlizard with razored limbs lunged from the shadows. Callum reacted first, shifting into a solid stance and bringing the Ram sword down in a brutal arc before Marcella could lift her weapon.

The beast split, corrupted magic fizzling out as its body hit the cobblestone.

<*Ha! See?*> Killeas shouted. <*You've got more than you think. You might be low on mana—but you're stronger now, thanks to our pact.*>

<*We are both pacted. Need I remind you?*> Fen said.

<*Yes, but it's clear who has the more charisma of the two; that and the sheer power that I add to this little partnership has to account for something!*>

<*You're never going to let us forget about you bringing down that airship, are you?*>

<*Did you bring it down, fox? Hmm?*>

Callum tuned the two out as they moved through the backstreets, stepping over rubble and the toppled remnants of what had once been statues, now broken and faceless. The stone still radiated warmth from earlier blasts.

Two lesser aetherbeasts appeared along the way. The first crawled along the side of a shattered wall, hunched, spined, and insectile, its too many yellow eyes blinking in erratic patterns. The second dropped from above, vaguely humanoid, its back slick with writhing tentacles that lashed at the air.

Callum didn't slow.

He drove his Ram sword upward through the spider-thing's torso, pinning it to the wall as it hissed and convulsed. Before its body hit the ground, he turned and met the second one mid-lunge, cutting clean through its midsection in a single, practiced stroke. The tentacles curled inward as it collapsed and fizzled into nothing.

Marcella was already airborne, intercepting a pair of winged creatures that had dropped from the smoke. Her frostblade crackled with cold light as she slashed one from the sky and froze another mid-screech.

She landed next to Callum again and they pushed on. Neither of them spoke. There was no need.

They came across a man fending off a winged leech-beast with a garden rake. Marcella cut it down with a single stroke, her frostblade severing its slick body midair. The man gasped out a thank-you and stumbled off into the fog, clutching his bleeding side.

Further on, a charred pile of armored corpses began to move. From beneath it, a slithering thing unfolded, thin and jointless, with a face like a lamprey and vertical yellow eyes grown straight into its skin. Callum crushed it with a pulse of wind before it could fully rise.

Soon, the street opened up, the entrance to the Great College just beyond when a demonic aetherbeast covered in twitching jagged, teeth-like armor landed in their path. Its lower body resembled a warhorse, but the torso above split into two thick necks, each ending in snarling wolflike heads with horizontal, tentacle-like fangs that writhed and clicked. Armor covered its body in jagged, twitching plates, teeth layered over bone, and bone layered over more teeth.

Its hooved legs splayed outward, cracking and snapping back together before it launched toward them.

"Oh, come on!" Marcella shouted, kicking into the air, wings flaring. She tried to swerve, but the beast twisted with startling speed and lashed out with its hind legs.

The blow caught her square in the hip. The crack of impact echoed across the street as she was hurled into a brick chimney, the structure shattering around her in a spray of dust and mortar. She slid down the wall, coughing, one wing dragging along the cobblestones as it faded out.

The two-headed monster wheeled toward Callum. Both muzzles snarled in unison, spittle hissing where it struck the cobblestones. Its tentacles writhed and curled, reaching as if eager to pull him apart piece by piece.

By then, Callum had split his Ram swords. <With me,> he told Fen and Killeas. Light blazed along the edges of his blades as he cut through the first rush of tendrils, the severed ends snapping back in pain.

Another strike came—fast, low, deadly. Callum pivoted aside, only to catch movement at the edge of the smoke.

A blur, quick and deliberate, sliced into the battlefield from the periphery.

The monster shifted immediately, both heads snapped toward the intruder. Tentacles lashed outward, abandoning Callum to strike at the newcomer.

He clenched his weapons tighter, the final surge of strength burning through his body. Whoever had just stepped in had given Callum the opening he needed.

CHAPTER 49

Hope is the last weapon drawn. Only reach for it when the others have failed.

—Bregor Gaston, poet, *Epitaphs for the Living*

The blur resolved.

Quinn burst from the smoke, vaulted up the side of a ruined building and landed on a slanted rooftop with feline precision. His aethercat's claws dug into the cracked tiles, holding him just long enough to pivot and launch.

He hit the monster's back and the two-headed beast reared up with a roar as Quinn landed full force. The pact didn't just amplify his speed, it multiplied his mass, turning him into a living weapon. The stone beneath the creature cracked from the sudden strain.

One of its hooved legs buckled.

Quinn didn't give it time to recover. He raked his claws through a nest of writhing tentacles, shredding them in bursts of dark ichor-like Corruption. More limbs coiled toward him, but he moved fast, carving his way across the beast's armored spine with precise, brutal strikes.

"Bring it closer to the ground!" Lynnafer shouted as she charged in from the right, her goose Weaponcore snapping forward. The mana-honed beak at its tip pecked and tore, each strike fast enough to split wood as it cut into the monster's legs. Together, they pushed the beast back toward the edge of the street, Quinn pinning it while Lynnafer's weapon jabbed at gaps in its hide.

"I'll check on Marcella!" Callum called to them as he scrambled over a heap of broken wall, boots sliding on loose stone.

He skirted the burned-out shell of an alleyway market, its charred beams still smoking, and pushed through drifting ash until he reached the base of a chimney where he found Marcella sitting with her back against the brick, head tipped toward the red-stained sky, armor streaked with soot.

For a moment, he thought his friend had gone somewhere far away, lost to the chaos around them, her eyes fixed on the red-stained clouds above. Then, furious tears started to fall as she continued to glare at the sky. "I didn't want you to see me like this," she said as he approached, her voice thick. "I'm so angry right now."

"About . . ." Callum glanced back to where Quinn and Lynnafer were forcing the demonic monster onto its side. "About that?"

She shook her head, wiping her cheeks with the back of her hand. "What? No. I saw them coming right before I was hit. In a way, it's sort of Quinn's fault." A sad snort seemed to bring her back. "I got distracted. But they'll handle it. Callum . . ." Marcella finally looked at him, eyes wet, pupils burning with a fury he had never seen from her before. "The Heart of Creation is gone. Do you know what that means?"

"I'm still processing it myself."

"Every day we wake up assuming the odds are more or less in our favor, that nothing will change by nightfall. Years can pass this way, the tide always coming and going as planned just as the tidekeeper logs in her charts. And sure, things have changed recently; there is always room for anomalies. We've visited abandoned campuses, learned new powers, chased sky lanterns into the unknown. You know what I'm saying. But nothing like this. Nothing like what just happened. At least not in five hundred years."

Callum crouched beside her. "I get it."

"What I mean is everything will be different from today forward. We've never experienced something like this."

"But our forefathers have."

"But—"

"And that's where you're wrong," he told her quietly. "Hear me out: Not too long ago, I woke up in Weatherby to gray clouds, nothing serious, nothing like the aetherstorm that followed. That night, it spawned terrible beasts that chased me into an abandoned building on my farm. By the next morning, I was pacted with Fen, told to reach the Archive of Destiny, told that I was the reincarnation of the Demonslayer, and that the Demon King would return. So . . . yeah, today is one of *those* days, one of those days that starts out relatively normal and, by the end, changes a person's life forever. I've been through it before. Recently. And . . ."

"And?"

Callum tried to meet her gaze with optimism. "If the world can change in a day, so can we."

Another tear slid down her cheek. "I'm just so angry we let this happen."

"We didn't. Someone else did."

"Killeas can destroy an airship—"

<*Damn right, I can,*> Killeas rumbled in his head.

Marcella kept going. "If Killeas can do that, we could have easily taken them out before this happened. Done to them what they did to us."

"But that's not who we are."

"Isn't it? Are we really this easy to fool?"

"I think there's more to it," Callum finally told her. "We're not on the High Council. We don't know how the Duke of Karna bent King Morninglade's ear."

"They were friends," she said bitterly, "friends since childhood according to Selene. The duke had him killed. Draven is proof of that. We saw him on the airship. He nearly took you to the Empire with him. Which means all of Karna has or will fall, considering its location on the border."

"You think the whole city is gone?"

She shrugged. "I have no way of knowing, but Karna is on the border, or what used to be the border between our two kingdoms. Which means the Empire has already taken some northern territory. Then there are the Badlands. Most of the Beast Masters seem to be here. There will be skirmishes there as well . . ." She closed her eyes and leaned her head back against the brick. "I just can't imagine what Selene must be going through."

Callum thought briefly of Weatherby, how quickly some would push back if they were told to join in a fight against the Valestra Kingdom. "Not everyone will follow." He offered his hand. "Come on. We keep moving. Keep fighting. It's the only way now."

Marcella took it. "You're right."

They crossed the rubble side by side and emerged just in time to see the last moments of the battle. Lynnafer stood near them, arms spread, her staff leveled like a fulcrum.

Quinn moved fast beneath the monster, low and relentless. He ducked a sweeping limb, carved through a mass of tentacles with his claws, then kicked off a broken pillar to launch himself up and onto the creature's two heads. With a roar, he slammed both claws into the base of one snarling neck.

The beast shrieked as mana cracked through its body. It stumbled, legs twitching, before collapsing in a heap of smoldering Corruption. Crystal shards burst free from its chest, glinting in the smoke. They shot toward Quinn; he caught them in his outstretched hand as if plucking sparks from the air.

"Nice. Regeneration," he said, glancing up at them. "Just what the cat ordered. Want some?"

"Don't mind if I do," Marcella said as she took one of the shards. "Thanks for the rescue, by the way. Even if you distracted me."

"Is that what you call crashing into a chimney?"

Marcella laughed. "Maybe."

"Eh, it was the least I could do," Quinn told her.

"How did you find us, anyway?"

"I followed my nose," he said with a smirk. "Erm, Tuck helped. And it was pretty clear where you were going when you flew out of the Vestige Arena toward the Heart. I'm going to go out on a limb here and say it was the two of you who brought down the airship."

<*There were more involved than two humans!*> Killeas told Callum.

"Killeas brought the airship down," Marcella said as if she had heard the gryphon's outburst.

"You're all heroes for that," Lynnafer said as she approached, her Weaponcore vanishing. "Seeing it come down rallied our forces. That's around the time we got control of the fight." She laughed sadly as she looked around to the madness that was now New Albion. "If you consider this control."

"Please take it." Quinn handed Callum the remaining Empowerment of Regeneration Shard. "I wouldn't say you look like you survived a tournament and perhaps the most infamous ambush to ever go down in Valestra history, but you certainly look like you could use a little boost."

Callum crushed the shard, the mana hitting like a cool rush of water through his veins, quenching the heat of fatigue still burning in his limbs. His shoulders lightened. Breath came just a little easier. Every cut, every bruise seemed to fade to the edge of awareness, not gone, but dulled enough to stand straight again.

"How bad is it?" Callum asked Lynnafer. "I mean—"

"It's as bad as you can possibly imagine," she said flatly. "The Heart of Creation has been destroyed. The king assassinated. There have been numerous deaths. And . . . the Soul Pythia has been taken."

Marcella swallowed hard. "The Pythia was taken?"

"She was on the airship, last anyone saw her," Lynnafer said. "I don't know how they got her."

"The Circle will figure something out," Quinn said. "I saw Rhea and some of the other Pythias-in-training already leaving the Calleva. When we came to find you all, everyone was regrouping in the center of the arena. Some of the instructors were even forming hunting parties to deal with anything left in New Albion."

"But the sky is still red," Marcella said, nodding up to the crimson-soaked sky. Somewhere in the distance, a bell tolled once—then stopped. "A sky like that has to mean something."

Fen took shape in a ripple of light beside Callum. "With the Heart of Creation destroyed, that's what we can expect."

None of them needed to say more. The four began the slow, battered walk back through the Great College and toward the Vestige Arena, Fen trotting ahead.

The campus was unrecognizable. Sections of stonework still smoldered. Collapsed archways spilled rubble across the pathways. Books lay scattered and trampled in the mud, their pages soaked with ash-stained water. The scent of burned wood and corrupted magic clung to every step.

In one courtyard, a fountain had frozen mid-explosion, the water now a jagged sculpture of ice locked in place.

They passed a field where students had once practiced sparring. It was now a makeshift triage site, filled with wounded people lined up on broken benches and stretchers made from doors. Master Shaper Luso Alpen limped by, robes torn and face smeared with soot, too focused on the injured to acknowledge them. Not far from him, Master Patrjohn Granadam, the Dean of the Great College, spoke with a pair of upperclassmen and pointed toward a smoldering tower on the opposite side of campus.

Callum and his friends came to the statue of the Demonslayer, which was now missing its head.

<*See?*> Killeas said as Callum paused in front of it. <*The warlock you fought was wrong. They have no respect for your namesake in their kingdom! What madness is this? Tell the fox to check around my poorly rendered statue and see if they did anything to it.*>

Callum didn't answer. He stared up at the headless statue, his heart sinking as Fen and Tuck circled the base, sifting through broken stone and scorched grass. Bits of shattered plinth littered the ground and a scorch mark ran along the statue's shoulder, just below where the neck had been sheared clean through.

The two aetherbeasts returned moments later.

"Nothing around here," Tuck said, sitting down with a sigh, his ears drooping. "Well, no heads anyway."

Lynnafer stepped up beside Callum, her eyes narrowing. "It wasn't random," she said. "That wasn't a blast or a falling beam. Someone meant to do this."

"And it looks to me like it was a clean cut." Quinn stood on his toes, peering closer at the break. "Deliberate. Surgical, even."

Marcella just stood there mouth agape for a moment. "They seriously took the Demonslayer's stone head. Why?"

"As an insult," Fen said, "as a reminder that the Demonslayer is no longer here, no longer *ours*."

"But he is," Marcella motioned to Callum, her gesture taking him off guard.

"Yes, yes," Fen said as he turned toward the Vestige Arena, "you are right. And they don't know what is coming their way once . . ." The fox never finished as a great plume of fire roared into the sky above the Vestige Arena, twisting before it settled into a hovering cloud of embers.

"What was that?" Marcella asked, wings unfurling in a sharp snap.

"It's fine," Lynnafer said grimly. "That was one of the protective wards misfiring. It happened earlier too. The Calleva is trashed, but there are still protective measures tied to the leylines—"

"Leylines which are in jeopardy," Quinn cut in as they started moving.

Callum took one last glance at the headless Demonslayer statue and followed the others.

The wreckage grew thicker the closer they came to the arena, where a collapsed tower made of ashglass still smoked from its fall. Off to the right, a student pacted with a winged gazelle used spiraling jets of water to douse a fire clinging to a cluster of dorm roofs. Farther along, Mastress Shaper Aena Gilford worked alongside three older students, shifting debris with combined Wind and Earth Affinity, the stone lifting in clean slabs while the air swept dust aside.

The space had been fortified for war inside the Calleva's outer gates. Beast Masters stood at key points along the tiered stands and around the field's rim, their melded forms towering, strange, and bordering on grotesque.

Selene hovered in the center of the Calleva, suspended above the crowd. Her armor was scorched and battle-worn, her wings flared slightly behind her to keep position. A hardened expression had settled over her face—composed, resolute, unshaken. She didn't look like a student; she looked like someone who had already stepped into power, especially with the flaming crown over her head courtesy of Lisalen, the Brightflame Phoenix.

Below her, citizens huddled near students and instructors, some clutching blankets, others gripping weapons or bandaged limbs. The weight of the day hung over all of them, visible in every quiet glance and every exhausted stance.

Callum spotted Master Cruedark among the crowd, speaking quietly to a pair of Second Years, who looked barely conscious.

Selene gestured and everyone stopped murmuring.

"The princess—" Marcella started.

"Queen," Quinn corrected.

A Beast Master landed in front of them before they could say anything else, the brute blocking their path. Broad-shouldered and horned, his frame corded with furred muscle, the man's meld had pushed far enough to blur the line between human and monster.

"We need to see the queen," Marcella said, bold as ever as she stepped forward and looked up at the towering Beast Master.

The man glanced back toward Selene. She spotted them instantly and spoke down to the crowd. Her words cut through the noise, and people shifted aside, clearing a path.

Sir Trindade limped into view, bruised and bloodied, one arm in a sling. His armor was battered, face streaked with ash, but his posture held.

"Good, you're here," he said without ceremony. "Come."

Sir Trindade led them to the front of the crowd, where Lynnafer joined Godric and Victrin Righexa, who stood near his mother, the Duchess of Ontaria. Marcella was just about to say something to them when Killeas appeared in a blaze of shadowy wind, startling everyone, Beast Masters included, several of whom surged toward Selene protectively.

"Relax, all of you," the gryphon said, voice carrying across the crowd as he rose a bit higher in the air, but not high enough to face Selene directly. "The Heart of Creation may have been destroyed, but we managed to take down one of the airships." His golden eyes swept over to the new Queen. "Impressive, right, Lisalen?"

<*Is he seriously calling her out at a time like this?*> Fen asked, voice filling with disdain. <*The nerve!*>

The crown of fire above Selene's head flared, yet the Brightflame Phoenix remained silent. Killeas returned to Callum, laughing as Fen scolded him for his outburst.

It was only a few moments later that Selene finally spoke, her voice clear and amplified, rising even above the tragic chaos that had overtaken the city. "Not everyone is here," she said solemnly. "But not all is lost."

A hush fell over the crowd.

"Today marks a turning point in the history of the Valestra Kingdom. What we do from this moment forward will shape our future—our survival and our livelihood. We will rally our forces. First, to protect New Albion. Then, to march on Karna. We will take the city back. We will take our kingdom back."

She let the words settle before continuing.

"Do not fear. We have strength left to call upon. Weapons. Archmages. Pacts forged in fire and purpose. The will of our people has not broken. And we will not let those who brought ruin to our gates, those who seek to open the Demonsrealm, destroy what has kept us strong for five hundred years."

<*This is our moment,*> Fen whispered in Callum's mind. <*The reason for my return.*>

For once, Killeas didn't comment.

Queen Selene's wings flared wide, catching the red light of the storm-choked sky above. She rose a bit higher above the crowd, her crown blazing bright with fire. "It is with a heavy heart that I say this now: the Second Demonswar has begun. Many of you will be tested beyond anything you've known. You will lose comfort. You will lose comrades. Some of you may lose your lives. But hope is still with us. And together, we will make it our weapon."

ABOUT THE AUTHORS

Luke Chmilenko is the bestselling author of Ascend Online and other fan-favorite fantasy epics, including the Warformed: Stormweaver, Hat Trick, and Shattered Reigns series. He has become a cornerstone of the LitRPG and progression fantasy genres, known for crafting vast worlds and delivering high-stakes magic and combat. Luke lives in Ontario with his wife and two daughters, splitting his time between writing, gaming, and plotting new stories faster than his hands can keep up.

Harmon Cooper is the bestselling author of nearly one hundred books across the LitRPG, cultivation, and progression fantasy genres, including the Pilgrim, Cowboy Necromancer, Cozy Abyss, Shadowborn Exile, and War Priest series. He began writing LitRPG in 2015 and hasn't looked back since. Born and raised in Austin, Texas, Harmon then lived in Asia for five years before relocating to New England and ultimately settling in Portugal.

RESPAWN YOUR CURIOSITY
follow us on our socials

 podiumentertainment.com
 @podiumentertainment
 /podiumentertainment
 @podium_ent
 @podiumentertainment

www.ingramcontent.com/pod-product-compliance
Lightning Source LLC
LaVergne TN
LVHW041621060526
838200LV00040B/1373